INTRODUCTION
IMAGINATIONS ON FIRE

Inspiration is a funny thing. One person can hear a song, hum along, and that's all. Another person can listen to the same song, an intense riff, a turn of phrase or play on words in the lyrics, and imagination opens up like a thunderclap.

The music of Rush has provided a great many of those thunderclaps to a great many authors. When we invited these contributors to choose a Rush song as the spark for a short story — loosely based, thematically linked, or directly inspired — we didn't know what we were going to get. The flood of creativity and literary excellence that came in shows just how important the music of Rush is to the imaginations of so many people. We gave the authors no specific guidelines other than to be inspired.

And they were. These stories range from stark dystopian struggles to uplifting triumphs of the human spirit, "straining the limits of machine and man." The underlying themes from a musical catalog that spans more than four decades come through in these stories as well: humans finding their strength, searching for hope in a world that is repressive, dangerous, or just debilitatingly bland. Most of the stories are science fiction, but some are fantasy, thriller, even edgy mainstream. Many of the big hits are represented here, but some authors chose truly unlikely sources . . . with wonderful results. We've also included reprints of two stories that had a significant impact on Rush history: the original fictional inspirations for "Red Barchetta" and "Roll the Bones."

Do you need to know the songs by heart to enjoy these stories? Not at all. In fact, if you had read the stories in another publication, you probably wouldn't even notice the Rush connection. If you like good fiction, you will love these stories. If you are also a fan of Rush, you will love them even more.

— Kevin J. Anderson
and John McFetridge

GREG VAN EEKHOUT **ON THE FRINGES OF THE FRACTAL**

inspired by "*Subdivisions*"

I was working the squirt station on the breakfast shift at Peevs Burgers when I learned that my best friend's life was over.

The squirt guns were connected by hoses to tanks, each tank containing a different slew formula. Orders appeared in lime-green letters on my screen, and I squirted accordingly. Two Sausage Peev Sandwiches took two squirts from the sausage slew gun. An order of Waffle Peev Sticks was three small dabs of waffle slew. The slew warmed and hardened on the congealer table, and because I'd paid attention during the twenty-minute training course and applied myself, I knew just when the slew was ready. I was a slew expert.

Sherman was the other squirter on duty that morning. The orders were coming in fast and he was already wheezing on account of his exercise-induced asthma. His raspy breaths interfered with my ability to concentrate. You really have to concentrate because after four hours of standing and squirting there's the danger of letting your mind wander and once you do that you can lose control of the squirts and end up spraying food slew all over the kitchen like a fire hose.

"Wasted slew reflects badly on you," said one of the inspirational posters in the employee restroom.

"What's eating you, Sherman?" I asked, squirting eggs.

He squirted out twelve strips of bacon. "Nothing. Don't worry about it. Not your problem."

I'd known Sherman for a long time. We'd grown up as next-door neighbors, had gone to the same schools, had the same teachers. This year we were both taking Twenty-Five Places That Will Blow Your Mind (geography) and Six Equations You Won't Believe (pre-college math) and You'll Have Itchy Eyes After Reading These Heartbreaking Stories (AP English). We did everything together, and, even though he was a little higher stat than I was, he never made me feel weird about it.

"C'mon, Sherman. Don't just stand there squirting in silent pain. Tell your pal Deni what's wrong."

He wheezed a while longer, really laboring. Then, like a miserable little volcano, he let it out: "My family lost stat yesterday."

The cold hand of dread fondled my knee. "How much stat?"

"All of it. Every last little bit. We got zeroed out."

Startled, I impulse squirted and missed the congealer entirely. Biscuit slew landed on the floor.

"My mom lost her job," he explained. "And my dad gained nine pounds. My sister got more zits. The swimming pool water was yellow when the Stat Commission came to audit. It was a bunch of stuff. Just a perfect storm of bad stat presentation." He rubbed his forearm across his nose. "I might as well be dead."

I could only agree with him.

Stat was determined by a complicated algorithm that factored in wealth, race, genealogy, fat-to-muscle ratio, dentition, and dozens of other variables from femur length to facial symmetry to skull contours. It was determined by the attractiveness of one's house. The suitability of one's car. You could lose stat from a bad haircut. You could lose it by showing up to school with food slew on your blouse. I had done that once during freshman year and never gained it back.

Stat was the cornerstone of our great meritocracy.

In olden days, one of the worst punishments society could exact upon you was outlawing. It meant you were literally outside the law. You had no privileges, no protections, no rights. Anyone could just up and kill you without consequence. Being declared no-stat was a lot like that. Without stat, Sherman's family would lose everything. Their house. The right to wear current fashions. To see the latest movies. To vote. And I could lose stat of my own just by being friends with a no-stat person.

My heart felt like a clammy potato. What was happening to my friend was worse than death. It was erasure.

I scraped congealed slew off the congealer, dumped it into various containers, and sent it down the slew chute to the drive-thru window.

"I just don't know what to do," Sherman said, squirting and wheezing.

I felt something surging within me like high-pressure burger slew through a lunch rush gun. This was a new feeling. A powerful feeling. The feeling that I could do something to break the patterns of my life and take Sherman along with me. The feeling that I could make a difference.

I was such an idiot.

"I'll tell you what we're going to do," I declared. Sherman

looked up from his station. Doubt and hope warred on his face. "We're going to save your life."

The next morning the alarm nagged me awake before dawn. It was early enough to hear the drones arrive, their rotors hurling morning birds from their paths. Delivery portals in the rooftops opened like flower petals and the drones dropped statpacks from their bomb bays. All over the division, people rushed to see what they'd been supplied with. I was usually in no hurry, but I needed to get an early start, so I gathered my share of my family's package and brought it to my room.

My stat was pretty low, so, as usual, it was knock-off brand shoes, last month's cut-off jeans, and a shirt the exact same brown as my skin. I could already hear the kids in the school halls calling me Miss Monochrome. There were keys for the day's new music releases from Top Three Radio, and some movies I didn't really want to see and nobody else did either.

But I was lucky. It could have been worse. This morning, for the first time since he was born, Sherman would get nothing.

I said goodbye to my family: my mom and dad and sister, just noises and voices behind closed bathroom doors. Showers. Hair dryers. Giggles and hijinks from *Morning Hard News*. I wondered if I'd ever hear them again. Swallowing the lump in my throat, I went next door to collect Sherman.

He was something of a demoralized wreck. My clothes were low-stat fashion, but he was literally wearing the same thing he wore yesterday. His hair was literally the same old parrot yellow. Yesterday's color. The sight of him only steeled my resolve. I could not let him live like this.

We loaded ourselves into my scuffed-up three-wheel grandma car and set out down the long, curving roads of our division.

We passed Cedar Grove Lane and Cedar Grove Court and Cedar Grove Place and Cedar Grove Way and made our way out to Cedar Grove Avenue.

We drove by Peevs Drugs, and Peevs Market, and Peevs Quik Oil and Tune-up, and Peevs 24-Hour Whatevers, and I didn't even slow down at Peevs Burgers.

"Don't you have breakfast shift in an hour?" Sherman said.

Sherman no longer worked at Peevs. They'd scraped him when he lost his stat.

"I called in sick. This is more important."

I grinned, thinking Sherman would thank me, but he only looked at me with something between wonder and disgust.

"You have no idea what you're doing, do you?"

I continued past the little circle of bricks and the water feature and the grass you weren't allowed to picnic on that marked the border of our division. "Taking a hit for a friend is never a mistake." That was a line from *Bomm and Gunn*, the first movie Sherman and I ever saw together at the Peevs Cinnecle. Bomm says it to Gunn, and then they both get shot to death by a gang of mutant cool kids. They go down with their middle fingers raised. Slow motion and everything.

It's pretty romantic.

Sherman just sighed from the passenger seat. "You're a pal," he said. Which were Gunn's last words, spoken through a dazzling arterial mist.

What I remember more than the movie was the popcorn. I couldn't afford any and Sherman could, so Sherman sprung for a big tub and shared it with me. That's the kind of thing that makes friends for life.

Sherman inserted my stereo key into the stereo and futilely searched the Top Three stations for anything other than the top three hits. "So what's the plan?"

"We're going to go see Miss Spotty Pants."

"Your . . . dog?"

"Miss Spotty Pants will know how to help us," I said, ignoring Sherman's tone of disbelief. There is little room for disbelief on a quest, I feel.

Sherman shook his head and made wheezy sounds of exasperation. "Then this isn't really about me and my stat. This is about you and your dog."

"It's about both of us, okay?"

Sherman stayed quiet a long time, thinking it over. "Okay, Deni," he said at last. "Okay. I fully support you in your misguided effort to redress injustices perpetrated against us."

I glanced at him. "Really?"

He shrugged. "Sure, why not? I'm no-stat. What have I got to lose?"

And so, after going past another Peevs Drugs and Peevs 24-Hour Whatevers, we arrived at Miss Spotty Pants's house.

She lived in a very nice house. There were eight bushes in the front yard, whereas my house had only four. Pillars supported a little roof thing over the door, which I suppose protected people from rain and birds. The fake stones in the lower outside walls were more three-dimensional than my house's fake stones.

The doorbell played some Bach or Beethoven or Boston or one of those other classical guys whose name starts with a B, and Miss Spotty Pants's new owner opened the door.

"Oh," said Mrs. Godfrey, with an uncomfortable smile. "It's you kids."

The Godfreys used to live across the street from me and

Sherman, but their stat had gone up high enough after work promotions that they were able to upgrade to a better division. Mrs. Godfrey looked quite different than I remembered. Her hair was bouncier and her teeth more symmetrical. But what really struck me were her pants. They changed length right before our eyes, rising above the ankles, charging halfway up her calves, then plunging back down and flaring out like trombone bells.

"Hey, Mrs. Godfrey," Sherman said. "What's going on?"

"Well, actually, this is a busy time —" she said, eager to get rid of us.

"No, I mean your pants. What's going on with your pants?"

She stood a little taller, a little prouder. "They're smart pants. They interface with the fashion channels and adjust themselves moment to moment as tastes evolve."

Tastes were evolving really fast.

"I was hoping we could see Miss Spotty Pants," I said.

"Oh, I . . . Well, as I said, this is a very busy time —"

"Is that Deni?" came a familiar voice from inside the house. There was a scrabbling and a galloping and then there she was, my old Dalmatian. She leaped through the doorway and almost knocked me off my feet. Standing on her hind legs with her paws on my chest, her butt wiggled so fast I thought her tail would fly right off and break a window. I scratched her behind her ears, which did nothing to kill her enthusiasm. I had to wipe my watering eyes.

When the Godfreys moved, they put in an application to take Miss Spotty Pants with them even though she'd been my dog since she was a puppy. She was a shelter dog, and you never know what you're getting with a shelter dog. But once her mods kicked in at about seven months old and she started talking and her extra spots came in, the Godfreys decided she was a really cool dog. And since the Godfreys had higher stat, they got their way.

Mrs. Godfrey didn't want to let us in, but when Miss Spotty Pants bared her teeth, she relented. Mrs. Godfrey even got Sherman and me a couple of Peevs Colas and left us alone in the living room with Miss Spotty Pants. The inside of the Godfreys' house wasn't all that different from the inside of my house, only better in every way. We sat on their better couch and drank their Peevs from their better refrigerator. After some more obligatory petting and scritching, Miss Spotty Pants curled up at my feet and asked me what had brought me and Sherman. We told her about how Sherman's family had been declared no-stat, and that we hoped she could help us.

She'd spent the first few months of her life in the pound, and she'd heard things from the other strays and rejects. Some of them came from far away, redolent with exotic, far-away scents, with odd dialects and strange ideas, and tales from distant lands. And when she came to our house, getting me up every two hours to pee, she spoke to me about what she'd learned in the concrete kennels.

She told me of lights and wonders. There was a city, she told me. And I asked her what a city was, and she wasn't sure. All she knew was that it was different than the divisions. She told me of towers that scraped the skies, and grand parks and boulevards teeming with people, a place of variety and a million smells and a million sounds and of things one could barely imagine.

"Miss Spotty Pants," I said, "how'd you like to go for a ride?"

She glanced around the Godfreys' living room, with its better TV and better sofa and better cola. And before I could ask again, she was out the door and in my car, panting with irrepressible glee.

Things got weird once we left our familiar divisions behind. So weird that at one point Sherman shouted for me to stop and pull over, and the three of us got out and stood on the sidewalk.

"Did you know this was here?" I asked Miss Spotty Pants.

"I never even imagined," she said, her voice a gruff whisper.

There, at the intersection of Spring Brook Falls Avenue and Brook Falls Spring Avenue, were a burger place, a drug store, a supermarket, and a convenience store.

Not a single one of them was a Peevs.

They were all something called a Wiggins.

Wiggins Burgers.

Wiggins Drugs.

Wiggins 24-Hour Whatevers.

We stared in wonder for what seemed like hours.

"No matter what happens from this point on," I said, "I will never forget this moment."

We went inside the 24-Hour Whatevers to buy fruit film snacks.

They were the same fruit film snacks you could get at Peevs.

We drove for days, taking turns sleeping in the backseat and subsisting on the fruit film. I wondered if my family missed my voice through their bathroom doors. After so many days on the road my brain began to change and time lost meaning. When we got out to pee at gas stations my feet felt disconnected from the ground. The car's odometer said we had driven hundreds of miles, yet, paradoxically, the farther we drove, the less distance we seemed to cover. Sherman and Miss Spotty Pants said they felt the same way.

"It's the fractal," said Sherman from the passenger seat. He stared ahead with red-rimmed eyes as if he was looking at something horrible and he couldn't look away, like maybe a ghost or a dead, brown lawn.

I remembered something about fractals. We'd covered them in Twelve Amazing Mathematical Concepts Everyone Should Know Before Eleventh Grade. A fractal is a pattern that repeats itself. Magnify it, and you'll see the same pattern as if you'd reduced it.

Yes, we were in a fractal. The little streets curving out from bigger streets like the bent legs of a millipede. The regularity and spacing of the houses, the stores, the divisions. It had become like a fever dream where you keep repeating the same bit of the dream until you feel your brain contract, squeezing your thoughts down into a hot little cage.

"We are stains," Sherman said. "And we are glorious." He had a weird glow in his eye, like the time he drank green milk-shake slew from the back of the walk-in freezer seven months after St. Patrick's Day.

Miss Spotty Pants stretched her jaws in a great big yawn. "What are you talking about?"

"We are stains. And stains are glorious, because a stain is a variation in the fractal. A stain doesn't repeat itself endlessly. A stain is unique." He was gaining boldness as he spoke, becoming more alive. "Being a stain shouldn't be a cause for humiliation and stat reduction. It should be celebrated."

Sherman was saying dangerous, subversive stuff. The kind of stuff that could cost you stat. But, like he'd said, he had nothing more to lose.

It was exciting and made me want to speed through the streets and do donuts in the cul-de-sacs.

We kept on until Miss Spotty Pants spied a dim glow on the horizon, and I aimed the car toward it. As the hours and days piled on, the light grew brighter.

"It's the city," she said. "It must be."

It turned out that she was right. Only, the city turned out not to be what we'd hoped.

It was Sherman's turn behind the wheel, and he'd fallen asleep and bumped into a fire hydrant at three miles an hour, waking me and my dog. We all got out of the car. Miss Spotty Pants peed on the hydrant while Sherman and I stared up at towers stained by rain and wind rising from fields of concrete like accusatory fingers, their windows covered with moss and lichen. The buildings were constructed from a dizzying array of materials. Glass and concrete and brick and marble. Back home, all was stucco. Stucco was the only element in the periodic table.

Weeds grew thick in the fissured, unnavigable streets, and we had no choice but to leave the car behind. We picked our way along the jumbled sidewalks, our voices hushed in fear and reverence. Miss Spotty Pants's ears pricked at the scrabbling and scratching sounds that came from the shadows in the fallen buildings. When something meowed I held onto her collar to prevent her from racing off on her own. But the only living thing we saw was a coyote down an alley. It carried a pink mannequin hand in its jaws and looked at us with its head cocked in curiosity before deciding we were bad news and trotting deeper into the shadows.

The city was a sad place, a lost place, a haunted place. But that didn't mean it was a bad place. If I closed my eyes, I could almost imagine what it might have been, alive with millions of people hurrying to jobs, or singing, or dancing, arguing, loving, fighting. A population as varied as the building materials, all smashing together like atoms and creating energy. Here, I sensed possibility. Squandered possibility, maybe, but possibility nonetheless. Crackled and crumbling, dust and destruction, but a place that inspired dreams instead of just processing desires.

"Dudes," I said, "the divisions suck."

Sherman and Miss Spotty Pants agreed that they did.

No matter what, we would not go back.

The city became less appealing when the bombing began.

With an eerie electronic *vorp* from the sky, a green spike of light struck the street. Bits of torn-up road sprayed everywhere, pelting us with gravel. We shrieked and ran like chickens with ignited BBQ lighters up their cloacas and scrambled toward the ruins of a pizza restaurant that was neither a Peevs nor a Wiggins but a Tonys, which might have been the name of an actual human being, when a bomb struck the roof. The windows blew out and felled the three of us with hot wind.

"Split up!" Sherman screeched, choking on black smoke.

"No, stay together!" I screamed back.

"Let's find a bank," Miss Spotty Pants suggested, a little more calmly.

"I don't even know where my ATM card is!"

I was a tiny bit traumatized by now.

"Banks used to be more than ATMs," Miss Spotty Pants said with an impatient bark. "They used to have inside parts, too, and they kept the money in vaults. We can shelter in one."

Purple sky machines with complex geometries sent down

more laser spikes. Blooms of white and red fell everywhere, blasting the structures to bits. Glowing red crab-like mechanisms descended upon the towers, crawling over them and eating their way down to the steel beams. Shards of glass fell, just glittering white flakes from this distance, like fairy dandruff, and we watched in open-mouthed fascination as the tower sank into itself with storm clouds of billowing debris.

Sherman and I saw the merits in Miss Spotty Pants's suggestion. We chicken-ran until we found a solid-looking ruin with the word *BANK* carved into a slab of concrete above the missing doors. Stumbling as the earth beneath our feet trembled, we scrambled through ivy and fallen ceiling until we found the vault.

We huddled there, shaking and crying and clutching one another as the machine tempest continued to obliterate the city.

At last the bombardment ended.

Leaving our shelter, we blinked at the sunlit sky like gophers peering out from their holes with hawks circling overhead. The bombs had finished the ancient towers, and even the debris-strewn streets and sidewalks had been reduced to little more than fine powder drifting against charred weeds.

We wandered along the red sediment that had once been bricks, trying to find my car. Miss Spotty Pants claimed she'd located where we'd parked it by smell, and I suppose it's possible that the blackened slab of half-melted blobby stuff had once been my car.

Sherman began to dig through the wreckage with his hands.

"What are you looking for?" I asked him, numb.

"Fruit film snacks," he said.

I shrugged and joined him, though when the best-case scenario is you get to eat another fruit film snack, you've really lowered your expectations in life.

Sherman started laughing a little.

"What's so funny?"

He scooped handfuls of dust and gravel. "We're the highest-stat people who live here," he said. "We're the cool kids."

"That's not a bad way of looking at it," I said, and I laughed, too.

Miss Spotty Pants called us idiots and bit both of us.

We weren't alone for much longer. More machines arrived.

First came the vacuums, some of them as big as the buildings the bombs had destroyed. They rolled in on massive treads and sucked up the dust. Through some internal process, they formed new bricks and slabs that they expelled through their rear ends. Giant metal octopi trailed behind them and arranged the recycled building materials into shapes that soon became familiar. Colossal devices rolled through and left bands of pristine green grass in their paths, like reverse lawn mowers. Other machines built roads, and swarms of little helicopters sprayed all the buildings with stucco.

The whole process took slightly more than six hours.

The final thing to go up was a billboard. It read *Oakview Springs, Good Living for Good Families, A Peevs Community*. Within a day, there was a Peevs Drugs and a Peevs Burgers and a Peevs 24-Hour Whatevers.

We chose a street at random, Meadowlark Avenue, and followed it to Meadowlark Way and turned down Meadowlark Lane. There was a still-empty house at the end of the cul-de-sac. Miss Spotty Pants pushed through the pet door and let us inside.

You have to live somewhere, after all.

After a few weeks, a family moved in. We never saw them,

because the house had more bedrooms and bathrooms than it had people, so it wasn't hard to hide. We subsisted on pilfered cereal and instant waffles and, of course, more fruit snacks. The family bought everything in massive quantities at Peevs BulkCo and didn't notice the small amounts that went missing.

One morning, I awoke to the sound of drones. Neither I nor Sherman nor Miss Spotty Pants was due statpacks because we weren't on the division's stat registry. But I wanted to go out and see the delivery anyway. Maybe out of nostalgia. Or maybe to remind myself that I'd accomplished what I set out to do, which was save Sherman from no-stat shame. I suppose that was even true if you squinted. The unexamined life was not worth living, wrote Socrates according to the Greek philosophy unit in Eight Ideas That Will Astonish You class. But then Socrates got to live in a real city.

So we tip-toed down the hallway, past shut bathroom doors. I heard the sounds of showers and hair dryers and chortles from *Morning Hard News*. It was almost like living with my own family. Maybe it even was my own family. Behind closed doors we are all the same.

Outside, we watched the drone swarm approach. The rooftop delivery ports opened like blossoms greeting the dawn, and the drones pollinated them with products.

"What do you think we look like to them?" Miss Spotty Pants said, squatting to pee.

Sherman pursed his lips, thinking about it. "We must look like stains."

I hoped we did look like stains. Like glorious stains without status, marring the perfection of the endless sprawl.

A PATCH RON COLLINS
OF BLUE *inspired by "Natural Science"*

On the whole, Galen considered himself to be happy.

Galen went to his office each day, stopping at the shop on 5th and Broadway for pancakes and coffee. He spent his good days with his multidimensional models (or his bad days in meetings), then he returned to his apartment to make dinner and to connect into his favorite shows.

He was good with this. It wasn't the life Galen thought he would be living, but he was comfortable. He could live this way forever.

Ishi leaned against the hood of the car and watched as Alex stood in the shallows. The wind was sharp, and the day was getting dark. The sky was that wicked slate color that only happens when the west coast overcast meets the ocean. Waves beat against the shoreline with a crescendo that made him feel like he was listening to electrojazz.

On the beach, Alex wore a dark sweatshirt with the words *Gem Machine* stenciled across her chest. Her platinum hair blew flat against her head. A pair of worn cargo pants were rolled to her knees, the bunched-up wads dark with sea brine despite the precaution. Her feet were bare. A wave crashed over her exposed calves. She looked cold but happy as she stared into the tide pool left behind.

"Come on," Ishi yelled, waving at her. "Time to go."

Without looking up, she waved back. Then she bent and took a shell from the pool. With a quick glance at the ocean, she straightened and picked her way up the beach, stepping around cracked shells and shards of driftwood that littered the sand. Rain began as she climbed the concrete stairway to the parking lot, a light rain, more a cold mist than a drizzle. It brought out the heat in her smile as she came near.

Ishi gave her a hug and they got into the car.

"Still sure you want to do this, babe?" he said.

She gave a crooked smile, her teeth perfectly straight. Then she sat back in the seat and stared over the breaking waves. A lace net of mist glistened in her hair. "More than ever," she said. "I need to do something important again."

Ishi ran his hand over her knee. "Then let's go."

That's when he knew this was really going to happen.

When Galen was at a party or any other social gathering he was unable to avoid, people who learned what he did for a living would sometimes ask how he felt about it.

"Do you think you're playing God?" they would say.

He always hesitated before answering. "No," he would say. "It feels more like being a parent."

"I can see that," they would reply.

Galen liked this answer because it made him sound wise. He also liked the fact that the answer was generally good enough to make people move on. He enjoyed what he did for a living. He was good at it. Talking about it made him uncomfortable, though, because it was his opinion that very few people actually understood themselves, better yet other people. On the other hand, this answer also gave him some anxiety because he knew even less about being a parent than he did about being God, and occasionally, of course, an inquisitive person would follow up with "That's interesting," or "Tell me more," and he would find himself embroiled in a conversation that made him even more uncomfortable.

"It's interesting to watch civilizations grow up," he would say in those cases, hoping this would be enough but knowing that once such an inquisitive person got this far, they inevitably went further. "It's interesting to see how societies start small and innocent, then grow more sophisticated," he would add when they responded with another "Oh, really?"

"It's like watching a hatch of tadpoles swimming around in their little ponds of muck, not particularly caring much how they got there. Or, if they ever do get around to asking those *where do I come from* kinds of questions, it's interesting to see how they always manage to make up the stories they need to get by. They're like kids playing in their fenced-in backyards, oblivious to the idea of something bigger outside."

"So they're just like us?" the inquisitive person would respond with a knowing chuckle as they sipped their martini.

"Yes," Galen would reply. "But they seem happy."

The conversation could go a few different directions at this point, but there always came a moment when the inquisitive person, who was invariably also a bit of an intellectual, would stop and say: "You know they're not *real*, right? You know they're just models?"

"Oh, I know that," Galen would reply.

He had discovered that this moment was sometimes a good point of dismount.

His eyes would slide left or right, looking for an acquaintance in the distance, or maybe indicating an appointment suddenly remembered. If, however, such a distraction were not available, he would proceed to compare his feelings toward his creations to the phantom sensations that war veterans often reported about missing limbs. "These people say they can still feel their hands or legs," Galen would explain. "Even though they know the hand or leg isn't really there. They say they can feel heat or cold in them, or the pain of a pinprick."

At this point, the inquisitive person would agree with him, but would then find their own acquaintance, or their own vital appointment that needed running off to.

Real or not, no one seemed to enjoy discussing pain.

Three hours later Ishi sat behind the drum kit as the band went on.

As always, they opened with "Willa Girl Wanna." Sarena did her guitar thing on the intro, and the crowd went dizzy. Crash laid a line of organ synth like a safety net underneath her riff, and the people roared.

Ishi ran the backbeat under the standard issue JazzMech unit.

For the first time in forever, the simple existence of the JMU didn't piss him off. He had hated the thing since the very beginning. Its receiver boxes were placed around the kit in their precise layouts, feeling like the footpads of some invisible spider of joy-sucking death that hovered over him as they played. Tonight, though, Ishi sat back and took in the plasticine feel of the entire place. He wallowed in the artificial sheen of money that covered everything in sight. "Live" performance made him ill now — it was music's equivalent to play-acting against a movie that was showing on the screen behind you. But tonight he sat back and waved his drumsticks in an overwrought caricature, and he grinned his ass off as the JMU ensured the band's trademark sound would nail the pleasure centers of every one of the eighteen thousand kids here who had paid their parents' cash money for the right to scream their lungs out at anything that happened.

And who could argue with success?

That's what Alphonse Cato, their manager, had argued a long time ago when one of the Machine's sponsors demanded the whole prepackaged thing to make the deal stick. Predictably, no one in the band had professed to like the odor of selling out that wafted from the contract, but Alphonse was sure it made sense.

"Think about the fans," he said. "Give them what they want!"

In the end, most of the band had come to see his view.

Ishi understood why.

Gem Machine had been so poor early on — the kind of poor most people can't actually describe, the kind that blankets a person's life and smothers their dreams if they aren't already too busy living them. So the idea of that kind of money just hanging there was like being given a guided tour of the Promised Land by Santa Claus. Alex was the last holdout, agreeing to the deal only when Sarena said she couldn't handle the grind anymore, and that if they didn't take the deal, she would ditch the band.

Not surprisingly, Sarena and Crash found they liked the whole mainstream thing just fine.

And the cash flow *was* great.

For a while, anyway.

But if Ishi would have known then what he knew now, if he could have felt the difference in the music . . . well . . .

Lights flashed. Smoke rolled on cue. The backing vocals slid in like gravy.

Ishi could picture J-Jezzie wired up in the booth pushing buttons and sliding settings like he was a conductor. The man was more than half machine, his brainwaves connected straight to the lighting system and his fingers able to call up sound with a simple twitch or a flex. When Jezzie was jacked-in, his eyes would glaze over and his face would get rigid. His hands moved and robots scurried over the board like mechanical cockroaches.

Ishi gripped his sticks properly, and threw a triplet into the break in Sarena's lead, even though he knew it would be lost in the rest of the show. The fans, bless their hearts, they screamed and yelled no matter what he did. But he played those runs to the best of his ability tonight, because that way at least *he* knew the music was still there, and because it had suddenly become important to him to do it right this one last time.

"The company is way behind on the Rift Gate project," Jada Hansho said to Galen.

She was standing at the control station of his containment

well, wearing a royal blue blouse, black slacks, and stylish shoes of some well-known make. Galen wore his powder-blue lab coat.

The row contained three other containment wells, machines that can perhaps best be viewed as a big tubs that hold a warped slice of space-time wherein almost anything was possible. But it was lunchtime so all of them except Galen's were empty. Around them, the windowless modeling center, with its thirty-five-foot ceilings, its hanging light fixtures, and the distant hum of an air handling system, felt like a secret cave. Galen had been deep in contemplation when she arrived (the changes he had made to the standard epigenome libraries hadn't worked as he had expected they would), so he had to replay the conversation back to himself to understand that Jada Hansho was reassigning him to the team responsible for modeling multi-dimensional gates.

"We need all hands on deck, or we won't hit our commitments."

He frowned. "Can I finish work on this project, first?" he said. "It won't take long, and I really hate to lose what we've accomplished so far."

"No can do," Hansho said. "I need you thinking about the Rift Gate every hour of every day. I want you dreaming about drop engines, time shifts, and transfer functions. This is important, Galen. MultiD says they can open a tri-gate. We don't believe it, of course. But if it's actually true, we're way behind."

Galen had been around long enough to know better than to put a rising star like Jada Hansho off her rails, but he didn't want to work on a project that everyone knew was a sham, regardless of the money it was bringing in. The Rift Gate project was a blight, it was their company sucking on the teat of a jointly funded government spending bill with hooks spread out over so many states and provinces that no politician anywhere could possibly manage to repeal it.

In theory, success in modeling a multidimensi result in opening interstellar space travel. That's wh was. Companies and governments wanted resource or some other such thing. They wanted faster-than wormholes, extradimensional passages that would fuel trade and maybe even discover partners beyond the ability to imagine.

The only problem was that none of the most respectable scientists in the field thought it would ever work. Not even Marcelle Ki, the French mathematician who made the final adjustments to the eigenvectors that resulted in the design and creation of the containment wells themselves. "The dimensions are doorways to other realms," Ki said, "not highways to our own future."

Of course, even if the theory was sound, Galen did not want to work on the Rift Gate project.

Galen liked his science smaller.

He wanted to understand how people worked. Why they did what they did. At one point he had actually wanted to help make a perfect society, but he knew that was a pipe dream. Still, he was happy to leave it to others to expand human understanding of the stars. He was more interested in understanding people. He liked the intimate feeling that came with making *his* models. He built unitary worlds, sometimes even just single planets, twisting the materials within them, changing small pieces of how life started, and watching the way these worlds grew.

He spent a year working with direct DNA modifications, creating worlds of life forms that were beyond the imaginations of most people — realms where eleven-armed birds controlled the planet, or where networked societies of gargantuan dolphins used their segmented legs to reign over land and sea. Mostly, though, direct DNA modifications still resulted in worlds run by human beings, or something like humans. Then he moved to the genome — adjusting the proteins and histones, and the rest of the chemical seas that make up the environment in which the DNA strand exists, and that would, theoretically, alter the way the base DNA would express itself — a study of nature vs. nurture, as it were.

His latest project, a universe that was now spinning away in the containment well, had been an experiment in adjusting a histone composite in hopes of increasing human kindness.

Though humans had managed to evolve in this run (something that was not always the case), his changes hadn't seemed to do anything to civilization in the grand scheme. But Galen wasn't finished with the progressions yet, either. The world in his containment well hadn't finished its cycle. Data needed to be regressed. There was still more to learn.

Galen chewed the inside of his cheek and looked at Jada Hansho. He could see no way out of her reassigning him.

For all his eccentricities, he was a top performer. In the early days, when social scientists and bioengineers were freighting eighty percent of the bill, he would never have been pulled to work on Jada Hansho's project.

But a lab, it seems, can become quite sanctimonious about withholding judgment as long as a research grant hangs in the balance.

Hansho was not taking "no" for an answer.

"All right. I'll shut it down," he said.

"That's great," Hansho replied.

Galen waited until she left the area before turning his attention back to the universe that still spun away in the middle of his containment well.

Alex was perfect, as always.

Perfect as she ran into the spotlight wearing her sequined pants, and her black and white top torn in just the right places to expose just the right amount of shoulder. Her lips were streaked with gloss. Her eyes were lidded in a hue of blue that Aul Larkin, the hottest fashion designer on the planet, had so precisely calculated would sell to women between eighteen and twenty-four years of age.

The crowd greeted her like she was Cleopatra. They rose to their feet as she strutted in the purple and silver beams Jezzie showered over her. They roared as she wiggled her shoulder and ran her sparkling painted nails through hair that tonight carried a shocking streak of magenta.

They were the G-Machine. The fucking G-Machine. Hear them roar.

Ishi could feel the gravitational pull of cash registers spinning as Alex opened her mouth to sing, and he could hear the producers and the Rez-Mark account reps clamp up in silent orgasm as the crowd went crazy.

Alex killed, of course. Totally killed.

Not many could tell the difference. The enhancement chips took her voice and ran it though compressors and digital shapers that ensured she had perfect pitch, and the timing algos made sure she matched the beat, just like they always did. There would be no imperfections. No raw edges. But Ishi felt the difference. He saw it in the way Alex held herself. He sensed it in her breathing pattern and the way she took her power pose on the edge of the stage as she waded into "Willa Girl Wanna." Raw desire flowed off her like it hadn't flowed since they were playing little clubs with misspelled marquees made up of plastic letters clipped together the afternoon before they came into town. That was what they wanted to do, both of them. That was how they wanted to play.

And it's what they would have done, too, if their contract had let them.

Instead, because they had been stupid, because they signed something they didn't fully understand, they were locked in. Forced in this direction. Forced to choose between a terrifyingly uncertain future of brilliance and a lifetime of wallowing in pseudo-art.

Ishi saw that Alex wanted to launch herself into the crowd.

It was there in the way her muscles clenched along her legs. There in the way her back arched as she looked over the fleshy sea of humanity that churned a proper arm's length away.

It didn't fit the script, but she wanted it. She needed it.

And she would have it. Soon. Yes, soon. But not now. Not yet.

Instead Alex pulled herself back from the edge, singing and clapping and dancing in her spandex and lace just as she had for a thousand shows before.

Ishi caught her eye as she passed.

A wry smile was her only acknowledgment that she saw him. Yes, she wanted to be free as much as Ishi did. Knowing that made the sticks feel real in his hands. He pounded the bass and felt vibrations like rain. Tears welled up. His chest grew tight.

They were so close.

"Willa Girl Wanna" finished, and while the group paused to give the crowd a chance to fill the recording with "natural" noise, Ishi reached under the seat, ripped off the tape, and pulled out the two vials that held the stuff of dreams. They had come from a renegade scientist overseas and cost more money than he knew existed.

Alex turned to him.

He threw one of the vials to her.

She grabbed it, ripped open the top to expose the hypodermic needle, then raised it up to let it shine in the silver beam of the spotlight.

The crowd went crazy.

Together, Ishi and Alex plunged the hypos directly into their hearts.

Software broke down. Enzymes decayed into acids that ate into proteins and ripped into cellular structures. Time stretched. Space boiled. The entities that had once been Ishi Castigan and Alex Sumpter sizzled in null space. There was pain but not pain. Joy but not joy. Images crossed their being, flashes of vision and smell and the taste of intense longing. Their bodies burst. Their minds melded. Behind them, eighteen thousand fans screamed and a business manager was left to calculate the return on a series of computerized vids and "best of" releases. Ahead of them stretched a future that raged in grand currents, endless loops, and patterns so complex.

Their hearts beat pulses across a universe made of universes.

Galen turned back to his containment well.

The problem, of course, was that the inquisitive intellectuals that sometimes surrounded Galen were wrong when they said the worlds he created were not real. Yes, they were *models*. Replicas. Scale duplicates. Clones, perhaps more than anything else. Half code and half material — strange systems made of subatomic mash and designed using the concept of multidimensional space warping endlessly within itself to create infinite physicalities that could be run forward rapidly in local time to study the effects of various new ideas. But they were not fake. Perhaps it was semantic, but these replicas were no more fake than he was. All these universes, all these worlds Galen created, and therefore all their life forms, the bacteria, and the mold, and the trees, and the protoplankton. The reptiles, amphibians, lungfish. The strange mutants, the bird-like things, and, yes, the people.

They were not models.

To Galen, all these worlds were *real*.

And this world he had in his containment well wasn't finished. The lives held within it hadn't completed their story. If he couldn't keep working on it now, maybe he could save it off somehow? Find a way to put it into a stasis that would let him come back to it.

This is what he was thinking when every readout in his containment well went alpha-ballistic.

He frowned and brought his eyebrows together.

The energy levels were off the chart. Internal temps were rising a degree every few seconds. The plasma core images dropped balance. The particle readers seesawed back and forth. The entire system's cosmic pressure spiked. Crap. He pressed a reset, but nothing good happened. He glanced into the well and saw his universe glowing blue and green. A gloppy bubble blistered from the side of the universe, a willowy, gauzy thing like the mass of a solar flare expanding outward like a Mandelbrotian jellyfish.

Numbers flowed across his control screen.

Holy crap.

Lost, Galen pressed the containment well's automatic shutdown.

The control panel went dark, the 3D holo display died away, and the hum of electronics faded into the background as the entire system ground to a halt.

Screens stared blankly at him.

The warped field inside the system may well be the realm of ultimate possibility, but right now it was nearly certain that something was totally fucked.

Galen put both hands on the control table and scanned the area around him.

No one had noticed. He took a very deep breath.

Christ, that was close.

Then he cursed. Now he was going to have to spend weeks justifying himself and resetting the machine. Even if he could find out what happened, there was no way the containment well could be used until he duplicated the problem and made sure they had it under control.

He rubbed his eyes and gritted his teeth as he looked into the containment well's pit.

Galen expected to see a charred-out husk of a universe. Instead, he saw colors churning, reds and greens and yellows, rotating, swirling like warped galaxies. Metallic flares shifted through the space inside a dark core. A beat pulsed. He swore he heard music. And he felt something more. As he watched this kaleidoscope of color and taste and otherworldly sensation churn before him, Galen Martin felt the presence of pure elation. He felt discovery. Beauty. Wisdom. Glory. Pain. He felt integrity.

He pulled his hands back off the table like they had been burned.

He sat down so hard on his seat that it rolled backward, and as he sat still he felt an elegance within him that consisted of a constant, gnawing yearning that ran deeper than anything he had ever felt.

Where is this from? Who put this here?

It was *his* containment well. *He* had created the world within, and yet he knew it was this world within that had hit him upside the metaphysical head with a multidimensional baseball bat that had him seeing emotions in colors and in a backbeat that still throbbed in his mind.

"Are you okay, buddy?"

It was Paulina Meridith, the woman who operated the containment well beside his. She was returning from lunch.

He glanced up at her, unable to shake the sensation. "Yes," he muttered. "I'm fine."

But he most definitely was not fine.

Galen stared at his containment well. The memory of that flare still burned. That flare was a birth of its own. That flare was . . . He didn't know what it was. But it felt like the most important thing in the world to him.

He found he couldn't breathe. The music came back to him, and he felt like flying. He wanted to throw himself out over the world and let it carry him on its shoulders. In that instant, Galen felt them. Two creatures. Two people, flying with bodies outstretched, branding themselves into his mind.

Ishi sailed into dimensions and through the infinity of universes. He and Alex became became one. They became many. Music flowed in white noise. Colors grew. Ishi tasted rose petals and something like sharp cheese. There was a sense that was neither taste nor sound, a touch that was not touch. He saw things that he could not have seen before.

And Alex.

Alex rode on her mosh pit. She soared in the waves of an ocean that flowed around her, waves that rolled up beaches and then pulled back to leave pieces of her in the sand that could be picked up again by later waves and then again by still others.

She reached out to touch entire worlds, exploring each, then dropping pieces of herself in their flow as she left life on these worlds to go on to the beat of its own pulse, but soaring as she left.

Soaring.

Always soaring.

Galen stood at the gateway to Hansho's cube, knowing exactly what he was going to do. He waited for her to pull herself away from the holomeeting. Her gaze caught him, and she grimaced. Excusing herself without hiding her exasperation, she disconnected and turned to him.

"What is it?"

"I'm done," he said.

Then he turned and walked through the sterile white hallway with its dark blue carpet, and its holoprint artwork, walked into the entry foyer, past the reception counter, and through the glass doors that led out into the open air.

He breathed in the scent of the hills around him and looked over the city.

The research center had been built on the crest of the slopes to the north of the city proper, and the building's porch gave a panoramic view of the skyline, complete with its massive brown and white pyramidal skyscrapers and the rows upon rows of other concrete and metal constructions that people had made. Traffic clogged the streets. People, and machines. The outskirts of the city were equally strange, a plasteel network of bubbled buildings and tubular vista jets that ran people from place to place.

How had he become so numb?

How had he let himself settle for so little?

Life was too short to waste on a Rift Gate project that was never going to pan out. Too short to stay in one place like he had been.

Tomorrow, he would take his learning to France. Perhaps see what Marcelle Ki thought of it. And if that didn't pan out, there were other scientists in small places where research was done despite dire sums of money or despite a lack of publicity. Other scientists who worked to make a difference rather than fill a grant quota. It might be a grind. Maybe it would take years to make a difference. Maybe he would never make a difference.

But he thought he would. There is progress, and there is progress.

And others saw the value of what he wanted to do.

The horizon stretched into the distance before him. The sky's overcast made the gleam of the solar farm to the west feel metallic. He looked up. How long had it been since he even paid attention to the clouds? He didn't know. But he looked up now. Really looked. The bottom of the overcast was smooth and solid, but curves of mist whirled in the weave of the clouds. Feathered wisps of vapor flowed in random currents of the wind.

Tilting his head just a notch further, Galen saw one patch of blue, open to the endless sky above.

BRIAN **THE**
HODGE **BURNING**
inspired by "Witch Hunt" **TIMES V2.0**

The first thing Jeremy had been taught, after he'd shown an aptitude for the craft, was the true meaning of *glamour*. A hint of it remained alive in the word today, coiled deep and slumbering, but still, the word had come a long, sorry way from its early days in a wilder world.

Once, glamour had nothing to do with beauty or elegance, style or charisma — not as people approached them today. When the word was young, to be struck by a glamour was to be bamboozled by an enchantment, a spell to deceive the eyes so that someone saw a thing as unalike its true appearance. To see it better was good, especially in pursuits of love, but worse could come in handy, too, sometimes. To simply see it as different, though . . . that could be the most useful of all.

Different was camouflage. Different was defense.

Their kind had neglected this once, and how the smoke had risen from the pyres. They had neglected it nearly to their extinction. Never again. *Glamour* . . . naught was more important for a fledgling witch to learn. They might teach him nothing else for years.

"I think they took the idea of defense-first from aikido," his brother Adam once told him. "The first thing they teach you there is how to fall."

But then, Adam knew a lot about aikido and nothing about the craft. Not firsthand, he didn't. Most sons never did. It was only the daughters, and often not even then. Only the daughters, and the very infrequent son like Jeremy Dane.

So say someone looked at him now, this afternoon, this very moment — what would they see? They'd see a fifteen-year-old peddling his bike, fast without being furious, recently tall enough to have to hunch over the handlebars and not looking any too comfortable about it. They'd see black hair that a lot of them would think should've been cut a month ago. They might notice the ridiculous feet, and there was no missing the nose, both intent on outgrowing the rest of him, parts he prayed would slow down so everything else could catch up.

They would see the truth; see him exactly as he was.

The backpack? They'd see that too. He wasn't skilled enough yet to hide it, so he'd just worked on enchanting the contents: six books, rescues and refugees all. Last month, the firemongers had torched a Carnegie library that had stood for a century. This hadn't come entirely as a surprise — firemongers enjoyed a good blustering threat almost as much as they enjoyed striking a match — so by the time the attack had come, a few of the librarians had squirreled away hundreds of favored books in the attics and crawlspaces and top closet shelves of their homes.

After the ashes were cold, it was just a matter of sending the survivors to sanctuary, a few at a time.

Jeremy had begged for the chance. Begged for it the way he imagined men in denounced books and movies begged for the favors of women. He had to start proving himself sometime. In all ways that mattered, this was war.

He'd chosen his route carefully for the run, his first. It was a good four miles of city streets between the nearest librarian's apartment and the coven house. The idea was to keep the distance as short as possible while not tempting fate by riding too close to anywhere the firemongers liked to congregate.

One mile down, then two. He zipped past office buildings and Greek restaurants, through neighborhoods and parks, around mailboxes and traffic lights. It was spring, a world in bloom again, and the weight on his back seemed to lessen with every block.

They caught up with him when he still had a mile to go, a carful of them that paced alongside the bike for a block before they decided, yeah, he was a suspicious one all right, and made their move. They swerved hard to cut him off, the car windows full of scowling faces, grinning faces.

He took a deep breath, slow in, slower out. He'd said the words; he'd seen the results in front of him as clear as sunlight; he'd dug to his innermost core and flexed his will with love. *They'll see what I want them to see.*

Five of them got out, all a few years older, around Adam's age. They all had a sameness to them. They didn't wear uniforms but dressed so much alike they might as well have. They wore pins, flags and crosses and a stylized flame with a logo that read *The Pyre*. They might have been in college if they'd had the inclination for it, might have played sports if they'd possessed the discipline. Instead, they had this.

"Let's see what's in the backpack," their leader said. Unlike the rest, he neither grinned nor scowled. His face was set with a look of cold, hard determination that he had a sovereign right to make sure nothing got past him, today or ever. "I don't like the way that thing hangs. It's too heavy."

When Jeremy didn't move fast enough to suit them, the fellow behind him yanked the backpack from his shoulders and they plunged in for themselves.

Out they came, one by one, shelf tags still at the bases of their spines: *Madame Bovary*. *Walking with Dinosaurs*. *The Art of Loving*. *Harry Potter and the Philosopher's Stone*. *The Catcher in the Rye*. *Zen Mind, Beginner's Mind*. All hiding beneath a glamour of titles these five couldn't possibly object to, the sort of bibles and manifestos that would feed them their diet of hostility and judgment.

They peered at the covers, squinting a moment, and tilting a book or two as if to rid themselves of a pesky glare from the sun. *But they'll only see what I want them to.*

"Where's your book on unicorns, too?" one of them said, and they all laughed. "Don't you know dinosaurs are a lie?"

His heart seemed to drop from his chest through his belly to the pavement. He'd tried. He'd tried so hard. He'd had it earlier, he was sure of it.

"*The Art of Loving?* Erich Fromm, what kind of name is that? You're too young for that, anyway," another said as he pawed through the pages. "There aren't even any dirty pictures."

That's because it's a psychology book, you fucking imbecile, Jeremy wanted to say, but this would only make things worse.

And that was how he lost them, all six books that would be ash by midnight.

Before these guardians of the pyre let him go, they told him his mind was a temple. You wouldn't pump sewage into a temple, would you? You wouldn't stand at the temple's altar and proclaim filth and lies, would you? Of course not.

They sent him home bloody. Not bad, nothing broken, nothing that wouldn't wash off. Just enough to get the lesson across, and a little more to remember it by.

He would've thought it would be their laughter he would hate the most.

It wasn't. Instead, it was the absolute, empty-eyed certainty of their conviction.

He returned to the coven house in failure, empty-handed except for the shame.

From the street, passersby who looked at the house saw only what they were meant to see. Three stories of tradition and grandeur, it sat far behind a spiked wrought-iron fence, lost deep in a sprawling neighborhood of gargantuan old homes and squandered fortunes. It gave every appearance of having been abandoned for decades, windows broken and boarded over, with rotted shingles dangling above starlings that nested beneath the eaves.

This was glamour writ large, an enchantment generations in the making. For those who knew how to look, it was a perfectly lovely manse, one of dozens around the world.

As soon as Jeremy slipped in through the back, some of the women, young and old alike, fussed over him. Others eyed him with quietly scornful disappointment, saddened more by the loss of the books than the bruises and the blood; what could you expect, anyway, sending a boy to do a witch's job?

"Go see Abigail," his mother told him, once she'd gotten over the shock.

"I don't want to," he said. Abigail was innately skilled with unguents and salves, but he wanted the lumps, the bruises, the scrapes. He wanted the aches left right where they were. If the thumping he'd received was meant to be a lesson, then let it be one . . . just not the kind the ignorant thugs had intended: *Never again*.

"I'm not asking for me," his mother said. "Do it for everyone else, okay? It doesn't help anybody to see you like that."

That was the downside to being here: a bunch of mothers, sisters, aunts, and grandmothers all up in your business when you wanted to be alone. Teamwork was the lifeblood of the place. Because no matter who they were and what they were skilled at, they were all daughters first. The Daughters of the Unburned — that was what they called themselves. They were all here, each and every one of them, because some woman, somewhere, during the Burning Times of long ago, got away.

After he was cleaned up, doctored, and bandaged, he wandered in search of solitude, but even in a place this big solitude was an increasingly scarce commodity to come by as the hallways closed in and the rooms filled up. It wasn't so much a home now as a library and museum. Be it book or film, painting or sculpture, recording or carving or photo, if it was destined for the flames, they wanted to bring it here. Sanctuary, for as long as it was needed.

The firemongers wouldn't run rampant forever — they never did — but whatever they destroyed would be forever lost. Sanity *would* return one day. The main thing it needed was something to return to. Every artifact on a shelf, cabinet, or wall was another victory over anyone who'd ever wielded a torch.

Even the house's population of animals left this growing collection alone. It was like they knew, and he loved them all the more for it.

If the dearth of privacy was the downside of being here, the menagerie was the upside. The animals all had free run of the place, and squabbles were few. Cats, mostly, then dogs, and a lesser number of such critters as ferrets and rats, and one inseparable duo of a parrot that rode the back of a hulking box turtle as they roamed the back gardens together.

Some were just what they were, no more and no less, while others were witches' familiars. He had no familiar of his own yet, and if today was any indication, he never would. What self-respecting spirit would want him? Sometimes it seemed that the most he would ever be good for here was tending all those food bowls and water dishes.

It was how he'd first shown an aptitude for the craft: hearing what animals had to say. Which, okay, was a good start and all, but not the place anyone would want to leave it. You wouldn't actually be able to *do* anything.

As the afternoon wore on and he'd endured one pitying gaze too many, he sought refuge in the science room, figuring no one would think to look for him there. It was filled wall-to-wall with books on everything from astronomy to zoology, at least half sent by teachers and professors from every grade level. Pyromania could make for strange alliances.

He found the section devoted to dinosaurs and ran his finger along the titles. There. *Walking with Dinosaurs* would've gone right there. He scooted aside the books that would have flanked it and gazed into the empty space until it gazed back. *Never again.*

As for solitude, though, the day again seemed intent on proving that he wasn't as smart as he thought he was. The voice came first.

So which would you rather hear? More coddling sympathy? Because I can do that until you're sick of it. Or hard truths?

Peering down at him from the top of the bookcase was a twenty-pound Maine Coon with a head the size of a softball and a tail as bushy as a feather-duster. Chaucer, they'd always called him. Chaucer had been the familiar of Jeremy's sister Lizzy for as long as he could remember, although he'd always gotten the impression the cat never had much use for *him*. Now, though, Chaucer gave every indication of having been waiting here for him all along.

"I'm already sick of sympathy," Jeremy said.

Are you sure? I can do sympathy until you're coughing up hairballs for me. As long as we're being honest, I wouldn't mind some help with that.

"Just let me have the hard truths."

Good. Maybe there's something in you to work with after all.

The thing about Chaucer, though, was that Jeremy could never be certain the cat didn't just have a knack for eyeballing him and taking credit for the dialogue already going on in his head.

Ready? Yawn and you'll miss it. One . . . two . . . three . . . atonement.

Then the cat sauntered away down the row of bookcases.

"That's it? One word? That's your hard truth?"

Chaucer swiveled his great head around to eyeball him again, in that dismissive way of cats who knew their own mind.

It's a very hard word for some people to digest. Chew on it awhile why don't you, and see what you find inside it.

After dark, Jeremy forced himself to watch the consequences of his failure.

At night, from the coven house's highest balconies and gabled windows, you could see far enough to observe the waxing and waning of the fires. Always the pyre in Settlers Square, and sometimes the pyre out in Silverstone Park. Jeremy was the only one who ever watched. Nobody else wanted to. They all had fire in their DNA, like a memory passed down through the generations alongside an aptitude for the craft.

He chose his balcony for view first, seclusion second. He sat on the edge of his chair and leaned on his crossed arms on the stone balustrade. The distant orange glow would swell brighter, and he would imagine what had fueled it. There goes *The Art of Loving*. So long, Harry Potter. *Walking with Dinosaurs* just met an end as fiery as any asteroid strike.

How did a thing like this even get started? Or rekindled, some preferred to say. It wasn't even legal, the burnings and the roustings, the break-ins and confiscations, but laws that weren't enforced might as well not have been laws at all. He'd never heard of a single arrest for it, let alone a prosecution. Depending on who you talked to, the firemongers either left the right people alone or had friends in high places.

And they'd been sly enough to start small. A few books here and there, and, they claimed, only the worst kind of indefensible smut. Few bothered to object. Kooks and crazies would always be around doing what kooks and crazies did. If the occasional bonfire helped them blow off steam, well, no harm, no foul.

Renewal, they called it.

Little by little, though, the fires got bigger, hungrier, yet it always seemed just one small step past reasonable, not worth the confrontation. If people wished to burn what they no longer wanted, better that than a landfill.

Cleansing, they called it.

Jeremy supposed that when it didn't stop, and seemed only to gain momentum, it must have been a comfort to a certain type of person, giving in and going along, no longer needing to be concerned with what to think. Because somebody else had already given matters all the thought that was ever needed. Just fall in line, and that way you always got to be right.

The smoke rose in the distance, and from here it looked anything but cleansing.

"Nobody blames you, you know."

When he glanced behind him, he saw Lizzy framed in the darkened doorway to the balcony. He'd have known her if she hadn't said a word. No one else here had hair like hers, blonde so pale it was nearly white, and luminous in moonlight. A moment after he turned back to the pulse of the fires, she was beside him and he'd never heard her move.

"If they don't, they should," he said. "But I know some of them do anyway, so come on, stop making your lies to me so obvious."

Lizzy was only four years older, but seemed decades farther along this path. He couldn't remember a time when she didn't make it look easy. She could heal, she could cloak, and no matter if the baby was human or animal, she could attend its birth and the process would go as smoothly as any mother could hope for.

"I've been thinking," he said. "Maybe I should go back home to Dad and Adam. Maybe I shouldn't be here. Maybe it was a mistake. Like a visit that got out of hand and I started thinking I belonged."

Two years, nearly? That was long enough to know. Better to admit it now, right?

Besides, this wasn't home. As much as he liked most aspects of it, the coven house wasn't home. For a majority of them here, it wasn't. Not yet, anyway. Only a small core lived here permanently — a few of the elders who wore the name of crone with pride, and a couple of widows, and a few younger ones who took to the place like nuns to a convent. The rest? They came and went. They had lives and families beyond. Their time here was like a soldier's tour of duty, especially these last few years because, make no mistake, these were burning times, and there was work to be done.

"You think you're in the way, is that it?" Lizzy said.

"In the way. Waste of space, waste of energy, waste of resources." He shook his head. "If I'm supposed to do this, I want to *do* it. I don't want to come away from here and all I can manage is a couple stupid party tricks that fizzle half the time. I want to be able to matter."

"How'd you get the idea you don't matter now?"

"There's not much future in being the token moonboy around here. After a while it just starts feeling pathetic."

You don't want this, Adam kept telling him two years ago. *You think you do, but you don't.* Even then, he was almost persuasive, just not very good at hiding that this was coming from more than a big brother's protectiveness. The rest was jealousy. Maybe he'd wanted it for himself once and was just recycling the arguments he'd used to convince himself how much better off he was without it.

They had a way of looking at things here: Men were of the sun, and women of the moon. Men were of fire, and women of the tides. Women had to forget the moon and tides to go over to the side of fire, and rare was the man who was truly born to the silver light, to the ebb and flow.

You only think you want this, Adam kept telling him. *You'll always be a freak and a little bit suspect in their eyes.*

"It takes longer for the men. You know that. It's always been that way. It comes on when it comes on. It clicks when it clicks," Lizzy told him. "You're not in anybody's way. You just don't have any patience."

She reminded him of a few of the sons who had gone before. In their own direct lineage, there was Abner Dane, a great-great-grandfather who'd displayed a miraculous command of any animal that walked, crawled, flew, or burrowed. Then there was Reginald Crowe, who with the same willow stick could locate an underground stream or mend a snapped bone. And there was no one who hadn't heard of Daniel de la Cour, who at the age of nearly fifty developed such an intuitive understanding of machinery he could diagnose and repair anything regardless of its complexity or size.

All of them, and dozens more like them, were men born to the moon, yet even they were subject to the whims of time and tide.

That was the problem, wasn't it? That was why their eternal foe had always had the upper hand. Flames devoured in minutes what had taken years to grow.

She'd called him impatient? As far as Jeremy was concerned, he had the best reasons in the world for it.

Lizzy meant well, he knew that. If she really wanted to help him, though, maybe she should work on figuring out a loophole around this handicap of having to operate on such a different scale of time.

He got a block away before he stopped and turned around to take his bike back to the coven house. Then he started again, this time setting off on foot.

Eventide was coming on, and nothing had ever felt more right in his life.

If there was one truth about the craft he'd learned, it was that it could be simpler in practice than it was in theory. There were those who insisted that a witch's power came straight up from the earth. Some said it was drawn from the moon, the reflected light of the sun made gentle, filtered of its scorching fire. Others swore it was absorbed from the air around them, like the buildup of an electric charge, while still others said it was powered by nothing more than the beating of their hearts.

He'd seen the arguments go bad, and couldn't think of anything sillier than people who agreed on so much becoming so furious with each other they refused to speak for days. The centuries had thrown at them armies of people shouting that their power came from a devil they didn't even believe in . . . and *this* was what they chose to divide them?

Why couldn't the answer be all, or any, or none of them? Why couldn't it vary from witch to witch, wherever the flow met you? Why couldn't it change with the years, different sources for different phases of your life?

So he chose to walk, guided by the beacon of a distant fire, closer with every thoughtful step.

Sometimes you had to remember that people believed they were telling you one thing but were actually telling you another. Impatient? That he was. Yet he'd never considered that impatience was what made him mount his bike and seek the shortest distance somewhere. That it was impatience that sent him skimming over the ground as if a path were something to be endured.

And so he walked, lured by the beacon of that distant fire, and began to suspect he'd never understood the ground underfoot at all.

As the blocks passed, it opened as if rising to meet a need, tendrils of power coming up through to him as sure and stubborn as the wild weeds that broke through sidewalks and streets. Where others might see only pavement, he walked as if through a field at summer's zenith. As night deepened, it revealed rather than concealed. This was the dark known best to poets . . . the dark that bloomed and sang, a dark traversed by noiseless feet and dusky wings.

It was his, too, by birth, and always had been.

It drew him onward until he reached Settlers Square, the place where the firemongers brought ideas to die.

No one from the coven house had ever been here. None of them had ever come close. They avoided so much as looking at its poisoned glow from their windows, as if to gaze at the pyre too long would be to invite it. He'd been hearing the mantra for years: *They may burn their own world around them, but they'll never burn us again.*

The square was, by any definition, the heart of enemy territory. Jeremy spiraled his way inside, a gradual path past dozens of jostling people consumed with so much gleeful rage it tainted the air worse than the smoke. They may not have been monsters on their own, but together they comprised one made of countless heads and arms and shouting mouths.

Whatever Settlers Square had been like before, it was now a plaza of dead grass and trampled flowers dusted with the ash of thoughts. In the center had stood some sort of statue, but all that was left was a concrete pedestal and the corroded stubs of the bolts that had held the effigy in place, like the roots of a pulled tooth. Even the nameplate had been pried out.

The pyre was the square's center now.

They'd made an aboveground pit with steel posts on concrete bases, contained by chain-link fence, all of it blackened by soot and nonstop heat. The interior was a thick bed of glowing embers littered with blackened pages. Whenever the fire waned, two grimy men on either side raked the embers like autumn leaves to expose them to fresh air so the flames would leap to life again.

Here and there, the charred wood of framed artwork jutted through the ash; elsewhere, it ran thick with the slag of melted plastic from the cases of music and movies and software, and the tarry sludge of vinyl albums.

A dozen steps from the pyre sat a dumpster filled with items destined to burn, and people took turns grabbing whatever they wished, whatever angered them most, and heaving it toward the center of the pyre. There was never a lack of volunteers, and they never seemed to tire of it. Their eyes gleamed with a mad and empty righteousness, and that was what frightened him most — it seemed to come from a place so deep no amount of ash could ever fill it up.

So that was how things worked here, at this perpetual fire that stoked itself.

He'd seen enough. It was time to act. Mirroring a sneer on his face, he took his place among them, as two more of the monster's arms.

Atonement . . .

He'd had a night and a day to gnaw on the meaning of the word. It didn't mean doing things right the next time. That was only what was expected of him in the first place. Instead, it meant making up for the loss. If he'd let ignorant thugs steal six books he'd been trusted to carry, then he would have to pull six others from the pyre.

That would be atonement.

That would set the balance right.

The hardest part was blending in, looking like he belonged. The mob was here for one reason, they did only one thing, and he would have to begin by doing it, too. Nothing could have made him feel sicker, for there was a part of him convinced that everything was alive in its way, no matter how inanimate it looked. Everything had a soul. And surely these pages, these paintings, these photos and songs, were at least as ensouled as forests and hills. They were extensions of the creators who'd dreamed them into being. It would be like burning these people by proxy.

He flung one book into the fire, and people cheered as they saw what he wanted them to see: a young man raised right; a crusader just like them, before he could even drive a car. He pumped his fist in the air as he hurled another, and if the mob saw a grimace of distaste cross his face, they'd have their own ideas of what was behind it.

Six books? No, make it eight now.

He chose the next one with care. *Feathered Dinosaurs: The Origin of Birds*. And in his heart he said the words. He saw the results in front of him as clear as moonlight. He dug to his innermost core and flexed his will with love.

"Hey, this can't be right." He showed it to the man next to him. "This shouldn't be in with the rest, should it?"

The man had a downturned mouth and fanatic's eyes. He peered at the cover and blinked as if it took him an extra beat to focus. "No . . . no, who would've put that in there? Leave that out."

While the burning went on without him, he reached for another — *Being Peace*, this one — and waved it at two others. "And this one! This shouldn't be here either. Somebody got careless."

Next he grabbed two at once, flexing a little harder so they looked like one. He got the approval of the others, and now he had a stack.

He didn't know when it went wrong, exactly, or why. If it was because he'd gotten greedy or careless, or if the fear had made his focus falter. Or maybe, as he'd wondered, there were people who were too dull witted to fool, who saw only with the eyes of the herd, and nothing behind their own.

All he knew for certain was that they were onto him, then

on him, as a big thick hand swatted the books in his arms to the ground. His focus was gone, his resolve was gone. All that was left was the fear. The harder he tried to get away, the more of them pressed forward to block his path.

They had fists, and he could deal with that no matter how much it hurt. He had before. When he went stumbling to the ground they used their feet, and if he curled up tight enough he could deal with that, too.

But then they had rope. Of course they did.

They bound him — wrists first, then his ankles, then his knees. They leaned in, leered in, they screeched and shouted inches from his face . . . and if he hadn't seen it for himself, he would never have guessed that so many people born to so many mothers, across so many different years, could look exactly the same.

They hauled him upright, holding on roughly to keep him from toppling to the ground again. Through the blur he sought faces, expressions, anything he could latch onto for proof that someone out there thought this was wrong. There was nothing for him. Nothing but agreement, nothing but unity. Nothing.

Why else would they be so eager to stoke the fire hotter?

Before these guardians of the pyre introduced him to it, they denounced him as a thief. They called him a conjurer, a defiler in their midst. They called him a sodomite, and he couldn't even guess why. They labeled him a cancer and a blight. You wouldn't tolerate cancer in the body, would you? You wouldn't let blight run rampant in the fields of the lord, would you? Of course not.

You would burn them out.

He was borne aloft by countless hands, swung back and forth by his shoulders and feet, and, at a count of three, let go. He passed through what felt like a hot summer wind before crashing back to scorched earth. His mouth filled with a charcoal taste of embers and ash, and the stink of them seared the inside of his nose. The heat became an inescapable cocoon atop a bed of coals, the blackened husks of books shifting beneath him as he writhed. He would not burn quickly this way. Instead, they meant to roast him. Through the shimmering waves of heat he saw that the grimy men with the iron rakes held them ready to jab him back to the center if he squirmed too far away.

The rest? They jeered as he screamed and fought for breath, cheered as his hair flickered alight. They laughed as his clothes began to smolder.

Yet somewhere within, beyond heat, past pain, a part of him remained focused. He'd never known a longing so refined. Cold — it was all he wanted, all he could remember wanting in his life. There was nothing else . . . just cold, pure and elemental. It was so close. He could smell it like a shaving of window frost under his fingernail. He could see it in the white of the moon, taste it like a brittle cube. In the crackling of embers he could hear the spreading of icy crystals.

Now, if he could only feel it.

So mote it be . . .

He may have been the last to know. The first hailstones would've been outliers, barely a distraction from the business at hand. Then a nuisance along the fringes. Until they hit harder, faster, closer together, and within moments the mob recognized it was caught in a downpour. Hail showered from the deepest regions of the sky, at first the size of marbles, then chunks as big as fists. The more the crowd scattered, the greater the deluge — bricks of ice, blocks of it, a hailstorm to split scalps and crack skulls.

They all ran, desperate for shelter. If they escaped the worst of it overhead, then they slipped on it underfoot. Some got away, some didn't. They lay where they fell, and bled where they lay, and moaned for god to save them.

On the pyre, by luck or design, Jeremy was spared the heavy blows. He was still pummeled, but only by the smaller stones, stinging, yet not much worse than rain. On him, around him, it poured down in buckets as the fire gave way beneath it. Embers hissed and ash turned to mud with a great dying breath of steam. He rolled in the hail as it melted, and nothing had ever felt so good.

Then everything went quiet again. He could hear every groan around him, every whimper, every drop of ice water slipping through the trees. He lay on his back and breathed cool air. He blessed the sky and whatever might lie beyond it.

In time, he freed himself. These people weren't very good at knots, either.

After that, he crawled from the muck and over the fence. He was a mess, but messes washed off. His head was stubble, a newborn's, but hair grew back. He was burned, but he knew healers, and they loved him because he was one of their own.

So this was what it was like to find a calling. This was what it was like to work *with* yourself, rather than against.

It made sense, finally. It was so clear now, why he needed to learn patience. Fire always burned itself out eventually, but ice had the patience of glaciers.

He gathered up what books he could, steering clear of the fallen, then limped for home. There was so much work to be done.

Revenge, the saying went, was a dish best served cold.

He didn't know if he would call it revenge or not. Even now, he didn't want to think that way. But by all the gods he would serve them cold.

MICHAEL Z.
THE WILLIAMSON
DIGITAL *inspired by "The Analog Kid"*
KID *and "Digital Man"*

The earliest scene Kent remembered from when he had real eyes
was a meadow in the mountains. Surrounded by trees, it sloped
away on all sides and, where there were breaks in the foliage, it
looked over the edges of a city below. It was hundreds of kilometers from home, and his mom or dad had to drive them there.
Sometimes they'd camp in a tent behind the cabin.

He couldn't remember who owned the cabin. He did
remember Joey and Atilla helping him build a treehouse. They
had three platforms, a rope ladder, and had even stocked it with
rocks to fight off "others," though, looking back, he couldn't
remember what others they'd ever need to fight. Atilla had used
twine instead of the rope he'd bought to haul the bucket of rocks
up. When it snapped, it gouged Kent's head open. He still had a
scar from the stitches. At the time, that had seemed the worst pain
imaginable. He'd since learned otherwise.

He remembered the trees down the hill being chopped to the ground and shredded by machines one summer. Then an oval tower got built. It seemed out of place, growing out of the hill. Argosy Apartments, it was called. They had ads about the gorgeous view, except they'd destroyed his gorgeous view to do it. They'd also destroyed the tree house. At night, he could look out over the geometric sprawl on the plain below, and the rushing lights of distant streams of cars.

Even here, the glare interfered with stargazing. He begged Dad to drive him over the peak at 2 a.m. so he could catch a meteor shower.

They still played there, but he tried to face the other way, uphill, so he wouldn't have to look at the concrete. He wanted to imagine he was exploring the wilderness, not surrounded by millions of people.

"You seem frustrated," Mom had said one evening.

"They put a building on the hill," he said. "It was all rolling trees, and now there's apartments."

"I saw," she said. "It's not the same, eh?"

"No."

"We noticed it, too," she said.

The next year, he sat in the back of the car as they drove for the summer house.

"Don't we take this exit?" he asked.

Dad said, "We're going to a different summer house."

"Oh?"

"It's a surprise."

They drove up and over the mountains, looking down on a

valley full of spruce trees. He had his wilderness back. There was a house here, too. They were two hours from the grid around the city, but here was wilderness.

The new house was all log outside, all wood panels inside, with rails and deck around it. It was like something out of a Western movie.

His father said, "This was your uncle Travis's, but he said he wasn't going to use it much, so he's letting us buy it from him."

"Can Joey and Atilla visit?"

"If their parents say so, yes."

He and Dad nailed timbers and plywood to make another treehouse, in the thick lower limbs of a larch. It shifted in the wind, which scared him at first, but it eventually became fun, then soothing.

Overhead, he had vivid blue sky by day, and black nights scattered with buckets of stars. He'd sleep out under them, unafraid of the blanket of night or the animals passing through. He knew every constellation and would watch until late became early for glimpses of meteors. That was where he was bound. No one could build apartments to block that view, if he could get into space.

Far down the hill, the high-speed train wrapped through the valley. He could only see it occasionally, and the road not at all.

It wasn't until later he realized Mom and Dad were rich. So were several of his friends. He showed pics of his summer house to kids at school. Reggie Hanaway grabbed him at lunch one day. "It's kinda not cool that you have a second house. A lot of the kids here don't even really have one, just apartments."

"I just like it," Kent protested. "I'd live there all year if I could. I don't care about money."

"Well, it isn't fair," Reggie insisted.

Kent guessed money mattered to people who didn't have it. Just as space mattered to him. There were three companies building ships to explore other stars. He wanted to be on one.

"You'll need lots of math," Dad had said. So he started reading sites on geometry and trigonometry, and used his chore money for proctored tests.

When he was sixteen, his parents let him drive some of the trip. It was tiresome, across the flat prairie and up into the hills, then the mountains proper. It had seemed so much shorter when he was young.

"I never realized what a thousand-kilometer trip actually was," he said.

"Ain't it, though?" Dad replied. "Turn off is just around the bend here. Slow for it."

"I got it," he agreed.

His uncle had died two years before. They owned the cabin outright now, and the barn of tools and equipment. They also had one of his old cars. It wasn't like modern vehicles. It had no fuel cell. The engine was over seven liters and guzzled gasoline. The brakes and suspension were a lot softer and slower than a modern car, and it had no navigation or feedback. You even had to change gears manually. It was simple in mechanism, and he learned how to maintain most of it with the shop tools. He watched old videos and read books on how to handle it on the road.

In between repairing the car, he lay in the grass and watched deer, elk, and bobcats amid the waves of grass. At night he looked at the stars.

The next year he took the van down into the town for a container of gasoline.

"Hi, Kent," he heard. It was Sheriff Okume.

"Hi, Sheriff."

"What do you need gas for?"

"I got my uncle's old car working."

"That old Hemi?" the Sheriff said with raised eyebrows. "Watch yourself. Those things were damned near uncontrollable."

"I will." He knew every bolt of it.

It took some time to clean the engine up and get gas flowing, but it fired with a cackle.

He realized later they probably shouldn't have let him take it.

It's my turn to drive, he thought.

The car swayed on turns. It was gorgeous, but heavy and ungainly. In a straight line it was like a rocket, and he loved the acceleration pinning him to the seat. He could imagine he was lifting for space. He nailed it on every straight. It didn't like turns, though. He'd studied inertia. This was a good example.

The curves came up fast, and he was scared. The tires whined on the edge of their envelope, and it took real strength to muscle around the bend, even with power steering. It held, though.

The next curve surprised him, and he braked, double-clutched, and downshifted. The tires skittered, and the car grabbed. He was learning it, becoming one with it. He would master it.

As he thought that, the road wound up before him into an

inside turn that gave way to a tight outside bend. He recognized it. He hadn't realized he was that far up the mountain already. He slammed the shifter, stomped the pedals, and heaved the wheel. He felt the car understeer and skid across the road, then gravity dropped away as he sailed into the open air over the spruces below. He had a moment to think about how pretty they were, and that he was flying, before they shot past him like feathery spears and a crashing bolt of pain ran up his spine into his head.

"Kent, can you hear me?"

"Ayeh." *That wasn't the right . . . what was . . .*

"You're safe. You're in hospital."

That was . . . what it?

"No . . . eyes . . . work . . ." he muttered. *The . . . words. Words. Hard to get.*

"You suffered some brain damage from the accident. It will take time to recover. Do you understand?"

Of course he understood. *He wasn't . . . wasn't . . . that word . . .*

He started crying. He felt someone hold his hand, then lean against him. It was Mom.

"Physcal therapost?" he asked.

"I'm a helper while you learn how to move again."

She sounded pretty. He wished he could see her.

He felt her hands and someone else's steady him upright and pull his arms onto rails. He clutched at those and managed to stay upright. He locked his elbows and let his lower body dangle.

"We're going to work on trying to walk today," she said. "It won't happen all at once. For now, just get used to being upright again."

He knew how to walk. All you did was walk. Except his legs didn't do anything when he tried. He tried to talk and made gargling noises. The words had stopped again.

"Remember, your left leg is a replacement," the helper said. "It might take some time. It's normal."

No, *what was normal was walking*. He looked at his legs and couldn't see them.

He thought really hard. Think, walk, think, walk. Sweat started rolling into the bandages on his face, and he started crying again. He was clenching his jaw, and his teeth hurt. His shoulders hurt.

Think, walk.

The helper reached over and put her hand on his, and gently pulled his fingers off the bar.

Think, walk!

His left leg moved a fraction. Then another. Then it slid forward the length of a foot. He could tell by where his knee was.

He heard her gasp something.

She'd said, "Already?"

He strained and growled and clenched until his teeth felt like they were being stabbed. Then his real foot slid forward to join the left.

His arms went numb and he fell, landing in a heap and busting his lip on the bar.

"Did it," he said.

When he woke up he was back in his room.

He knew when the doctor came in. He'd already learned to identify people by the sound they made and their presence in the room.

"How are your words, Kent?"

"Better," he said. "I can remember a lot of them. What happened again?"

"You had a concussion and traumatic brain injury. Sections of your brain died. Do you remember what today is?"

"Eye day. New eyes." He was frightened, but he needed to see.

"Yes. We can't transplant. Your optic nerves were too badly damaged. We'd have to put artificial nerves in anyway. So your eyes are artificial, too."

"Yeah."

It took a long time for his eyes to come back, because they weren't eyes. He saw grainy upside-down images. Then he saw right-side-up images. Finally, they colored in. He noticed that things focused perfectly in front, but not outside of a circle of direct vision. He could see better, though. There were colors here he'd never known before. He asked about it.

"Yes, the imagers are designed to cover the entire spectrum that's theoretically visible to humans, and a little more for harmonic resonance."

"What does that . . ."

"You'll learn later."

He saw things differently than before. His memory of lighted streets in veils of fog wasn't the same as what he saw now. Now he could see the droplets and tiny rainbows of light through them.

His senior year had him in tears.

He was still finishing junior year work he'd been doing at home, because he'd missed most of the school year itself. But more than that, he remembered he'd been a clocker in trigonometry. He'd been starting on calculus and gearing up for differential equations, in high school.

Now, geometry had him in fits of frustration.

"But what is the answer?" he asked as Mr. Siles helped him plot another graph.

He followed with his eyes as Mr. Siles pointed. "That. Minus fifteen to seven point three."

"But which one?"

"All of them, Kent."

He knew this, but he didn't. "How can more than one be an answer?"

"How many integers are between one and ten, not counting them?"

"I . . . oh."

He'd been stupid. How could he not know that?

Mom and Dad didn't even mention the car, but it hung there, a subject never raised. It has been valuable, historical, and his uncle Travis's. All the additional support he'd needed on top of the medicine had cost them the summer house and land. In a shove of the accelerator, he'd destroyed part of his family's history. He was an apartment kid now.

He'd also destroyed his future. He was too far back in math to get into the programs he needed for space. He could dream, but he was trapped. He didn't want to work in one of the towers that blocked the stars.

"Hey, Kent, want to come cruising?"

"Sure," he said. He couldn't drive again yet, and wasn't sure he wanted to. But Marc had a sweet convertible, and it was a warm night. He needed to get out of the house.

He realized part of the reason they took him along was freak factor. At the Coff-In coffee shop parking lot, high school and college kids milled about. Since he was wearing shorts, his left prosthesis was visible. It almost matched the skeletal wheels, seats, and window frames of Marc's Turbo V.

Shortly, a burning hot blonde ran fingers along the door ledge, looked at him, and asked, "Did you get the shades to match the car, too?"

"Not exactly," he said, and took off his shades to show the metal orbits underneath.

"Oh, wow!" she said, more impressed than bothered.

Jackpot.

Yeah, it was shallow, and what did he care? He'd lost his real eyes and suffered a lot of pain. This was only fair.

"What's your name?"

"Casey," she said.

He could walk with a limp. He could see adequately. He'd even done well enough to get accepted to Avalon University, but that meant nothing now. His eyes especially needed ongoing tuning, and they occasionally aberrated enough to need a reboot. He wouldn't be going to space.

So he threw himself into cybernetics. There had to be a way to integrate stabilization protocols and circuits onboard. Then, of course, they'd have to be micronized. Materials did funny things at that scale. Cryogenic cooling was not an option for an implant.

It was properly graduate work, but he didn't want to wait. Class, study, then independent research. The grad students were aloof, but finally accepted his determination. He thought some of that was pity for his "condition." That should have irritated him, but they let him work so he swallowed it.

His apartment mate kept nagging him.

"Kent, man, you need rest," Andy would tell him at four in the morning.

"I need study."

"You're going to pass."

"Passing isn't enough." He had to clock it.

And he had to get to the gym. The left leg needed to work like the right one, and he needed more muscle tone. He pushed weights until muscle failure, feeling the burn.

He still talked to Casey, but they weren't dating.

She'd asked, "But what job are you going to get in the real world?"

"If I can't crew a ship, I'm going to one of the stations," he said.

And that was it. She wanted to remain on Earth.

The farm in the hills wasn't his anymore. Still, he made a point to drive up and take in the view from roadside, and from the public land farther up. There was a quite nice meadow there, and the view was even more vivid, if slightly artificial, with his eyes. He even went in winter to see the endless quilt of snow. He drove cautiously, sedately, with all the automated controls engaged, wincing every time someone passed him and volted up the mountain.

His sophomore year he got a spot of good news. The deep space projects changed the rules. They said they'd take certain prosthetics if they were stabilized.

That was his field. That's where he'd put all his effort.

His work was already known. CyRe Inc. and Omega sponsored some of his research and provided prototypes. He was in his second year of his doctorate when, completely apart from his thesis, one of his papers led to the micronization of monitor and adjustment circuits that just might be powered by bioelectricity. He received patent co-credit, and references.

A recruiter from CyRe called and offered him a position.

"Thank you very much, and I expect I'll take it, or something similar," he said. He'd probably have to. Better a rat in a race than in a cage.

"What would convince you?" she asked.

"If you had deep space operations," he said. "I put my life into this because I want to get there and couldn't with the prostheses I had. I probably can't now, even with the improvements they're making, but I don't want to commit until I have to." He wanted the lights of space, not of an industrial park.

"I'm sorry that we don't," she said. "But I'd like to keep in contact as you get closer to completing your doctorate."

"Please do," he said. If he couldn't go, he could help others, whether they wanted to reach space or just live normal lives.

An hour later, his phone rang again.

"This is Kent," he answered.

"Mister Eastman, my name is Najmul Hasan. I'm with HR at Prescot Space Resources. Ms. Luytens at CyRe gave me your information . . ."

He would have to make a point to visit Ms. Luytens. He'd never met her, but she was the most beautiful woman in the world.

Prescot even wanted to pay him. He promised to consider their offer seriously and respond within three days. He lasted two days before accepting, and barely avoided screaming that he'd do it for free.

He was going to space.

Prescot had heavy industry in the asteroids and wanted to jump to other systems. They worked with JumpPoint on theoretical physics he only vaguely understood. But they were going to space. They had a ship ready for trials, a destination, and wanted crew.

When he went to the mountains in August, he took a specially programmed sensor suite along. He hoped he'd need it.

This time he had control of the car. It was modern, safe, and handled any surface. It was better than his uncle's historical beast in every measure, but it lacked character.

Still, it took him along the road and up the mountain. He didn't let it get near the edge of control. Any time he felt traction feathering, he eased off. His future wasn't in race cars. It was in spaceships.

For the next two years, he learned how to fly an interstellar ship. The math was simple, really. The tough part was adapting his eyes so he could control them with internal feedback. The lack of eyelids was still more hindrance than help. Then, some of the flight controls were operated by tracking the pupils. He had no pupils. Four cyberneticists created an interface that mounted to the sides of his eyes and used induced microvoltage to mimic tracking. He wasn't involved with that because he was working on the ship's bionetic systems. He had to grit his teeth and trust in four strangers to make things work without ruining his eyes or bouncing him from the mission.

The tracking worked. The module was slim enough, but protruded from the sides of his head like bug eyes. He looked properly cyborg with those installed. That almost seemed fitting.

He was paired up with Lance Naguro for training. Together they worked on astronautic computers and onboard mission controls. They still had to learn to astrogate and pilot. The days started at 0500 and often went until dinner. They sat at consoles matching those of the *Seren Wrach*. The flight, with the JumpPoint, should last about a month. They might remain in system for a year longer. These couches would be their work stations. They were smaller than any cubicle, but they'd be in space.

About a month in, Lance said, "Kent, if you'll pardon the terminology, you're a machine. Do you ever sleep?"

"Yes." Some nights he saw treetops and a dark void. Some nights it was a dark void with stars. Other times it was a cubicle in a building. That was scarier than the first one. "But I want to do this."

"There's no doubt," Lance said. "I think you're pretty well guaranteed to be Lead."

He shrugged, "Lead, Second, as long as I go. Or the next flight. But I'm going. I'll volunteer to remain in place for the second mission, too."

Three months later, he got notice.

Lead Engineer, Astrogation and Project Control: Kent Eastman.

So then he had a crash course in flying, and cringed at the term. He went up in sailplanes and propeller trainers with instructors, then into jets, and finally, a converted military fighter. He discovered the loss of a leg let him pull more Gs — he had fewer extremities for blood to pool in. That, and his eyes worked past where flesh eyes grayed out from the same issue.

Parachuting terrified him, every jump. It took ten jumps to qualify for escape procedures, but he took ten more. It didn't reduce his fear. Falling would forever be his phobia. Gravity fell away, and he saw spruce trees.

It was only logical, he insisted to himself, that he buy a Hawkwing HangJet.

It did handle a lot like a hang glider. Then, if you dialed up the thrust, it turned into a tiny aircraft. You could drop from a plane or throw yourself off a mountain. He knew he had to do both.

The drop from the jumpship wasn't as scary with the jet. He pulled the lever that snapped the wing struts open, thumbed the igniter, and felt the engines shove. Here on the coast, he could see the endless waves of the sea. It wasn't space, but he felt there was a bond. He flew in broad loops around the dropzone and stirred up a wave of leaves when he touched down.

After that first open-air flight, he loaded the kit into his car and, with Lance along, drove up to where the farm had been. It now belonged to some wealthy producer who'd kept all the buildings but had built a castle farther in the trees. He messaged ahead to be sure he was expected and welcome.

The police lights surprised him. Had he been . . . ? *Damn.*

It was Sheriff Okume, who said, "Doctor Eastman, do you know why I pulled you over?"

The sheriff had helped save his life fifteen years before. He owed the man.

"I am so sorry, sir. I wasn't even paying attention."

Smiling and shaking his head, Okume said, "We already had one wreck this year. Slow down, okay?"

"Yes, sir. Have a good day."

Yes, he'd slow down. For now.

Lance chuckled, and he realized his fellow astronaut didn't know the details. He shrugged and drove.

He pulled through the electronic gate and bumped across the meadow.

There was his sensor pillar, with a hawk soaring down past it to snag a mouse from the grass. The pillar was untouched, and had two years of panorama. He pulled the pins mounting it to the steel post, and opened the trunk.

"Okay, Lance, you take it back down."

"You're sure?"

"Yup," he said, grabbing the HangJet, and closing the trunk. "I'll beat you down."

His phone rang. Even up here.

"Hey, Mom."

"Kent! What's the site for your interview? I want to make sure I catch it."

Indeed. That was in twenty minutes. He told her, and started laying out his gear for his first earth launch.

The hawk watched him curiously from a half kilometer away. His eyes were slightly better than the bird's.

On cue, the stream channel called.

"This is Kent."

"Doctor Eastman, are you ready?"

"Sure."

"Okay, we'll start recording . . . now, and intro, and we're on.

"We're live with Doctor Kent Eastman, before he leaves Earth and heads for another star system. Hi, Kent."

"Hi, Alex."

"How do you feel about leaving Earth? Sad? Or eager to get away?"

"Well, both of those. I'll miss my family and friends, and my favorite places, but I'm leading the way where I hope others will follow."

"What are your final preparations before you leave Earth for several years, possibly forever?"

"I'm actually at a remote place in the wilderness that's been an inspiration to me for a long time. I brought a stereo-holo-imaging setup so I can create a full surround image of it to take with me. It's been running for two years, so I can visit any season I want, or just let it run at its own pace. There's audio as well. I just wish there were some way to preserve the scents."

"So you're taking a bit of Earth with you?"

"A small bit that's very personal to me, yes. We have entire matrices of images, video, music, and film, and we'll get updates as we go. But this archive is something for me."

"Can you take a listener question now?"

"Sure."

The voice was that of a teenager. "Doctor Kent, I had ocular implants two months ago. I've been blind since birth. I'm just starting to see things now, and I guess it'll be years before everything syncs. It's almost dizzying. I managed without sight just fine, but now I realize there's that much more, and I will be able to see more than most people. How did you get from recovery to where you are now?"

He knew which eyes the boy meant. His research had helped create them. A small shiver of satisfaction ran through him.

"You have to be driven," he said. "Whatever you want to do, it has to be a passion that possesses you. You have to live it, dream it, wrestle it. If it doesn't mean that much to you, it's not your destiny, and you have to find what is. Never settle for less. Of course, it might take a long time to get there, and there might be detours. But you have to make the path."

He'd expected a half-hour long interview. Those were typical. At forty minutes he realized this one was running long. He sat back in the grass and pulled his hat brim over his eyes. The evening sun was still bright in the clear sky.

After an hour, he got up and started prepping for departure. He had to do so before it got too dark.

A young woman in the Seychelles wanted to know what courses had been hardest.

"I had to take high school math twice," he said, as he mounted the wings on the frame. "I had a traumatic brain injury from the accident that destroyed my eyes. It was so frustrating, I got so angry, knowing I'd learned all this and it was gone. Once I got through that . . ."

"The rest was easy?"

"No, not at all. But I knew it wouldn't stop me. All I did was math. If you're going into space, math and science are critical, even if you're in a social science. The more you can do to help the mission crew, the better." In fact, ballistic math had been easy after all he'd done.

"So what do you think you'll find there, Kent?"

"I have no idea," he said. "Something different. Somewhere I've never seen." He realized he'd barely seen Earth.

"I understand that. Exploration." The interviewer concluded with, "Thanks again, Dr. Eastman, and good luck and safe skies."

"Thanks very much, Alex. Good luck down here."

He took one last long look around in the still, cloudy evening, smelling the spruce, the mountain grasses, the tang of the fuel in his jet.

He donned the harness, checked every item religiously. He'd never been gigged in training on that. He took the list line by line, every time.

The meadow dropped away to the east, sloping steeper and then down a shallow cliff to the land below. He'd chosen this spot from memory. It was a safe, almost perfect launch zone.

He gripped the controls, flexed the wings, and read the HUD.

He had the one booster for launch, so he had to make it count.

He started the turbines and heard them spool. With the auto-igniter engaged, he jogged, ran, sprinted for the slope, and leapt. The wings caught air.

The booster cracked and roared and shoved him across the mountainscape as the turbines ran up. He angled slightly down to gain more velocity, watched the revs climb, and felt the thrust drive into sustained flight range.

He arced wide right, looking for the ribbon of old asphalt below. He found it, woven through the trees, and rose above it, looking . . .

There. That bend, those trees. That's where his journey had started.

He took a tight banking turn around the bluff, feeling Gs increase as he drove into the thermals rising up the slope. The trees had recovered, though there was a visible dip where the car had shorn their tops down. The maples glowed red and orange in their fall livery. The wind whistled past his helmet, causing ripples down his jumpsuit and down his spine.

And now it begins again, he thought.

Leveling off with arms out, he made a long, smooth descent, until the treetops whipped past only meters below, and the wind scoured his cheeks. He kept his enhanced vision on the path ahead. It wouldn't do to crack up now. He had an appointment to make.

The clouds parted, and bright beams of golden evening sunlight drenched the landscape. The trees gave way to shaven fields, and he ran thrust up until the wings thrummed in resonance, then eased off until consumption and velocity curves guaranteed he'd reach the landing zone. The sky ahead was indigo fading to a velvety violet. The sun was at his back, melting into the mountains.

It's my turn to fly.

The road unwound behind him. Before him were the stars.

The *Moving Pictures* liner notes for "Red Barchetta" include the intriguing acknowledgment "Inspired by 'A Nice Morning Drive' by Richard S. Foster." For years I had the vague misconception that "A Nice Morning Drive" must be a classic science fiction tale from the 1940s. After all, the story in the song sure *sounds* like it. Not until much later did I try to track it down, only to learn that it had been published in — of all places — *Road & Track* magazine in November 1973. Not the sort of thing *Road & Track* normally runs . . . but Neil Peart read the story and was inspired to write the lyrics to one of Rush's all-time most popular songs.

Of course, we had to reprint it in this anthology.

— KJA

RICHARD **A NICE**
S. FOSTER **MORNING**
inspired "Red Barchetta" **DRIVE**

It was a fine morning in March 1982. The warm weather and clear
sky gave promise of an early spring. Buzz had arisen early that
morning, impatiently eaten breakfast, and gone to the garage.
Opening the door, he saw the sunshine bounce off the gleaming
hood of his fifteen-year-old MGB roadster. After carefully
checking the fluid levels, tire pressures, and ignition wires, Buzz
slid behind the wheel and cranked the engine, which immediately
fired to life. He thought happily of the next few hours he would
spend with the car, but his happiness was clouded — it was not as
easy as it used to be.

A dozen years ago things had begun changing. First there
were a few modest safety and emission improvements required
on new cars; gradually these became more comprehensive. The
government requirements reached an adequate level, but they
didn't stop; they continued and became more and more stringent.

Now there were very few of the older models left, through natural deterioration and . . . other reasons.

The MG was warmed up now and Buzz left the garage, hoping that this early in the morning there would be no trouble. He kept an eye on the instruments as he made his way down into the valley. The valley roads were no longer used very much: the small farms were all owned by doctors and the roads were somewhat narrow for the MSVs (Modern Safety Vehicles).

The safety crusade had been well done at first. The few hare-brained schemes were quickly ruled out and a sense of rationality developed. But in the late '70s, with no major wars, cancer cured, and social welfare straightened out, the politicians needed a new cause and once again they turned toward the automobile. The regulations concerning safety became tougher. Cars became larger, heavier, less efficient. They consumed gasoline so voraciously that the United States had had to become a major ally with the Arab countries. The new cars were hard to stop or maneuver quickly, but they would save your life (usually) in a 50-mph crash. With 200 million cars on the road, however, few people ever drove that fast anymore.

Buzz zipped to the valley floor, dodging the frequent potholes which had developed from neglect of the seldom-used roads. The engine sounded spot-on and the entire car had a tight, good feeling about it. He negotiated several quick S-curves and reached 6000 in third gear before backing off for the next turn. He didn't worry about the police down here. No, not the cops . . .

Despite the extent of the safety program, it was essentially a good idea. But unforeseen complications had arisen. People became accustomed to cars which went undamaged in 10-mph collisions. They gave even less thought than before to the possibility of being injured in a crash. As a result, they tended to worry less about clearances and rights-of-way, so that the accident rate went up a steady six percent every year. But the damages and injuries actually decreased, so the government was happy, the insurance industry was happy and most of the car owners were happy. Most of the car owners. The owners of the non-MSV cars were kept busy dodging the less careful MSV drivers, and the result of this mismatch left very few of the older cars in existence. If they weren't crushed between two 6000-pound sleds on the highway they were quietly priced into the junkyard by the insurance peddlers. And worst of all, they became targets . . .

Buzz was well into his act now, speeding through the twisting valley roads with all the skill he could muster, to the extent that he had forgotten his earlier worries. Where the road was unbroken he would power around the turns in well-controlled oversteer, and where the sections were potholed he saw them as devious chicanes to be mastered. He left the ground briefly going over one of the old wooden bridges and later ascertained that the MG would still hit 110 on the long stretch between the old Hanlin and Grove farms. He was just beginning to wind down when he saw it, there in his mirror, a late-model MSV with hand-painted designs covering most of its body (one of the few modifications allowed on post-1980 cars). Buzz hoped it was a tourist or a wayward driver who got lost looking for a gas station. But now the MSV driver had spotted the MG, and with a whoosh of a well-muffled, well-cleansed exhaust, he started the chase . . .

It hadn't taken long for the less responsible element among drivers to discover that their new MSVs could inflict great damage on an older car and go unscathed themselves. As a result some drivers would go looking for the older cars in secluded areas, bounce them off the road or into a bridge abutment, and then speed off undamaged, relieved of whatever frustrations cause this kind of behavior. Police seldom patrolled these out-of-the-way places, their attentions being required more urgently elsewhere, and so it became a great sport for some drivers.

Buzz wasn't too worried yet. This had happened a few times before and, unless the MSV driver was an exceptionally good one, the MG could be called upon to elude the other driver without too much difficulty. Yet something bothered him about this gaudy MSV in his mirror, but what was it? Planning carefully, Buzz let the other driver catch up to within a dozen yards or so, and then suddenly shot off down a road to the right. The MSV driver stood on his brakes, skidding 400 feet down the road, made a lumbering U-turn, and set off once again after the roadster. The MG had gained a quarter mile in this manner and Buzz was thankful for the radial tires and front and rear anti-roll bars he had put on the car a few years back. He was flying along the twisting road, downshifting, cornering, accelerating, and all the while planning his route ahead. He was confident that if he couldn't outrun the MSV then he could at least hold it off for another hour or more, at which time the MSV would be quite low on gas. But what was it that kept bothering him about the other car?

They reached a straight section of the road and Buzz opened it up all the way and held it. The MSV was quite a way back but not so far that Buzz couldn't distinguish the tall antenna standing up from the back bumper. Antenna! Not police, but perhaps a citizens band radio in the MSV? He quaked slightly and hoped it was not. The straight stretch was coming to an end now, and Buzz put off braking to the last fraction of a second and then sped through a 75-mph right-hander, gaining ten more yards on the MSV.

But less than a quarter mile ahead another huge MSV was slowly pulling across the road and to a stop. It *was* a CB set. The other driver had a cohort in the chase. Now Buzz was in trouble.

He stayed on the gas until within a few hundred feet when he braked hard and feinted passing to the left. The MSV crawled in that direction and Buzz slipped by on the right, bouncing heavily over a stone on the shoulder. The two MSVs set off in hot pursuit, almost colliding in the process. Buzz turned right at the first crossroad and then made a quick left, hoping to be out of sight of his pursuers, and in fact he traveled several minutes before spotting one of them on the main road parallel to his lane.

At the same time, the other appeared in the mirror from around the last corner. By now they were beginning to climb the hills on the far side of the valley, and Buzz pressed on for all he was worth, praying that the straining engine would stand up. He lost track of one MSV when the main road turned away but could see the other one behind him on occasion. Climbing the old Monument Road, Buzz hoped to have time to get over the top and down the old dirt road to the right, which would be too narrow for his pursuers.

Climbing, straining, the water temperature rising, using the entire road, flailing the shift lever back and forth from third to fourth, not touching the brakes but scrubbing off the necessary speed in the corners, reaching the peak of the mountain where the lane to the old fire tower went off to the left . . . but coming up the other side of the hill was the second MSV he had lost track of!

No time to get to his dirt road. He made a panicked turn left onto the fire tower road but spun on some loose gravel and struck a tree a glancing blow with his right fender. He came to a stop on the opposite side of the road, the engine stalled. Hurriedly, he pushed the starter while the overheated engine slowly came back into life. He engaged first gear and sped off up the road just as the first MSV turned the corner.

Dazed though he was, Buzz had the advantage of a very narrow road lined on both sides with trees, and he made the most of it. The road twisted constantly and he stayed in second with the engine between 5000 and 5500. The crash hadn't seemed to hurt anything and he was pulling away from the MSV. But to where? It hit him suddenly that the road dead-ended at the fire tower, no place to go but back . . .

Still he pushed on and at the top of the hill drove quickly to the far end of the clearing, turned the MG around, and waited. The first MSV came flying into the clearing and aimed itself at the sitting MG. Buzz grabbed reverse gear, backed up slightly to feint, stopped, and then backed up at full speed. The MSV, expecting the MG to change direction, veered the wrong way and slid to a stop up against a tree. Buzz was off again, down the fire tower road, and the undamaged MSV set off in pursuit. Buzz's predicament was unenviable. He was going full tilt down the twisting blacktop with a solid MSV coming up at him and an equally solid MSV coming down after him.

On he went, however, braking hard before each turn and then accelerating back up to 45 mph in between. Coming down to a particularly tight turn, he saw the MSV coming around it from the other direction and stood on the brakes. The sudden extreme pressure in the brake lines was too much for the rear brake line, which had been twisted somewhat in his spin, and it broke, robbing Buzz of his brakes. In sheer desperation he pulled the handbrake as tightly as it would go and rammed the gear lever into first, popping the clutch as he did so. The back end locked solid and broke away, spinning him off the side of the road and miraculously into some bushes, which brought the car to a halt. As he was collecting his senses, Buzz saw the two MSVs, unable to stop in time, ram each other head-on at over 40 mph.

It was a long time before Buzz had the MG rebuilt to its original pristine condition of before the chase. It was an even longer time before he went back into the valley for a drive. Now it was only in the very early hours of the day when most people were still sleeping off the effects of the good life. And when he saw in the papers that the government would soon be requiring cars to be capable of withstanding 75-mph head-on collisions, he stopped driving the MG altogether.

AUTHOR'S NOTE

Back in the early 1970s, as I was writing "A Nice Morning Drive," little did I know that my story would end up in *Road & Track* magazine, or that Neil Peart would be inspired by it to write "Red Barchetta." Although I had heard the song on the radio when Rush released the *Moving Pictures* album, I didn't realize the connection until 1996 when a fellow in my office tried out the internet by searching my name. His search found a Rush fan website, and we all marveled at the connection.

Then it wasn't until 2006 that I read Neil's book *Ghost Rider* and realized, among many other things, that he and I were both lifetime car aficionados, rode the same model BMW R1200GS motorcycles, and enjoyed writing. Or that we were both members of famous and groundbreaking "power trio" bands. (Okay, in my case the Surftones are really just a carport band hoping to someday graduate to garage band status.)

One thing led to another and, before I knew it, Neil, Michael Mosbach, and I were tearing around the backroads of West Virginia on our motorcycles having a great time and getting to know each other. Less than a week later, I attended my first Rush concert, accompanied by my college roommate and best friend Buzz — the hero of "A Nice Morning Drive." Neil and I have been great friends ever since.

In between writing the story in 1972 and meeting Neil in 2007, I managed to finish graduate school, become an actuary, serve as the Chief Actuary for the U.S. Medicare and Medicaid programs, race cars with the Sports Car Club of America for ten years, and have a most enjoyable life with Nancy, my wife of almost forty-four years, and many friends. I read Neil's "NEP News" stories religiously, and he reads my RSFTripReporter.net stories (occasionally catching spelling errors in the process), and we get together whenever our wanderings put us in the same part of the country.

I hope you enjoyed "A Nice Morning Drive" and its connection to "Red Barchetta."

— Richard S. Foster

DAVID FARLAND

PLAYERS *inspired by "Tom Sawyer"*

Solomon Isaac fought down his fear as he opened the cab door. His legs wobbled beneath him like reeds, and his head felt almost as if it were floating, disembodied.

What do you think you're up to, buddy? he asked himself. *Going to the effing Middle East to close a movie deal. You're just a little Jew boy, and you're going to get hurt.*

He swung his travel bag from the cab's rear seat, and his elbow brushed the pistol in his concealed belt holster. *Damn! Good thing I noticed it before the TSA did.*

He wondered where to hide the gun. There was no time to take it back to his house, or even to the office in Hollywood.

He slid his gaze across the façade of Burbank's Bob Hope Airport then studied the potted palms near the front door.

"Sir?" the driver said through the open passenger window.

84

Sol eyed the meter, pulled out his wallet, peeled off a hundred-dollar bill. "Keep the change."

"*Gracias.*" The cabbie pocketed the bill, closed the window, and eased away from the curb.

As the cab's taillights receded in the gathering dusk, Sol studied the palm trees, took a calming breath. *Too bad I can't take it. I'd feel a lot safer if I were packing heat.*

He strode to the nearest palm. The tree was large, with a few red chrysanthemums planted in the loose humus at its base. He picked a spot near the largest bush. *That'll be easy to recognize when I get back.*

The secret to getting away with . . . questionable things, Sol knew, was to be bold, to act as if what you were doing was proper. It wasn't *chutzpah* that he needed, exactly, but it was something damned close.

He worked the holster's paddle off his belt. He scrutinized the compact, .45-caliber Smith & Wesson for a moment, loathe to place it in the soil; he wanted to wrap it in something first.

He'd purchased a few travel-size toiletries before calling the cab. He unzipped his carry-on and snagged the white plastic bag off the top. Dumping the toiletries into his carry-on, he slid the pistol, holster paddle and all, into the store's bag and knotted the top. *That's better.*

A businessman walked past him into the terminal, and Sol ignored the man.

Instead, he scooped a hole with bare hands, as if he were a gardener. The dry landscaping mulch got under his fingernails despite the fact he kept them trimmed short. He had no difficulty scooping a cache large enough to contain the handgun, but he grimaced at the soil as he worked. *I feel like some idiot movie pirate, doing this.*

With the hole filled and mulch chips smoothed to conceal the spot, Sol straightened. A woman exited the door, but she wouldn't have been able to see him. He brushed himself off and hurried into the terminal.

A glance at his gold wristwatch showed he still had an hour to catch his flight to Atlanta, so he detoured to the nearest men's room to thoroughly scrub his hands and inspect his charcoal-gray suit for splinters of mulch.

Once settled in first class, on Delta, Sol retrieved his iPhone and reread the message which had arrived that morning:

Next time you are in our region, His Highness Prince Farhan would like to meet with you. He has expressed interest in backing your current film fund. Cordially, Mr. Ahmed bin Al-Muhmahd bin Al-Rashad, Attorney at Law.

Sol had immediately replied that, as it happened, he was traveling to Dubai the next day. When Mr. Ahmed confirmed that Prince Farhan would be pleased to meet him there, Sol assured him that he would make contact when he arrived in country. Then he'd swiftly booked a flight, by way of Atlanta, and a room at the Riqqa Ali Babba, a mid-priced hotel in downtown Dubai. Arab businessmen, Sol had learned, preferred not to set solid appointments until both parties were in the same locale.

He smiled at the lawyer's use of "His Highness" in reference to his Saudi client. In his mid-thirties, Prince Farhan had a secret love for American movies, and too much oil money scorching holes in the pockets of his dishdasha. Farhan doubtless belonged to some obscure "cadet branch" of the Saudi royal family, what Sol thought of as a shirt-tail relation.

He's probably got about as much royal blood as a goat does. Sol allowed himself a slight smile. *But maybe three years of courting the kid is finally going to pay off.*

Good timing for Bronc and that blockbuster he's filming. If I can cut him loose from the Chinese mob, I may be able to persuade him to take me on as a partner.

Sol watched the boarding passengers shuffle past first class, some nudging children wearing souvenir t-shirts from Universal Studios or Disneyland. Sol felt a pang of longing, then one of bitterness. He'd always wanted a family, but Regina, his wife of almost twenty years, couldn't be bothered with kids.

Regina the Vagina. Sol scowled and shifted to stare out the oval window. A lengthy video he'd received last week had confirmed his suspicions that she was cheating on him. A hidden camera had caught her, still voluptuous at thirty-nine, screwing some blond bastard who appeared to be younger than Farhan. A movie star wannabe from some pissant town in the Midwest, no doubt.

He'd watched the man fondling Regina's augmented breasts and wanted to shout, "Hey, asshole, I bought those!"

Time for a divorce. In Hollywood, some men said that you should marry three times. The first time for sex. The second for a family. The third for true love.

He'd married Regina for the vagina and had hoped that she'd bear him a muppet or two. She'd disappointed him in that respect.

Now he suspected that he'd lose half of what he owned when he divorced Regina. But that wasn't the worst of it.

The video had arrived anonymously, but Sol knew very well that his partner, the moneyman behind his company, Free Bird Entertainment, had sent it. Glenn Northwood had made his first few million as a military contractor developing both offensive and defensive cyberwarfare systems.

Spying on me, too, aren't you, you effing old goat?

Northwood shared none of Sol's aesthetic tastes in film. All he wanted was easy money.

"The real money, Sol, old boy, is in porn," Northwood had said more than once. "Forget art. You've got all the right contacts. You've got genius directors, and line producers who know how to squeeze a quarter out of every dime. You really want to make art films, then make porn your art. We videostream it from Bosnia, and it'll make a killing compared to those so-called 'real' movies Hollywood makes. You've just got to think of yourself as the goose who keeps laying golden eggs."

What a load of crap! Sol bridled at the thought. *I've got to get out of this hellhole before I lose my edge — or worse, my soul.*

He'd be forced to give up a fortune to Northwood when he quit Free Bird. At the moment, he didn't god damn care.

Close the deal. That's all that matters.

He tried to calm his breathing. Sol had met with Prince Farhan a few times before, but had never so much as shaken hands. Farhan had stopped in at LAX, and they'd met aboard Farhan's private jet so that Farhan wouldn't have to contaminate himself by touching infidel soil. It went without saying that the devout man wouldn't shake hands with a Jew.

It was a mark of Sol's urgency that he'd even *considered* traveling to an Arab country, let alone gone through with it.

Only as the aircraft began its climb out of Burbank did he fully register what he was doing.

What the hell were you thinking, Sol? You're a Jew, and a pornographer on top of it. Exactly the type of guy your typical jihadi would love to stuff into an orange jumpsuit and behead with a dull, two-inch blade on YouTube.

When the generously curvy, blonde flight attendant asked what he'd like to drink, Sol ordered a scotch neat and nursed it most of the way to Atlanta.

He didn't sleep much through his connecting flight to the United Arab Emirates. He spent part of it with iPhone in hand, brushing up on Arab business protocol and the usual compliments and wishes for blessings upon one's hosts that accompanied the opening of meetings. He spent the rest of the flight questioning his sanity.

When the pilot announced that they were beginning their descent into Dubai, Sol's palms dampened. He wiped them on the linen napkin that had accompanied the dinner service, which he'd only picked at, and forced himself to peer out the window.

The setting sun lay on the surface of the Persian Gulf, lighting a cloud-streaked sky with peach and orange, and casting a path of golden fire across the ripples to the shore.

Minutes later, as the aircraft banked into its final approach, Sol spotted the Burj Khalifa, the world's tallest tower, like a needle rising among the glittering lights of the modern city.

"We just missed the sunset call to prayer," the pilot said as the aircraft taxied to the gate. "The last call will come after dark."

Sol suppressed a shudder. He wasn't a religious man, but a line from his mother's favorite Psalm of David passed through his mind. *Yea, though I walk through the valley of the shadow of death . . .*

He had only his carry-on, no baggage to claim. Mouth dry, he acknowledged the flight attendant at the aircraft's exit with a courteous nod.

The terminal, an oval tunnel bright with stainless steel and glass, might have belonged to any major airport in the States or Europe. Except for the palm trees towering like guards along the slideways, and men wearing white dishdashas and red-and-white checkered keffiyehs milling among the travelers.

I'm walking through the valley of the shadow of death.

Sol squelched the thought and made his way briskly to a currency exchange booth, where he traded a few hundred dollars for Emirati dirhams. The young woman at the counter spoke English with only a trace of an accent. She smiled and directed, "That way, sir," when he asked where he might find a taxi.

Upon emerging from the terminal, he found the cabs lined up at the curb, as at any other airport. They were white Toyota Camrys with stylishly colored tops. He slid into the back seat of the one in front.

The driver, a wiry young man in his mid-twenties with a sparse, black beard, stared at him through the rearview mirror as he requested, "Riqqa Ali Babba Hotel."

The driver pulled away with a squeal of tires, his eyes fixed on Sol instead of the lane out of the airport.

He kept driving, but his eyes hardened as he stared at Sol and began to scowl. After two hundred yards, he wetted his lips and said with a heavy accent, "You are a Jew!"

The driver's black eyes took on a manic glint. "A dog Jew in my taxi!" He seemed genuinely put out. "Now I will have to cleanse it before —"

"Don't be ridiculous," Sol snapped, and felt relief that the abrupt wash of fear didn't reveal itself in his voice. He puffed out his chest. "Keep your effing eyes on the road."

He remembered something that his father used to say: "If you're going to lie, do it with dignity."

The driver blinked, peered at the road, and the cab careened through the busy twilit streets as if the driver couldn't be rid of his passenger quickly enough. At the gilded entrance of the Riqqa Ali Babba, he refused to take the fare from Sol's hand. When Sol dropped the bills in the front seat, the young man spat on them before he squealed away, sending up a spray of grit.

Sol drew a few deep breaths to compose himself as he strode inside.

The lobby rose up in a thirty-story atrium, down the center of which hung a massive wind chime, giant geometric shapes of colored glass and shiny metals that clinked and tinkled in an artificial breeze. White orchids and exotic vines bloomed in three-foot-high vases placed among groups of richly upholstered chairs and gold-edged tables.

The aromas of pastries and strong Arab coffee wafted from a coffee bar down the lobby as Sol crossed to the registration desk. He glanced toward its ornate gazebo. *I could certainly use a cup or two of that right now.*

Checked in, and with steaming coffee cup in hand, Sol took an elevator to the fourth floor. As he opened the door to his room, the softened light from a lamp in one corner assured him it would be adequate and practical, with an executive-style desk and a king-sized bed, but it lacked the luxurious amenities that the ad had showed in the suites above the atrium.

Behind the desk, the partly opened curtains revealed a sliding glass door onto a narrow balcony and a view of the Burj Khalifa's lower levels, sparkling from within against the settling night.

Sol showered and shaved before he called Mr. Ahmed. *It wouldn't surprise me if they want to meet tonight.*

Almost breathlessly, he considered the films in his slate, rehearsing the pitches for each one. He had the log lines down by heart, along with the enhanced pitch. Some of the films he'd been wanting to make for twenty years.

He inhaled. *You won't screw up this sales meeting,* he promised himself. *This is an opportunity. These films need to be made, and Farhan is going to want them. He just doesn't know it yet.*

Sol made the call. The lawyer sounded pleasant and relaxed when Sol announced himself. "Ah, Mr. Isaac, very good, I trust you had a pleasant flight?"

"Yes, it was, thank you," Sol replied.

"Very good," Ahmed said again. "Where are you staying? We will send a limo at 10:00 tomorrow morning to bring you to the Mishari Al-Khaled Law Firm for our business meeting."

The cab driver's savage, black eyes burned through Sol's memory. "I'd appreciate that, Mr. Ahmed."

He'd barely concluded the call when a wail began outside, a caterwaul that made the hair at the back of his neck stand on end. He froze and listened.

"*Allahu akbar, Allahu akbar,*" called a clear tenor voice. Stillness fell on the streets below. "*Ash-hadu an-lā ilāha illā Allāh . . .*"

Last call to prayer for the night. Sol let out his breath.

But the cab driver's menacing stare slid into his memory once more, and he threw the bolts on his door. *No telling how cheaply guest information might be bought down at the front desk.*

When the predawn call to prayer tore Sol from sleep about an hour before his wake-up call and he couldn't drift off again, he got up and pressed his shirt using the iron and board from the closet. He could've had the hotel valet service do it, but having someone he didn't know bring it to his room offered too easy an opportunity for some kind of attack. Besides, he had yet to see a hotel valet do as impeccable a job as he could himself.

Returning to his room after breakfast to clean his teeth and collect his slim leather binder, he paused to throw open the sliding door to the balcony. A morning breeze swept in, bearing familiar traffic noise, traffic fumes, and the faint, salty scent of the Persian Gulf. The light was blinding. Sol pulled the curtain closed and headed to the elevator to meet Prince Farhan's car.

A white stretch limo pulled up promptly at 10:00, and a uniformed footman opened the gleaming door to the passenger compartment. "Please enjoy a cup of coffee, Mr. Isaac," he said, gesturing to the intricate silver coffee service set out on the bar. "The law firm is across the city."

"Thank you. I believe I will," Sol smiled. *One can never be too alert going into the lion's den.*

He calmed himself and glanced occasionally through the tinted windows as the limo eased through Dubai's busy streets. He had film concepts to pitch, five of his own as well as Bronc's Chinese blockbuster, and he wanted to present each one with the grace and power it deserved.

The limo pulled up to a modern high-rise with a classic Arab façade. The footman opened the building's tinted-glass door and motioned Sol inside. After the sunlight the lobby seemed half dark, and Sol didn't see Mr. Ahmed until the lawyer had drawn up close and extended his hand.

"We are glad you could join us," the lawyer said, smiling beneath his thick mustache. "Come this way, please. We will be meeting in the penthouse garden this morning."

As an elevator whisked them to the top of the Mishari Al-Khaled law building, Sol adjusted his red-patterned tie and brushed a speck of lint off the front of his conservative dark-gray suit. When the door shushed open, Mr. Ahmed gestured Sol to exit before him.

He stepped into what first appeared to be a palm grove.

Mid-morning sunlight filtered between leaves almost as broad as his body, casting cooling shadows over the glass-topped table and the half-dozen men sitting around it.

All but one wore red-and-white checked keffiyehs, large, dark sunglasses, and neatly trimmed mustaches and goatees. *Like photocopies of the stereotypical Saudi male*, Sol thought.

Only Prince Farhan, clearly the youngest man present, stood out. He wore a black, gold-trimmed robe over his pressed linen dishdasha, and a plain white keffiyeh that identified him as a *hajji*.

The other men stood when the prince did, and Sol, dry-mouthed, offered, "*Salaam alaikum*, Your Highness."

Farhan smiled. Almost a grin from behind his sunglasses, and not without genuine warmth. "*Kaif halak*," he replied, offering his hand.

As a twenty-something, Prince Farhan could have been a male model, Sol decided. Now in his mid- to late-thirties, his face had only begun to soften under the excesses of extreme wealth.

"Thank you for meeting with us," Farhan said. "I will allow Mr. Ahmed to make the introductions to my colleagues."

Colleagues? Sol wondered. *Probably a pack of ISIS commandos.*

Moving around the circle, greeting each man in turn and looking directly into their shaded eyes in the Arab way, Sol couldn't help wondering if they secretly burned with the same loathing as the cab driver had.

Introductions finished, Farhan gave a small nod. A steward emerged from the shadows beneath two tall palms, bearing a gold coffee service on a tray large enough to cover most of the table. Then he beckoned to Sol. "Come, sit here beside me, Mr. Isaac, and we will talk about investing in your films."

Sol settled into the white wicker chair placed close at the prince's right elbow, planted his black leather shoes firmly on the mosaic floor tiles, and accepted a glittering gold coffee cup from the steward. It would likely take hours to come to actual negotiations, he knew.

There would be pleasantries about their respective families — the children, in other words. Sol spoke of his nephews at such meetings. Sports were a safe topic. And luxury automobiles and yachts. And the arts. Especially films. They would talk long about films, and eventually Sol would pitch his concepts.

At that point, the prince would nod to Mr. Ahmed. The key decision-maker in the gathering became a silent observer while his assistants hammered out the deal.

So Sol's eyebrows rose almost to his slightly receding hairline when the lawyer, cradling his own steaming cup, leaned forward. "It is most unfortunate," he began in an apologetic tone, "that we must forego the traditional courtesies on this occasion, Mr. Isaac, especially when you have come so far. His Highness must return home this afternoon. It is a family matter of great importance, a new son expected to enter the world by this evening."

"That's wonderful news, Your Highness," Sol said, smiling as he turned to address the prince. "I believe this is your fourteenth child?"

"My fifteenth, and my ninth son." Even behind the sunglasses and keffiyeh, there was no mistaking the younger man's pride at the impending birth. His broad smile displayed movie-star-perfect teeth and crinkled the small, pale scar near the corner of his eye.

But Sol's gut twisted under his ribs. *This is completely off. Why did Farhan agree to a meeting at all when he knew the birth was imminent? There's something else going on here.*

"We must, as you say in your film production, 'cut to the chase,'" Ahmed was saying.

"Very well." Sol's gaze swept the circle. He felt every pair of unseen eyes boring into him, noted the expressionless straight lines of every mouth. He cleared his throat, leaned forward as well. "I have a bundle of six films for which I'm seeking backing. Five are my own concepts, stories that will empower people and make the world a better place."

The excitement he always felt for his art began to swell, edging out the uneasiness still lurking in his gut.

"I don't know if you're aware of it, Your Highness, but I'm a student of neurolinguistic programming," Sol said. "I'm fascinated with how its modeling assists people to increase the use of all their senses, to enhance learning, and enables one to see himself as having already achieved his life's dreams."

His pulse had quickened and his voice rose slightly. He glanced about the circle again. Spotted puckered brows above four pairs of sunglasses. *Puzzlement, or curiosity?*

It didn't matter, he decided. But he consciously toned down his voice when he continued, "I've selected five little-known films, small masterpieces if you will, which I have rewritten to demonstrate the impact of NLP on people's lives.

"The first is based on a Mexican film released in 2000, *Amores Perros*. It's unique in that it contains three separate stories connected by a single event, a tragic car crash.

"In my remake, the separate stories revolve around three young girls from different social classes who all witness an assassination — the single connecting event. In dealing with the resulting trauma, each girl finds NLP. They never meet, but each rises to a position of influence, one as a medical doctor, one as governor of her state, and one at the head of a powerful drug cartel."

Sol paused, scanned the group once more. A couple of the mouths had pursed in addition to the wrinkled brows, and one jaw had set. His heartrate quickened, but he pressed on.

"A second story is drawn from a film set in the United Kingdom. *Ginger & Rosa*, which was released in 2012, begins with the births of two girls in London on the same day America dropped the atomic bomb on Hiroshima."

Three of the men seated across from Sol shifted in their wicker chairs and slid sidelong glances at one another.

Sol sipped coffee to moisten his mouth.

Silence hung over the table like the dust motes adrift in the shafts of sunlight that pierced the palm fronds.

"Yes," Ahmed said, almost an interruption, "we are familiar with your slate. But," he asked in apparent confusion, "there is now a *sixth* film?"

Of course, he had sent them a prospectus, but in Hollywood producers never actually read the damned things. They preferred to hear it "from the horse's mouth," as they say.

Sol sat back in his chair and smiled. "That one is being filmed as we speak, by my protégé in China, and that one," his smile tightened, "is going to be a blockbuster."

He felt the tension lift, saw it in relaxing mouths and easing forehead creases. So he added, "Bronc is doing fabulous work. It's a big fantasy —"

"How much will you need to produce the films?" Ahmed asked. There was something in his voice that said, "I know all about this movie," and Sol sat back.

His current business partner wasn't the only person in Hollywood who resorted to corporate spying. Sol suspected that the Arabs knew all about the project . . . even the unfortunate attachment to the Chinese mob.

Sol needed $60 million, but he knew the haggling process would whittle down his opening request. "One hundred million to do all six," he said. "The majority of that would be spent on

Bronc's film, of course. We'll bring the computer graphic design work to the States, though some of the B-shots can be rendered in Asia. This is a huge fantasy, one that we can sell as an indie tent-pole property to Paramount or Warner Brothers domestically, but if we do it in 3D, it will make all of our money back in China alone. We're talking a billion dollars in global box-office potential — and perhaps seven billion in merchandising revenue . . ."

The lawyer, the only one besides Sol not hidden behind sunglasses, slipped a meaningful look to the prince.

At that moment, a singsong cry rose on the morning air.

"Ah, the call to prayer," Ahmed said. "You will please excuse us, Mr. Isaac."

"Certainly," Sol nodded. He rose while Prince Farhan stood and led his entourage to the elevator.

When its door closed, he sank back into his wicker chair. Listened as the call rolled on around him. *Like a damn banshee. And just when we were getting down to business.*

Twenty minutes later, Sol stopped pacing through the potted palms at the sigh of the elevator opening and returned to the table in the garden's center. Like the others, he remained standing until Prince Farhan resumed his seat.

As Sol sank into his wicker chair at the prince's side, Farhan said, "I am eager to see the Chinese film completed, Mr. Isaac. We will come to a fair agreement."

Sol had learned, through his years of contact with the prince, to read the context in Arab communications. "Yes" meant "possibly," concessions were traded for concessions, promises were made to do certain things with the understanding that a genuine effort might qualify as fulfillment, and one would never receive an outright refusal. Preserving each other's dignity and saving each other's face remained paramount.

Sol knew better than to attempt a hard sell, too. It was considered rude.

As the discussions wound on, mostly between Sol and the lawyer, Prince Farhan removed his sunglasses and leaned on the chair's arm nearest Sol. He appeared pensive, as if the joy at his new son's arrival had evaporated in the midday heat. Sol's earlier uneasiness returned under the young man's steady gaze, but he couldn't place the shadowed expression in his eyes.

He resorted to his NLP training. There was fear in the man's eyes, and that slight slump in the shoulders . . . resignation?

Sol decided to give it his best shot, to try to reel Farhan in.

"Look," he said. "I don't think that you need to make films for money. You've got more than enough. Nor do I . . . sense that you want to make them for art's sake, exactly. But there's a lot that one can achieve with a film."

One of the Arabs who had not spoken, the one with the hard jaw, said, "To send a global message?"

"Exactly," Sol said. "To change the world, to touch people, one heart at a time. Back in the 1920s and '30s, my people were not . . . exactly popular in America. We were beaten, persecuted. But some of us saw the potential for movies to change the world, to slowly change human perceptions.

"Your Highness, your own people are facing some of the same kinds of stereotyping. A few of your people are terrorists, so all of you get the same label." Sol knew that he was pushing, knew that he shouldn't do it, but said, "But what if we worked together? What if your movies educated the world about your culture, taught others to see the . . . the beauty in it, the humility and honor?"

One of the men began to speak, but the prince held up his hand. "Would you consider casting a Moslem star in a role? For example, could a Moslem man be cast in the role of Wu Li?"

That question shocked him. In Bronc's film, Wu Li was a powerful protector, a mythic figure come to life, a man whom enemies thought of as a monster while his friends thanked the gods for his presence.

"Wait a minute," Sol said. "Your cousin?"

He did not need to speak anymore. To voice the question was to make a promise.

Then Sol's jaw dropped a little in amazement. These bastards understood that a story doesn't just entertain, it transmits culture, and they needed that. Perhaps they even believed that they needed him — to have the Moslems and the Jews making movies together.

He had an epiphany. He envisioned a truly global market, one where he used his connections with Jewish-run studios to distribute films in the West, where Mr. Chin sewed up Asia and India, and where — to his surprise — Moslem filmmakers brought the same picture into the Middle East, Africa, Malaysia, the Philippines . . . the profits would be incalculable.

Oh, man, I've been played, he thought.

He'd imagined that he was the only player in the room.

Ahmed said, "We can provide you twenty million at this time, Mr. Isaac."

Only twenty? That's a third of what I need. Sol contained his disappointment. "That will barely cover production of Bronc's tent-pole film," he said. "It won't allow me even to begin any of the others."

"The Chinese film must be our highest priority right now."

There's the unspoken, face-saving refusal. Sol said, "I understand," though he was thinking furiously, trying to make sense of this. He realized that he was out of his depth.

"We will do all we can to increase our backing in the future."

Followed by the non-binding promise. "I appreciate that," Sol said.

Negotiations ended, everyone stood and began to drift toward the elevator, and the lawyer said, "I will send a term sheet to your office."

"Very good," Sol replied.

The elevator door opened, and Prince Farhan moved calmly toward Sol. Still appearing subdued, he said, "Thank you for coming to meet with us, Mr. Isaac."

He reached out and shook Sol's hand in farewell, something that he'd never done before. Then the prince unexpectedly clasped Sol's right shoulder with his left hand and leaned in to kiss him quickly on each cheek — a gesture reserved, Sol knew, only for close friends and business partners.

Surprised but gratified, Sol said, "My pleasure, Your Highness."

Only when Farhan stepped back did Sol recognize the shadow in his eyes. It said, "I'm truly sorry that I must kill you."

Shaken, Sol allowed Ahmed to escort him back down to the limo. He second-guessed what he'd just seen. Perhaps Farhan was only worried about his son's birth.

Or maybe Sol's eyes were showing him one thing, while his ears told another.

The lawyer shook his hand once more as the footman opened the car's door. "We appreciate your coming, Mr. Isaac. We will email the terms to you within the week."

Sol responded cordially and slid into the limo.

Disappointment clouded his view through the vehicle's tinted window for most of the drive. *Only twenty million. How do they expect me to create a blockbuster on that?*

On the other hand, Bronc's told me that his Chinese filmmaker is planning to siphon off most of the money to keep as profit, and cheat the investors — people like Farhan. Maybe Farhan knows that. Maybe he's just denying that effing mobster what he really wants.

The corners of Sol's mouth quirked up. Then they stretched into a broad smile. He sat back and clasped his hands behind his head. *Yeah, I got myself a movie deal!*

The sight of two taxis parked at the hotel's entry, as the footman let Sol out of the limo, sent a prickle across the back of his neck.

Now you're being paranoid, he told himself. But he made a swift survey of the spacious lobby as he paused at its doors.

A young man in a rumpled dishdasha stood at the front desk, his back to Sol. Three more lounged in a nearby group of chairs. Otherwise, the lobby was empty.

One youth peeked up from his cell phone when the in-rush of air from the opening door set the nearest pieces of the wind chime tinkling. The prickle Sol had felt moments earlier raced down his spine.

He made fleeting eye contact with the young man, a hard look that warned, "I know you're there," before he strode toward the elevators.

The elevator door was made of slabs of polished stones set into a mosaic, tones of gold and camel. It looked as if it had been installed within the last week. Sol hope that the door would open quickly.

The scuff of a step behind him alerted Sol to someone's approach as he punched the UP arrow. He pivoted. Found himself facing the cabbie with the manic eyes. He didn't have to mask surprise; he'd been expecting something like this.

"You left your wallet in my cab, sir," the kid said loudly enough to be heard at the front desk. He held a cheap billfold of cracked brown reptile skin in his palm.

"That's not mine," Sol said.

Over the cabbie's shoulder, he saw the three youths from the lobby sauntering toward them. One carried a lumpy black garbage bag.

Behind him, the elevator whooshed open. Sol sprang inside, still facing the kid, already punching the CLOSE DOOR button.

The cabbie lunged, got one shoulder through the closing doors. They recoiled, and he braced them open long enough for his accomplices to charge inside.

He glared at Sol, baring his teeth. "Now, Jew, we will go to your room," he snarled, "and we will show you how we deal with those who pollute the sacred lands of Allah." He pressed 4 on the panel.

The desk clerk will have given him my room number, too, Sol realized. So much for Arab laws of hospitality.

As the elevator began to rise, one of the other three drew a pistol with a silencer from his jacket pocket and trained it on Sol's belly.

When the 4 lit up and the doors hissed apart, the cabbie snapped something in Arabic and poked his head out. He squinted up and down the thick-carpeted corridor, then glared at Sol. "Go. There is a housekeeping cart in the hall. If you shout or run, my brother will shoot you."

Better to be shot than what the Libyans did to Ambassador Stevens.

Sol broke into a cold sweat, and his heart rate rocketed.

At the door marked 422, the cabbie smirked as he slid a room key out of the battered reptile-skin billfold. "Service is very good at this hotel."

Housekeeping had already serviced Sol's room. The youth with the bag upended it on the bed's brocade coverlet. Sol glimpsed a roll of black duct tape, a tangle of red-coated electrical wire, and a box cutter.

They're going to behead me with the box cutter.

"Bring that over here," said the cabbie, and pointed at the large, leather-upholstered swivel chair behind the desk.

Heart pounding and palms sweating, Sol rounded the bed, avoiding looking at the objects dumped on it. Despite putting space between himself and the gunman, he could still feel the barrel shoved into his kidney.

As he sidled between the polished desk and the closed, gold-threaded curtain, something clicked in Sol's head. *They've given me a weapon.*

Sol pushed the chair around the side of the desk, feigning submission. The chair's swivel base rolled off the protective mat and caught in the deep carpet as he'd known it would. He wrestled the chair forward, ignoring his captors' murderous gazes and the way they edged toward him bunched together in the narrow space between the bed and the TV cabinet.

"Hurry up, dog!" the cabbie ordered.

Clear of the desk, Sol seized the chair near the top of its high, padded back. Fear-spurred adrenaline alone gave him enough strength to hurl it into them.

All four staggered. The one who caught the chair's bulky seat in his midsection landed hard on his ass, and Sol heard a pop.

Lightning seared his right side. A bullet half-spun him around. He clapped a hand over the spot, felt wet heat ooze between his fingers. *Damn it, I'm hit.*

"Filthy dog Jew!" The cabbie scrambled clear of the fallen chair, his features contorted in fury. He leaped headlong, outstretched hands hard as claws.

At that instant, Sol spotted the pistol loose on the carpeted floor. He dove after it, fingers reaching, grasping.

He heard a thunk as the cabbie struck the desk behind him, a swish of fabric, then a short, muted yell at the edge of his awareness that seemed to come from outside.

The meaning of the yell didn't connect until, shaking and panting, he leveled the handgun at the other three. They stood motionless, mouths agape, eyes wide and fixed on something behind him.

Sol risked a glance over his shoulder as he shoved himself to his feet. Saw the curtain, pushed over the balcony rail, fluttering in a midday breeze.

A chuckle escaped him, a slightly hysterical sound born of receding adrenaline. "Karma's a real bitch, kids." He chambered a round and played the weapon across their chests. "There are two ways out of this room: through the window like dickhead, or through the door. Would you rather take your chances with Allah or hotel security?"

All three bolted for the door, shouting in frantic Arabic.

Sol locked it behind them with his bloody left hand, thumbed on the pistol's safety, and punched the button for hotel security on the desk phone. "You've got three terrorist wannabes on your premises," he informed the man who answered, "probably heading down to the lobby right now."

He gave descriptions, then wondered if the cabbie had survived his fall. This was only the fourth floor, after all. Sol leaned out the sliding glass door, blinking against bright sunlight.

"You'll find the fourth guy on the swimming pool deck," he added in the driest tone he could muster. "He tried to exit via my window. I don't think he'll be going anywhere."

"Are you all right, sir?" The male voice sounded anxious.

"Fine," Sol lied, though the crease across his ribs had begun to throb. "If you need further information, please fax a deposition request to my home office." He provided the number. "I have a flight to catch." *As soon as I patch up this wound . . . I just hope they don't put the hotel on lockdown.*

Most of the bleeding had slowed, but Sol knew, after a brief examination, that a little exertion would start it up again.

It looked like a fairly superficial wound. He hoped to god that it would stop bleeding.

He mopped drying blood off his side with his stained shirt, wrung it out, and stuffed it in the wastebasket. *It's a total loss. I'll have to wear yesterday's shirt home. But I need a bandage.* He surveyed the bathroom.

His gaze fell on a fluffy snow-white washcloth lying in a decoratively folded figure beside the sink. *One hundred percent Egyptian cotton.* He smiled grimly. *That'll do in a pinch. Now, something to hold it on . . .*

The roll of duct tape and the box cutter still lay on the bed. Sol stepped over the office chair, collected tape and cutter, returned to the bathroom. A couple of strips, about eighteen inches long, secured the washcloth tightly to his side. He eyed his handiwork in the mirror.

My suitcoat will conceal that. But tearing it off when I get home is going to be a bitch. He grimaced at the thought.

Ten minutes later he emerged in the lobby to find it full of local law enforcement officers. Outside the glass façade, a string of police cars with flashing lights hemmed in the pair of taxis. A quick scan revealed no sign of Sol's assailants. He adopted an expression of mingled puzzlement and curiosity as he crossed to the registration desk.

An attractive young woman, who hadn't been there earlier, inquired, "Checking out, sir?"

"Yes." Gaze lingering on the taxis, Sol asked, "Is your airport shuttle available?"

The only thing sure in life is change, Sol knew. On the flight back he made plans to finance his movie. By noon he planned to serve his wife with divorce papers. He'd need to be careful with his business partner, though, give no hint that he was parting ways until he'd secured funding for this new film.

Everything he had in the world was riding on this one throw of the dice. He had to make it good.

He forced himself to keep still and planned on a doctor visit. Dr. Kahn from down at the Temple could be trusted.

All in all, the future was looking up.

Sol's flight into Burbank touched down a few minutes before the early sunset.

Even in the more comfortable seats of first class, his grazed side had begun to throb. He'd bought some Tylenol — without any codeine — after clearing Security at the Dubai airport. He dreaded sitting through the night until his morning flight.

Upon leaving the aircraft, he stopped in a men's room long enough to pop a couple more pills, shake wrinkles from his jacket, and comb his hair before he left the terminal.

The streaky, red-lit sky cast the row of palm trees along the road out of the airport into inky silhouettes, like backdrops for some beach flick. Sol turned to the potted palm outside the entrance and spotted the distinctive geranium plant at its base at once.

Shadows shielded him as he scooped into the soil with both hands. He touched plastic within moments, gathered the folds in his fist, and pulled.

A black garbage bag burst from the soil. No mistaking that

it contained a handgun, but he furrowed his brow. *My bag was white, with the store logo.*

Sol poked around for a few more minutes, digging deeper and then searching a wider area. *No joy.*

Growing impatient, he seized the black bag in both hands and tore it open with a tug. He winced at the jab in his side as a black matte-finish pistol tumbled onto the disheveled earth among the geraniums. He picked it up with care, turned it in his hands, and scrutinized it in the minimal light.

A .45-caliber Glock 30 SF subcompact with a ten-round clip.

Well, that's a trade up. Sol chuckled aloud. "Karma, you are indeed a fine lady!"

SOME ARE BORN TO SAVE THE WORLD

MARK LESLIE

inspired by "Losing It"

With all of the strength left in him, Bryan lifted his arm and extended his hand.

His knuckles cracked as his fingers stretched to their limits. But he was still half an inch shy of his mark.

"I won't go down this way!" tears of rage streaked down his face as he wheezed an exhalation of stale, dry air that burned both his lungs and his throat. "White Vector will not die today!"

Despite the futility of his situation, he wouldn't give up.

He had simply come too far.

As a young child, Bryan spent more than his fair share of time cowering in the dark while listening to the sounds of his drunken father beating on his mother and calling her a useless, lazy bitch.

His father hated his life and took it out on his wife, since Bryan's mother always ensured, when Daniel Rand got into those moods, that Bryan was hidden away.

He was a scrawny child and easily frightened. And lying there in the dark under the bed or in a nearby closet, he kept wondering if he might ever grow big enough, or strong enough, or brave enough to stand up to his father and save his mother from the pain and humiliation.

He did his best to cover his ears so he couldn't hear the sound of fists hitting flesh nor his mother's cries of pain. To drown out the slaps and punches and cries, he replayed stories from the comic books he constantly escaped into, stories driven by truth, justice, and the American way. He dreamed of one day being able to stop bad people from harming good people.

Especially his mother.

The supernatural powers he had dreamed about began manifesting themselves when he was midway through puberty. It was during the times when he had lain in the dark listening to the horrible sounds and kept wishing as hard as he could and with all of his might that his father would just leave them, would just pick up and leave, never to return.

One night, those feelings burning within him, Bryan stepped out of his hiding place and stood quietly looking at his father.

His old man turned, spittle running down his chin from the curses that accompanied each strike of his fist. The burning hatred in his father's eyes was clear, and Bryan tensed, waiting for the attack — but it never came. His father merely stared him down while the rage seemed to deflate right out of him. As he watched the heated anger fade from the man's eyes, Bryan felt a confidence flowing within, a boundless sense of energy and strength.

"Enough!" Bryan said, expelling the word and the energy he felt pent up inside.

As if to punctuate his word, the dome and light bulb in the ceiling above his head exploded.

Without saying a word, Bryan's father looked at his son, the broken light fixture, his unconscious wife, and then back to his son. He made a move as if to step forward, but stopped almost as if something invisible was preventing his progress.

More than anything, Bryan wished that his father would just go away, just leave.

After a minute of silent staring, his father turned, walked out the front door, and disappeared into the night never to return.

It took several days of pondering the scene before Bryan realized the power that must have existed within him. It wasn't immediately apparent, because the force-flow of power had appeared in odd fits and starts — the way acne would appear without warning, or his prepubescent voice would crack at random.

By his early twenties, he had mastered the odd ability to focus and channel ambient energy life force from his body and from those around him either into himself, providing super-human strength, dexterity, and agility, or to affect objects with a telekinetic-like power. He would never be meek and helpless again.

Bryan tried to take in a deep breath, but he might as well have been sucking a mouthful of crackers into his lungs for all the good it did. The breath of air was devoid of the vital oxygen his body needed.

He was out of oxygen and, sadly, almost out of time.

But he had gotten out of life-and-death struggles before.

Hundreds of them.

White Vector was, after all, the people's hero who had always found a way.

This is no different than that day on the bridge, he thought.

It was a stifling hot summer day when he had first donned the white skin-tight costume with the crimson shorts, the vector-based, round four-color swirl on his chest, the red leather boots, and the red hooded mask.

After several years of carefully planning out his costume, his name, and exactly how he could put them to use, he was about to step out into public prepared to change into his alter ego, White Vector.

That July afternoon, wearing the outfit under his street clothes, the hood tucked into his knapsack, was a day he had ultimately been needed.

He didn't have the ability to fly like Superman, nor to scale walls or swing from building to building like Spider-Man, nor even to race through the city streets in a super slick Batmobile like Batman, so public transit was the quickest way to get about the city. He got around by bus, subway, or train.

He had been riding the Q60 bus from Queens to Manhattan when a transport truck blew a tire and drove a station wagon up against the guard rails with such force that it crashed through, the back half of the car dangling precariously over the edge.

After taking a quick visual survey to ensure his passengers were physically unharmed after the sudden stop, the bus driver opened the doors and ran toward the station wagon.

Bryan took that moment to slip outside, pulling his backpack off while ducking below the bus windows and behind the steel wall of the transport truck. There, he pulled the hooded mask over his head and then quickly removed his shirt and pants and stuffed them into his knapsack before tossing it under the transport.

He wondered if he'd ever get those street clothes back; it never seemed to be an issue where Peter Parker or Clark Kent stashed their civvies.

In his mostly white-and-red costume, Bryan — now transformed into White Vector — walked back around the front of the bus and watched the bus driver finish pulling the male driver and female passenger out of the station wagon.

The driver had a bleeding gash on his forehead and was stumbling away from the car looking dazed. The passenger, who seemed uninjured, was turning back to the car as if she wanted to climb back in, but the bus driver held her by the arm.

"My baby!" she cried. "He's in the back. In his car seat."

The car was teetering, slowly rocking, looking as if any sort of extra weight on it would send it plummeting down into the river.

"Don't worry, ma'am!" Bryan said, stepping between the woman and the car. "I'm White Vector. And I'm here to help. What's his name?"

"Bobby."

"Stand back, please! It's going to be okay." Bryan said, then turned toward the car. "It's okay, Bobby! I've got you. You'll be safe."

The front of the car was pitched up almost two feet in the air in its teeter, and Bryan grabbed onto the steel bumper and let the power that flowed through the blood in his veins send an extremely focused concentration of strength into his arms and upper body. He also siphoned slivers of strength from those nearby. Each power siphon didn't last more than a minute or two, but it was often enough for him to perform some superhuman activity.

He pulled at the car's bumper, and the entire vehicle began to slowly slide back onto the bridge, one inch, then two.

"Oh my god!" someone shouted. "He's lifting the car!"

With a wail of scraping metal, the bumper Bryan was holding was no longer attached to the front of the car. The vehicle slid back quickly, farther back than it had been sitting before.

The car was now dangling at a nearly ninety-degree angle to the bridge, and, inside, Bobby was wailing even louder for his mommy.

"Do something!" Bobby's mother screamed.

Bryan shuffled over to the side nearest the open door, dropped down onto the pavement, and peered through the triangle of space between the car, the door, and the edge of the bridge. He couldn't climb into the car because the extra weight would send it toppling down. But he wondered if he might be able to lie on the bridge, stretch his upper body inside the car, and grab the child and pull him to safety.

Inching his way forward, he finally got to a point where he could lean most of his upper body into the car without putting any of his weight on the vehicle. He reached down past the back of the driver's seat toward the car seat. The only sounds, besides the wind, were Bobby's cries and the gentle creaking of the car as it continued to shift and rock.

With his arm fully extended, he was still a good three inches away from reaching the buckle. The child, who looked to be less than two years old, was crying harder and louder than before.

"Damn," Bryan muttered. His arm just didn't reach far enough. *But my mind can.*

Bryan took a deep breath, concentrated on the unseen energy flowing through his body, on the anxious energy pumping out of Bobby's mother, the bus driver, and even the nearby passengers from the bus. He could feel their life force and drew strings of it into his mind, wrapping it into a tight ball.

Then, with a focus that completely blocked everything else out, Bryan propelled the ball forward in a pencil thin, compacted blast of air.

The force was enough to depress the buckle.

Pop.

The straps on either side of the buckle released.

Bryan's head immediately filled with a lightning burst of white-hot pain, and it took everything in him not to yell out or move his body in any way that would touch the vehicle.

Now the hard part.

Bryan drew in more energy and channeled it down through his extended arm. He could feel the mystical power throbbing through his arm, and he pushed out an energy field that wrapped around the toddler's body.

When he felt the child securely within his grasp, his mind pulled back and up, and the toddler levitated forward, up, and out of the car seat toward Bryan as if carried by unseen hands.

The pressure in his head grew to a pounding series of quakes, and he could feel the blood vessels in his nose bursting.

Blood trickled down his chin and splashed onto the toddler's face as he telekinetically pulled Bobby up close enough to grab a handful of the toddler's shirt and finish pulling him the rest of the way up. Wailing, Bobby grabbed at Bryan's forearm and held on as he was slowly lifted up.

Bobby's shoulders cleared the window, the toddler kicked out and hit the steering wheel with his knee.

The car teetered at a much sharper angle.

Bryan pulled the child in and as close to his chest as he could, shielding the boy's body while the car pitched backward, finally breaking free of the tentative hold the bridge and railing had on it and plummeting into the cold waters more than a hundred feet below.

Bryan felt his energy leaving him, a side effect he recognized that came immediately after he drew in and expended such a burst of energy. He could just manage to roll onto his back to present the screaming toddler to his mother.

Not a bad first public use of his powers.

It would be just like that child on the Queensboro Bridge, Bryan thought, reaching his arm far forward.

He was so close; but it was just out of reach, and the lack of breath was causing a tightness in his chest.

He tried channeling what little energy he could gather from his ailing body into the end of his right arm like he had done that first time he had played at superhero.

But the power wouldn't flow.

It wasn't like before.

Ever since his stroke, the one that had incapacitated his left side, he had been unable to get the energy, the power to flow anywhere near his left side. It was as if that part of his supernatural powers had died somewhere as an even more critical side effect.

He had, of course, seen the degeneration coming well before the stroke had hit.

Understanding enough about physics, Bryan knew that for every action there was an equal and opposite reaction. For the force to flow, he knew the energy had to come from somewhere. He just had never properly counted the ultimate cost to playing hero for so many years.

The plane was headed for a crash course into the side of the Goldman Sachs building in the Paulus Hook neighborhood, and there was nothing anybody could do about it. A freak accident during takeoff involving a series of birds striking both engines and causing them to fail created a scenario so oddly similar to the one in early 2009.

Only, in this case, the pilot wasn't able to get the plane on course for a relatively safe landing in the Hudson. There simply wasn't enough power.

Bryan had been on the Staten Island Ferry when the plane started to go down and, along with his fellow New Yorkers, had been stunned to see a plane coming in so low over the city. It was impossible to see such a sight and not immediately think about that September day in 2001.

It was a rush-hour ferry, and as Bryan stood in the crowd of commuters, watching the plane swoop down, he reached out and grasped at the tentacles of energy from the thousands of fellow passengers, quickly and subtly pulling just a little bit of life force from each of them.

He channeled the gathered mass of energy and reached out to try to gently push the plane slightly off of its crash course into the tall office tower. His head rumbled with the force of concentration and the distance involved in manipulating the force, and he grasped onto the rail of the passenger ferry. But he managed to nudge the plane just enough so it didn't strike the side of the building and then, body quivering, guided it down for a landing in the cold and choppy waters of the Hudson River.

The plane splashed down with the nose pointed down, and it must have immediately begun taking on water.

Exhausted and actually weeping from the throbbing pain in his head, Bryan began to again channel fragments of power from those around him and funneled it into another mass. With the fresh collection of power, he snaked out invisible tentacles of energy that he used to hold the aircraft afloat until all of the crew and passengers could be rescued by nearby commercial boats and FDNY marine vessels.

Providing additional buoyancy to the plane from such a distance proved to be a feat beyond anything Bryan had attempted before. But he managed to hold on for the fifteen minutes that it took to complete the full rescue.

Then, as his vision blurred and the pain surged, more intense than he had ever felt it, he collapsed to the deck of the ferry.

Everybody around him assumed he had fainted from witnessing the incident.

It wasn't until he woke up in the hospital a day later that Bryan learned he had had a massive stroke.

Somehow, the power he had been able to channel must have drained some portion of the natural tidal pools of his life energy. Of course that energy was limited. He must have always known; he'd just ignored it, been a slave to the driving obsession that he make a difference, that he be the hero.

That choice had left his body weak well before its natural time, and though he was merely in his mid-sixties, he looked like he was in his late seventies or even his early eighties.

Now he didn't have enough of his own life energy to reach his oxygen mask. And there was nobody close enough that he could draw life force from.

With his lungs burning from the lack of oxygen, and dizziness beginning to lap at his mind, Bryan stared at the tipped canister of oxygen, at the thin line of transparent yellow tubing just out of reach.

Less than an inch from his trembling fingers, the oxygen hissed.

Teasing him, tantalizing him from just beyond his feeble reach.

The steady hiss mocked him.

Reminded him of another sound. The applause from an appreciative crowd gathered in the streets on the day White Vector had received the key to the city.

It was thirty years ago, just half a decade after he had made his first appearance at the Queensboro Bridge.

White Vector had established a pattern of daring rescues — assisting the fire department with saving people unable to navigate their way out of burning buildings, lifting debris to free people who had been pinned or trapped from collapsed construction sites, weather damaged buildings, or vehicular accidents, and even providing emergency CPR. Channeling energy allowed Bryan to kick-start a failed heart without having to perform traditional compressions.

Surprisingly, there were very few confrontations with bad guys. Sure, he had thwarted the occasional mugger, robber, and even pickpocket, but most of the good White Vector had done had been akin to the work of New York's Bravest rather than the work of New York's Finest.

Bryan remembered the pride he had felt standing on the stage beside the mayor as the gray-haired gentleman presented a speech about him and a recent schoolhouse rescue by him and FDNY

Rescue 1 two weeks previously; White Vector alone had been responsible for saving no fewer than one hundred lives.

"And, asking nothing in return for his selfless acts, White Vector worked diligently along the brave men and women of Rescue Company 1, repeatedly ignoring the danger and running back into the burning school to retrieve every single person trapped inside.

"This most recent act is, of course, just one of many times that White Vector has stepped forth as a hero to the fine citizens of our glorious city. Which is why I am not only presenting him with the key to our city, but am also instituting him as an honorary member of New York City Fire Department Rescue Company 1."

The crowd responded with a thunderous burst of applause.

As the echoes of old applause rang through his head, Bryan's mind continued the dizzying spin, whirling, descending into a sea of darkness.

His eyes, bloodshot and unfocused, tried desperately to target onto the oxygen line that eluded him and he hacked out choking breaths.

The most difficult thing Bryan had ever done had been to stay alone and single, to purposely avoid getting close to anybody, either as a friend or as a lover. It was a conscious decision made to protect others, keep them distant and safe from his vigilante life.

So he had consciously decided to live the course of his life alone.

No love.

No family.

No legacy to speak of.

The ultimate price of his secret identity, his hidden life as a hero.

Despite the parades, the celebrations, the lines of kids seeking

White Vector's autograph, the cheers and the applause and the notoriety, he realized that it would all end alone.

Simply because, as a feeble old man with barely any strength or any super ability left, his oxygen line had popped off and he was unable to reach it.

It was too humiliating.

Bryan had, of course, just in the past few years, known humiliation.

Public humiliation.

His ability to save the day had been significantly lessened ever since the stroke he had had that morning on the Staten Island Ferry.

With a weakened left side, Bryan had to concentrate hard just to try to walk in a normal fashion when he was visible to the public, and his heroic acts were more akin to rescuing kittens or kites from trees than anything worthy of a comic book plot. His main gig was giving inspirational talks at local public schools denouncing bullying.

So when he arrived at the scene of a bank hostage situation, and Officer Mahoney explained that there were three gunmen and five hostages, his first thought was wondering whether or not he should just leave it to the police. They had, after all, been doing just fine before he arrived.

But when the officer in charge, the one with the bullhorn, informed the bandits inside that White Vector was now here, that burst of pride took over.

Bryan stepped past the barricades of police cruisers and walked right up to the bank. He channeled the energy of the surrounding police officers, cognizant of how much additional effort just pulling energy in required, and used the energy to heighten his senses.

Halfway to the bank building, he could hear two of the robbers talking, panicked that he was approaching them so calmly, and was able to determine their approximate location behind the walls and through the bright reflective glass of the bank.

This type of sensory enhancement typically helped him in combat because it made him more sensitive to picking up subtle changes in a person's chemistry and heartbeat before they acted; it gave him the split second of additional time he needed to have the upper hand in any sort of hand-to-hand combat.

Only, this time, while he was able to easily syphon energy to enhance his senses, his agility was still that of a recovered stroke victim.

So when he entered the door and the gunman to his far right fired, he wasn't able to dodge out of the way. And his reflexes were so slow that sending a blast of energy into the air to deflect the bullet just inches after it left the chamber didn't happen. The bullet made it all the way to Bryan, his late-acting energy bolt barely slowing the bullet as it punched into his right arm.

He had slowed the bullet down enough so that it didn't break his skin; but it still hit him hard like a good solid punch in the arm — something that, thirty years ago, he could have shrugged off the way one might shrug off a mosquito.

This one, though, hurt tremendously, putting him off guard.

What had he been thinking just walking straight into the building?

Sure, years ago, before the stroke, he could have easily sent energy bursts to disarm as many as half a dozen gunmen, then used his temporarily enhanced senses and increased strength to subdue the bad guys.

But that had been before.

Now, Bryan questioned what he was doing.

That's when the second gunman, the one directly in front of Bryan, fired.

He hadn't fired at Bryan, though. He shot one of the hostages. An older woman. One of the tellers. The bullet went into the back of her head and exited her face in a sickening explosion of blood, skin, and bone.

"I told you we weren't fooling around here!" the gunman shouted as the woman collapsed forward onto the cold tile floor.

The other hostages screamed, and another gunman, the one on Bryan's left, fired. His bullet struck a second victim, a middle-aged man in a gray suit, in the stomach. That man bowed over, clutching at his midsection, and crumpled to his knees.

Bryan rushed at the gunman directly in front of him, channeling his rage and energy into his right arm. He batted the man's gun away just as he was attempting to fire another round at Bryan. The shot went wild and ricocheted off the ceiling. Bryan drove his fist into the man's face, knocking him out with a single blow.

He paused to pull in a short burst of energy from the man he had just felled before turning to his right and looking at the first gunman, the one who had fired at him when he entered. That gunman aimed at Bryan. This time, Bryan was ready for the shot and pushed a burst of energy straight at the bullet.

But instead of stopping the bullet, the energy deflected it into the the neck of an older gentleman who had been sitting up against the wall.

Bryan rushed at the shooter, slapped his gun-hand away, and elbowed him in the gut. As the man fell, Bryan sent a mental air-shove, launching the man across the lobby where he struck his head hard against a marble pillar.

The third gunman seized that opportunity to rush out the front door.

And that's where, immediately outside the front door, he was apprehended by New York's Finest.

Three of the five hostages had been shot.

Because Bryan had been too feeble to properly handle the situation.

Bryan took in a deep breath, felt the trembling in his bones, the throbbing in his head from the energy it had taken. His upper lip was matted with blood from the burst vessels in his nose.

But here was another damp and sticky part of his body. He had lost control of his bowels.

Not the best thing to happen when you were wearing a mostly white costume.

Like in that humiliating moment in the bank, the one that had ended his career, Bryan felt his bowels let go again.

And, as the lack of oxygen made him feel as if every single nerve was being torn apart, the ripples of the surrounding darkness started to intrude.

Just as he began to let go, a clean and cool burst of oxygen filled Bryan's lungs.

He hacked and choked, feeling the sweet breath that filled his airways.

At that point he realized that someone was standing over him —the someone who had moved the oxygen mask back onto Bryan.

Bryan slowly opened his eyes, the light a stabbing pain, but could make out the shape of a young man with short, dark hair standing before him.

"Mr. Rand," the young man said. "Can you hear me?"

"Y—yeah," Bryan breathed out, his throat still sore and raw. "Yes."

"You're going to be okay."

The man grabbed Bryan by the wrist, pressing his fingers into the underside of it. "I'm just going to check your pulse, Mr. Rand."

"Who . . . are . . . you?" Bryan said.

"I'm the new nurse that has been assigned to this ward. I'll be taking care of you now, Mr. Rand. My name is Robert."

As Bryan's vision came into focus he could make out the sharp jaw line and ruggedly handsome features of the young man, likely in his early thirties. Bryan looked down from the young man's face to the gold pocket watch he held in his hand, using it to keep time of Bryan's pulse.

"Robert?"

"Yes."

"Nobody . . . uses a . . . pocket watch . . . any . . . more."

"This was my grandfather's watch, sir." Robert said. "He received it when he retired from the fire department. He passed it along to me when he died."

"Fire . . . fighting," Bryan gasped, "is a good calling."

"Yes," Robert said. "And it's something I've wanted to do for as long as I can remember. I was in a car accident when I was quite young. I don't remember it, but my mom liked to tell me the story of how White Vector saved me. I wanted to be like him, and like my granddad, too. Only, my asthma means I failed the physical three times. So I became a nurse." He shrugged. "At least I can still make a difference."

His vision much clearer, Bryan looked up at the blue-green of the young man's eyes and recognized a conviction he hadn't seen since he was Robert's age and stood staring in a mirror.

He also recognized the tingling he'd first felt when he discovered his power. Something in the young man pulled at the remaining power left in Bryan's body.

As his foggy mind became clearer with each fresh breath of oxygen into his lungs, Bryan knew.

It was not over.

Succumbing to the gentle pull, Bryan pushed the mystical power that had coursed through his body in the young man's direction. The world-weight that he had carried on his shoulders started to let go as he could feel Bobby's body accept the gift naturally, but his confused eyes told Bryan that he didn't seem to understand what was happening.

That's okay. He soon will.

"Bobby," Bryan whispered.

"Yes, Mr. Rand."

"I want you . . . to have something, son."

"What's that, sir?"

"The top drawer . . . of my . . . nightstand. Open it. There's a . . . brown leather box inside."

Robert moved over, opened the drawer, and looked inside.

"Take it out. Open it."

Robert did as requested.

While he did so, Bryan thought back to the day he had packed that leather box.

Bryan's companions at the NYPD had honored him by not mentioning the condition they'd found him in, Mahoney covered him in an EMT blanket so that nobody except the first few cops into the building had seen what he'd done to himself.

And, since not every hostage situation always worked out perfectly, there was no blatant blaming or accusing White Vector of any wrongdoing. With the exception, of course, of a few city reporters who had never been on the side of vigilante justice and used the incident as an excuse to further their position.

But Bryan knew better.

He knew that he could not be counted on to be the people's hero any longer.

He was a danger.

Weeks later, with trembling hands, he carefully folded the freshly laundered suit and tucked it into the box. Burning tears fell from his eyes and onto the white silk as he placed the key to the city on top of it.

Though he was firm in his resolve, he hadn't realized how difficult it would be to know he would never again put the costume on, never again come to anybody's rescue.

He shut the box, and the most significant part of his life with it.

Robert's eyes lit up as he opened the box.

"This," Robert said, "looks like the key to the city. And this white top, and red mask. It . . . it was *you*." He looked up from the brown leather box and down at Bryan. "You're the one who saved me that day."

"I was," Bryan said. "Once. That costume, that key belonged . . . to White Vector . . . to me. But . . . I'm no longer him . . . I'm giving it to you."

Bryan knew that his days were numbered, that there would not be many more sunrises before him. But the young man who stood before him was his sign that it didn't have to end with him.

Bryan would teach Robert everything he knew. White Vector, the hero that the world needed, the people's hero, would live another day in the eyes, heart, and mind of the young man who stood over him.

The sun would rise once more.

RANDOM ACCESS MEMORY

In the car on the way to the prison, Marcus went over the file one more time. Dale Beechum had been convicted of killing seven people over two years. Four women and three men. He'd killed them all over North America, three different provinces and four states. But he was fairly easy to catch once there was enough evidence to correlate. In fact, he knew he was going to be caught and was cooperative with the cops in Toronto when they picked him up. He'd said, "What took you? I never expected to get to seven."

There were four other people in the car, sitting in a circle around the central hub. Marcus would have preferred a private pod but these government contracts never paid much for expenses. Still, Toronto to Kingston, 165 miles, less than an hour, not too bad. The pod had picked him up in front of his apartment building and joined the train on the 401 expressway a few minutes later. Once they'd cleared the city, there was a lane for driver-vehicles left over from years ago and another lane for first-class private pods with the middle lane taken up by the two-hundred-pod train.

Marcus watched the interview with Beechum again, flipping through to parts he'd marked as relevant; Beechum saying, "All this surveillance, all the technology, the DNA, I barely covered my tracks." During his interrogation he never questioned any of the evidence, but he never addressed it, either, never added to it. The interviewer, a man Marcus had worked with a couple of times, Darren Keneally, went over everything, asking Beechum about each detail, and Beechum either said, "Yes, that's true," or, "No, that's mistaken."

As the train approached Kingston a couple of pods broke away and the ones behind pulled up immediately and closed the gap. Marcus looked out the window and watched the train disappear around the bend of the highway, a couple hundred pods inches apart, looking like a single vehicle.

The prison was the first stop in Kingston and, as he was getting out, Marcus had the feeling the rest of the passengers weren't happy making the stop, but he figured that's what they get on the cheaper run; you want non-stop, you get a better contract and you pay for non-stop.

It took half an hour to get through security and then Marcus walked by himself through the corridors, following the maze-like route he'd been down half a dozen times before. When he got to the guard office he stopped in front of the security check and waited a moment, then pushed open the door.

There was only one guard on duty, a woman with blonde hair pulled back in a bun, who said, "Mr. McKenzie, I'm Sgt. Fowler."

"Nice to meet you."

"We've met," she said. "I was the intake guard the last time you were here."

"Oh, I'm sorry, I don't remember."

"I didn't expect you to." She stood up from the desk and motioned to one of the monitors. "Beechum."

"Yeah, I recognize him," Marcus said. "I watched his interview again on the way here."

Fowler looked directly at the monitor for a moment, and she couldn't hide her disgust. She looked at Marcus and said, "Do you know what he does in there all day?"

"No, what?"

"He touches himself. He masturbates." She wasn't happy about it, of course. "Five or six times, just on my shift, probably more overnight. It's disgusting."

"Well, it's what I'm here to stop."

"Are you going to cut his dick off?"

"No," Marcus said, "that wouldn't stop him thinking about it."

Fowler said, "I don't care what he thinks about, I just care what he does."

"He's looking through his souvenirs," Marcus said. "Most serial killers keep something. Jewelry, articles of clothing." He shrugged a little and added, "Panties, bras." He paused and looked at Fowler, then said, "Sleepwear. Or even body parts. Skulls, fingers, skin."

"Souvenirs?"

"Yes, souvenirs. Trophies. Mostly these days we get video. That's been going on for a while, actually — pictures, way back when it was Polaroids. Still pictures, you know?"

"I know, yeah."

"Beechum didn't keep any physical trophies but, as you see, he's still got the memories, and he still enjoys going over them."

"Oh, he enjoys them all right."

"So I erase them."

"Good. Can you wipe his brain completely?"

Marcus smiled. "No. I mean, people are still working on that. That's where this came from, the idea you could wipe someone's brain and then build it up again. The research goes way back — it turns out the wiping out is possible but the building back up, or the planting of false memories, that's trickier."

Fowler looked at her monitor and said, "You wipe as much of that sick brain as you can."

"The contract only calls for the memories of the murders," Marcus said. "His proceeds of crime, as it were. Of course, if it was up to me," and he shrugged a little. In truth he didn't really care one way or the other, but it was his experience that people contracted to law enforcement and incarceration usually wanted the maximum penalties, and not just because that would get the most profit — they seemed to have a personal interest in it.

"I get it," Fowler said. Marcus thought she was going to add something about wishing they could bring back capital punishment, so many of the guards he met did, but she just said, "So, do you need anything for the procedure?"

"No, I'll just set up in the visiting room."

"How long will it take?"

"Depends on him," Marcus said. "Usually these guys want to drag it out, mostly just so they have someone to talk to, I think, but then often they can't help themselves and they blurt it all out right away."

"But you already know what he's going to say?"

"I think so. Sometimes they surprise me. One guy confessed to another murder he hadn't even been charged with."

"Well, if you're telling me he's thinking about one of his

every time he rubs one out, it's a lot more than the file says." She shook her head and sat back down at her desk.

Marcus laughed a little, and he was thinking he liked this Sgt. Fowler. He said, "I booked the room for today and tomorrow but I may not need it that long."

"Well, it's right through there. Oh, I guess you know that."

"I do, thanks."

The visiting room looked a lot like the living room in the apartment Marcus had in Toronto. Or like the hotel room he'd be in later that night. He sat down on the couch and opened his kit on the small table. A few minutes later, the door opened and Dale Beechum walked in.

He was a white man and pretty much average everything — height, weight, sandy blond hair, clean shaven, thirty-one years old. He extended a hand and said, "Hi, you must be Marcus McKenzie."

"Yes." Marcus had planned to stay back and not engage, but he found himself taking Beechum's hand and giving it a shake.

Beechum said, "I wish we were meeting under different circumstances."

"Well, here we are."

They stood facing each other until it started to get awkward and then Beechum said, "Should I sit?"

"Oh, yes, of course."

Marcus sat back down on the couch across from the chair and said, "I'm sure you've gone over the information yourself."

Beechum said, "I have, yes. Quite thorough. Very technical."

"Do you have any questions?"

"Do you have any answers?"

Marcus wasn't sure what he meant, so he ignored the question and said, "I have a little speech I usually give, I explain that I've done this many, many times before and that there's nothing new or special or even interesting about you or what you've done, but I have a feeling you'd just be bored."

"I'm often bored." Beechum shrugged a little, accepting it, his boredom.

Marcus was thinking this Beechum was, as warned, pleasant and even a little charming. Not disarmingly charming like some of the criminals Marcus wiped, not one of those guys who was very good at being a friend, very understanding and helpful. This guy was coming across as curious and a little distant.

"All right then, basically what we're going to do is remove some of your memories."

"Of the murders, right."

"Yes, and maybe more if you want."

"Why would I want that?"

"Anything that may be causing you stress or guilt, anything you'd like to do without."

"Anything I'd like to do without?" Beechum seemed surprised. "I don't want to do without anything."

"You're not having any trouble sleeping? You're not wracked with guilt or shame?"

"I used up all my guilt at the trial. I traded it for all I could."

"So, all you've got left to trade are your memories."

Beechum nodded and said, "Doesn't sound like a very good deal, though, does it? Seven for two. Maybe it should be more hours or I should hold something back?"

"I don't negotiate the terms of the contract," Marcus said. "I'm just the technician."

"Just a clerk," Beechum said. "A nothing clerk."

Marcus leaned back on the couch and said, "The terms of the contract call for you to give up the memories of the seven murders and in exchange you'll be able to spend two extra hours a day outside of solitary."

"Yes, that's the deal. What do you think of it?"

"I've seen worse," Marcus said. And he had, but he'd seen better deals, too. "All right. We can start right away."

Beechum nodded and leaned forward to pick up the headset. It looked a little like a woolen hat with wires coming out of it. He said, "And you won't just erase everything in my head?"

"Of course not."

"But how would I know?"

Marcus said, "What do you mean?"

"Well, if you just erased all my memories, how would I be able to tell? I'd take this little hat off and ask you where I was and why I was here." He looked at Marcus and said, "And who I am."

"It doesn't work like that."

"But it could."

Marcus shrugged a little and said, "I've never tried to do that."

"I see."

"A lot of this is really up to you," Marcus said. "The more detail you give me, the more precise you are with your memories, the more precise I can be about what gets erased." Marcus waved his fingers over the touchscreen on his kit.

"Yes, it's more an art than a science," Beechum said. "I saw that in the info packet."

"I'm not so sure it's an art, but experience does help and I have a lot of experience. I can be very precise."

"Not all your experience is with . . . criminal memories?"

"No," Marcus said. "This kind of work makes up a small percentage of my contracts, actually."

"Of course, government work doesn't pay very well, does it?"

"I'm very experienced," Marcus said. "You're not getting shoddy work here."

"Oh, I didn't mean to imply . . ." Beechum paused and then said, "I'm sure you're very professional, it's just my head you're messing with and all."

Marcus said, "There was a lot of public interest in your case, public pressure, that made it political and that gave you a negotiating position."

"Yes, and that reporter who won't let the story fade away and keeps the outrage level so high."

"This will put an end to that, as well."

"And he'll move on to something else, get people all bent out of shape."

"If no one cared, if no one ever talked about you, then you'd never have been able to even offer giving up these memories for extra time out of solitary. Or maybe you would have only been able to get a student in here, someone still learning the technique, experimenting on you."

"That was offered," Beechum said. "They even offered me four hours out if I let a student, 'get some practice' on me, I think they said."

"So, you didn't take that offer and now you have someone with a lot of experience."

Beechum considered that for a moment and then said, "When you were a student, did you screw up a lot?"

"No, I didn't."

"How do you know?"

"What do you mean?"

"Did you experiment on each other, with other students, I mean, when you were learning the techniques?"

"A little, yes."

"So, for all you know you had a lot of memories erased? Oh, I'm sure," Beechum added quickly, "they were innocuous, little unimportant things."

Marcus said, "Yes. Now, let's get started."

"Oh right," Beechum said, "time is money and all that. How long do I get?" He turned the little hat over in his hands a few times before pulling it down over his head.

"As long as you need."

"Well, I'm sure I can't take up too much of your time, Marcus." Beechum was smiling a little, and Marcus was impressed with the act. He knew it was an act, of course. He knew Beechum was working him, being his friend and hoping that Marcus would get distracted enough to leave him a few memories, a few souvenirs.

Marcus was playing along. He said, "We have plenty of time." He was looking at his controls then and he said, "We can continue to get to know each other so I can get a feel for your patterns."

"After everything I have to tell you, you'll want to get these images out of your head, too."

"They're not real to me."

"But you'll still be haunted by them."

Marcus said, "No, I won't be."

"I guess you do have experience with this kind of thing."

Marcus had the feeling that Beechum was still faking his detached casualness about the whole procedure. He said, "Yes, but that doesn't mean I'll be any less precise. Just the exact memories."

"So that I can't replay them in my head anymore?"

"Right."

"But really," Beechum said, "what's to stop me from making up new fantasies and pretending they happened?"

"Nothing's stopping you, you're free to make up whatever you want. It's not the same thing, though, it's not a real memory."

"But wouldn't it serve the same purpose? I mean, an illusion, no matter how convincing, is still just an illusion. At least objectively. But subjectively — quite the opposite."

"No, you're free to make up whatever fantasies you like," Marcus said. "There's been outrage over your acts, over what you actually did, and those memories, those souvenirs, are what people have been demanding you give up."

"So nothing I think will be held against me?"

"That's right."

Beechum looked dubious for a moment but then quickly his easy smile returned and he said, "All right then, I guess we should start."

"We already have." Marcus tried for an easy smile, too, but wasn't sure he pulled it off. "So now let's get to the matter at hand. We'll start with the first murder."

"Adrianna, yes. I remember her."

"You remember them all," Marcus said. "That's what we're here to fix."

Beechum smiled. "I first saw her on the carousel in Lakeside Park, do you know it?"

"No."

"It must be two hundred years old. It still has an original Looff lion, very beautiful." He paused for a moment and then said, "Will I be able to remember that?"

"Do you have a different memory of it?"

"Oh yes."

"Then you'll still have those."

"That's good."

Over the next six hours, Beechum described his crimes, from

the moment he identified a victim all the way until he disposed of the body. Marcus had heard it all before, almost every single detail, just not all from one murderer. There was nothing new or unique or original about any of the rapes or the killing, they were just the same images movies and video games had been peddling for decades. Beechum could've just stayed home and saved everyone a lot of trouble. Of course, that wouldn't have been real.

With two murders still to detail, Marcus said, "All right, we should probably stop here for today."

Beechum said, "Quite a day."

"Yes, quite."

Marcus closed up his kit and stood up.

Beechum rubbed the side of his head and said, "I don't feel anything."

"It's not surgery."

"So, really, the memories are still there, I just can't access them?"

"Yes."

"So," Beechum said, "though it's just a memory, some memories last forever."

"That sounds familiar."

Beechum laughed and said, "It's from a song. A good one, you probably know it."

"I doubt it."

A guard was at the door then, and Beechum said, "Well, I guess I'll see you tomorrow," and left, reluctantly, to go back to his cell.

On his way out, Marcus passed through the guard station and Sgt. Fowler was still there. She said, "I don't envy you your job, spending all day listening to him."

"It's not that hard," Marcus said. "The criminals are all kind of the same, they blend together after a while. Of course, they do make the corporate jobs I get seem a lot easier."

Fowler said, "I finish my shift in an hour, would you like to get some dinner?"

Marcus was surprised but recovered and said, "That sounds nice, where would you like to meet?"

She suggested the restaurant in the lobby of his hotel, and he said that would be fine.

After a pleasant-enough dinner, Marcus and Sgt. Fowler ended up in his room at the hotel. He wasn't quite sure how it happened, he didn't remember inviting her, but he was pleased with the way things went. They drank a bottle of wine at dinner and then another in the room and ended up in bed.

When they were finished, Marcus watched Sgt. Fowler — Kristen — finish herself. She said, "Do you think you'll be done tomorrow or will you need another day?"

"I'll be done tomorrow."

"Will you leave then or will you stay another night?"

Very businesslike.

"If I stay another night I'll have to pay for the room myself."

Kristen said, "You didn't negotiate much slack."

"The government contracts never allow for much."

"Do they allow for room service? Any kind of per diem?"

Marcus rolled onto his side so he was looking at Kristen and said, "If I had known something like this would happen I would've held out for a little more." Then he winked and said, "But I can manage a couple of drinks, if you'd like one."

"I would."

She got up from the bed and walked the few feet to the mini bar. Then she crouched down and looked back over her shoulder, a very sexy pose, her naked back, the curve of her ass, the glint in her eyes — Marcus was especially surprised it had such an effect on him after the actual sex — and she said, "Whiskey?"

He managed to say, "Yes," and watched her touch the keys on the screen and open the little door to get out the glasses.

She stood up and walked back to the bed with a glass in each hand and her head to one side so her blonde hair fell over part of her face. Marcus found that incredibly sexy, too.

"I guess on the corporate jobs you get real scotch from little distilleries in Scotland, places that have been there for hundreds of years." She slid back into bed.

Marcus said, "Yes, sometimes. The bizboys are always trying to impress me. Well, not just me, everyone they talk to, I guess." He held up his glass and they had a little toast — he wasn't sure what it was to, crappy government contracts, maybe? The whiskey was better than he expected, but he was thinking that might have more to do with the company.

"They must have some wild memories to be wiped out."

"Not very often. It seems like the more money people have the more they fixate on the little things." Marcus took another sip. "What seems like the most pointless slight, some little insult at a party or a meeting that didn't go a percent the way they wanted to, and there I am getting a decent day's pay to get rid of it."

"Sounds like you deserve every cent," Kristin said, "listening to people whine like that."

Marcus laughed a little and said, "I'm glad to hear someone say I deserve it."

"But they never confess big things to you, they never want to erase the memory of some crime or some terrible insider deal they made or anything like that?"

"No, never anything like that." But then something flashed for Marcus and he started to say something but stopped.

"What is it?"

"Nothing." He looked at Kristen, who was sitting up with her back against the headboard, and he found himself looking up at her breasts. "For a second I thought there was something, but it's gone."

"You mean you can't remember?"

"No, I was probably thinking of a movie." He turned and moved up a little so he could look into her eyes, but they were as distracting as her breasts. He said, "But it's gone now."

"So, nothing juicy, no great scandal or conspiracy? Oh well."

Marcus reached past her to put his glass on the bedside table and then pressed his face into her bare stomach, nuzzling her skin, and he said, "We'll have to make our own scandal."

Kristen rolled him off onto his back and then draped a leg over him, saying, "That should be easy." She climbed on top of him and leaned down and kissed him on the mouth.

Afterward, Marcus watched Kristen finish herself, and she fell asleep only a few minutes later.

But Marcus couldn't sleep. He kept thinking about the memory just beyond his grasp. The more he thought about it, the more his insomnia played tricks on his brain. He was sure it wasn't a movie or a book he'd read but he was also sure it wasn't real. He really didn't have any idea what it was. He heard music but didn't know what it was, and then there was an image of a carousel. But then it was gone.

At some point he must have fallen asleep, because when his

alarm went off it woke him up and Kristen was gone. She'd left a note on his phone that said, "Thanks, that was fun. Today is my day off but if you have to stay another night, call me."

"You need excitement," Beechum said. "You need chaos."

Marcus said, "I do?"

"Everyone does. And if they don't experience it themselves they live vicariously through others."

Marcus looked back at the file and said, "As you were saying, you met the young woman on the rock climbing vacation?"

"Now that was boring. No better than the simulation I did at home but ten times the price."

"But you didn't speak to her that day?"

"People need real adventure," Beechum said. "All us plain, dull people, we have a real love for adventure."

"You found out she worked at the distribution centre nearby?"

They were on the last murder and Marcus was happy about that. The job was proving to be more difficult than he'd expected. Not the grisly details, he was used to those, but Marcus was beginning to have trouble keeping his mind from wandering. He was thinking of Kristen, of course, and already planning to get the next contract that would bring him back to the prison — never mind the low rates — but he was also thinking about what they'd talked about. There was something about the corporate account, the scandal, the conspiracy.

Beechum was saying, "But to maintain control we need a little chaos, we need something that requires control — security is the word we use, but control is what we mean. Don't you agree?"

"So you were trying to impose control on her?"

"No, not at all. I'm the chaos." Beechum waved his arms and said, "I was the chaos. I was a small part of it, for sure, one tiny false flag blowing in the wind, but I did my part."

Marcus said, "But you killed real people." The phrase false flag tweaked something.

"I did, yes," Beechum said. "Their stories are real. I think ..."

"Oh yes, they're real." Marcus had already erased many memories from the families of some of the victims. One of the families was wealthy and an online fund had been set up to pay for some of the others who wanted it. Most people say they would never want that, never want to lose the memory of a loved one, but the pain can be too much, even many years later.

Marcus continued, looking at his notes, "Describe the day you spent with Nadia."

"Day and night," Beechum said. He perked up then, looking a lot more lively. "And another day."

The details flowed out and Marcus erased them.

At the end of the day, Beechum removed the hat, stood up, and stretched and said, "Well, you're right, I didn't feel a thing."

"The contract includes two callbacks if memories do start to resurface."

"What if I don't tell anyone?"

"They'll find out," Marcus said. "They always do."

"Do memories resurface often?"

Marcus had finished packing up his kit. He looked at Beechum and didn't feel anything for the man, not even hatred after everything he'd described the past two days. "Not very often, no," Marcus said. "But memory is a tricky thing, a lot of it depends on what triggers what. We can never be sure exactly which triggers hit which memories. Sometimes if the same trigger gets hit over and over the memory does resurface. But, as I said, not very often. Usually the brain just moves on, skips to the next memory as it were, and you never even know anything is missing."

"So really, I can't access the memories, but they're still there?"

"Yes."

"So," Beechum said, "the song got it wrong — it's not that some memories last forever, all memories last forever."

"But not all memories get triggered," Marcus said. "Music is a strong trigger, try and avoid it."

"A life without music," Beechum said. "I can't imagine that."

"Music isn't that important to me."

"Too bad, it makes life better."

In the pod on the way back to Toronto, Marcus heard the line out of his head again, something about memories lasting forever, and he looked it up. "Lakeside Park." He'd heard it before. It was a trigger, all right. Images of fireworks and fires on the beach. He listened to the song a few times, trying not to sing along out loud, there were three other people in the pod and they all looked hard at work.

For Marcus the trigger was at first a pleasant one, his father playing the song in the car. Back in the days when his father actually drove the car, pressing a pedal with his foot and turning a wheel with his hands. Marcus smiled at that memory, thinking he was lucky to be alive, the way his father loved to drive with that old music playing so loud, singing along, not looking at the road.

Then the memory became darker and began to slip away.

Marcus could see his father and some other adults looking very serious, talking quietly and looking over their shoulders.

And then it was gone.

Entering Toronto, the pod detached from the train and drove into an industrial area filled with warehouses and distribution centers. Marcus was thinking it was too bad he hadn't paid extra for a solo car. But when the pod stopped in front of a bunker-like building no one else was making a move. The door opened and a man Marcus had never seen before said, "Hello, Marcus, this is your stop."

"I don't think it is."

"Of course it is."

Marcus didn't want to make a scene, and he was sure it would all get sorted out easily enough, so he stepped out and the pod drove off.

The man said, "That was a tough assignment, serial killer."

"Not particularly," Marcus said, and then, "How did you know about my assignment?"

"You just need a quick tune-up, nothing serious."

The man was smiling, but Marcus was focusing on the security team standing behind him.

"I don't think I do."

"You're having trouble sleeping."

"Not in my own bed," Marcus said. "Just when I travel." And he almost said something about when he didn't sleep alone, and then he started to understand.

"Yes, some memories are starting to surface," the smiling man said. "We can't have that, can we?"

"No," Marcus said, "we can't."

Walking into the building, Marcus started to see something. A man talking, telling him about a scandal, or what a scandal it would be, a conspiracy, if only people knew. But now they never would. Security. Control. Chaos.

If he could just concentrate on it for a while Marcus was sure he could remember. He saw his father behind the wheel of the car. Then they were in a park, Marcus by himself and his father talking with some other people.

"Won't take but a few minutes," the smiling man said. "Get you home for dinner."

The song was the trigger. Marcus could keep that memory, not say anything about the trigger, that wouldn't be erased. Then later he could try to find the real memory.

He was going to have to make music a more important part of his life.

RACE LARRY DIXON
HUMAN *inspired by "Marathon"*

THE ARRIVAL

Motorsports legend Luis Bergandi was whisked from the private hi-strat airstrip by chromed aircar. The fame game in the 2060s required being shuttled around in an aircar, alas. Luis disliked aircar dynamics; they were vector thrust vehicles, and he was a racer used to millimeter-precise handling. In anything but a straight line, aircars lurched about with the elegance of drunken blimps, and it was legal for them to use up two lanes. Consumer-grade utilitarian airtrucks barely needed a road, and autonomous military GEV convoys were now ubiquitous, but they tended to have dedicated routes. Self-important People-Of-Means loved taking high-end luxury aircars on regular streets, though, or for taking shortcuts across open terrain, such as farmers' fields, to avoid traffic. Luis thought of such POMs by their technical name, "dicks." No, no ostentatious chromed hulk was his style; a crisp, low car or 'cyc was where his heart was at.

"Mr. Bergandi?"

A man ducked through from the aft compartment. A perfectly manicured, half-gloved hand with white-plated nails was proffered, and Luis reflexively grasped it. The man's face was perfectly photogenic, well sculpted, and framed by jet-black hair. The implant dots on the man's temples were the same bright white as the nail plating, with the same tiny metal logos.

"Mr. Bergandi, I am Levon Novel, head press director for the Circuit. I have a liaison volunteer for you!" He twisted and gestured as if hard-selling an appliance. He seemed more game show host than the director of anything. "This is Naomi Paikea!" Levon listed off Naomi's "quallies" like they were bonus features. Luis nearly asked if Naomi came with an extended warranty, rude though it would have been. Finally, Luis edged in, "Naomi, it is a pleasure to meet you. I hope that I will not be a burden."

Naomi was dark skinned, slender, with a spritely face that reminded Luis of dear Björk, back in the "All Is Full of Love" days. It couldn't be coincidental, considering how much her white armored-and-cooled jumpsuit resembled the machines in the video. Naomi's suit was so new it still had labels on the ports. Her shimmery brown hair was cupped by the retracted helmet. Naomi bobbed her head — some Oceania in her family maybe? Samoan? — and answered with a chirpy, "You won't be a burden at all! And if we wear you out, I can get a shuttle or scoot-chair over with just a call." She made a gesture way past its time: pinky and thumb extended, ear to chin.

"Isn't Naomi the best? She is super-pro. I got her from a Degreed Interns program. After all, I can't be everywhere!"

Levon strained to project empathy toward Luis, and wrinkled his face. Luis assumed it was how Levon thought old people's expressions looked when they were happy. However, Levon's face simply didn't flex that much.

Anagathics helped, but Luis's heavily crinkled, sun-browned face still marked him as an early adopter of such age-halting medical miracles. Decades ago, people gawked due to his celebrity as The Legend, Luis el Legendario, *el mejor piloto*, ten-time World Champion. Lately, he was stared at as a combination of being an antique, being famous, and, truth be told, people's unease over someone who genuinely *looked* old, while they themselves might appear young for centuries to come.

"We have everything ready according to the plans you sent us," Levon continued, with a conspiratorial whisper. "*Everything*."

THE WELCOME HOME

Luis strode slowly down the roadweave. He could summon Olympic-athlete sprints with his exosuit, but he savored these moments, taking them at a contemplative pace. The press camera-drones gathered above, but Luis largely ignored them. He bent down easily thanks to the silent servos and graphene muscle in the exo, and laid a palm on the sun-heated surface. Luis peered down the gently curving sweep, breathing deeply through his nostrils. His gaze followed the racing line he'd driven thousands of times until it vanished into a flat decreasing-radius downhill right-hander. He could read the story of every tire mark, scrape, and scuff as far as his precision nuspec eyes showed him, as easily as a programmer could read code. The deep, even waves of sand beyond the wide, striped runoff was a better balm for him than any beach. The grassy slopes beyond the crash barriers, surrounded by bleachers and skyboxes, were more beautiful to him than New Zealand, Ireland, or maybe even his beloved Argentina.

Naomi's shouldercam kept a fix on Luis, but she stayed well back, while the news drones kept their legal distance. *Give me this*, Luis thought, with a smile on his face. *Be patient during my communion. Let me walk the track a while.*

The technology changed, the courses changed, but whatever continent he was on, whatever hemisphere, Luis Bergandi was at home as long as he was embraced by a racetrack.

THE WALK-AND-TALK

Luis stood, stretched, then stepped to Naomi's side. He was surprised to see she had a glossy sticker of a hyacinth macaw on her shoulderplate. "Eighty minutes until the interviews in the Porsche blockhouse, Mr. Bergandi. You'll have ten-minute breaks between press sessions until nine. I have full-caf waiting, and *dulce de leche* ice cream will be brought to you each break." Naomi had done her homework.

"Good, then there is time to see Dio and get things going," Luis responded warmly. "I can see you've worked at this track before. Tell me, Naomi, do you like this kind of racing that we do?"

Naomi paused, choosing the right words. "I've worked 'cyc and club races here, but I studied endurance racing's history to prepare for you. I came in assuming it was just driving around in a twisty circle, but it's bigger than that. There's more . . . majesty to it than I expected. I think I can like it more."

Luis laughed. "You make me happy, Naomi. Come, come, let's get into the paddock before anyone sees us." He waved a hand up at the camera drones following them, swatting as if they were flies. Obviously, by now over a million people had seen them. The drones halted at the invisible fence 12 meters from the paddock gate and landed on a charging shelf in a neat row.

Luis slipped between two massive modular transport trucks and paused. "Let's do bumpers and spots," he said, "then documentary roll." Naomi tapped at her tablet and her shoulder cam, exempt from paddock restrictions, bezel-flashed ready. Naomi finger-counted him down. Luis ran through a dozen variations on "This is 'The Legend,' Luis Bergandi," and "Welcome to the Circuit of the Americas!" Then Luis shifted to a more evangelical manner. "Prototype Endurance races — and, before it scandal-imploded, Formula One, which led to the much saner World F-Zero-One Series — weren't about merch, spectacle, and hype. The drivers were celebrities, yes, idolized by fans, and they idolized me, which was quite nice. But our racing was not completely about fame or out-driving someone else, nor about sponsorship, mindspace, and cam-time. This is a sport for humanity. Our prototypes are testbeds for world-changing technology. Aerodynamics, body materials, suspension systems — everything that might benefit consumer vehicles, aerospace systems, and nanomedicine is stress-tested in this racing." He walked, patting the side of the transporter, and Naomi's shouldercam stayed steady as she followed. "These are laboratories. Safety systems for vehicles from automated loaders to turbine trains, from Moonbase to Mars, are pioneered in race headquarters, fabricated, and brought here with these mobile labs. Microlatency telepresence used for remote robotic surgery was developed for slotcar links. Impact gel, magnetorheostatic fluid, and even the nanotube radiator fibers that keep your clothes cool in summer came from this. If the technology can survive the rigors of endurance racing, it makes its way into consumer items. Here, there is competition and excitement, and the ultimate goal of it? To keep your grandmother safe and comfortable driving around town. We all want to win but, just as importantly, we all want *you* to win." Luis smiled widely for several seconds, useful for a fade cut.

Naomi stood still for a few breaths and then pulled the clip up on her tablet and copied it to Levon's suite. "That was . . . I didn't see that coming. Sent."

"I'll give some history next. People love to hear an old star blather about the past," Luis snickered. He paused in place for a few beats, then resumed ambling. "The Ottos and slotcars made their debuts around the time of my seventh World Championship. Ottos were racing robots built to advance technologies that were impractical with living drivers. They were meant to be even competitors but, while they seemed fair on paper, they started with advantages in aero, weight distribution, and so forth. They were nicknamed 'Ottos' for the engineer Nikolaus Otto, of course, and for being *auto*matic. But, the name had a sinister connotation, too: that of Evil Otto, an invulnerable, unstoppable adversary from a classic video game."

Luis stopped walking, framing himself between the transporters and support pavilions. "Ottos seldom failed, and I found them to be brilliant opponents. Like chess against a computer, there was a strange purity in the game. By their fifth year, though, they were unbeatable. This was endurance racing, and the Ottos simply never got tired. It was successfully argued that the Ottos and slotcars had an unfair advantage because they did not carry the shape and weight of a human being. The rules committees declared that every vehicle that did not carry a live driver had to accommodate a human-shaped eighty-kilogram robot in a racing position. These imitation drivers were nicknamed 'asimos.'"

In Argentine tradition, Luis spoke with hand gestures as much as his voice. "The Ottos still outran nearly everyone. They certainly ended my career as a champion." He smiled and shrugged. "What could be done? They were legal, and I lost to them."

Luis rounded a few steps and leaned back against a datapost, crossing his legs at the ankles. "Then there were the slotcars. Toy slotcars had little plastic drivers molded into them, and, of course, the driver drove them by remote control. With our slotcars, the living driver is linked to the car's asimo using a sensory suite in the pit complex — a simulator that could make the driver feel all the cues from their car. Slotcars had the same restrictions as the Ottos — asimo and all. We greeted this with joy. Drivers, often friends of ours, who were incapacitated from injury could compete again, or instruct. A double-amputee Marine veteran who could never pass the physical to be in a race car campaigned against me for two years with a slotcar and beat me twice. Slotcars made for magnificent comebacks and brought in talented new-comers. I was proud to lose to them — from time to time."

Luis waited, until Naomi gave a "got it" signal. She told Luis, "I expected to escort a slow, cranky old man around all day. This is epic."

Luis chuckled back, "Oh, we racers have a saying: 'The older I get, the faster I was.' Our stories wind up more epic the longer we have to embellish them. Now, take me to the Victor Pit and you'll meet your cranky old man."

THE GARAGE

Naomi guided Luis to the *Victor*-bannered garage, and Luis cued Naomi to cease recording. Upon entering the shade, a big white man in a straining coverall surged toward Luis.

"*Papito*. You are here at last," Dio Panoz wheezed, hugging Luis. Dio looked much less like the big-muscled welder of his youth than he did an indulgent churro vendor. "Armed teams have unloaded transporters at the ballroom for weeks. What are you up to with my money, eh?"

Luis released the hug and chuckled, "With less than half your money. You'll see. Everyone has had time to clear their schedules for it. You all got the invitations, what was it, twelve days ago, Naomi?" She flicked at her tablet and nodded.

"And no one in motorsport would refuse an invitation from El Legendario Luis?" Dio asked. Luis held up a hand in mock humility as they walked deeper into the pit building. "Please, just La Leyenda is fine." Dio laughed back.

Naomi offered, "So far the only press leaks are from dox sources. They know the contents are insured for a billion-plus dollars, and they've traced the route of the shipments to museums, and one board did acquire a loadout list from the Petersen. The press consensus is that it's an invitation-only car show. There've been microdrone attempts to get inside, all shut down by ECM curtains. There are also betting pools over what vehicles will be in the show." Dio and Luis looked impressed. Naomi just grinned back, holding her tablet up. "What? You have your jobs, I have mine."

A printed-composite, woven-carbon skeleton chassis leaned against a pit wall, trading reflections with a gunmetal-and-gold racing machine so sleek it was clearly designed to make the air wonder what just happened to it. "I appreciate the technical notes you sent, Dio," Luis commented while crouching beside the Victor GT38. He lifted a wheel arch to show Naomi. "The paint weighs more than the graphene body. The body's as strong as five centimeters of titanium. The tires have numuscle embedded in alternating tread layers. When all the numuscle layers are relaxed, the tire is a sticky racing slick. For light rain, the numuscle flexes and it becomes a widened-sipe intermediate, and flexed fully it's a

deep-grooved rain tire. All without coming in for a tire change."
He tapped the GT38 and then the spare chassis next to it. "It has
its racing suspension, and the driver is in a protective tub with its
own suspension system. The tub swivels on the car's centerline up
to twenty-three degrees in turns to help with lateral Gs. In a crash,
the car disintegrates in a specific order, and the driver tub ejects."

"Sweet. Why bother to paint it though? You can get colored
graphene."

Dio answered that one. "The 'paint' is a flexible binder. Its
micropits cheat turbulent airflow, but, mainly, it contains the
graphene. In high-speed impact, graphene sheet fragments into
clouds of flying razors."

Naomi replied, "Paint is good. I'd go with the paint option."

Luis stood and reflexively brushed down his exosuit. "I would
love to drive this, Dio. Your *pilotos* are lucky. And yes, before you
ask, I have your strategy. And yes, it is within close reach of the
rules."

Dio chewed a bite from a brownfat bar. Brownfat bars were
common these days and they weren't illegal in the sport, so if Dio
wanted a spare tire for an energy reserve, there it was. It wasn't
doping, or implants, or a rigged ULS suit.

THE PAST DISASTER

Ultra Life Support suits were mandatory for all crewmembers,
but those suits were strictly to spec nowadays. ULS mods, doping,
and the human need to find an edge were responsible for the
infamous 2028 Spa-Francorchamps Meltdown.

The owner of the leading human team equipped his entire
crew with mil-spec ULS gear and networked them. It was meant
to be an emergency-response safety measure, but it was outside

the manufacturer's design. Their car caught debris in Hour 18, just after dawn, and limped for the pits. One of the crew, jumpy on stims, jolted from a nap and triggered a panic reading from his ULS, which alerted the other suits. Those suits responded by boosting adrenaline, and calorie burn, so they could better respond to the presumed threat. That transmitted to the other suits in the network, and recursion began.

Their pit was like a kicked termite mound. By the time their car arrived, the crew chief was screaming incoherently, three crewmembers ran up carrying two tires each, two crewmembers brought body panels, one ran around adjoining pits pleading for water bottles while already carrying two, and the fuel captain just stood, shuddering, with the fuel line over his shoulder aimed back into the open garage bay. One of the crew snapped, threw tools at the car, and then stormed off — over the pit wall, onto the live course, wielding a torque wrench in his hand like a club.

Luis was second in the pack bearing down on the crazed crewman on the straight. He braked hard behind the Otto he'd been chasing, and shut the car down. He could see stewards, cops, and medics exhausting themselves trying to catch the high-as-balls race crew, while press drones swarmed. The armored crewman beat on the Otto in front of Luis, sobbing. Luis knew that while it all looked like a Benny Hill act, what had just happened was a knife in the sport. And it was a bleeder.

There were Ottos on every side and aft of him. Luis removed his helmet, popped his harness, and stood up in his seat, witness to a deadly farce. He had been a World Champion, and now, on a good day, he might have gotten twentieth place. A sad madcap was just globalcast. In mere moments, his sport became a punch-line due to desperation. The leading human team had resorted to juicing, uppers, and stims for a chance to beat the machines.

The aerial shot he saw later taught him that his time as a champion had passed. All of the Ottos, independent of each other, had stopped in a perfectly spaced geometric pattern with twenty centimeters of space between them — surrounding Luis's car.

You can't escape us, they implied. *Our software lets us run with precision you will never achieve. We can draft your wake, and when you turn in for the apex, we will fill your mirrors. Terror will hit you. You will instinctively overbrake or swerve. You will lose your momentum and your line. And as you overreact and tire out, we will be right there. Twenty centimeters ahead of you. Twenty centimeters beside you. Twenty centimeters behind. All day and night.*

THE SHOW BEGINS

Luis sat with his eyes closed, seemingly in silent prayer, after the last interview. He always looked meditative while lost in regrets. Both his hands clasped his full-caf.

Naomi chimed in, "Attendance at the banquet is one hundred percent. Six are telepresenced by bot-talkers." Luis looked up to her then absently wiped his face down, removing no-shine spray. "There are still no press leaks. Your presence, and the mystery of the ballroom, is trending strongly. Mr. Novel is working it hard."

Some energy returned to Luis's face. "Everyone there! It is one of the best things you could tell me, Naomi. You are so very good at helping this old man. You're patient."

"I'm fascinated. I've worked with celebs before, and they were just tiresome to be around. You're . . . it's just weird. You know how famous you are, but you're humble."

Luis stood and stretched. "Ah, Naomi. When you have crashed at 260 kilometers per hour, broken your body, and are on your third facial rebuild, vanity vanishes quickly. Fame's relative. Fame is a tool one is given. I use the fame I am gifted with to educate and help people. I am owed regard by no one, but it is bestowed by people who wish me to have it. We gain nothing by pushing others down, but good things happen when we lift others up."

Naomi ventured, "So you're saying your fame does more for others than for you? That's sharp." She offered Luis his now-antique team jacket from his last World Championship.

"Oh, I'm not stupid, I like the ego part of fame," Luis chuckled as he shouldered the jacket on. "But in practical use? Fame opens doors where little else would. It is not a sprint race, this life. When you are given fame, you enter a life of strategy. Celebs who use fame as a bludgeon do not last long; it burns them out. We who nurture fame, and are considerate of it, are able to do more in the long run."

"The long run's a bigger deal now that everyone's living longer, I guess. This jacket's older than I am," Naomi commented, helping him straighten the waist, then covered her mouth, making Luis chuckle. "I'm so sorry!"

"No, it is true, I am sure! It is all right. But like this? This jacket is to remind everyone I am La Leyenda, the champion. What we show to others frames and defines our fame. It is craftsmanship. You could take me to the event in a limo, but I requested we walk in the open wearing this, so they see the great *piloto* still walking strongly, wearing a reminder of what a man can do."

"You have the mind of a publicist. No wonder Levon likes you."

"He likes you, too, Naomi. He was desperate for me to approve of you, and he knew you would be on camera with me in every wide shot. You'll come to be known by the blue macaw sticker. You'll be interviewed about what it was like assisting me. Levon is building your fame, too."

Naomi stood wide-eyed but didn't disagree.

THE BANQUET ROOM

Media drone swarms cruised with them at the legal distance of ten meters. Luis strode with confidence and, at the brightest-lit part of the walk, paused to wave up at all the cameras. It was a slow wave with a big smile that would play well as a clip or a still.

Levon Novel awaited them at the main doors, in formal whites with a checkered-flag ascot. "Mr. Bergandi! I hope Naomi has been helpful."

"Helpful? She has been indispensable. You should hire her at double salary."

Levon chuckled with him but eyed Naomi. "Yes, yes. Well. Ah, everyone inside is in formal wear, sir."

Luis picked at his jacket and replied, "This is as formal as I get tonight," and strode in. Naomi fell in step on one side, Levon on the other. Naomi rattled off popstats from her tablet through the halls. "I also wasn't joking, Levon. Hire her at double," Luis asserted. Naomi stifled a laugh and keyed the banquet hall door open.

A spontaneous standing ovation greeted the trio. Over half of the attendees were legends themselves, and all in sleek dresses, tuxedos, or formal kilts. Team leaders, techs, drivers, and team owners were there from the race car and slotcar teams. Six tall bots were in formal dress as well, in black-and-chrome housings, with their faces mapped to the distant attendees.

Luis pointed at one of the bot-talkers. "Rico, you are probably still in your underwear." Rico's grinning face answered, "Nomex underwear, Luis. Can't stop tradition." The applause died down as Luis clapped his hands and called for calm. The trio stepped up to the short stage. Levon stuck an amp-patch on Luis's collar. Luis's voice boomed. "I hope you enjoyed the meal and the wine. The burgundy was Château Bergandi, and the white was Château

Élan. I learned from the Panoz family: no matter how good a racer you are, it never hurts to have a vineyard to fall back on."

Everyone chuckled; that broke the ice. "So many friends here, new and old. You are here for more than a speech, you are here for a show, and I am your host. I have put myself into this project for most of a year, called in many favors, and I am confident in how it will go. I was asked to develop a strategy for the upcoming race. But what will surprise you is it was not a strategy for just one team. I was asked to develop a strategy for all of you." Murmurs at the tables ramped up. Luis had a sip of wine, then continued.

"You all respect me, admire me, or trust me. What you are about to experience is a card that I can only play once in my life. I ask you all to keep what happens tonight a locked-down secret for the next five days." There were nods of assent from every table. "By now you have noticed there are no Otto invitees. It is for a simple reason. I was asked to develop a strategy for beating them." The murmur spiked again. The houselights dimmed and Luis was subtly spotlighted.

"We humans stepped into the cosmos. We sent probes, and then people. Many of those probes were vehicles. We put cars on the moon, and cars on Mars. Cars are on Titan, Io, Ganymede, Enceladus, and Europa, even Mercury," Luis began. "Automated or remote-controlled vehicles mine away on the moon, expanding the base. But if you say the phrase 'Cars on the moon,' nobody thinks of bot miners toiling away; people think of the Apollo lunar rovers. We have brilliant rolling laboratories and basebuilders on Mars, but say 'Cars on Mars' and people think of Chariot One's famous ramping jump, with the astronauts raising their arms up in midair. I laugh every time I see that."

"People are proud that there are robots exploring and mining. The lab-bot cars show us amazing things. And, in our races, the Ottos gather data that saves lives. I do not devalue their data gathering. But, as you all know on some level, no one wants to see test mules whiz by, driving themselves, feeling nothing. Race fans watch races because they want to imagine what it is like to be the driver. Fans project themselves into the driver's seat. They want to be the *piloto*. Compare memories of the Chariot and the lunar rovers with the hundreds of probe vehicles, and we find in ourselves that we don't dream of the hardware. We want to be the astronauts."

Luis gestured upwards with his wineglass. "Look up to the moon, and it isn't just a big round rock, it's a place people are. Walk around on. Sleep on. Drive around on. Live on. Same with Mars. The feeds from the Sagan, Korolev, Hadfield, and Tyson bases make us happy. Their adventure becomes our adventure. We know that human beings are tromping around out there, cracking jokes and pulling pranks."

Planning and timing. Pace the race.

"It feels good to be what we are, doesn't it? Being on posters and shirts, and signing autographs. I feel a bit sad for them, that Ottos can't sign autographs. Hell, they would avoid even driving over the paper." Laughter from the tables confirmed he owned the room. "The more the Ottos dominate, the less viewership we get. We are good testers and researchers, superb engineers, brave *pilotos*. But, as people, we want the world to watch us. We want our victories to be seen and admired. We want to be winners, and we want to inspire others. We want glory, not a day job. We want to feel triumph and bask in the view from the podium."

Luis could read emotions from every face and heard sighs and murmurs. He said, softly, "We want our youthful dreams to come true. We want to be among our heroes."

He set the wineglass down and nodded. Levon and Naomi split off around the tables and keyed opened the ballroom doors. Luis led everyone in.

THE LEGEND'S TREASURE REVEALED

Luis stepped into the only light in the ballroom, a meter-wide pinspot, while all the attendees made their way in. "We need to remember why we are here, on a race team, or behind a wheel. We must remember why we do this, and what made us want to." Luis gestured widely. The lights ramped up in the vast room. Tuned spotlights came on, seemingly randomly, on a vast room of treasures. Luis imitated Enzo Ferrari's voice, though few here would recognize it: "*Bella, bella, bella.*"

The attendees blurted expletives, whistled, and shouted. Arrayed before them all was a voluptuous Talbot-Lago in French Blue, a scarlet Ferrari 166 MM from Luis's own collection, Baja Trophy trucks, vintage motorcycles from Aprilias to Ducati Monsters to Can-Am Spyders, and two legendary BMW Boxers. A sidehacker special stood next to a salt lake belly tanker in SoCal colors, and a happy little Miata kept them company. The massive spear-like Bloodhound SSC gleamed. A 1963 DB5, a repro Ferrari 330P4 and matching 250 GTO, the LeMans-winning 2003 Bentley Speed 8, and a longtail McLaren F1 clustered with a JPS Lotus 79 on loan from the Andretti family. A copper-liveried 2022 Bentley Speed 12 faced off with a 2029 Corvette Z18. The Sebring-winning Mustang GT1000 from 2032 dared anyone to come near, and Clark's Lotus 49 looked like a toy next to it. There were over a hundred race and road cars, drag bikes, movie cars, and hot rods. In one corner was an exact replica of Mars Ventures's Chariot One and a copy of a NASA Lunar Rover. Beside every few vehicles, someone in formal wear or a vintage racing suit stood. Every vehicle was as bright as a dream, as if new.

The noise from the crowd grew to shouting levels as the attendees fanned out. Even the bot-talkers were swearing or just gasping. Luis looked to Naomi, then Levon. Finally, when Dio nodded, grinning, Luis's amplified voice rang out.

"This is your gift from me, to all of you. Some of you have only seen pictures of these, but you know their history. For an hour or so, reunite with your dreams. My curators are experts on everything here, and they'll answer any question. Some are even their owners or mechanics, and they have the keys. Now is no time to be shy, my friends. Have fun."

Luis tapped down his amp and let himself be led away. Once clear of the ballroom, a rush of fatigue came over him. He slumped into a chair and was brought an *aranciata* to sip. They left the ballroom doors open. Before ten minutes had passed, someone tried to start the E-Type. It turned over, its V12 tapping along in its lovely super-sewing-machine way. More whoops and laughter. Then there was an explosion, loud enough that it made a couple dozen attendees cry out, and the explosion lasted and lasted. That would be the 427 Cobra starting up. The laughter got louder. The black custom twin-supercharged Pantera cleared its throat. Then the Lola T70. The incomprehensibly loud open-pipe Chaparral 2 fired up, then, after it shut off and people could hear again, came the almost timid-sounding rattly Talbot, probably dribbling a liter of water from its exhaust. Engines shut down, others started, and doors were slammed and opened as the teams and drivers turned into little kids playing with toy cars.

Luis's smile broadened as meals were brought in for the trio. He tipped his drink to his companions. "*Salut*," he said to his con-spirators and finished the last sip.

"You've got skills, Mr. Bergandi."

Luis answered, "No one can be a champion just by being a good driver, Mr. Novel."

THE SECOND PLAY

An armed detail wheeled in hardcopies of The Strategy and set one before each seat in the secure conference room. Luis thanked them, simply said "Showtime" to Levon and Naomi, and strode into the ballroom. The ventilation had worked overtime to clear the exhaust. Luis tapped his amp back on, and stepped onto the platform in front of a silver E-Type, so everyone could see him as he spoke from the heart. A subtle pinspot highlighted him. Luis spoke slower than before, pulling in a storyteller cadence.

"Do you remember how it felt on that first grid?" Luis began softly. "The helmet was too heavy. You tugged at your gloves and made fists around the steering wheel. You wished you could afford a coolsuit. Your suit was already soaked. You wanted to look around, to see if you could find some clue how to beat your competitors by glancing, but instead your HANS rig stopped you from turning your head. All you could do was wait there, so cramped, so hot, looking ahead through your windscreen. And then . . . your eyes went out of focus. We all felt it. Our eyes stopped mattering momentarily, and we felt everything else: every seam in our firesuit, every bind in our belts, every trickle of sweat, every moment of our breathing. We became something new, fully immersed. We were enveloped by that moment and the realization that, yes, this is it, this is real. I am in a race car, on the grid of a real racetrack." Luis switched between "we" and "you" to build empathy. "Officials walked by with clipboards, and you heard the sound of a muffled PA system, then your team did a radio check. And you knew they were talking to you, but you were so deep in that moment that they sounded distant. You inhaled a deep breath. Your gloves released from the wheel then gripped again. You had practiced, you had studied. Your breathing became controlled again. Color returned to the world as it widened in your vision. You replied to the radio check, and ahead of you all, the steward raised his clipboard. You lifted the toggle covers on your go panel and clicked the switches in sequence. The clipboard dropped, and the official walked out of view. Your thumb pressed the START button. You were a racer. This was your time." He emphasized that with a victory fist, tucked against his chest, then after a few breaths Luis continued.

"And you were terrible at it."

Everyone laughed, and a few got the giggles. "You misjudged apexes, forgot to check your mirrors, and some of us even did some mowing. None of us made podium, but — we were changed. It was not that we got a trophy; it was that we had actually done what billions of people only played at in games. We were racers now. Even last place was a victory, because we'd dared to be there at all. 'Coming in last' beats 'never tried.'" A smattering of applause and some "hell yeahs" from the Mank & Foose team came from that. "And 'has been' beats 'never was.' You can trust me on that." Luis laughed along with a few dozen other relics like himself.

"I am happy to bring these treasures to you. Celebrated in song, immortalized on posters. There is one in particular that I want to highlight." Luis gestured as he stepped sidelong to wind up standing at the nose of the car. "This," Luis proclaimed, presenting its long, silver bonnet, "is a Jaguar E-Type coupe. It is considered the most beautiful car of all time." By the sound of it, pretty much everyone agreed.

This was a pivotal moment. If he spoke poorly, the momentum

would be lost. He paused for effect. "And, technically . . . everything about it is wrong," he stated.

A few curse words came from the crowd. Luis picked up the pace. "It is the most beautiful car ever, to human eyes, but as engineers, look at its elements. Its aerodynamics are questionable at best. Its temperature management will cook your calves, and it's likely to leak any fluid, at any moment, in any amount. The nose is in terrible proportion to its headlights; its bumpers laughable. Parts of it are made up of kilos of shims. Its rear hatch is a bubble worthy of growing prize tomatoes. The side trim is pointless, too shiny, too wide, the fenders too tall. The badges cause drag. And yet." He held up a hand to the heavens. "And yet. It is beautiful." He laced his fingers lightly in front of himself. "It stirs something inside us. It is not something a computer and simulators would create at all; instead, it is an E-Type. By criteria of functional design, all of its individual elements are wrong. But when they are put together it *feels* exactly right."

Dio nodded firmly. Clearly, he loved the Jag. Dio's head was not the only head nodding. Luis continued, now walking around the group, past a Countach, then a 1967 big-block Stingray with cannon-sized sidepipes. "You can take in the numbers. For some, form and function produced genuine beauty, like the Skyactiv and the Furai 16. They feel right." By now, Luis led a crowd of devotees. He raised his hands now like a preacher, fingers spread wide. "You can get into these legends, smell their interiors, and wonder about their quirks and personalities. Why does the Talbot smell of castor oil? Why are there sweater fibers in the Barchetta seats, there? Why is there a money clip riveted on the Cobra's dash? You'll wonder. You'll care. Something about one or more of these legends catches you. It is not data any more. It is a story.

"My friends, I will tell you who my heroes are. I am impressed by the podium finishers, certainly. But, as an endurance racer? Eighth place and back, that is who I admire. The middle-of-the-pack or the back-marker drivers know at some point that they will not win that race. They could give it all up and quit racing, never knowing the view from the podium except in daydreams. But instead they keep going. They don't have a chance at a trophy, but they go the distance. They are *true* racers. They know in Hour 23 that they are a hundred laps down, yet they stay out there, pushing. They could quit at any time, and no one would blame them. Most people will glance at the results of a race and glance at the top five and they're done, but I, I read all the way down. And sometimes I whisper, 'Thank you.' The ones who don't win are my heroes because they did win, in the best way: they had the willpower and the passion to not give up.

"We as racers feel we must do this, or else we are lessened. An Otto can data-collect, but it can feel no thrill. To an Otto you are a point cloud, a thousand scans a second, a shape mapped out. It cannot know you. It cannot care. It is there to test things, and all you will ever be is a variable in its algorithms. It cannot know passion, nor behave irrationally, nor do anything for fun. They've no childhood heroes to remember or dreams to fulfill. They cannot be moved to tears by wonder."

Luis completed his circuit of the room with that and stopped at the ballroom doors. "Team leaders and owners, with me, to the conference room."

THE THIRD PLAY

The guards locked the room behind them. Naomi rested with her back against a wall, one foot up. Luis wasted no time once everyone was seated or parked. "Ayrton Senna said, 'If you are doing something like motor racing, you either do it well, or forget it.' I will paraphrase him: 'Do it well, or be forgotten.'"

Luis put his hands on the table and leaned forward. "Each of you fought your way here. We have faced tragedy, adversity, weakness, and loss. You have seen our budgets drop, the attendance drift away, the grandstands emptier year after year. We can handle losing a race, or crashing a car. What we can*not* abide are neglect and indifference and, above all, irrelevancy."

"I studied the challenge from untold angles, and one morning I realized what was wrong the whole time. It is what we missed for years. I am putting my fortune and reputation on this statement. In my analysis from every angle but one, the Ottos cannot be beaten." The room's mood sank. "Your best *pilotos* will never be able to exceed the precision and smoothness of even the most poorly built Otto. The vague despair everyone feels is that we've lost to these machines, and the fact is we have." Luis stood up again, raising his chin. "Interest in our sport wanes because the top ten or twenty finishers are always Ottos. The human drivers feel like monkeys driving billboards around, while dodging the robots that leave them eighty laps behind. And as long as you race against Ottos as if they were your equals, you will never score a victory."

Luis adjusted his jacket. "People have lost interest in our sport because they want astronauts, and what we offer them are robots. I spoke to a great many people about this. Most said if they looked at our standings at all, it was just to see who the highest placing human was."

All were being politely quiet, but it was clear that a thousand questions were ready to explode from them. It was time for Luis to set the hook. "It was as I studied the Ottos' nature — that is to say, why they were there at all — that I realized their essential weakness, and our essential strength. We all race by certain rules, and breaking rules comes with penalties. Ottos cannot break rules, nor can they even bend them. Think of the implications of just this one thing. An Otto has lightning-quick collision-avoidance systems. They react faster than you can, to any obstruction, always. Why are the collision-avoidance systems there?"

Mank answered first. "So they don't get hit." Luis prompted for more from him. "So they won't hit anything else."

Luis replied, "Those systems must react to demanding variables, so they are sent to race, where their reactions are put to the test. They must, by their nature, always try to avoid you. An Otto will always back down if it senses a collision with you. It has no choice."

Mank laughingly countered, "Your strategy is to just ram them?" and before Luis could reply, the Glickenhaus team leader stood up, her eyes shining. "No. No, he's not saying you should ram them. He's saying you *can't*."

Dio had the beginnings of a grin. Luis continued the pace. "Don't go out and race in stupid ways that will get you flagged off the course or penalized into oblivion, no. But the key is, if you try to race on the Ottos' terms, you'll always lose, so the way to win is not to try to win an Otto's race." Luis straightened his jacket. "The essential truth of an Otto is that it is not a racer, it is a *simulation* of a racer. Competing with an Otto as if it were a racer is a guaranteed failure. But if you drive contrary to how Ottos operate, you will suddenly tax the Ottos' abilities. You will be more like the rest of the real world: unpredictable. Ottos will work to evade you as much as work to lap you. In this way, you help the Otto teams to help humanity, because consumer cars aren't driven by precision racers trying to beat precision robots.

"The fact is, this sport will be gone soon, rendered irrelevant to the fans, unless you *all* follow my strategy. I repeat, this must be all of you, or none. It is that important. The choice is yours. Open the envelopes now, please."

Luis sat down while everyone opened the Strategy envelopes. The room filled with questions, arguments, and incredulity. He thought of it as a chicane to be navigated briskly. Not a problem.

The Strategy opened with, *A machine only has as much power as you give to it. This is the way to tell the world, "I am a racer. These machines are irrelevant to me. They are robots. They serve a function, so let them serve it. But now, watch what racing really is.*

THE GRID, RACE DAY

The Circuit of the Americas was five and a half kilometers long. Its twenty turns were designed after the greatest turns of circuits around the world, with sweeping high-speed straights and nearly 40 meters in elevation changes, with esses, hairpins, roundhouses, and sprint-straights. This race was to be twenty-four hours long, forty-eight entries, with half attrition expected.

The sixteen top spots were Ottos. The stands were sparsely filled, despite wonderful weather. The first human drivers on the grid were Glickenhaus, then Bowlby, then Crider and Tesla, trailed by malfunctioned-in-testing Ottos, humans, and slotcars. The last entry, "Garage 100," was always an extreme experimental. This time it was a narrow eight-wheeled chromed arrowhead with two low-diameter, low-profile tires per nacelle. The design appeared to be machined from a solid block of billet understeer.

The megascreens showed ten minutes to start.

THE FORMATION LAP

The yellow laser ghostwall across the pit-row exit flashed twice a second. Engines started, turbines whined, alert signals sounded from the silent electrics. The Ottos filed out of their pits virtually in unison. The illuminated body panels on each vehicle flashed in a test sequence on approach to the ghostwall. The cars exited the pit lane and formed up according to their qualifying time. Tires were brought to temperature, and variable-form bodies adjusted wings, fenders, and intakes in response to humidity and air density. The pace car, this time a Bentley Magnique, led the pack around Turn 20, into the start-finish straight. The speed slowed to a rules-mandated 120 kph, a crawl compared to what each vehicle was capable of, and midway down the start-finish straight the pace car slowed to just 40 kph. All the vehicles were in their grid positions, approaching the flagstand.

Luis, this race's guest of honor, held the green start flag tightly at his side, high on the flagstand. As was traditional, all the drivers and asimos raised their arms to wave to the fans and to the flagmaster as they crawled along. Every slotcar asimo, and every human driver, waved fingers wide. Then, as they approached the flagstand, they clenched their hands into fists. Media commentators wondered what was going on. The fists stayed raised until the uphill approach to Turn 1. The media chatter built up. What could it mean? Even the silver arrowhead, with no one behind her to see the gesture, passed the pit exit with her fist raised. Luis smiled broadly. He glanced down to pit row where Dio gestured rudely up to him.

Luis laughed out loud and readied the green flag.

THE RACE

The cars came around the Turn 16, 17, and 18 roundhouse in starting formation, compressing to a tight version on the approach to Turn 20. The pace car took a sudden sharp left and its lights went out. Only race cars and Ottos were on the track now.

Engine sounds intensified. The ready lights on the flag stand shone brightly as the vehicles accelerated to near race speeds. The green laser ghostwall under the flagstand line snapped off. Luis waved his flag vigorously in a figure eight, and racing machines howled into full throttle. The Ottos pulled away and screamed uphill to Turn 1, all within meters of each other.

But back there — The Strategy was engaged.

The media commentators were nearly speechless. The spectators screamed and stood. The Ottos vanished around Turn 1, off on their own, against each other.

Luis smiled, tears in his eyes. Every human-controlled race car on the track set their speed-limiters to 60 kph. They stayed in their starting order but tightened up, filling the empty gaps where the Ottos had been. By now, the Ottos were far away, reaching 260 kph in the esses, but except for their roboticists, sponsors, and programmers, nobody on or off Earth cared about the Ottos. All cameras and all eyes were on the cars on the main straight.

The spectators jumped and danced, and in the paddock, everyone who could get a view, did. Vendors climbed atop their trailers to get a glimpse. Every screen at the Circuit showed the tight grouping of human-controlled racers approaching the virtual wall of the pit exit where the climb to Turn 1 started. When the flagger at Turn 1 flashed the yellow-striped blue flag, suddenly their engines shrieked. With the Ottos on the far side of the track, the human racers fulfilled their agreement with Luis. In The Strategy, the green flag was the official start for all vehicles, but because the human-controlled cars were bunched together closely, the flagger at Turn 1 would inevitably wave the blue-and-yellow "check behind you, traffic is close" flag, and *that* is what they would treat as their start flag.

Lightning flashed to the south. There was always rain sometime during this summer race, but that distant thunder was lost amidst the howl and growl of racing machines, and cheering. Levon and Naomi laughed out loud in the media booths, watching the media metrics soar. Channels were switching over live, interrupting their other broadcasts. Others were trying to catch up. In a moment neither of them expected, Levon and Naomi hugged each other, then backed off, wondering what just happened, but they liked it, whatever it was.

Luis sat on the old aluminum stool in the flagstand, and rested the Start flag across his lap. Luis's Strategy was not about fuel metrics, driver-changes, and pit times. It was about mattering to people. Defiance was part of human nature. So was a love of novelty, admiration for audacity, and some rule-breaking. Every Otto would, by the numbers, win this race. But the Ottos' placings would be ignored by the general public because the humans just did something *really* novel, *really* exciting. They rebelled against emulating machines and took their series back on their own terms.

Every hour the race went on, the Ottos passed the humans, but the humans were *all* driving differently this time than they had in the past few years. They were racing each other, and treating the Ottos as secondary interests. The humans took racing lines that were more adventurous than usual, knowing the Ottos would either back off or swerve away. Over the team comms, and from the slotcar driver pods, drivers were laughing.

Of *course* it was a publicity stunt, unashamedly so. And it was hilarious. It was exciting. It was broadcast to the moon and to Mars. It made clerks, doctors, farmers, kids, and astronauts want to be in a race car. It wasn't all about data-collecting, sponsorships, and championship points. It was *fun*. There was far more to racing than prize money and numbers on a scoreboard, after all.

HOLLYWOOD DREAMS OF DEATH

TIM LASIUTA

inspired by

"I Think I'm Going Bald"

HOLLYWOOD, 1936

Lazlo Delorean wiped the knife clean after pulling it out of the prostrate man on the ground. He smiled a sardonic smile and looked around the room then, with a brush of his hand, pushed his flowing hair back into position.

"You made me do it, Lyle," said the actor. "Just couldn't keep the secret. What happens behind closed doors in Hollywood stays behind closed doors. You should've known that."

Delorean put the knife into a velour bag and glanced one more time around the room. He stepped over the body and looked at the framed photos on the wall. Friends and coworkers' images in black and white signed *To Lyle Davies, with love* adorned the walls.

"Ahh, Olivia De Havilland. Claudette, my darling. We could have made a beautiful couple. Errol. Bogart. Cooper," the actor murmured. "You all had secrets, too. No one will know them now."

The police arrived at the trailer of the dead makeup man within minutes. In a city built on celluloid lies, a place where rumor replaced truth as the most valuable commodity, the media frenzy was unlike anything else on Earth.

The murder of RKO's top makeup artist moved through Tinseltown like light through a vacuum, and the police cordon came up almost as fast as the first studio moguls appeared on scene.

"Mr. Selznick, come this way," a studio runner called to a sleepy-looking man stumbling out of a limousine beside the soundstage and makeup trailer. "Follow me, please."

A full squadron of policemen manned the cordon while Inspectors talked to potential witnesses and examined the scene. Bright lights illuminated the crime scene perimeter. Despite the lateness of the hour, a full crowd had gathered behind the line and murmured among themselves. "I heard it was suicide . . . He was having an affair . . . Lyle was a lovely man, wouldn't hurt a fly . . . I hope they get whoever did this . . ."

Inside the trailer, the Hollywood detective force had gathered to examine the crime scene. Clearly used to crime in a community that thrived on exploitation, the head investigator, George Braham, ordered the trailer shut and gag orders issued to the studio.

"Believe me, Mr. Selznick, you don't want this getting out," said the tall, handsome police inspector. "This is the third murder in the studio over the last five or six weeks, and the second this month. I think you've got a murderer on your payroll, sir, or someone doing real-life research."

The studio head looked around the crime scene and back at

the inspector, then grinned. "I agree we do have a problem. Have you seen our last two pictures?"

The inspector frowned. "This, sir, is no time for jokes. You have two dead people in three weeks. TWO. And you can crack jokes?"

Selznick's demeanor changed. "Sgt. Braham, I have a studio to run, and while I lament the loss of Mr. Davies and Miss Penny, I will do my job and you will do yours. If you have any questions, contact my secretary. She knows everything."

A young officer stepped in the way of the departing studio executive. "Sir. This is a closed investigation. You cannot leave until the inspector says so."

Selznick turned around and stepped into Braham's personal space and blew cigar smoke into his face. "What do you want me to do?"

The inspector stepped back.

"What can you tell me about Davies?" asked the sergeant. "Give me the skinny and you can go be a producer again."

Selznick sneered and began to sing like a canary.

Lazlo Delorean was a Hollywood legend. For more than a decade, his face had graced the movie posters that drew crowds around North America. While not having the rugged star appeal of a young John Wayne or Errol Flynn, his flowing blondish hair and deep blue eyes were pure gold for Hollywood programmers.

And he knew it.

Delorean stared in the mirror, gently turning his head from left to right, then up and down, staring at his face with a critical eye.

"Let's face it, Lazlo," he said, running a hand over his flowing hair. "The face that made a million women swoon in their seats, and it's all yours. And hers," he added looking back into the bedroom, where Delila Delorean lay seductively on the bed waiting for her husband.

They had wed five years previously after a torrid romance on the set of a John Ford film where Delila had played the part of a settler's wife and Delorean was second lead to a young John Wayne. Back then, Lazlo had just come off a successful series of detective films in the vein of Dashiell Hammett's *The Thin Man*, and in the interim, Ford had approached him for his film.

Delila, on the other hand, was fresh out of the Midwest and straight off the bus. Wide-eyed and dream driven, the young actress gravitated to RKO and gleaned a bit part after she caught the eye and the couch of an ambitious assistant producer. One day on the set of the Ford film and the aspiring starlet was lost to Lazlo, and he to her.

That was then.

"Darling, come to bed. You've been gone for two hours already and baby wants her cuddles," said Delila sleepily. "I want to run my fingers through your gorgeous hair."

A switch clicked inside the model-turned-actor and a spring returned to his step. He looked at his wife and smiled deeply, then took a step toward her, dropping his robe.

"Say it again, Delila. This time, purr when you say my name," he murmured.

"Lazzzzzlllooooo . . ."

The sun rose a few hours later to a satisfied Lazlo lying in bed. His wife was snuggled up to him with her head resting against his chest. She breathed softly while he breathed more heavily. He reached over and stroked her hair.

Meanwhile, back at RKO, Braham and the squad of Hollywood detectives continued to examine the makeup studio of the late Lyle Davies. One man dusted for fingerprints on the photos and smiled impishly when he discovered lip marks on several of the starlets. Another had been examining the desk by the mirror for traces of blood and fibers. He was puzzled as he turned his attention to the carpet.

"Detective," said the young man. "How do we look for evidence in a zebra-print shag carpet?"

The senior investigator was standing away from the scene lost in thought.

"Detective!" the young man asked again, drawing him from his dream-like state.

"Good question. Have you ever thought of hiring a Native guide? Keep digging and something will turn up. Get that photographer, Costello, to take as many shots as he can," said the detective. "That's how you learn. Evidence can hide anywhere. When I was a young detective, a murder weapon was hid in a trunk under a chiffon dress. Once we discovered it, it was an open-and-shut case."

With the body gone, Braham was trying to determine the hidden mystery behind the murder. He walked in and pretended to stab a phantom. He did it again, and again, and then snapped his fingers. In a soundstage across the lot, a choir struck up a rhythm.

"The victim knew his killer," exclaimed Braham. "If he didn't, there would have been struggle marks and makeup all over the place. The scene was clean, telling us he knew whoever killed him. We couldn't find the murder weapon, but if we had to look, every soundstage is full of knives."

Behind the desk, a voice piped up. "Sir, if you recall, the crime scene was similar to Miss Penny's. Perhaps we do have the same killer?"

Braham sat down on the couch in the trailer and pondered the idea. "I said that last night, but I was only half serious. But it may be . . ." continued the investigator as he launched into a soliloquy from *Hamlet*. "To sleep, perchance to dream . . ."

The police cars roared down Rodeo Drive screaming emergency and turned left into a prestigious crescent and through a series of gates. Designed to be a home away from home for Delorean, this was his refuge, his Xanadu.

Three police cruisers screeched to a stop in front of the Victorian-style home, and policemen opened the doors and ran to the front door. The Hollywood detectives had been at this game for more than two decades, and they salivated inwardly at the potential of a scandal like the Fatty Arbuckle case on their watch.

Braham stepped out of the lead cruiser and walked to the door. He knocked and almost immediately a wizened butler answered with a question on his lips. "How may I help you, sirs?"

Taking a step into the mansion, Braham looked around as he spoke to the butler. "Sir, we are here to arrest Lazlo for the murders of Davies, Penny, Slater, and his wife, Delila. Where is he?"

From the living room to the left, Lazlo walked into the foyer dressed in a silk evening housecoat. He was sipping a cognac and had his arms around a Hollywood starlet. He was immediately surrounded by the detectives. Braham put the cuffs on him. Lazlo glared at the police inspector.

"I'm innocent," he yelled. "I'm innocent. Alfred, call my lawyer and the press!"

Braham and the police officers sped away from Lazlo's home and drove toward headquarters. The inspector had been through star arrests and the piranha-like feeding frenzy of the tabloid press. He feigned annoyance, but he secretly thrilled at the prospect of the confrontation. Perhaps it was his love of Shakespearean drama, which he engaged on the weekends secretly. Perhaps it was his sense that stardom did not mean entitlement. Either way, he had bitten off a big assignment this time and he was determined to see it through.

By the time the police had arrived at the station house, it had started.

Flashbulbs exploded as the three cars arrived on scene and the handsome actor was taken out of a vehicle into the station house. Braham's men ran interference as he took Lazlo in through a side door, past holding cells, and to a processing desk where an officer removed the cuffs and logged Lazlo in.

Outside, the reporters and photographers were working themselves into a frenzy. Braham stepped up to the mike.

"Ladies and gentlemen," said the inspector, "tonight, at 8:10 p.m., the Hollywood Precinct arrested Lazlo Delorean on suspicion of committing multiple murders. I'll take your questions."

A dozen hands went up. A bedraggled middle-aged man stuck his hand up.

"Karl, from the *Hollywood Reporter*," said Braham. "Your question?"

The reporter moved through the crowd and stopped in the front row. "Do you think these charges will hold? Or will they disappear like the Loch Ness Monster?"

The crowd laughed.

"Karl, we have solid evidence to link Lazlo with the four

murders," offered the detective. "We do not intend the murders to go unsolved or, worse yet, have this investigation turned into a Dick Powell murder mystery film."

More hands went up.

"Any idea when you'll have more information?" asked an attractive reporter from the *Los Angeles Times*.

Sgt. Braham turned to where the voice came from. "By tomorrow afternoon, there will be a full press conference with more details."

The press dispersed and the lies began.

June 1933 was a good year for Lazlo.

He had just finished a film with Fay Wray after her triumph in *King Kong*. Something had started that Lazlo could not control, yet he would grow to understand intimately.

The Passion of Gilbert was written by Hollywood's most prolific scripter and starred Hollywood's hottest leading man and woman, yet beneath the romantic skin, sinister undertones resembled real life.

Wray and Lazlo's love scene was torrid. In pristine sepia tone, the glint in Lazlo's eye and the emotion Wray portrayed had struck a nerve.

"Gilbert," said the young actress, her eyes boring deep into her lover's soul as Lazlo moved to put his arms around her. He oozed sexuality while the actress tilted her head back slightly to expose her pale white neck. He began kissing it gently.

During rehearsal it had not always gone so smoothly. Studio crews had witnessed his disdain for the lighting and the lack of a gentle breeze, which would have showcased his hair.

"Raoul, more light and, please, a little more breeze," Lazlo would say with conviction.

Every time, the director would deny the request with a wave of his hand and walk away muttering, "Talk to Selznick."

It only took one temper tantrum and he won.

"What Lazlo wants, Lazlo gets," became the buzzword at RKO. Meanwhile for extras and studio services, it was "stay away from Lazlo."

After Lazlo's arrest, RKO Studios rereleased his early films with great economic success. *Yukon Quest* struck gold in a second run, and *Noonday Sun* raked in bushels of greenbacks. The unreleased romantic comedy, *Panacea*, was soon a bonafide hit in the cinema chains.

"A great send-off for a suspected murderer," said *Variety*.

"The last great film of Hollywood's most handsome murderer," added the *Los Angeles Times*.

"Ghost of Lyle Davies seen in Grauman Theatre screening of *You Only Die Once*," the banner of the *Hollywood Reporter* screamed to readers.

July 6 was the first day of the trial.

The downtown Los Angeles courtroom was packed with press members and, outside, the overflow gallery was packed as well. Judge Garrett was the presiding official, and the state had appointed Mary Pason. Lazlo had secured the best his fame could buy, Counsel Gavin Bates who, only a year earlier, had successfully defended a man caught with a knife in his hand on the charge of murder and got him released on his own recognizance. Lazlo knew he had a winner on his hands.

Lazlo walked into the courtroom, and the ladies swooned. He smiled and looked around the room. Judge Garrett banged his gavel to bring order to the courtroom, read the charges, then called Counsel Bates, who presented his opening argument.

"Ladies and gentlemen of the jury, I maintain that Lazlo Delorean, being of sound mind and body, is innocent of the charges of murder of Lyle Davies, Nora Penny, Brenda Slater, and Delila Delorean," intoned Bates. "At the times of those murders, he has alibis that can be substantiated and verified. In fact, we hold that these crimes should be classified as unsolved and my client be allowed to continue his acting and modeling career."

Legal counsel for the state Pason stared at Lazlo, who sat beside his lawyer. Clad in a tuxedo, the actor cracked the smallest of smiles in an attempt to penetrate her cold veneer. Pason shook her head slowly and turned to look at the jury.

"Members of the jury, we live in a culture that worships beauty," said Pason, looking back at Delorean. "When one of these demigods is arrested and accused of heinous crimes, we have to look past the beauty, the perfect image, and the illusion. I will prove that Delorean is a vicious, violent killer who is guilty of four murders. He was found with the weapon in his possession."

Pason walked back to her desk and picked up four pictures and showed them to the jurors. "Lyle Davies, makeup artist. Dead at the hand of Delorean. Nora Penny's life taken. Brenda Slater, killed with the same knife used to murder Davies and Penny. Last, Delila Delorean, wife of the accused, found dead in her bed while her husband supposedly was playing tennis," said Pason. "Your job is to see past the lies and listen to the evidence."

The casting call for *Top Hat* went out in November 1934, and Lazlo, on a brief hiatus from the Hollywood life, had arranged for his agent to come by the house.

"Phillip," said Delorean. "Can you make a call to see when I can audition to work with Astaire?"

His agent laughed while the men watched the birds fly off the swimming pool in the back of the estate.

"Seriously, Lazlo?" he said. "I mean, you know the rumors. Astaire has said he doesn't want to work with you."

Delorean grimaced. "I know. I do want to try to spread my wings. Too many romances, too many Westerns. They're bad for my skin and that gets in the way when I pose for movie posters and magazine covers. You can only do the same pose so many times."

Phillip smiled in agreement and struck a pose while Lazlo pretended to take a picture. "I will see, but be on your best behavior on the lot," warned the agent.

Delorean's audition was a failure. Compared to the grace of Astaire, Lazlo danced like a duck with a limp, although he was cast as the manager.

For Delorean, though, it was good. Three weeks of work on his contract, and three weeks with the delightful Brenda Slater, who was his personal massage therapist and dance instructor and, if rumors were true, his most current secret flame.

Two years into his marriage to Delila, Delorean's passion for his wife had cooled while his demands for attention and hers for privacy grew.

"Lazlo," said Slater, lying on the divan in her studio-supplied therapy trailer. "You know, once this film is done, so are we."

Delorean stood by the window looking over the back studio lot toward the Hollywood Hills and the vineyards that still dotted the far reaches of his view. He turned to look at the beauty clad only in a scarcely there night jacket and breathed deeply.

"Yes, that may well be true," said the actor. "But we will always have *Top Hat*, won't we?"

Lazlo walked toward Slater slowly and shook his hair slightly, wiggling his hips seductively.

"Yes, we will, but there is one thing I have to ask you, darling," said Slater softly as she stood up and moved her lips toward his head . . .

A knock at the door broke the atmosphere. Then the door came tumbling down as Delila stepped over the debris holding an ax.

"So sorry for the mess, darling. I'm sure Lazlo will make it up to you somehow," said Delila, who threw the axe down then slapped the actor across the face and kicked the divan over before security arrived and restrained her.

The actress fought and wiggled in the strong grip of the men as she looked at her husband, who had a red welt forming on the right side of his face.

"You think I didn't know," she said, seething with anger. "You thought I would take your dalliances and accept them."

Still looking surprised, Delorean tried to speak.

"What do you have to say now, lover boy?" she screamed at the top of her lungs. "Oh, I know, 'Someone, a little more breeze on my hair now.' Is that it?"

The stunned actor regained his composure and steeled his nerves. "How dare YOU! I am a STAR!" screamed Lazlo.

Delila tried to break free from the grip of security again and arched toward the actor. "And I am your wife! Remember?"

Turning to the security guards, who had now stopped struggling with his enraged wife, he glared at the pair of men. "Remove this woman from this trailer! Now!"

Slater stood up holding her nightie around her tightly and looked for a housecoat. Grabbing one off the end of the divan, she tied it up quickly and slapped the actor on the other side of his face.

"This is MY trailer, Delorean," she howled before kicking the actor in the shins and privates.

A second set of security guards had by now entered the trailer, and held back the second woman while Delorean writhed on the floor.

"I've been kissed better by Silver!" screamed Slater.

A crowd had gathered outside the trailer attracted by the raised voices that echoed between the buildings.

"Get OUT!" she yelled. "You, too, Delila. Take your Samson and get out. NOW!"

Delorean and his wife were led to their vehicles parked in the employee lot. In the distance, the pair could hear Slater ranting to anyone who would listen. An uneasy silence fell between the couple and the security guards, who were now joined by two more men and met by Selznick at Delorean's limo.

"Lazlo," he said, defeated, "take some time off until this blows over. I'm not sure what happened, but Slater is trouble. She took down a top dog over at MGM last year. She kisses, and tells anyone who will listen."

Selznick waved the limo on and stood with his hands in his pockets. Delila spun her convertible out of the studio lot.

"Oy vey. RKO just hit gold . . . thanks, Delorean," he said as he turned and walked to the office, whistling as he walked.

The second day of trial raised the public ante.

"Oh, Lazlo is a stable, professional actor to work with," said Adam Hale, a portly actor under contract to RKO and co-star of numerous adventure films. "I've never seen him lose his cool, but I did see him lose his car keys once after too many Key Limes at the Coconut Club."

Clark Gable was the second-last witness on the second day. "Lazlo is a great guy to spend a day with on the yacht," said the handsome actor. "As a matter of fact, he can hoist the mainsail as fast as Flynn can. The big difference though is that even Flynn's hot air couldn't power a ship like Delorean's could."

Lazlo was five years old when his mother died.

Marta, or Mariessa as her father called her, had been a delicate child and remained frail beyond her years. Born with weak bones, she was raised in a shielded environment and treated as "special" by her parents. Despite her infirmity, his father, Daniel, fell in love with her at first sight at the community church service in their home village in Italy.

They married six weeks later and had their first child when she was nineteen. Lazlo was loved by his family, but, because of her condition, Marta was told not to have any more children. Reluctantly, the couple agreed. They moved to America for better opportunities, and settled in the Los Angeles area, where his father got a job as an extra in the fledgling film industry to provide for his wife and child.

One Tuesday afternoon, Lazlo bounced home from his friend's place to ask for a drink of water, opened the door, and yelled into the kitchen. "Mama, can I have a drink of . . ."

His mother turned to look at him. Her birth condition had taken its toll, and it was the first time he had seen his mother's true condition. She froze, wig in hand, and her patchy scalp burnt itself into his memory like a sepia print of the Frankenstein monster.

Brenda Slater was found murdered in her car a week before Christmas. Witnesses reported hearing sounds of a quarrel earlier in the evening.

The Hollywood tabloids jumped all over the death of Slater and sensationalized her passing, but the Hollywood Police Department was more than interested, and Sgt. Braham paid another visit to RKO studio boss David O. Selznick.

"Well, hello . . ." offered Selznick, forgetting the police officer's name.

"Braham, sir. Sgt. Braham. Here to ask you some questions about the Slater girl," the tall police officer replied.

Selznick offered him a seat and a drink.

"Thank you," said Braham, taking a sip. "Well, what can you tell me about Slater? Did she have any fights or any enemies? Her murder seems so random."

The movie mogul sat behind his desk and smoked a Cuban, blowing smoke rings in the air. He pondered the question. "Well, she came to us from MGM a couple of years back," said Selznick. "Very accomplished professional, but she had a tendency to start scraps with our marquee stars. She got along with Wayne, Cooper, Dix, and Grant but got into a quarrel with Delorean here and Gable at MGM after some quality time together."

Braham's eyebrows lifted in interest. "You mean she and Delorean were . . ."

Selznick coughed. "Just friends, but they parted differently."

Day three of the Delorean trial was a tabloid writer's dream.

Not since the Academy Awards had Tinseltown royalty gravitated so strongly toward a public gathering. Photographers crawled the hallways and galleries of the courtroom with cameras ready to capture their favorite actor or actress in the event they were called to the witness stand.

Mary Astor was one of those.

"I am not one to speak ill of my coworkers," said the dark-haired beauty on the witness stand. "While on camera in *Sin Ship*, he was a gentleman. Off camera, he was not. I understand vanity, but he made Cleopatra look like a campground queen."

Others echoed the same sentiments.

"Well," said a young starlet on the witness stand, "I don't think anyone thought of Lazlo the same after he was 'escorted' off the studio for his rendezvous with Slater. Actually, I don't think he really was the same after that. He was more irrational than before."

The starlet looked over at Delorean with dreamy eyes, then turned back to the jury. "You know, he's sure easy on the eyes, but hard on a lady," said the girl. "Kind of like a loose cannon. I was in a film with him once, *The Lady* in '35, and once was enough for me. But, boy, what a love scene."

Director Marion Cooper was called to the stand and was

sworn in. Pason paced the space in front of the director briefly, then started her questioning.

"You, Mr. Cooper, are a close friend of Mr. Delorean's?" asked Pason.

Cooper nodded. "Yes, ma'am, I am. We have known each other since he started his career in Hollywood. In fact, he has been in several of my films with RKO. *King Kong* was his most famous film with me."

"What has his behavior been like during your friendship with him?" asked Pason. "In particular, what has he been like over the last four years since his 'incident' and the beginning of the murders he allegedly committed?"

The jury murmured among themselves.

"Leading question, your honor, assumes guilt of client," offered Bates to the judge.

The judge looked over at Bates, then over to Pason. "Please rephrase the question, Ms. Pason," said the judge.

Throughout the courtroom, the press scribbled, and the courtroom artist, Paul S. Powers, captured the scene for the dailies.

"How has Mr. Delorean reacted to the murders, Mr. Cooper?" asked Pason.

Cooper leaned forward in the witness stand. "He was devastated as you would expect him to be. She was his wife. With her death, he has taken time away from the spotlight to mourn. He was also very concerned he was being wrongly accused and that his career would take a hit it could never recover from."

Pason walked over to the evidence table and reached for an item. Lifting it up, the lawyer showed a knife with complex engraving on the hilt and an Asian angle to the blade. She turned to the director.

"Is this knife familiar to you, sir?" asked the lawyer slowly, turning the knife in her hands.

Cooper looked closely at the blade. "We used one like this in our production of *Comanche Stallion*. Delorean's character, Dobe, used it. There are quite a few on the studio lot. There could be five others, or none. Props go missing all the time."

Pason questioned the director further. "What were his knife skills like in the film?" asked the lawyer as Cooper pursed his lips.

"Very good, like he had handled knives all of his life," said Cooper.

Pason asked one final question. "Having known the defendant for many years now, do you feel he is he capable of cold-blooded murder?"

Cooper looked over at his friend, and back over to the jury, then back to the lawyer.

"On film? Convincingly. Offscreen, I can't say yes or no for sure," said Cooper. "I really can't."

The discovery of the body of Delila Delorean made national news.

She was found in the kind of scene that Hollywood special effects people love: a pool of blood, a room in disarray and a semi-nude victim with stab wounds. The media jumped into the fray, publishing pictures of Delila on the front page under sensational headlines. HOLLYWOOD STAR FOUND DEAD IN HOME . . . HUSBAND SUSPECTED . . .

Detective Braham was first on scene with his crack homicide squad. He was getting used to dealing with Delorean, and it was rapidly becoming old.

"Detective," said one of the police officers on duty. "We have Delorean in the living room. He's expecting you."

Braham looked around the mirrored bedroom. Antique furniture adorned the corners, and mirrors were sandwiched between mahogany wood panels. A painted fresco inspired by the masters completed the decor. It was the body of Delila that was the centre of attention, not the decor.

"Death be not proud," he murmured softly as he kneeled beside the bed and looked closely at the wound, then around the room once more from his haunches.

His lieutenant looked over at him. "Shakespeare?"

Braham shook his head. "No, John Donne. Less cheery, like this scene."

The tall detective gazed around the room, stopping to the left of the bed. He stood up and examined the cracked mirror. Around the room, small cracks shattered the illusion of integrity of the mirrors.

"Sorry for your loss, Delorean," said Braham, entering the living room, where a distraught Delorean sat on the Italian leather couch. "It must be a shock to find your wife this way, killed in your own bedroom."

The actor looked up with tears in his eyes. "I was playing tennis with Fairbanks and, for a change, I won," he said. "I came home and called for her. She didn't answer. I found her in the bedroom. Dead."

Braham listened carefully. "Can you give us Fairbanks's phone number?" asked the detective.

The actor nodded to his butler, Alfred, who returned with the number.

"Thank you, sir," replied Braham. "Were you and your wife fighting today or yesterday?"

Delorean nodded slightly. "A little, she had come back from the hairdresser. She said she looked in the mirror and didn't like the way she looked, her eyes didn't look so bright. She wanted to go to the hairdresser again, to have them redo her makeup," said Lazlo. "I told her not to go, that it would be fine tomorrow. She didn't listen. She went back, I found Fairbanks, we played tennis."

Braham nodded and squinted toward the sun coming through the living room window. "We all have those days, Lazlo," commented the detective.

Lazlo's face twisted slightly. "That's what hair and makeup is for!" he said, raising his voice, looking into the face of the detective with a hint of rage in his eyes. "Hair and makeup!"

The final day of the trial had arrived and, with the mounting media circus, anticipation was high for red carpet appearances. No one disappointed as cameras flashed, and once again Tinseltown shone in the most dire circumstances.

Finally, it was time for Lazlo to take the stand, and he walked the path to justice like it was a catwalk, smiling at the ladies in the audience and catching the glances of his former costars and witnesses. The actor was sworn in and took his place in the dais of truth. Bates had the first opportunity to question him.

"Lazlo Delorean, are you guilty of the murders of Delila Delorean, Brenda Slater, Lyle Davies, and Miss Penny?" asked Gavin Bates.

Delorean calmly replied, "I am not."

"In fact," said Bates turning to the jury, "my client can explain his presence elsewhere when the murders occurred. In each case . . ."

Soon, it was Pason's turn.

"Sir, you are very well known for your hair and romantic appeal," said Pason, walking in front of the podium. "In fact, your image adorns hundreds of movie posters and magazine covers. For evidence, I present this one."

Pason hands a copy of *Movie Love Monthly*, the January 1935 issue, with Delorean holding an unnamed model in his arms mid-kiss. Lazlo smiled.

"Ah, one of the good ones," he commented.

Pason's face showed confusion. "Good ones?"

"Yes, the photo shoot had good light, and the breeze was just right for my hair," he replied. "The actress was good, but . . ."

The actor brushed his hand over his hair, to straighten it out.

"What was the name of the actress you posed with?" asked Pason.

"I cannot remember," he replied, shaking his head. "They all blend together after a while."

Pason looked at the star, then over to the gallery where Mary Astor sat fixated on the star trial.

"Who is that woman over there?" she asked.

Lazlo looked over and smiled. "Mary Astor."

"So she was special to you then," suggested the lawyer.

Lazlo nodded while Astor returned the smile with a glare. "Yes."

The lawyer looked up to see the actress leave, prompting murmurs from the audience. "And now?" asked Pason.

Lazlo searched the room and looked at the lawyer. "A nice prop," said Delorean. "Interchangeable with any pretty face."

Pason looked at the crowd, and spoke to her cocounsel for a moment, only to return to the questioning area.

"Lazlo, I saw you in *Comanche Stallion*. Loved the film, actually, but I thought your knife work was sloppy, not real," she said, then continued. "In fact, your last three films, including *Panacea*, have been good, except for your hair. It looks like a half-drunk hairdresser gelled it and combed it once."

Bates called for a dismissal of the comment. He was denied.

"In *Panacea*, your costar, Vivien Leigh, outshone you, hair included," continued the lawyer. "I bring one review in that states, and I quote, 'Lazlo has lost his edge, and his hair is waning. We are not a fan.'"

By now, Delorean was fidgeting in his seat and had started to wring his hands. He moved his hands across his hair to smooth it.

"How is your hair these days, Lazlo?" asked Pason. "Rumor has it you may soon be a fallen star. In fact, perhaps you are so vain that, as Astor put it, you 'make Cleopatra look like a camp-ground queen.' You also have a temper you cannot control."

Lazlo started to fidget uncontrollably.

"We have one more piece of evidence, taken from your home, Lazlo. One that you could not hide, despite your best efforts," said Pason presenting a bottle of hair growth tonic. "We found it mislabeled, in your wife's effects. In fact, we double-checked the inventory of the other murder scenes and, in each case, a bottle of tonic was in each room. In fact, we believe you killed each of the victims because they were jealous of your hair . . ."

Lazlo stood up.

"All lies . . . all lies!" exclaimed Delorean. "I killed them because they were going to reveal my secret!"

The audience gasped as Lazlo reached out and grabbed the lawyer by the throat. The police in the room quickly responded, and the actor was handcuffed.

After a five-minute recess, the judge called the trial back to order and the jury was sent out to deliberate. They returned with a guilty verdict on all four counts of first-degree murder.

Delorean hung his head low while the verdict sunk in. He looked at the jury that convicted him. He looked at the crowd that once adored him. He looked at the judge, then back to the media who were at the back of the room eating up every word and picture he gave them, even in defeat.

"I suppose you want to know why I killed them," screamed the murderer. "You see . . . it all started when they couldn't keep a secret. Nora, Penny, Lyle 'I'm going to tell everyone' Davies, Brenda 'Blackmail' Slater, and, finally, Delila 'You're so vain' Delorean, my late, quiet wife . . . Everything was fine until they tried to make me say it!"

Delorean was led away to prison still ranting. "I kiss better than Silver!"

Five days later, officials found Lazlo Delorean in his cell, dead by his own hand. Hollywood mourned the passing of a bright star. In accordance with his last wishes, his tombstone bore a simple inscription: *Lazlo Delorean, 1900–1937.*

In the official report released one week after his death, prison officials reported hearing the actor crying himself to sleep in his cell and murmuring, "I think I'm going bald. I think I'm going bald."

DAVID NIALL **A**
WILSON **PRAYER**
inspired by "The Trees" **FOR "0443"**

Boz worked as quickly as he could with sweat-slick fingers, teasing the broken ends of wires into place and soldering them with the tip of a homemade iron. The tools were crude, barely adequate to the task. If he made a mistake, shorted a lead to the wrong element, he'd be too late, and "0443" would be lost. Working with his hands inside the tool bag, while pretending to shuffle and inventory the contents, added a level of difficulty that nearly drove him mad. His fingers shook, and he hesitated, breathing deeply. He pushed the last lead into place and applied the heat.

The parts were from a phone, a relic hidden and passed from hand to hand since banned by the Fairness Act. Not many components remained and being caught with them would be a serious offense. He might lose his number. Boz knew if that happened, he would have to find a way to terminate, but at the same time he had to take the risk.

There was a soft sound behind him and he turned. Cherie had entered their shared quarters. She saw him, smiled, and then stopped, standing very still.

"Move," he said softly. "Keep moving. Don't let them notice anything different, or you'll trip the bug."

"What . . ."

"I have to finish this. There are only a few minutes left."

Fear flashed through her expression like dark lightning, but she recovered quickly. She crossed the room, bent, and kissed him gently on the forehead. Then she turned and headed for the kitchen. He heard her opening and closing cabinets and knew she was making coffee. She wasn't doing it because she wanted coffee, but because she wanted the ritual.

Boz closed his tool bag, concealing his creation in one hand as he tugged the straps tight with the other. Then he turned in his seat and pressed a button on the console in front of him. A tray slid out of a recess in the wall. He laid his fingertip on the scanner and the screen lit. An image filled the monitor, just for a moment — the familiar HAS logo (he had been taught that this stood for Human Access Screen but had long suspected the acronym had other meanings). A bright, generically cheerful voice welcomed him.

"Welcome, 9628356."

Boz said nothing. At home, he was Boz. With Cherie and a few close friends. To the world, he was 9628356. To the system. Moving slowly, keeping his actions as casual as possible, he reached for the music controls. At the same time, he slipped his fingernail into a panel on the side of the tray and tugged. It popped open, and he held his breath. No warnings. He had not been discovered.

The music would start soon. He leaned casually to the side, palming the device he'd created, glanced at the panel, and saw what he was after. Two wires protruded slightly, not far enough to catch on the tray as it slid in and out, had been carefully stripped, a bit at a time, so that bright copper shone through their plastic insulation. He had seconds.

Two curls of wire protruded from his device. He hooked them over the bare points in the wires, let the small circuit card swing down and out of sight, and leaned back. He watched the screen expectantly.

Anyone monitoring his actions might have believed he was merely anticipating the music. No warnings appeared on the screen. No lights flickered. Sound rose slowly from the speakers in the walls. He recognized the first strains of "0443" and his heart nearly stopped.

He wanted to lean down again and check the connection. He wanted to know if it was working, but he knew that if he did check, it would be lost forever. They would see. They would send someone to yank him out of his life and his home. They might erase his number and take his words. They might take Cherie, change her number. He had to trust his skill, the things he'd remembered and those he'd learned.

He knew there were others. He'd found the clues they'd left. He'd collected and passed on the artifacts. Forbidden secrets. Lost science. It passed beneath the radar of the system like a network of spirits, a dimension of its own. There had been a term in the past — "darknet" — for a network of dark, private things hidden from the government and other prying eyes. Boz's darknet consisted of small caches of antique tech, stolen bits of wire, components slipped in and out of pockets and left where others could find and access them. Folded bits of paper with schematics and designs. Even snippets of verse, lyrics, prose, and occasional drawings. Signed drawings, not with numbers, but names. All forbidden.

There might be ten others — there might be a thousand.

Maybe all of them — every single number in the system — had something hidden away, something special that they were scared to death to share or pass on. For all they knew, the system was fully aware and allowed their small indiscretions to keep them in line — the illusion of individuality.

Somewhere out there was a singer. Her voice called to Boz in ways that the endless streams of music he'd been fed from the console's speakers had not. Her song had begun its cycle one year to the day in the past, and the very next day Boz had started gathering parts.

Musical compositions were allowed only a single year of existence. They were played in a steady, repetitive cycle, no one piece or artist granted a moment longer than another. Books and stories were the same. You could write, if the urge came upon you, but you couldn't save it. Once you typed it into the console, it was part of the system, stamped only with your number. It would be there for a year, but no one could read it twice. If you were caught singing or reciting things that you'd read, your access was cut off until the next cycle, so that you would forget.

The only things that were constant were the histories and the laws, and every citizen jacked into the system knew them by heart. The rules existed to protect. The histories existed to remind them of all that had gone before. Equality was the only true hope for survival. Total equality. Stories came and went. Songs sifted through the collective consciousness, and then faded, replaced by new voices and new tunes. Nothing but numbers differentiated them one from another.

Boz knew the mantra. No one would be worshipped. No one would be held above any other, except, as it had always been — someone was. Rules only exist when they can be enforced. Men and women were kept equal by people who believed in their own right to make that decision. Boz and his peers knew them only as The Noble — a title that, in itself, denied the truth of the equality it purported to serve. The rules were so simple and calming on their surface.

Music is for entertainment.

Writing is for sharing, and moving on.

Names and labels only encourage pride and inhibit equality.

We are one. Except, there were those overseeing that unity, and so it was false.

The song started. The urge to close his eyes, lean back, and enjoy it was almost overwhelming, but he was afraid to react. He'd heard the song 364 times and this was to be the last. To react to that — to show emotion at the passing of one work while ignoring the others — would send up a flag.

He heard Cherie moving around in the next room. There were times they could talk, places where it was allowed — between couples — to share in private. He wanted to go to her and explain himself. He wanted, more than anything else in the universe, for her to understand, for *any* other to understand, but he had to wait. She had to wait.

Sweat beaded on his upper lip, but he didn't brush it away. He concentrated on the music, letting it draw him out of the moment. It was a complex piece, starting softly with a smooth melody and moving into sequences of more powerful notes. There were no lyrics, but the voice was high and sweet, finding vocal tricks and subtle shifts that somehow conveyed their message without words. He had been surprised since the moment it first drifted through his console that they hadn't cut it. Too controversial. Too different. But then, music was a very subjective experience, and sadly, he knew, most of those who heard it wouldn't even notice.

The last strains of "0443" died away. He felt the muscles in his arm twitch, but he forced himself to remain still. He let the next song play halfway through, and casually opened the screen to the story he'd been reading. It was a disjointed ramble, fantasy carefully wound around a thin plot without deep meaning or serious intent. It was a very safe story, and he skimmed the text without really seeing it as the music continued through three more forgettable songs. He leaned forward and saved his place in the story.

At the same time, he bent slightly, flipped the small device up and off of the wires, and palmed it. He turned off the music, and the console slid slowly back into the wall. He held his breath, afraid he might have dragged the wires out too far, and that they would catch, or short, without their cover in place. He couldn't lean down to retrieve that yet either, but he knew he could in a few moments. He leaned back, stretched, smoothed his pants, and managed to slip the small solid-state recording device into his pocket as he did so.

He rose and left the room, heading into the kitchen for coffee. Cherie sat at the table. She had the kitchen console open and was watching a vid of fish swimming placidly through a coral reef. Such calming uncredited programming was always available. There were other shows — films and serials — but, like the music and the books, they were available for a set cycle of time then gone forever. Never the same actors in any two programs. There were no names. For all the viewers knew the people in the dramas *were* those characters. It was difficult to discuss any particular program with others because the numbers that differentiated them were long and intricate, worse by far than the music, and they did not run at the same time or in the same sequence in all homes at once.

Everyone had a purpose. Skills were valued. All the education one might desire was available and encouraged. In isolation. Boz worked within a pod — a group of individuals with disparate abilities. They completed tasks that required their combined efforts, sometimes supplemented by a new member, or in smaller groups as they were called away to collaborate with others. There was no competition between artisans of the same skillset. There was no way to know if you were as good as or better than others performing the same duties. There was no impulse to excel, no fear of falling short. Work was completed, for the most part, in a state of utter stagnation.

Now he had a purpose, though he was not certain what it would lead to. He had the song. He had no way to listen to it, but it existed. He wondered if there was another, somewhere, who had been equally driven, but driven to create a device to play music or display stories and essays, words and thoughts. He wondered if there might be an entire society hovering just beneath the surface of the system, feeding ideas from one to the next, building something unique while the world rolled bleakly onward. He thought about writing about such a network, thought about what it might be like to create that world in his mind, write it down, and submit it to the system . . . but he knew that he would not. If they were out there, he'd be doing them harm, and he'd likely disappear from the grid forever. If he was wrong . . . he might disappear, and the idea would die as well. And there was the song. Now it wasn't just his own thoughts he protected, but the work of another. Something with meaning. Something worth saving.

He took his coffee to the next room and sat down, sipping slowly. The carcass of the phone he'd used to create his recordable drive had been built into a section of a console he'd been called to perform maintenance on. It wasn't the first time he'd found something that didn't seem to belong. He'd learned not to react. The first time had been years earlier — a coil of wires wrapped around components not connected in any way to the system he'd been servicing, tucked in behind a large transformer. He'd yanked it out and stared at it stupidly, and moments later men had appeared, calmly taking it from him and disappearing back into the halls of the complex.

It wasn't until later that same night that the implications had hit him. It had been put there to be found, but not by the system. He'd allowed something precious to disappear from the world. Somewhere out there was another person he had failed.

When he'd found the phone, he'd calmly worked around it, giving no indication that anything was different. Since none of those working with him had his expertise, and it was secreted into the case of the machinery, there was little likelihood another would notice. It had taken his entire day to work the instrument free while calmly going about his normal duties, and a heart-stopping moment of near panic as he palmed it along with one of his tools and slipped it into his bag.

Not long after the confiscation of the wires and components, he'd begun working at the seams in the bottom of his tool bag. It was constructed of double-layered canvas. Over time he was able to cut a slit from one end to the other, very thin. This left a pocket where something could — if it was thin enough — be slipped beneath the inner lining. Unless the search was very thorough, which it usually was not, it was possible to smuggle small items in and out of each workspace.

Boz had done this exactly three times. Once for the phone, and once each for bits of wire and a tiny roll of tape that had been unrolled from the end of a spool and stuck to the underside of a circuit board. The number who had left it must have unrolled it, rolled it back up without the tube, and turned in the empty tube for a new roll. It was clever and inspiring.

The phone had come home in the lining of his bag and

remained there for months. He'd worked with it, always inside the bag, during the time he normally spent organizing and inventorying his tools, careful not to spend too much time at any one point. What was left of the phone he intended to install in another unit, in another room, along with his recording.

There was no way he would ever be able to build a player. Probably, he was never going to hear "0443" again, though the strains of the song were currently playing in an endless loop through his mind. He knew, over time, it would fade. Memory would warp the melody and rob him of the haunting tune bit by bit until it was nothing but a ghost of itself.

But it would exist. He intended to leave the drive in an inconspicuous circuit, the two wires necessary to hook it into — something — dangling free, but tucked up where they could not be seen. One day, he knew, it would be found by another tech. If he was lucky, it would prove interesting enough to be passed on. If a time came when it was possible to resurrect the things that were being cast aside in the wake of the world, "0443" would remain, ready for a rebirth. Maybe the woman who had sung it would remember. Maybe she would be alive to know that someone, somewhere, had heard her and loved the music.

Cherie came and sat across the table from him. For a moment or two they sat in silence, sipping their coffee. Then, on impulse, he stood and circled the table, wrapping her in his arms and leaning in to whisper in her ear . . . but instead of whispering, he hummed the melody of "0443."

She didn't tense up, as he'd feared. Instead she opened her hand very slowly. Inside was a small scrap of paper. On the paper, in very fine print, he saw lines and words. He couldn't make them out because tears welled in the corners of his eyes and blurred his sight, but it didn't matter. The words were preserved. They were secret, and sacred. They were hers, and she'd shared them, and somehow he knew that she would pass them on. She closed her hand, and he turned her face to his, kissing her deeply. Without another word he led her off to the one room where they were absolutely alone. Already, he was dreaming of the next thing he would save — the next thing that would matter.

He had a momentary flash of vision, lines intersecting other lines, secrets reaching out to other secrets, like fingers grasping, or a tapestry that had been unraveled drawing back in on itself. It comforted him. As he slid the door closed on their bedroom and lay down beside Cherie, he closed his eyes — just for a moment — and sent out a silent prayer to the voice behind "0443."

He knew he'd begin his search the next day for something new. Something to believe in. In the back of his mind, The Noble's laws echoed and pulsed, and he tried to ignore them.

Music is for entertainment.

Writing is for sharing, and moving on.

Names and labels only encourage pride and inhibit equality.

He only hoped that wherever the words and the music, the technology and the art lay hidden, others would continue to pass it on. He hoped the cleverness of his recording would bring someone a smile, and that the music would live again. He thought that when he hid the recording, he'd sign the case. Not 9628356, but Boz. No one would know who he was, but that didn't matter. It wasn't just the art, he knew, but the artist. He wished that he knew who had sung "0443" because he could have added her name to the cache. It would have to be a collaboration.

Then he drew Cherie close and they began a collaboration of their own — a creation that the system had not found a way to control, or deny. He put his heart and soul into their coupling, sharing himself fully. The lie in the system was that they were all one. The truth of the moment was that if the lie ever became truth, as it did for the two of them in that moment, it would set them free.

When Rush was working on their *Roll the Bones* album, Neil told me he had written lyrics that were inspired by a story he'd read a long time ago called (something like) "Roll the Bones," but he couldn't remember enough details to be able to track it down. When he described the story a little more, I thought I knew which one he was talking about.

I dug through my library, found a copy of Harlan Ellison's seminal SF anthology *Dangerous Visions* (1967), which included the original appearance of Fritz Leiber's "Gonna Roll the Bones," which won both of science fiction's most prestigious awards, the Hugo Award and the Nebula Award, in the year of its publication. I photocopied the story and sent it to Neil, who agreed that, yes, this was the story he remembered.

But I didn't want to stop there. Fritz Leiber was an elderly gentleman at the time, a legend in the field, and I had met him a few times. I did a little more research and tracked down Fritz's address and sent it to Neil, in case he wanted to write him a letter. I didn't expect Fritz Leiber to be a Rush fan, but I thought he'd at least like to know that his story had inspired an album. Alas, I had found an old address for Fritz, and Neil's letter came back undeliverable after a long delay. So I did more investigative work, found where Fritz had moved . . . and he passed away shortly after that, before Neil could send him a new letter. "That's the way that lady luck dances."

Considering the influence this story had on Rush, the anthology would not be complete without including it. Please note that this story was published decades ago and is a product of its times. Some language may be offensive.

— KJA

FRITZ LEIBER **GONNA ROLL**
inspired "Roll the Bones" **THE BONES**

Suddenly Joe Slattermill knew for sure he'd have to get out quick
or else blow his top and knock out with the shrapnel of his skull the
props and patches holding up his decaying home, that was like a
house of big wooden and plaster and wallpaper cards except for the
huge fireplace and ovens and chimney across the kitchen from him.

Those were stone-solid enough, though. The fireplace was
chin-high at least twice that long, and filled from end to end
with roaring flames. Above were the square doors of the ovens
in a row — his Wife baked for part of their living. Above the
ovens was the wall-long mantelpiece, too high for his Mother to
reach or Mr. Guts to jump anymore, set with all sorts of ancestral
curios, but any of them that weren't stone or glass or china had
been so dried and darkened by decades of heat that they looked
like nothing but shrunken human heads and black gold balls. At
one end were clustered his Wife's square gin bottles. Above the

mantelpiece hung one old chromo, so high and so darkened by soot and grease that you couldn't tell whether the swirls and fat cigar shape were a whaleback steamer plowing through a hurricane or a spaceship plunging through a storm of light-driven dust motes.

As soon as Joe curled his toes inside his boots, his Mother knew what he was up to. "Going bumming," she mumbled with conviction. "Pants pockets full of cartwheels of house money, too, to spend on sin." And she went back to munching the long shreds she stripped fumblingly with her right hand off the turkey carcass set close to the terrible heat, her left hand ready to fend off Mr. Guts, who stared at her yellow-eyed, gaunt-flanked, with long mangy tail a-twitch. In her dirty dress, streaky as the turkey's sides, Joe's Mother looked like a bent brown bag and her fingers were lumpy twigs.

Joe's Wife knew as soon or sooner, for she smiled thin-eyed at him over her shoulder from where she towered at the centermost oven. Before she closed its door, Joe glimpsed that she was baking two long, flat, narrow, fluted loaves and one high, round-domed one. She was thin as death and disease in her violet wrapper. Without looking, she reached out a yard-long, skinny arm for the nearest gin bottle and downed a warm slug and smiled again. And without a word spoken, Joe knew she'd said, "You're going out and gamble and get drunk and lay a floozy and come home and beat me and go to jail for it," and he had a flash of the last time he'd been in the dark gritty cell and she'd come by moonlight, which showed the green and yellow lumps on her narrow skull where he'd hit her, to whisper to him through the tiny window in back and slip him a half pint through the bars.

And Joe knew for certain that this time it would be that bad and worse, but just the same he heaved up himself and his heavy, muffledly clanking pockets and shuffled straight to the door, muttering, "Guess I'll roll the bones, up the pike a stretch and back," swinging his bent, knobby-elbowed arms like paddle-wheels to make a little joke about his words.

When he'd stepped outside, he held the door open a hand's breadth behind him for several seconds. When he finally closed it, a feeling of deep misery struck him. Earlier years, Mr. Guts would have come streaking along to seek fights and females on the roofs and fences, but now the big tom was content to stay home and hiss by the fire and snatch for turkey and dodge a broom, quarreling and comforting with two housebound women. Nothing had followed Joe to the door but his Mother's chomping and her gasping breaths and the clink of the gin bottle going back on the mantel and the creaking of the floor boards under his feet.

The night was up-side-down deep among the frosty stars. A few of them seemed to move, like the white-hot jets of spaceships. Down below it looked as if the whole town of Ironmine had blown or buttoned out the light and gone to sleep, leaving the streets and spaces to the equally unseen breezes and ghosts. But Joe was still in the hemisphere of the musty dry odor of the worm-eaten carpentry behind him, and as he felt and heard the dry grass of the lawn brush his calves, it occurred to him that something deep down inside him had for years been planning things so that he and the house and his Wife and Mother and Mr. Guts would all come to an end together. Why the kitchen heat hadn't touched off the tindery place ages ago was a physical miracle.

Hunching his shoulders, Joe stepped out, not up the pike, but down the dirt road that led past Cypress Hollow Cemetery to Night Town.

The breezes were gentle, but unusually restless and variable tonight, like leprechaun squalls. Beyond the drunken, white-washed cemetery fence dim in the starlight, they rustled the scraggly trees of Cypress Hollow and made it seem they were stroking their beards of Spanish moss. Joe sensed that the ghosts were just as restless as the breezes, uncertain where and whom to haunt, or whether to take the night off, drifting together in sorrowfully lecherous companionship. While among the trees the red-green vampire lights pulsed faintly and irregularly, like sick fire-flies or a plague-stricken space fleet. The feeling of deep misery stuck with Joe and deepened and he was tempted to turn aside and curl up in any convenient tomb or around some half-toppled head board and cheat his Wife and the other three behind him out of a shared doom. He thought: *Gonna roll the bones, gonna roll 'em up and go to sleep*. But while he was deciding, he got past the sagged-open gate and the rest of the delirious fence and Shantyville, too.

At first Night Town seemed dead as the rest of Ironmine, but then he noticed a faint glow, sick as the vampire lights but more feverish, and with it a jumping music, tiny at first as a jazz for jitterbugging ants. He stepped along the springy sidewalk, wistfully remembering the days when the spring was all in his own legs and he'd bound into a fight like a bobcat or a Martian sandspider. God, it had been years now since he had fought a real fight, or felt *the power*. Gradually the midget music got raucous as a bunny-hug for grizzly bears and loud as a polka for elephants, while the glow became a riot of gas flares and flambeaux and corpse-blue mercury tubes and jiggling pink neon ones that all jeered at the stars where the spaceships roved. Next thing, he was facing a three-story false front flaring everywhere like a devil's rainbow, with a pale blue topping of St. Elmo's fire. There were wide swinging doors in the center of it, spilling light above and below. Above the doorway, golden calcium light scrawled over and over again, with wild curlicues and flourishes, *The Boneyard*, while a fiendish red kept printing out, *Gambling*.

So the new place they'd all been talking about for so long had opened at last! For the first time that night, Joe Slattermill felt a stirring of real life in him and the faintest caress of excitement.

Gonna roll the bones, he thought.

He dusted off his blue-green work clothes with big, careless swipes and slapped his pockets to hear the clank. Then he threw back his shoulders and grinned his lips sneeringly and pushed through the swinging doors as if giving a foe the straight-armed heel of his palm.

Inside, The Boneyard seemed to cover the area of a township and the bar looked as long as the railroad tracks. Round pools of light on the green poker tables alternated with hourglass shapes of exciting gloom, through which drink girls and change girls moved like white-legged witches. By the jazz-stand in the distance, belly dancers made *their* white hourglass shapes. The gamblers were thick and hunched down as mushrooms, all bald from agonizing over the fall of a card or a die or the dive of an ivory ball, while the Scarlet Women were like fields of poinsettia.

The calls of the croupiers and the slaps of dealt cards were as softly yet fatefully staccato as the rustle and beat of the jazz drums. Every tight-locked atom of the place was controlledly jumping. Even the dust motes jigged tensely in the cones of light.

Joe's excitement climbed and he felt sift through him, like a breeze that heralds a gale, the faintest breath of a confidence which he knew could become a tornado. All thoughts of his house and Wife and Mother dropped out of his mind, while Mr. Guts remained only as a crazy young tom walking stiff-legged around the rim of his consciousness. Joe's own leg muscles twitched in sympathy and he felt them grow supplely strong.

He coolly and searchingly looked the place over, his hand going out like it didn't belong to him to separate a drink from a passing, gently bobbing tray. Finally his gaze settled on what he judged to be the Number One Crap Table. All the Big Mushrooms seemed to be there, bald as the rest but standing tall as toadstools. Then through a gap in them Joe saw on the other side of the table a figure still taller, but dressed in a long dark coat with collar turned up and a dark slouch hat pulled low, so that only a triangle of white face showed. A suspicion and a hope rose in Joe and he headed straight for the gap in the Big Mushrooms.

As he got nearer, the white-legged and shiny-topped drifters eddying out of his way, his suspicion received confirmation after confirmation and his hope budded and swelled. Back from one end of the table was the fattest man he'd ever seen, with a long cigar and a silver vest and a gold tie clasp at least eight inches wide that just said in thick script, *Mr. Bones*. Back a little from the other end was the nakedest change-girl yet and the only one he'd seen whose tray, slung from her bare shoulders and indenting her belly just below her breasts, was stacked with gold in gleaming little towers and with jet-black chips. While the dice-girl, skinnier and taller and longer armed than his Wife even, didn't seem to be wearing much but a pair of long white gloves. She was all right if you went for the type that isn't much more than pale skin over bones with breasts like china doorknobs.

Beside each gambler was a high round table for his chips. The one by the gap was empty. Snapping his fingers at the nearest silver change-girl, Joe traded all his greasy dollars for an equal number of pale chips and tweaked her left nipple for luck. She playfully snapped her teeth toward his fingers.

Not hurrying but not wasting any time, he advanced and carelessly dropped his modest stacks on the empty table and took his place in the gap. He noted that the second Big Mushroom on his right had the dice. His heart but no other part of him gave an extra jump. Then he steadily lifted his eyes and looked straight across the table.

The coat was a shimmering elegant pillar of black satin with jet buttons, the upturned collar of fine dull plush black as the darkest cellar, as was the slouch hat with down-turned brim and a band of only a thin braid of black horsehair. The arms of the coat were long, lesser satin pillars, ending in slim, long-fingered hands that moved swiftly when they did, but held each position of rest with a statue's poise.

Joe still couldn't see much of the face except for smooth lower forehead with never a bead or trickle of sweat, the eyebrows were like straight snippets of the hat's braid and gaunt, aristocratic cheeks and narrow but somewhat flat nose. The complexion of the face wasn't as white as Joe had first judged. There was a faint touch of brown in it, like ivory that's just begun to age, or Venusian soapstone. Another glance at the hands confirmed this.

Behind the man in black was a knot of just about the flashiest and nastiest customers, male or female, Joe had ever seen. He knew from one look that each bediamonded, pomaded bully had a belly gun beneath the flap of his flowered vest and a blackjack in his hip pocket, and each snake-eyed sporting-girl a stiletto in her garter and a pearl-handed silver-plated derringer under the sequined silk in the hollow between her jutting breasts.

Yet at the same time Joe knew they were just trimmings.

It was the man in black, their master, who was the deadly one, the kind of man you knew at a glance you couldn't touch and live. If without asking you merely laid a finger on his sleeve, no matter how lightly and respectfully, an ivory hand would move faster than thought and you'd be stabbed or shot. Or maybe just the touch would kill you, as if every black article of his clothing were charged from his ivory skin outward with a high-voltage, high-amperage ivory electricity. Joe looked at the shadowed face again and decided he wouldn't care to try it.

For it was the eyes that were the most impressive feature. All great gamblers have dark-shadowed deep-set eyes. But this one's eyes were sunk so deep you couldn't even be sure you were getting a gleam of them. They were inscrutability incarnate. They were unfathomable. They were like black holes.

But all this didn't disappoint Joe one bit, though it did terrify him considerably. On the contrary, it made him exult. His first suspicion was completely confirmed and his hope spread into full flower.

This must be one of those really big gamblers who hit Ironmine only once a decade at most, come from the Big City on one of the river boats that ranged the watery dark like luxurious comets, spouting long thick tails of sparks from their sequoia-tall stacks with top foliage of curvy-snipped sheet iron. Or like silver space-liners with dozens of jewel-flamed jets, their portholes a-twinkle like ranks of marshaled asteroids.

For that matter, maybe some of those really big gamblers actually came from other planets where the nighttime pace was hotter and the sporting life a delirium of risk and delight.

Yes, this was the kind of man Joe had always yearned to pit his skill against. He felt *the power* begin to tingle in his rock-still fingers, just a little.

Joe lowered his gaze to the crap table. It was almost as wide as a man is tall, at least twice as long, unusually deep, and lined with black, not green, felt, so that it looked like a giant's coffin. There was something familiar about its shape which he couldn't place. Its bottom, though not its sides or ends, had a twinkling iridescence, as if it had been lightly sprinkled with very tiny diamonds. As Joe lowered his gaze all the way and looked directly down, his eyes barely over the table, he got the crazy notion that it went down all the way through the world, so that the diamonds were the stars on the other side, visible despite the sunlight there, just as Joe was always able to see the stars by day up the shaft of the mine he worked in, and so that if a cleaned-out gambler, dizzy with defeat, toppled forward into it, he'd fall forever, toward the bottommost bottom, be it Hell or some black galaxy. Joe's thoughts swirled and he felt the cold, hard-fingered clutch of fear at his crotch. Someone was crooning beside him, "Come on. Big Dick."

Then the dice, which had meanwhile passed to the Big Mushroom immediately on his right, came to rest near the table's center, contradicting and wiping out Joe's vision. But instantly there was another oddity to absorb him. The ivory dice were large and unusually round-cornered with dark red spots that gleamed like real rubies, but the spots were arranged in such a way that each face looked like a miniature skull. For instance, the seven thrown just now, by which the Big Mushroom to his right had lost his point, which had been ten, consisted of a two with spots evenly spaced toward one side, like eyes, instead of toward opposite corners, and of a five with the same red eye-spots but also a central red nose and two spots close together below that to make teeth.

The long, skinny, white-gloved arm of the dice-girl snaked out like an albino cobra and scooped up the dice and whisked them onto the rim of the table right in front of Joe. He inhaled silently, picked up a single chip from his table and started to lay it beside the dice, then realized that wasn't the way things were done here, and put it back. He would have liked to examine the chip more closely, though. It was curiously lightweight and pale tan, about the color of cream with a shot of coffee in it, and it had embossed on its surface a symbol he could feel, though not see. He didn't know what the symbol was, that would have taken more feeling.

Yet its touch had been very good, setting *the power* tingling full blast in his shooting hand.

Joe looked casually yet swiftly at the faces around the table, not missing the Big Gambler across from him, and said quietly, "Roll a penny," meaning of course one pale chip, or a dollar.

There was a hiss of indignation from all the Big Mushrooms and the moonface of big-bellied Mr. Bones grew purple as he started forward to summon his bouncers.

The Big Gambler raised a black-satined forearm and sculptured hand, palm down. Instantly Mr. Bones froze and the hissing stopped faster than that of a meteor prick in self-sealing space steel. Then in a whispery, cultured voice, without the faintest hint of derision, the man in black said, "Get on him, gamblers."

Here, Joe thought, was a final confirmation of his suspicion, had it been needed. The really great gamblers were always perfect gentlemen and generous to the poor.

With only the tiny, respectful hint of a guffaw, one of the Big Mushrooms called to Joe, "You're faded."

Joe picked up the ruby-featured dice.

Now ever since he had first caught two eggs on one plate, won all the marbles in Ironmine, and juggled six alphabet blocks so they finally fell in a row on the rug spelling "Mother," Joe Slattermill had been almost incredibly deft at precision throwing. In the mine he could carom a rock off a wall of ore to crack a rat's skull fifty feet away in the dark and he sometimes amused himself by tossing little fragments of rock back into the holes from which they had fallen, so that they stuck there, perfectly fitted in, for at least a second. Sometimes, by fast tossing, he could fit seven or eight fragments into the hole from which they had fallen, like putting together a puzzle block. If he could ever have got into space, Joe would undoubtedly have been able to pilot six Moon-skimmers at once and do figure eights through Saturn's rings blindfold.

Now the only real difference between precision-tossing rocks or alphabet blocks and dice is that you have to bounce the latter off the end wall of a crap table, and that just made it a more interesting test of skill for Joe.

Rattling the dice now, he felt *the power* in his fingers and palm as never before.

He made a swift low roll, so that the bones ended up exactly in front of the white-gloved dice-girl. His natural seven was made up, as he'd intended, of a four and a three. In red-spot features they were like the five, except that both had only one tooth and the three no nose. Sort of baby-faced skulls. He had won a penny — that is, a dollar.

"Roll two cents," said Joe Slattermill.

This time, for variety, he made his natural with an eleven. The six was like the five, except it had three teeth, the best-looking skull of the lot.

"Roll a nickel less one."

Two Big Mushrooms divided that bet with a covert smirk at each other.

Now Joe rolled a three and an ace. His point was four.

The ace, with its single spot off center toward a side, still somehow looked like a skull — maybe of a Lilliputian cyclops. He took a while making his point, once absent-mindedly rolling three successive tens the hard way. He wanted to watch the dice-girl scoop up the cubes. Each time it seemed to him that her snake-swift fingers went under the dice while they were still flat on the felt. Finally he decided it couldn't be an illusion. Although the dice couldn't penetrate the felt, her white-gloved fingers somehow could, dipping in a flash through the black, diamond-sparkling material as if it weren't there.

Right away the thought of a crap-table-size hole through the earth came back to Joe. This would mean that the dice were rolling and lying on a perfectly transparent flat surface, impenetrable for them but nothing else. Or maybe it was only the dice-girl's hands that could penetrate the surface, which would turn into a mere fantasy Joe's earlier vision of a cleaned-out gambler taking the Big Dive down that dreadful shaft, which made the deepest mine a mere pin dent. Joe decided he had to know which was true. Unless absolutely unavoidable, he didn't want to take the chance of being troubled by vertigo at some crucial stage of the game.

He made a few more meaningless throws, from time to time crooning for realism, "Come on. Little Joe." Finally he settled on his plan. When he did at last make his point the hard way, with two twos — he caromed the dice off the far corner so that they landed exactly in front of him. Then, after a minimum pause for his throw to be seen by the table, he shot his left hand down under the cubes, just a flicker ahead of the dice-girl's strike, and snatched them up.

Wow! Joe had never had a harder time in his life making his face and manner conceal what his body felt, not even when the wasp had stung him on the neck just as he had been for the first time putting his hand under the skirt of his prudish, fickle, demanding Wife-to-be. His fingers and the back of his hand were in as much agony as if he'd stuck them into a blast furnace. No wonder the dice-girl wore white gloves. They must be asbestos. And a good thing he hadn't used his shooting hand, he thought as he ruefully watched the blisters rise.

He remembered he'd been taught in school what Twenty-Mile Mine also demonstrated: that the earth was fearfully hot under its crust. The crap-table-size hole must pipe up that heat, so that any gambler taking the Big Dive would fry before he'd fallen a furlong and come out less than a cinder in China.

As if his blistered hand weren't bad enough, the Big Mushrooms were all hissing at him again and Mr. Bones had purpled once more and was opening his melon-size mouth to shout for his bouncers.

Once again a lift of the Big Gambler's hand saved Joe. The whispery, gentle voice called, "Tell him, Mr. Bones."

The latter roared toward Joe, "No gambler may pick up the dice he or any other gambler has shot. Only my dice-girl may do that. Rule of the house!"

Joe snapped Mr. Bones the barest nod. He said coolly, "Rolling a dime less two," and when that still peewee bet was covered, he shot Phoebe for his point and then fooled around for quite a while, throwing anything but a five or a seven, until the throbbing in his left hand should fade and all his nerves feel rock-solid again. There had never been the slightest alteration in *the power* in his right hand; he felt that strong as ever, or stronger.

Midway of this interlude, the Big Gambler bowed slightly but respectfully toward Joe, hooding those unfathomable eye sockets, before turning around to take a long black cigarette from his prettiest and evilest-looking sporting-girl. Courtesy in the smallest matters, Joe thought, another mark of the master devotee of games of chance. The Big Gambler sure had himself a flash crew all right, though in idly looking them over again as he rolled, Joe noted one bummer toward the back who didn't fit in — a raggedy-elegant chap with the elflocked hair and staring eyes and TB-spotted cheeks of a poet.

As he watched the smoke trickling up from under the black slouch hat, he decided that either the lights across the table had dimmed or else the Big Gambler's complexion was yet a shade darker than he'd thought at first. Or it might even be — wild fantasy — that the Big Gambler's skin was slowly darkening tonight, like a meerschaum pipe being smoked a mile a second. That was almost funny to think of — there was enough heat in this place, all right, to darken meerschaum, as Joe knew from sad experience, but so far as he was aware it was all under the table.

None of Joe's thoughts, either familiar or admiring, about the Big Gambler decreased in the slightest degree his certainty of the supreme menace of the man in black and his conviction that it would be death to touch him. And if any doubts had stirred in Joe's mind, they would have been squelched by the chilling incident which next occurred.

The Big Gambler had just taken into his arms his prettiest-evilest sporting-girl and was running an aristocratic hand across her haunch with perfect gentility, when the poet chap, green-eyed from jealousy and lovesickness, came leaping forward like a wildcat and aimed a long gleaming dagger at the black satin back.

Joe couldn't see how the blow could miss, but without taking his genteel right hand off the sporting-girl's plush rear end, the Big Gambler shot out his left arm like a steel spring straightening. Joe couldn't tell whether he stabbed the poet chap in the throat, or judo-chopped him there, or gave him the Martian double-finger, or just touched him, but anyhow the fellow stopped as dead as if he'd been shot by a silent elephant gun or an invisible ray pistol and he slammed down on the floor. A couple of darkies came running up to drag off the body and nobody paid the least attention, such episodes apparently being taken for granted at The Boneyard.

It gave Joe quite a turn and he almost shot Phoebe before he intended to.

But by now the waves of pain had stopped running up his left arm and his nerves were like metal-wrapped new guitar strings, so three rolls later he shot a five, making his point, and set in to clean out the table.

He rolled nine successive naturals, seven sevens and two elevens, pyramiding his first wager of a single chip to a stake of over four thousand dollars. None of the Big Mushrooms had dropped out yet, but some of them were beginning to look worried and a couple were sweating. The Big Gambler still hadn't covered any part of Joe's bets, but he seemed to be following the play with interest from the cavernous depths of his eye sockets.

Then Joe got a devilish thought. Nobody could beat him tonight, he knew, but if he held onto the dice until the table was cleaned out, he'd never get a chance to see the Big Gambler exercise *his* skill, and he was truly curious about that. Besides, he thought, he ought to return courtesy for courtesy and have a crack at being a gentleman himself.

"Pulling out forty-one dollars less a nickel," he announced. "Rolling a penny."

This time there wasn't any hissing and Mr. Bones's moonface didn't cloud over. But Joe was conscious that the Big Gambler was staring at him disappointedly, or sorrowfully, or maybe just speculatively.

Joe immediately crapped out by throwing boxcars, rather pleased to see the two best-looking tiny skulls grinning ruby-toothed side by side, and the dice passed to the Big Mushroom on his left.

"Knew when his streak was over," he heard another Big Mushroom mutter with grudging admiration.

The play worked rather rapidly around the table, nobody getting very hot and the stakes never more than medium high. "Shoot a fin." "Rolling a sawbuck." "An Andrew Jackson." "Rolling thirty bucks." Now and then Joe covered part of a bet, winning more than he lost. He had over seven thousand dollars, real money, before the bones got around to the Big Gambler.

That one held the dice for a long moment on his statue-steady palm while he looked at them reflectively, though not the hint of a furrow appeared in his almost brownish forehead down which never a bead of sweat trickled. He murmured, "Rolling a double sawbuck," and when he had been faded, he closed his fingers, lightly rattled the cubes — the sound was like big seeds inside a small gourd only half dry — and negligently cast the dice toward the end of the table.

It was a throw like none Joe had ever seen before at any crap table. The dice traveled flat through the air without turning over, struck the exact juncture of the table's end and bottom, and stopped there dead, showing a natural seven.

Joe was distinctly disappointed. On one of his own throws he was used to calculating something like, "Launch three-up, five north, two and a half rolls in the air, hit on the six-five-three corner, three-quarter roll and a one-quarter side-twist right, hit end on the one-two edge, one-half reverse roll and three-quarter side-twist left, land on five face, roll over twice, come up two," and that would be for just one of the dice, and a really common-place throw, without extra bounces.

By comparison, the technique of the Big Gambler had been ridiculously, abysmally, horrifyingly simple. Joe could have duplicated it with the greatest of ease, of course. It was no more than an elementary form of his old pastime of throwing fallen rocks back into their holes. But Joe had never once thought of pulling such a babyish trick at the crap table. It would make the whole thing too easy and destroy the beauty of the game.

Another reason Joe had never used the trick was that he'd never dreamed he'd be able to get away with it. By all the rules he'd ever heard of, it was a most questionable throw. There was the possibility that one or the other die hadn't completely reached the end of the table, or lay a wee bit cocked against the end. Besides, he reminded himself, weren't both dice supposed to rebound off the end, if only for a fraction of an inch?

However, as far as Joe's very sharp eyes could see, both dice lay perfectly flat and sprang up against the end wall. Moreover, everyone else at the table seemed to accept the throw, the dice-girl had scooped up the cubes, and the Big Mushrooms who had faded the man in black were paying off. As far as the rebound business went, well, The Boneyard appeared to put a slightly different interpretation on that rule, and Joe believed in never questioning House Rules except in dire extremity — both his Mother and Wife had long since taught him it was the least troublesome way. Besides, there hadn't been any of his own money riding on that roll.

In a voice like wind through Cypress Hollow or on Mars, the Big Gambler announced, "Roll a century." It was the biggest bet yet tonight, ten thousand dollars, and the way the Big Gambler said it made it seem something more than that.

A hush fell on The Boneyard, they put the mutes on the jazz horns, the croupiers' calls became more confidential, the cards fell softlier, even the roulette balls seemed to be trying to make less noise as they rattled into their cells. The crowd around the Number One Crap Table quietly thickened. The Big Gambler's flash boys and girls formed a double semicircle around him, ensuring him lots of elbow room.

That century bet, Joe realized, was thirty bucks more than his own entire pile. Three or four of the Big Mushrooms had to signal each other before they'd agreed how to fade it.

The Big Gambler shot another natural seven with exactly the same flat, stop-dead throw.

He bet another century and did it again.

And again.

And again.

Joe was getting mighty concerned and pretty indignant, too. It seemed unjust that the Big Gambler should be winning such huge bets with such machinelike, utterly unromantic rolls. Why, you couldn't even call them rolls, the dice never turned over an iota, in the air or after. It was the sort of thing you'd expect from a robot, and a very dully programmed robot at that. Joe hadn't risked any of his own chips fading the Big Gambler, of course, but if things went on like this he'd have to. Two of the Big Mushrooms had already retired sweatingly from the table, confessing defeat, and no one had taken their places. Pretty soon there'd be a bet the remaining Big Mushrooms couldn't entirely cover between them, and then he'd have to risk some of his own chips or else pull out of the game himself — and he couldn't do that, not with *the power* surging in his right hand like chained lightning.

Joe waited and waited for someone else to question one of the Big Gambler's shots, but no one did. He realized that, despite his efforts to look imperturbable, his face was slowly reddening.

With a little lift of his left hand, the Big Gambler stopped the dice-girl as she was about to snatch at the cubes. The eyes that were like black wells directed themselves at Joe, who forced himself to look back into them steadily. He still couldn't catch the faintest gleam in them. All at once he felt the lightest touch-on-neck of a dreadful suspicion.

With the utmost civility and amiability, the Big Gambler whispered, "I believe that the fine shooter across from me has doubts about the validity of my last throw, though he is too much of a gentleman to voice them. Lottie, the card test."

The wraith-tall, ivory dice-girl plucked a playing card from below the table and with a venomous flash of her little white teeth spun it lot across the table through the air at Joe. He caught the whirling pasteboard and examined it briefly. It was the thinnest, stiffest, flattest, shiniest playing card Joe had ever handled. It was also the Joker, if that meant anything. He spun it back lazily into her hand and she slid it very gently, letting it descend by its own weight, down the end wall against which the two dice lay. It came to rest in the tiny hollow their rounded edges made against the black felt. She deftly moved it about without force, demonstrating that there was no space between either of the cubes and the table's end at any point.

"Satisfied?" the Big Gambler asked. Rather against his will Joe nodded. The Big Gambler bowed to him. The dice-girl smirked her short, thin lips and drew herself up, flaunting her white-china-doorknob breasts at Joe.

Casually, almost with an air of boredom, the Big Gambler returned to his routine of shooting a century and making a natural seven. The Big Mushrooms wilted fast and one by one tottered away from the table. A particularly pink-faced Toadstool was brought extra cash by a gasping runner, but it was no help, he only lost the additional centuries. While the stacks of pale and black chips beside the Big Gambler grew skyscraper-tall.

Joe got more and more furious and frightened. He watched like a hawk or spy satellite the dice nesting against the end wall, but never could spot justification for calling another card test, or nerve himself to question the House Rules at this late date. It was maddening, in fact insanitizing, to know that if only he could get the cubes once more he could shoot circles around that black pillar of sporting aristocracy. He damned himself a googolplex of ways for the idiotic, conceited, suicidal impulse that had led him to let go of the bones when he'd had them.

To make matters worse, the Big Gambler had taken to gazing steadily at Joe with those eyes like coal mines. Now he made three rolls running without even glancing at the dice or the end wall, as far as Joe could tell. Why, he was getting as bad as Joe's Wife or Mother — watching, watching, watching Joe.

But the constant staring of those eyes that were not eyes was mostly throwing a terrific scare into him. Supernatural terror added itself to his certainty of the deadliness of the Big Gambler. Just who, Joe kept asking himself, had he got into a game with tonight? There was curiosity and there was dread — a dreadful curiosity as strong as his desire to get the bones and win. His hair rose and he was all over goose bumps, though *the power* was still pulsing in his hand like a braked locomotive or a rocket wanting to lift from the pad.

At the same time the Big Gambler stayed just that — a black satin-coated, slouch-hatted elegance, suave, courtly, lethal. In fact, almost the worst thing about the spot Joe found himself in was that, after admiring the Big Gambler's perfect sportsmanship all night, he must now be disenchanted by his machinelike throwing and try to catch him out on any technicality he could.

The remorseless mowing down of the Big Mushrooms went on. The empty spaces outnumbered the Toadstools. Soon there were only three left.

The Boneyard had grown still as Cypress Hollow or the Moon. The jazz had stopped and the gay laughter and the shuffle of feet and the squeak of goosed girls and the clink of drinks and coins. Everybody seemed to be gathered around the Number One Crap Table, rank on silent rank.

Joe was racked by watchfulness, sense of injustice, self-contempt, wild hopes, curiosity and dread. Especially the last two.

The complexion of the Big Gambler, as much as you could

see of it, continued to darken. for one wild moment Joe found himself wondering if he'd got into a game with a nigger, maybe a witchcraft-drenched Voodoo Man whose white make-up was wearing off.

Pretty soon there came a century wager which the two remaining Big Mushrooms couldn't fade between them. Joe had to make up a sawbuck from his miserably tiny pile or get out of the game. After a moment's agonizing hesitation, he did the former.

And lost his ten.

The two Big Mushrooms reeled back into the hushed crowd.

Pit-black eyes bored into Joe. A whisper: "Rolling your pile."

Joe felt well up in him the shameful impulse to confess himself licked and run home. At least his six thousand dollars would make a hit with his Wife and Ma.

But he just couldn't bear to think of the crowd's laughter, or the thought of living with himself knowing that he'd had a final chance, however slim, to challenge the Big Gambler and passed it up.

He nodded.

The Big Gambler shot. Joe leaned out over and down the table, forgetting his vertigo, as he followed the throw with eagle or space-telescope eyes.

"Satisfied?"

Joe knew he ought to say, "Yes," and slink off with head held as high as he could manage. It was the gentlemanly thing to do. But then he reminded himself that he wasn't a gentleman, but just a dirty, working-stiff miner with a talent for precision hurling.

He also knew that it was probably very dangerous for him to say anything but, "Yes," surrounded as he was by enemies and strangers. But then he asked himself what right had he, a miserable, mortal, homebound failure, to worry about danger.

Besides, one of the ruby-grinning dice looked just the tiniest hair out of line with the other.

It was the biggest effort yet of Joe's life, but he swallowed and managed to say, "No. Lottie, the card test."

The dice-girl fairly snarled and reared up and back as if she were going to spit in his eyes, and Joe had a feeling her spit was cobra venom. But the Big Gambler lifted a finger at her in reproof and she skimmed the card at Joe, yet so low and viciously that it disappeared under the black felt for an instant before flying up into Joe's hand.

It was hot to the touch and singed a pale brown all over, though otherwise unimpaired. Joe gulped and spun it back high.

Sneering poisoned daggers at him, Lottie let it glide down the end wall . . . and after a moment's hesitation, it slithered behind the die Joe had suspected.

A bow and then the whisper: "You have sharp eyes, sir. Undoubtedly that die failed to reach the wall. My sincerest apologies and . . . your dice, sir."

Seeing the cubes sitting on the black rim in front of him almost gave Joe apoplexy. All the feelings racking him, including his curiosity, rose to an almost unbelievable pitch of intensity, and when he'd said, "Rolling my pile," and the Big Gambler had replied, "You're faded," he yielded to an uncontrollable impulse and cast the two dice straight at the Big Gambler's ungleaming, midnight eyes.

They went right through into the Big Gambler's skull and bounced around inside there, rattling like big seeds in a big gourd not quite yet dry.

Throwing out a hand, palm back, to either side, to indicate that none of his boys or girls or anyone else must make a reprisal on Joe, the Big Gambler dryly gargled the two cubical bones, then spat them out so that they landed in the center of the table, the one die flat, the other leaning against it.

"Cocked dice, sir," he whispered as graciously as if no indignity whatever had been done him. "Roll again."

Joe shook the dice reflectively, getting over the shock.

After a little bit he decided that though he could now guess the Big Gambler's real name, he'd still give him a run for his money.

A little corner of Joe's mind wondered how a live skeleton hung together. Did the bones still have gristle and thews, were they wired, was it done with force-fields, or was each bone a calcium magnet clinging to the next? This tying in somehow with the generation of the deadly ivory electricity.

In the great hush of The Boneyard, someone cleared his throat, a Scarlet Woman tittered hysterically, a coin fell from the nakedest change-girl's tray with a golden clink and rolled musically across the floor.

"Silence," the Big Gambler commanded and in a movement almost too fast to follow whipped a hand inside the bosom of his coat and out to the crap table's rim in front of him. A short-barreled silver revolver lay softly gleaming there. "Next creature, from the humblest nigger night-girl to you, Mr. Bones, who utters a sound while my worthy opponent rolls, gets a bullet in the head."

Joe gave him a courtly bow back, it felt funny, and then decided to start his run with a natural seven made up of an ace and a six. He rolled and this time the Big Gambler, judging from the movements of his skull, closely followed the course of the cubes with his eyes that weren't there.

The dice landed, rolled over, and lay still. Incredulously, Joe realized that for the first time in his crap-shooting life he'd made a mistake. Or else there was a power in the Big Gambler's gaze greater than that in his own right hand. The six cube had come down okay, but the ace had taken an extra half roll and come down six, too.

"End of the game," Mr. Bones boomed sepulchrally.

The Big Gambler raised a brown skeletal hand. "Not necessarily," he whispered. His black eyepits aimed themselves at Joe like the mouths of siege guns. "Joe Slattermill, you still have something of value to wager if you wish. Your life."

At that a giggling and a hysterical tittering and a guffawing and a braying and a shrieking burst uncontrollably out of the whole Boneyard. Mr. Bones summed up the sentiments when he bellowed over the rest of the racket, "Now what use or value is there in the life of a bummer like Joe Slattermill? Not two cents, ordinary money."

The Big Gambler laid a hand on the revolver gleaming before him and all the laughter died.

"I have a use for it," the Big Gambler whispered. "Joe Slattermill, on my part I will venture all my winnings of tonight, and throw in the world and everything in it for a side bet. You will wager your life, and on the side your soul. You to roll the dice. What's your pleasure?"

Joe Slattermill quailed, but then the drama of the situation took hold of him. He thought it over and realized he certainly wasn't going to give up being stage center in a spectacle like this to go home broke to his Wife and Mother and decaying house and the dispirited Mr. Guts. Maybe, he told himself encouragingly, there wasn't a power in the Big Gambler's gaze, maybe Joe had just made his one and only crap-shooting error. Besides, he was more inclined to accept Mr. Bones's assessment of the value of his life than the Big Gambler's.

"It's a bet," he said.

"Lottie, give him the dice."

Joe concentrated his mind as never before, *the power* tingled triumphantly in his hand, and he made the throw.

The dice never hit the felt. They went swooping down, then up, in a crazy curve far out over the end of the table, and then came streaking back like tiny red-glinting meteors toward the face of the Big Gambler, where they suddenly nested and hung in his black eye sockets, each with the single red gleam of an ace showing.

Snake eyes.

The whisper, as those red-glinting dice-eyes stared mockingly at him: "Joe Slattermill, you've crapped out."

Using thumb and middle finger — or bone rather — of either hand, the Big Gambler removed the dice from his eye sockets and dropped them in Lottie's white-gloved hand.

"Yes, you've crapped out, Joe Slattermill," he went on tranquilly. "And now you can shoot yourself" — he touched the silver gun — "or cut your throat" — he whipped out a gold-handled bowie knife out of his coat and laid it beside the revolver — "or poison yourself" — the two weapons were joined by a small black bottle with white skull and crossbones on it — "or Miss Flossie here can kiss you to death." He drew forward beside him his prettiest, evilest-looking sporting-girl. She preened herself and flounced her short violet skirt and gave Joe a provocative, hungry look, lifting her carmine upper lip to show her long white canines.

"Or else," the Big Gambler added, nodding significantly toward the black-bottomed crap table, "you can take the Big Dive."

Joe said evenly, "I'll take the Big Dive."

He put his right foot on his empty chip table, his left on the black rim, fell forward . . . and suddenly kicking off from the rim, launched himself in a tiger spring straight across the crap table at the Big Gambler's throat, solacing himself with the thought that certainly the poet chap hadn't seemed to suffer long.

As he flashed across the exact center of the table he got an instant photograph of what really lay below, but his brain had no time to develop that snapshot, for the next instant he was plowing into the Big Gambler.

Stiffened brown palm edge caught him in the temple with a lightninglike judo chop . . . and the brown fingers or bones flew all apart like puff paste. Joe's left hand went through the Big Gambler's chest as if there were nothing there but black satin coat, while his right hand, straight-armedly clawing at the slouch-hatted skull, crunched it to pieces. Next instant Joe was sprawled on the floor with some black clothes and brown fragments.

He was on his feet in a flash and snatching at the Big Gambler's tall stacks. He had time for one left-handed grab. He couldn't see any gold or silver or any black chips, so he stuffed his left pants pocket with a handful of the pale chips and ran.

Then the whole population of The Boneyard was on him and after him. Teeth, knives and brass knuckles flashed. He was punched, clawed, kicked, tripped, and stamped on with spike heels. A gold-plated trumpet with a bloodshot-eyed black face behind it bopped him on the head. He got a white flash of the golden dice-girl and made a grab for her, but she got away. Someone tried to mash a lighted cigar in his eye. Lottie, writhing and flailing like a white boa constrictor, almost got a simultaneous strangle hold and scissors on him. From a squat wide-mouth bottle Flossie, snarling like a feline fiend, threw what smelt like acid past his face. Mr. Bones peppered shots around him from the silver revolver. He was stabbed at, gouged, rabbit-punched, scrag-mauled, slugged, kneed, bitten, bearhugged, butted, beaten and had his toes trampled.

But somehow none of the blows or grabs had much force. It was like fighting ghosts. In the end it turned out that the whole population of The Boneyard, working together, had just a little more strength than Joe. He felt himself being lifted by a multitude of hands and pitched out through the swinging doors so that he thudded down on his rear end on the board sidewalk. Even that didn't hurt much. It was more like a kick of encouragement.

He took a deep breath and felt himself over and worked his bones. He didn't seem to have suffered any serious damage. He stood up and looked around. The Boneyard was dark and silent as the grave, or the planet Pluto, or all the rest of Ironmine. As his eyes got accustomed to the starlight and occasional roving spaceship-gleam, he saw a padlocked sheet-iron door where the swinging ones had been.

He found he was chewing on something crusty that he'd somehow carried in his right hand all the way through the final fracas. Mighty tasty, like the bread his Wife baked for best customers. At that instant his brain developed the photograph it had taken when he had glanced down as he flashed across the center of the crap table. It was a thin wall of flames moving sideways across the table and just beyond the flames the faces of his Wife, Mother, and Mr. Guts, all looking very surprised. He realized that what he was chewing was a fragment of the Big Gambler's skull, and he remembered the shape of the three loaves his Wife had started to bake when he left the house. And he understood the magic she'd made to let him get a little ways away and feel half a man, and then come diving home with his fingers burned.

He spat out what was in his mouth and pegged the rest of the bit of giant-popover skull across the street.

He fished in his left pocket. Most of the pale poker chips had been mashed in the fight, but he found a whole one and explored its surface with his fingertips. The symbol embossed on it was a cross. He lifted it to his lips and took a bite. It tasted delicate, but delicious. He ate it and felt his strength revive. He patted his bulging left pocket. At least he'd start out well provisioned.

Then he turned and headed straight for home, but he took the long way, around the world.

BRAD R. **SPIRITS**
TORGERSEN **WITH**
inspired by "Mission" **VISIONS**

Alberto stood with his stomach pressed to the chest-high chain-link fence. Winner of the grand prize at his high school's science fair, Alberto had been just one of two Miami city kids given a Kennedy Space Center VIP pass. Both he and his parents had waited until they had enough money saved up to make the trip. It had been hard, since Alberto's father was still out of work. And his mother's job cleaning rooms at the hotel didn't pay very much. But Alberto was their only son, and he'd been so excited to see a launch. An actual, real-live launch! Now that he was here, he kind of couldn't believe it.

In the far distance, a colossal tower of metal — painted white and black in parts, or left an unfinished, rusty orange down the middle — rose into the blue morning sky. Gentle wisps of condensation and moisture drifted from the sides of the mighty multi-stage rocket. Alberto knew from his studies that countless gallons of fuel inside the rocket had to be kept cold, so that the fuel would stay liquid.

On the outside, two solid-core rockets were strapped to the main rocket boosters. The workhorses that would help push the big rocket most of the way into space before falling off and letting the big rocket's liquid-fuel engines do the rest.

Alberto thought it one of the most glorious things he'd ever seen in his life.

"If I didn't know better, I'd say you were staring at a pretty girl," said Alberto's father, who playfully nudged his son with an elbow.

Alberto turned and smiled up at Papa. "I wish they'd let us get closer!"

"Then we'd be so close, the fire might burn us," Alberto's Mama said.

They each stood protectively at Alberto's back. Behind them were two dozen other adults who'd also come with their children and were all cordoned off in a special boxed seating area separated from the bleachers nearby. Some of the adults had suits and ties on and wore various ID cards.

Alberto didn't know who they were, but he assumed they were important people.

The only adult who seemed out of place was the blonde lady in the wheelchair. Unlike everyone else, she seemed sad. As Alberto surreptitiously watched her — through a gap between his mother and father — he noticed the woman's eyes. It was like she was trying *not* to look at the rocket, but her gaze kept drifting back to the mobile launch pad in spite of herself. She would fixate for an instant, then she would dip her head and stare into her lap, dabbing Kleenex at her nose.

Alberto tugged at Papa's sleeve and motioned for him to lean over.

"Who is she?" Alberto whispered.

Papa looked around, then noticed where Alberto's eyes were aimed, and cleared his throat.

"She's the astronaut who had the accident," Papa said low enough that only Alberto could hear. "She was supposed to be going on this flight — to Mars. But now she can't."

Alberto's heart jumped slightly in his chest.

He remembered. He'd seen it on the news. A car crash. Very serious. Just a month before the launch. He didn't remember the astronaut's name, but now that he looked at her again — staring past Papa's ear — he remembered her photograph from the internet. Beautiful.

She kept dabbing her nose with the Kleenex, while her shoulders gently shook.

Alberto's eyes suddenly began to swim with warm fluid. It was cruel. Not going to Mars! How he would have given everything in the world to have that chance — and she'd had her opportunity taken from her by a stupid accident.

Alberto reached a hand up to his eyes — to stop the tears from dropping over his fifteen-year-old cheeks . . .

. . . and all that came away was wetness.

Sharlene McTavish sniffled and held her anguish close to her heart, trying to stop the pain. But it was no use. Sitting in the VIP section and seeing the massive multi-stage Space Launch System vehicle begin its final countdown had been too much. Even for her normally steely nerves. All the thousands of hours in Air Force training, flight school, her master's and doctorate programs in engineering, and flying every kind of jet she could get her hands on, had all been wiped out in the length of a single slow-motion car wreck that had left her upside down and pinned — and unable to feel her legs.

Every member of her astronaut selection group had come to see her in the hospital. In their eyes Shar had witnessed sympathy, and also a tacit message: *glad it's not me.*

The doctors had all told Shar she was lucky. It could have been much worse.

Now that the launch was happening without Shar, she wasn't sure what "worse" looked like. The mission was proceeding — a backup astronaut going in Shar's place. They would ride the mighty SLS rocket into space, link up with the transit vehicle — *Wanderer* — and spend the next month and a half being pushed to Mars by *Wanderer*'s experimental engines. Once in orbit around Mars, two-thirds of the crew would descend to the surface in the specially engineered landing stage and make history.

Astronaut McTavish? Grounded. Permanently. Not kicked out of NASA necessarily. Her knowledge and expertise were far too valuable to them. She would be helping to design more ships like *Wanderer*, though there would never, ever be the chance to actually fly on a mission. Not now.

Shar felt astounding, unutterable grief. Like a bird who has lost its wings.

Shar had argued with them. Oh, she'd argued hotly. There was no need for legs in space. Even if Shar couldn't walk, she could stay aboard the *Wanderer* and keep the ship running while the expeditionary crew explored the Martian surface, preparing for the first permanent settlement there. What use was it keeping

Shar off the flight roster? Just rotate someone else into her slot for the descent. She'd be fine in orbit. At least give her that!

But NASA rules were NASA rules. The flight surgeons would not hear of it. She was gently — but firmly — told that there could be no exceptions.

And so, all that was left for Shar was to sit helplessly and watch the launch.

Her friends and her husband — Jason — had all argued against it. But she'd felt obligated to come for the sake of the team. Jason was at her side now, his hand resting lightly on her shoulder as she cried quietly. His thick, manly fingers squeezed ever so gently. He felt guilty, she knew. The traffic accident had been his fault. He hadn't hit the brakes in time, coming around that sharp corner on the road to Washington, D.C. The car had rolled. Maybe things would have still been okay if Shar had not momentarily unclipped her seat belt so that she could fish in the back seat for her phone.

When the rumbling of the SLS's huge engines began, Sharlene's vision was too blurry to see clearly. She forced her head up and watched through smeared vision as the stupendous machine roared up and into the sky, white columns of billowing smoke roiling off the bottoms of the solid boosters.

The rocket rose, and rose, and rose until it was merely a dot in the sky, trailing vapor and spent fuel.

A different hand suddenly came to rest on Shar's left forearm, which she'd locked like an iron bar across the armrest of her slim-profile wheelchair.

Shar turned her head and looked up.

A handsome teenage boy looked down at her. His face was wet like hers.

Shar simply stared at him, her eyes blinking furiously. "Do I —"

"We're so sorry," a man interrupted, gently tugging the teenager away.

The boy's father?

"He didn't mean to disturb you," a woman said.

"It's quite all right," Shar blurted, and she realized her voice was hoarse. She hated how weak she sounded. Defeated. Broken.

The teenage boy's watering eyes remained locked onto Shar's as he was ushered away.

Jason's hand — still on Shar's shoulder — squeezed again . . .

. . . and Alberto looked up from his desk to realize that Papa was shaking him awake. He'd slumped over his books, the light still on, at his little room's single desk.

"It's after midnight," Papa said.

"Sorry," Alberto replied. He straightened up in his chair — stiff muscles saying *ouch* as he moved — and yawned.

"I think you've put in enough hours," Papa said. "You've been preparing for exams all month. It's just a preplacement test. You always get excellent grades on all the others. Why is this one extra important?"

"This one might help me get set up for a good medical school," Alberto said.

"That's years away," Papa said.

"I just want to be ready," Alberto replied defensively.

His Papa just looked over the top of his glasses, not saying much — but the emotion in his eyes was enough.

"Yes, sir," Alberto said, and obediently closed his book, shut off his tablet device, and hastily undressed and climbed into his bed.

They were now living in a bigger house than the one Alberto had been born into. With Papa working again, and Mama doing night management at the hotel — instead of cleaning rooms — the family had more money than ever before.

Many of Alberto's new friends had money, too. They had a lot of toys, and video games, and other things which were all fun, and sometimes even interesting, but Alberto had other thoughts on his mind. And he knew from the way Papa's eyes spoke words that didn't need saying, that Papa was worried about his son.

"It's a big world," Mama liked to say when they ate dinner. "You should relax and have a little more fun! Maybe even go out with a girl some time?"

Fun. Girls. For Alberto, fun was getting four-point-oh on every report card. The achievement itself was what mattered. And girls? *Hah!* As confusing as they were alluring. He didn't want to have to be distracted by that stuff. Too many of his friends already were, and Alberto considered it a cautionary tale. After all, he had serious things to do. Knowing he was at the top-most limit of the evaluation system was what counted. That's how a man with plans got to have scholarships — and only a scholarship would get Alberto into one of the major medical universities where he could start learning how to make a *real* difference.

"Good night, son," Papa said, slowly closing the door.

Alberto lay in darkness, his eyes half-open, staring . . .

. . . at a ceiling which was shadowed by the street light filtering in from the bedroom window.

Jason was at work — until very late most days. Shar missed him terribly. She didn't make a great deal of money at NASA, but it would have been enough for them, even without Jason's job. However, he was determined to move them to a parcel of land way out in the country. Something he'd picked out years ago. Not expensive to buy but plenty expensive to build on, being so far from utilities and conveniences.

"It will be wonderful," Jason said. "Right there on the shoulder of the mountain."

"But what about my job?" she asked.

And that's about as far as the conversation usually got.

It was an uncomfortable thing between them. She had doggedly hung on to her spot on the multinational Mars Permanent Settlement Project. Helping to plan the retrofitting of *Wanderer* upon its return to Earth orbit and assisting in the planning and assembly of *Journeyman*, the second Earth-to-Mars-to-Earth ship. How many hours had she spent staring at computer screens, her fingers flying over the keys?

Too often, though, she regretted being so single-minded. She suspected it was one of the reasons why Jason was away at work all the time now. Her workaholism had bred his workaholism. And tonight he was gone from their bedroom — when Shar felt like she desperately could have used some warmth and tenderness.

She rolled over and pulled Jason's pillow into her arms, stuffing her nose into the fabric. It smelled faintly of him. A manly kind of trace aroma that made her heart beat just a bit faster.

Of course, love-making had never been the same since the accident. Neither Shar nor Jason let on, but she'd known it for years. And he had, too, she thought. Such a silly thing to have lodged between them. But it was impossible to avoid the obvious. Her legs were withered sticks now, and she could feel nothing below her pelvis. Jason was gentle and tender, but always held back — as if

Shar were still barely a week out of the hospital, and he might break her. She didn't like being treated like she was fragile.

Closing her eyes, Shar regretted the fact that the accident had taken so much from her life. And though the doctors were always talking about therapy and treatments, it was pretty obvious that things couldn't ever be fixed. Spinal injuries were just like that. And the more she dwelled on regretting the past, the more her energy was sapped from the future.

Shar clamped her eyelids shut . . .

. . . then opened them again. Alberto was exhausted. This was the chemistry final. Having always done remarkably well in high school, he had discovered that college-level work was much different. They wanted you to learn and know so much more, in a much shorter period of time. Of course, he was also slotted into one of the toughest premedical tracks in the nation. And Alberto's A-grade work in high school was barely C-grade work in this school far across the country, away from the comfort of his home in the suburbs outside Miami. Sleep was a luxury he sometimes couldn't afford — not if he wanted to keep at the top of his class.

A little flashing alert in the bottom of Alberto's computer screen told him that he had only a few minutes left. And still so many questions to go! His heart began to beat fast because it was obvious that he was going to have to rush things. And rushing never, ever went well. This wasn't just multiple choice. Alberto had to explain himself. Show through his words that he understood the concepts laid out in the coursework.

His fingers pounded the keys furiously . . .

. . . so that the *clickity-clackity* noise filled Shar's small NASA office.

The framed photo Shar used to keep — of her wedding day, with Jason — was now absent from the desk's corner.

She'd let him off easy. It hadn't been an acrimonious separation. One day he'd come home to discover that Shar was moving closer to work. A tiny studio apartment, with easy public transit options for getting to and from the NASA office.

"We can figure this out," Jason had said, his face flushed.

"It's not about figuring it out," Shar had told him gently. "It's about us going in different directions. We've *been* going in different directions for a long time. We can't keep beating around the bush, or pretend that everything is just going to be all right. It's not that I don't love you, Jason. It's that I don't think loving you is enough anymore."

He hadn't argued with her much. Which essentially cemented her hunch that she'd been right about how tenuous their affection had become. He'd increasingly had his world — focused on his dream of the country house, far from the NASA office. And Shar had had her world — pushing forward on the building of new machines, new ships, and new technology designed to grow and foster the tiny fledgling colony on the surface of Mars.

Shar's little office was covered in high-resolution color print-outs of digital photos from the colony. Unless she had known better, she might have suspected that they came from Utah or New Mexico. The rocks and soil stretched dryly in every direction, with an orange sky that faded to red and purple when the sun went down. Shar watched every digital movie that the colonists could send back. She spent hours talking to the people from crews which had returned. Some of them were friends from the original *Wanderer* mission. Others were just getting back from their first assignment. The colony wasn't ready yet for year-round habitation, but with Shar's help, it would be soon.

Shar leaned back in her thin-profile wheelchair and watched the three-dimensional machining animation on her screen. In the span of thirty seconds, a five-hour printing and milling process played out in quick-time. Her fingertips swiveled the finished product around on the screen.

If ever the colony was going to survive unaided — in case something interrupted the supply line from Earth — they were going to need to be able to build replacement parts by themselves. The automated manufacturing units being planned for the newer missions were supposed to be able to fashion almost any part, of any shape, from any refined material. Even solid steel. Every colony component that could break or wear out was going to have to be programmed into the databases on those units. Then the units were going to have to be tested relentlessly, to be sure they worked as they were meant to.

To include being able to manufacture the parts to replace the units *themselves* if it came down to it.

Satisfied with her work, Shar closed the animation and put her computer on standby. It was only a little bit after ten at night. The cafeteria was closed, but she could go get some sandwiches from the twenty-four-hour desk, which had a refrigerator constantly stocked with cold foods for the staff who often needed to eat at odd times.

She brought her hands down onto the familiar hoop grips on the sides of her chair's two wheels . . .

. . . and the chair rolled into the office.

Alberto stood silently, his pastel-blue hospital scrubs fresh and clean. Life as a young resident was proving to be even more challenging than school itself. This wasn't just book learning and cadavers anymore. These were real people. With real problems. The paralysis specialty therapy program at Collingsworth General was among the most advanced research programs in the country. Alberto had slaved for years to qualify for this job and, now that he was here, he could see why they weren't just taking anybody.

"Good morning, Mr. Gerald," Alberto said with a smile.

The man in the wheelchair — Philip Gerald, forty-seven, wounded in combat, VA disability case, elective referral for experimental therapy — grunted.

"Doc," Philip said, stopping his chair at the foot of the exam table. The man's head was shaved bald, and a walrus-like mustache adorned his upper lip. His sea-blue eyes were sharp but held no humor. As always, his manner was direct. No nonsense. A relic from his years in the Army, or so some of the nurses had said when he'd initially been referred. Alberto liked working with Philip, because Philip would often tell stories from his time spent overseas. And he wasn't afraid of trying anything new.

"If it'll get me my legs back," Philip once drawled, "hell, I'll kiss a rattlesnake on the lips and call her my girlfriend!"

Without needing to be told, Philip allowed myself to be maneuvered up and out of his chair by Alberto and one of the medical assistants. They had Philip lying on his stomach on the exam table, and Alberto peeled up the man's t-shirt to reveal the plastic-covered network of wires that ran up and down Philip's spine. The wires branched off and penetrated the skin at different points — though there was no blood, nor any scabbing.

"Any changes since last week?" Alberto asked.

"Naw," Philip said, his voice slightly muffled. "Just dull little prickly sensations where I remember my legs *used* to be. It's been like that since the third day after the implant."

Alberto allowed himself a frown. The direct nerve induction system wasn't working nearly as well as everyone had hoped.

Alberto wasn't yet experienced enough to perform any of the surgeries himself, but one day soon he would be. Still, he couldn't help feeling like the entire induction technology initiative was a dead end — an attempt to solve the problem without considering more elegant solutions.

"Okay," Alberto said. "I'm going to change the battery, and we'll take the signal up just a tick."

"Dial to eleven if you want," Philip said, chortling. "There ain't nothin' you can break that hasn't already been broke by a bullet."

"Right," Alberto said. "I just want to be careful."

"Roger that," Philip grunted.

Alberto snapped the cover off a small, slim-line plastic box, then he took out the rechargeable battery inside and placed a fresh one in. When the battery quietly snapped into place, Philip's legs jerked.

"Did you feel that?" Alberto said hopefully.

"Feel what?" Philip replied.

Alberto suppressed a sigh. Yes, he was definitely going to have to find a way to get his alternative theory into the lab. This hardware-based implant program wasn't going to do the job — not the way Alberto envisioned it should. Too clumsy. Prone to breakage and the problem of the batteries always running low. If it was going to work, it needed to be able to last a lifetime.

Alberto pulled his patient's shirt back down and, together with the medical assistant, began to lever Philip back into the chair . . .

. . . which was difficult, even in the wheelchair-accessible stalls. Shar had never quite gotten over what a chore it was, simply going to the bathroom. So much levering, careful positioning, and work. Her arms were like the limbs of an oak tree now, after so many years of learning to get around on her own. It was tough, but then Shar had learned toughness. After the heartache of the divorce itself, nothing had hurt her more deeply than losing her legs.

But life had gone on. As it must. She'd become almost obsessed with keeping her spot on the development team. She was their sharpest veteran mind. A twenty-year pro. Never one to mince words or play nice if she felt the safety or efficiency of the colony project might be compromised. Yelling across conference room desks was one of her best skills — a skill she'd had to learn through doing.

But nobody could say she didn't get results.

The Mars colony was almost ready for full-time use.

Shar wheeled herself out of the stall and up to the low-hung accessible sink, washed and rinsed her hands, toweled off, and scooted out of the bathroom and into the hallway beyond.

This was her third building, in her third decade with NASA. As always, her office was small, but she kept it papered from floor to ceiling with fresh color printouts from the Mars colony's cameras, which were forever beaming data back to Earth, through the satellite uplink system that tied Earth to its diminutive sister world.

Humans had been living and working on Mars for a long time. There was occasional talk about shutting the project down — getting money was a never-ending battle, given the fact each incoming president had new priorities. But after the initial push to get the colony established, nobody dared pull the plug now. The public had become invested in it. If the American people had grown bored after the first few Apollo moon landings, the real chore for the Mars colony effort was to keep enough people interested so that enough congressmen and senators would keep the American end up.

Who wanted to be the elected official blamed for letting the Russians or Chinese have the Mars project all to themselves? It wasn't exactly polite talk — both countries were supposed to be America's friends now. But the undercurrent was there: *don't let the other powers make America look weak!* Shar didn't care what leverage it took, just so long as nobody canceled anything.

And not because she was in it just for her job. There had been offers aplenty from different aerospace research firms — ever since Shar made those guest appearances on that science popularizer's television and webcast show. But this was her life. It was her investment in eternity. She wasn't going to quit now.

Shar rolled down the hall and spun through her office door.

The visions of Mars — captured, wondrous — greeted her like paintings of the Grand Canyon.

To some, Mars looked no more inviting than Death Valley.

But to Shar? Mars was a vision of paradise.

She rolled to her desk and pulled up her display, ready to engage in the next ground-to-orbit conference call. She put her headset and mic on, adjusted her monitor's tiny camera, and waited for the little instant messenger program to . . .

. . . blink green. That was Dr. Alberto Crespo's cue. He adjusted his suit jacket and walked out onto the stage in front of the massive projection screen that showed what was already displayed on his tablet computer in his hand. He used his fingers to maneuver and expand the tablet's little media program until a computer-generated image of nerve and scar tissue cells filled the screen.

"You see," Alberto said, "the problem isn't just getting the impulses to skip over the site of the damage. The problem is repairing the damage itself. Now, we've made a lot of progress this century, working on cloning heart valves, ears, kidneys, and other parts of the body — all from stem cells provided by the patients. Once grafted into the subject, these perform much better than any prosthetic or transplant. But nervous tissue has always been a challenge. What I am proposing we try, is this — "

The screen was slowly washed over with a yellowish fluid. Little by little, the scar tissue cells began to dissolve.

"Break the damaged portion down," Alberto said. "Do it cell by cell. No microsurgery at all. And once the damaged portion is gone — thanks to the decombinational immersion process — we can plant stem-generated bud cells into the gap, and they will replace the missing tissue, reintegrating with the existing cells. No scarring left at all."

The computer image was now washed through with what appeared to be brown fluid. Gaps in the computer-generated image were seeded with smaller bright blue cells, which began to multiply. Once the gaps had been filled totally, the blue cells faded to match the color of the surrounding regular cells.

"The amount of time it takes to repair the break depends on the extent of the damage," Alberto said. "But I am confident we can begin elective trials within twenty-four months."

There was a low drone of sudden conversation that swept

through the auditorium. Alberto had been preparing for this moment for three years. Laboratory results had all been positive. He knew it worked. What they needed now was proof in a human subject. Beyond merely publishing promising papers in medical journals.

Alberto waited for the talk to die down, before he proceeded to speak further . . .

. . . at which point Shar almost knocked her computer monitor off her desk, reaching for the little knob that controlled the speaker volume. Morning news was usually a light affair, but today she was seeing something rather astounding. A video of a paraplegic wearing a military veteran's ball cap slowly standing up out of his wheelchair for the first time since being shot in the war.

A crawl ribbon at the bottom of the video shouted — in all-caps lettering — about the new medical breakthrough being tested in California.

The man who'd stood up out of his chair — bushy mustache lifted up in a triumphant smile — raised his fist and pumped it victoriously.

The image of the man was replaced with the face of a different person, wearing a white physician's coat.

"Dr. Crespo," said an off-camera reporter, "what do you think this means for rehabilitative programs across the country? How many people do you think this can help?"

"Well," said the doctor, "it depends on how quickly we can duplicate this success at other facilities. Not everyone has the necessary equipment at this time. It's all still experimental. But I am confident that with federal approval for widespread application, every major surgery center in the country will be able to start doing what we've just done."

Shar didn't wait.

She was already furiously scanning the internet for Dr. Crespo's name. It took two minutes to locate his email address, then she was typing up a letter of introduction.

She mouthed the words as she punched keys.

"Dear Dr. Crespo. You don't know me, but . . ."

". . . sincerely yours, Dr. Sharlene McTavish, lead engineer, MPSP, NASA."

Alberto sat back in his chair.

He'd gotten barraged by such emails ever since the news of his breakthrough hit. Almost all of it he'd had to forward to the hospital's public relations person, but when he saw the NASA address he got curious.

Now he suddenly remembered, all the way back to the time he'd watched his first space launch. The years had passed quickly. Or slowly, depending on how one measured endless plowing through textbooks, term papers, tests, more papers, more tests, grades, applications, slogging through residency, and finally emerging on the other side as perhaps the world's preeminent researcher on nervous system rehabilitation. The little phone on Alberto's desk chimed quietly. Alberto picked it up. Another text from one of his colleagues, Dr. Nalls. A tall woman. Earnest and direct. He knew she had designs on him — and they weren't designs of a professional nature.

As always, Alberto found women to be as irksome as they were attractive. He didn't play the relationship game very well.

Interested parties came, and went. Kayla Nalls had been the most persistent yet. But Alberto resisted. When would he possibly find time for a family? Especially now that his work mattered more than ever before.

Speaking of which . . . Alberto called up a search engine and looked up Dr. McTavish's name.

He immediately got video footage of something she'd done for a pop science show. Alberto wasn't familiar with the host. But as soon as he saw the face of the woman in the chair — chatting seriously about the problem of refining industrial-grade ores on the Martian surface — he knew.

It really is her!

Did she remember him? Did she have any idea how much of an impression she had made on him at the launch, that day he'd stood in the VIP seats and watched her heart be broken at the sight of the launch? He'd felt an immense and overwhelming sorrow on her behalf. For the fact that the universe could dangle a dream so close to someone then snatch that dream away without a care. Alberto had gone home that night and promised himself that someday — for the sake of people like the disabled astronaut — he'd be able to make things better.

An idea quickly sprang into his head. Alberto smiled. He wouldn't tell her about how he remembered her from the launch. Not yet.

Alberto began to type . . .

. . . and the message ended with, "Your bosses might not go for it, but I know they're going to need a good surgeon when the Mars colony goes full time. Tell them to contact my people, and we can set it up as a joint-research project. With the foundation I am working for. It'll be great public relations for both parties, and the news will be all over it. As a human interest story. 'The astronaut who gets her wings back.' And maybe she takes a new friend with her?"

Shar stopped reading the message, her heart thudding wildly in her chest.

It was a good idea. No. It was a *perfect* idea.

She clicked the Forward button . . .

. . . and the electronic message that came back told Dr. Crespo that the procedure was complete. He slowly unhooked his diagnostic machinery and put it away on the cart nearby.

Shar stared up at him from the gel-mattress bed.

"I don't feel anything yet," she said. "Is it done?"

"Patients report that sensation returns gradually over about a week's time. You'll have to stay flat on your back in that bed, though. No shifting or moving. When you're ready to get up, you'll know it. Though your muscles won't be in any shape to carry you without a lot of physical therapy."

Shar ran a hand over her bony thigh, through the fabric of her medical gown. She'd moved heaven and earth to fly to where Dr. Crespo was working. Now that the last stage of the process was complete, she was equally nervous and excited to see if the treatment really would give her her legs back. It had worked for many others at this point. Would it work for her?

He watched her — brown eyes, kind and intelligent. Young. At least compared to her. Did he have a wife? There was no ring on his finger. Something about his face kept telling Shar that she'd met him somewhere before. Though she couldn't guess where. Her brain searched and searched, trying to make the connection, and failed every time.

"I'll check in on you every day," he said. "Please try to be patient."

"Patience is my middle name," Shar said. "I've waited this long, I can wait a little longer for a miracle!"

Dr. Crespo smiled at her, and turned to walk through the door . . .

. . . into the hallway where the other astronaut trainees were gathered for their group photo. The application process had been streamlined — thanks to NASA working the public relations angle — but Alberto had still had to work as hard as any of them to earn his spot. All McTavish had been able to get him was the promise that he'd get a shot. All else had been up to him. The physicals. The mental assessments. The vomit comet — a horrendous jet ride which had pushed Alberto's stomach and nerves to the limit. And finally, the board's announcement of the results.

When Alberto took his seat for the photo, he noticed a woman hobbling into the room, still on crutches. Sharlene wasn't up to full strength yet. She had months of rehab ahead of her: working up the muscles and tendons which had sat useless for so many years. But already he could tell she was stronger. She was grinning, and he smiled at her, giving her a thumbs-up. Then he turned to face the camera . . .

. . . and blinked as the flashes went off, over, and over, and over again.

Alberto walked slowly — his puffy space suit making him heavy and bulky in Earth gravity. Together with the other mission members slated for the launch, he crowded into the big elevator which would take them up to the top of the tower. Then they'd cross the bridge into the launch capsule.

Shar wouldn't be on this flight. She'd already gone ahead of him, six months in advance, as per the public relations plan. It had been a huge deal on the news, and on the internet. Almost three decades after being grounded, astronaut is finally able to pass her flight duty physical and *walk* across the gantry for her first launch.

Shar had not been NASA's oldest astronaut. That honor still belonged to the late John Glenn, who'd flown at almost eighty. But Shar was the oldest astronaut to have landed on Mars to date. And Alberto couldn't wait to join her on the surface. Just a few months traveling across interplanetary space . . .

. . . and Alberto was down. He was home. Or at least what would pass for home during his time on the Martian surface. The girders and bubbles of the colony dotted the landscape. Men and women in space suits were busy assembling more buildings, inflating still more bubbles, or directing roboticized machinery to do the work for them.

With all of them in suits, it was almost impossible to tell who was who. Then, with a little inquiry, he located the astronaut he wanted.

Shar was perched on a red rock outcropping overlooking the

colony site. Her hands were poised on her hips, and her face bowl was aimed so that she could survey the entire surround.

Alberto hopped up to her — still clumsy in the Mars gravity.

"Astronaut McTavish," Alberto said through the suit-to-suit wireless.

Shar turned to face him.

"Dr. Crespo!" she exclaimed. "I knew you were coming on the next flight! I'm sorry I didn't come out to the landing field to greet you properly. I still can't quite believe I'm here. It seemed impossible."

"Science has a tendency to make *anything* possible," Alberto said, smiling. "If we put our minds to it."

"Indeed," Shar said. "Thank goodness for people like you, who have the pride and the drive to make the impossible into reality for the rest of us."

Alberto knew then that it was time to tell her. He'd kept it all to himself, all these months. He hadn't even let his family know. His parents had completely forgotten about the woman in the wheelchair at the first launch.

"Well," Alberto said, both sheepish and bursting at the same moment, "it helps when you have someone who inspires you."

"A girlfriend?" Shar said, turning her suit so that she could look at him through the clear bowl of her helmet.

"You might say that, after a fashion," Alberto replied, grinning.

"She'll miss you, being up here," Shar said.

"Nope," Alberto said, "because she's standing directly in front of me."

Then he laid it all out. The first launch, how he'd touched her arm, and how they'd locked eyes as Papa slowly pulled him away.

"Oh my lord," Shar said, sniffling back fresh tears.

"I wanted to wait for a special occasion, to let you know. I figured my first day on Mars was the best time."

She hugged him — as tightly as their two suits would allow. There were thirteen years between them, though it suddenly felt like zero.

Her voice was wavering when next she spoke. "I can't ever repay you," she said. "It's an impossible debt."

"I'm here, aren't I?" Alberto said, lifting his arms out and twirling once, his palms lifted to the pinkish sky. "This is enough!"

Shar laughed loudly. "Well, Doc, you ready to get to work?"

"I've been waiting for it my whole life," he replied.

Together they bunny-hopped back down to the site and rigged up their tools.

MERCEDES LACKEY
inspired by
"Freeze"

INTO THE NIGHT
A SECRET WORLD CHRONICLE PREQUEL STORY

Chicago was actually one of Vickie Nagy's favorite cities. It was August, though, so of course it was ridiculously hot and ridiculously humid. *That's what happens when your city is on a big fat lake and bisected by a river.* Under other circumstances, she'd have been working her way through the museums, the Adler Planetarium, and the Shedd Aquarium.

Unfortunately, she, Hosteen, and her parents were here to work. Even her quick run through the Lincoln Park Zoo had not been for pleasure.

Well, there was no question of why FBI Department 39 had gotten this assignment. The local head of ECHO — the Extrahuman Coalition for Humanitarian Operations, the official metahuman organization — had asked for the FBI's help after two of her metahumans had investigated the string of disappearances around Lincoln Park and come up missing themselves. ECHO had been called in after three Chicago PD detectives had gone investigating . . . and went missing. Which was after six people around Lincoln Park had vanished. All of them gone without a trace, after doing things like taking out the garbage, going to the corner store, or going out to the car. Three of the six had left wallet, keys, and two-way pagers behind in their houses.

While six ordinary people gone missing could have been a serial killer, or even some sort of gang violence, three missing detectives plus two missing metahumans pointed one way and one way only.

Magic.

Oh it might have been a metahuman criminal, but metahumans usually worked big, and loud. They liked to make a splash. They didn't just quietly murder people and spirit away the bodies. That had been Director Eames's take, anyway, which was why he had assigned 39 to the job. *Mom always said he had good instincts.*

"Finished with your walkabout?" asked her father, as she came up to where the white panel van had been parked. It was a good spot, just off the alley under some tall, overgrown lilac bushes, next to the garage of a currently vacant house. The area around Lincoln Park, once you got past the high-rise apartment buildings facing it, was pretty much residential: two- to four-story buildings, some all apartments, some stores below and apartments above, and the occasional single- or double-family building. Good for parkour, once you found a way up to the roofs. Next to staff fighting, parkour was probably Vickie's favorite thing to do for exercise. And it sure didn't hurt that most of the creatures she and her parents hunted couldn't swarm up walls or leap rooftops the way she could.

"Yep," she said, and climbed into the van. It was cooler in there than in the alley, thanks to her mom, who'd created a little magic-powered heat-exchanger for it. Obviously they couldn't keep the van running to power the AC when it was *supposed* to be unoccupied, and she'd probably pass out from heat exhaustion if there wasn't some form of cooling in it.

It was crowded in there. Moira Nagy had her unruly bright red hair more or less confined in a ponytail and was wearing a jogging outfit, Alexander Nagy was in jeans, an old vest, and a t-shirt. Hosteen Stormdance was in a generic gray coverall with a faded nametag that read "Joe."

"Well, I guess it's time to get this party started," she said. Mom passed her the three ECHO-tech headsets they were going to use — safe in their hardshell plastic boxes with silk lining. She took them out, one at a time, and held them in both hands, concentrating on the complex equations that insulated the sets from their wearers. It had been fun figuring that out.

She was here precisely because of what she *was*: the only magician she knew of — possibly the only one in the whole world — who could work with technology. That was why Director Eames had let a teenager work with three seasoned FBI agents in the field ever since she was old and strong enough to protect herself. Well, that and the fact that her mom and Hosteen would fry even common electronics if they touched them, and even her dad, though he wasn't a magician himself, would glitch them after a couple of hours.

And the more complicated the gadget, the worse the damage. If any of the other three members of Department 39, otherwise known as the "Spook Squad," had tried to do *anything* with the high-tech gadgets in this van, there would have been a very messy, and very expensive, serial meltdown. The amount of difficulty a magician could have with tech varied — some, like her parents and Hosteen, could operate ordinary things as long as they didn't directly touch sensitive electronics, while others couldn't even drive a car without seizing the engine. But that same tech would lie down, roll over, and fetch for Vickie. She couldn't simply work with tech, she could interface magic with it. That part, she was only just beginning to explore, but it had all her teachers at school very excited, though not half as excited as she was.

"This is a better version of the spell to protect this stuff from you guys," she said, handing over the headsets to her mother, father, and the Navaho magician, Hosteen Stormdance, who was her godfather. Or . . . whatever that equivalent was for the Dineh. "It'll hold for about ten hours now. Your batteries will run out before the spell does."

"Well done!" Alex Nagy grinned. He was an exceptionally handsome man, blond, clean-shaven, compact with a lot of wiry muscles. Both her parents were shorter than Hosteen. *Which is why I'm a shrimp.* But in looks, Vickie took after her father.

"All right, then," Alex continued. "Sooner we get started, the better."

She nodded. All three of the adults were going to split up and cover as much of the neighborhood as they could, using their varied talents and knowledge to try to pick up some arcane traces. Once it was dark, Alex — who was actually a hereditary werewolf, not a magician as such — would come back to the van, shapeshift, and literally *sniff* any magic out in wolf form. And he would probably be covering four times as much territory as the others. To avoid alerting the neighborhood dogs, he'd carry a charm with him that Vickie had already put another of her spells on. She had given it the rather long name of *We be of one blood, ye and I*, from *The Jungle Book* — the mantra that animals saluted each other with to signal a truce. The dogs would feel it, and wouldn't go apeshit when a two-hundred-pound wolf ran by their yards.

"The guy running the liquor store on the corner knows what we're doing here, and you have permission to use his bathroom," Alex said. "Use the door in the alley. Short-long, three times."

Vickie nodded again. Besides being a technomage, she was primarily a geomancer whose talents specifically worked with the earth. She'd be doing a general sweep of the area for as far as she could reach from inside the van — a bit like a radar-sweep, but she would specifically be looking for a magic imprint *on the ground*. It wouldn't be as effective with all this asphalt and concrete as she'd like, but she also wouldn't be on the move the way the others were. She could actually sit here in the van and *concentrate*. The others would have to be watching out for non-magical trouble, because even though this was a pretty good neighborhood, it was Chicago, and you could get mugged at night anywhere in a city.

"Time to move out, team," said Hosteen, in his deep, quiet voice. One by one they left the van, until Vickie was alone in the dark and the cool. She locked the door, made sure she knew where everything was, and settled back in the radio operator's seat far in the back.

She flexed her fingers, reached under the seat for her kit, and set up her obsidian scrying plate. Time to go to work.

Her father came back at dusk, just long enough to shift form, get his charm-collar on, and slip out again; he couldn't use the ECHO-mike in this form, but he did have a special earpiece designed to fit in his wolf-ear that was also shielded against magic. At that point, she only had to monitor the check-ins from her mother and Hosteen and try to pick up . . . anything . . . within the limited range her own earth-magic could manage, choked off as it was by asphalt and concrete. It wasn't impressive, no more than a circle of a few blocks in diameter. And it could only work for something that was actually on the ground. Disappointing. If they'd been closer to Lincoln Park, she could have extended her reach all the way to Lake Michigan.

I need to find a way to hack into traffic and ATM cams. Or something.

By midnight, Vickie was beginning to feel that her sleep cycle was off. The only help for that was a lot of caffeinated drinks . . . which meant that at about 2 a.m., she needed to pay a visit to the liquor store. To make a deposit, not a withdrawal.

She "disengaged" the heat-exchange spell — a spell, of course, being a *process*, as she had been told all her life, and not a *thing*. It needed energy to run, so why waste the energy when she wasn't in the van? Then, just to be safe, she ran another little spell that killed her scent. There was no reason to go leaving a trail to and from the van. It took less energy than the scrying spell, and it was something she'd only just figured out. *Practice is good.*

The humid heat hit her in the face like a slap with a wet towel as she opened the rear door and eased her way out, locking the door behind herself. It felt as if the city was crouching all around her, steaming. It would be three hours until predawn, and the sun seemed like a distant memory. Vickie knew from experience that this was the longest part of the night, the time when minutes dragged unless you were actively doing something. It was hard to feel like an important member of the team when all you were doing was sitting in the back of a nice cool van. Even if the team couldn't do what they were doing without you.

The signal on the back doorbell was short-long-short-long-short-long. The owner himself, a burly, muscular man in a red t-shirt, with a Paul Bunyan beard and surprisingly kind eyes let her in, and when he let her out again, he watched her from the door all the way to the alley before he went back into his store, which was awfully nice of him. Not that she couldn't take care of herself. She was a black belt in aikido and was one exam away from being a black belt in staff, and she had a knife on her and with it she could regularly best the saber master using his sword. But she was under five feet tall, waif-like, and he probably had had every protective instinct in his body go off when he'd seen her.

Leaving the alley, she began to slip as quietly as she could through the darkened streets, avoiding the pools of light from the streetlamps. Just in case something was watching. She had every sense cranked up, and she moved in spurts, in an uneven number of steps, to avoid establishing a pattern that anything or anyone who was listening might pick up. *Nature moves chaotically. Only humans move in cadence.* It was good practice, and it forced her to wake all the way up.

It was a good thing that she was being super cautious, too. Because she heard something trying to get into the van just as she got within eyesight of it, and she stopped abruptly where she was next to a brick wall.

It was not the noise that a car thief would make. It was more like . . . the sound of claws trying to pry open a door.

Her palms began to sweat, and she pressed herself back into an alcove where someone could leave a trash can out of the way. *I need mage-sight*, she decided. No matter how hard she peered into the slot where the van was, all she could see was a faint gleam of grille and a glint off the windshield, a glint that changed as the van moved. There was *definitely* something there.

Things in mage-sight were visible by the amount of magic they gave off. Because the van had had spells working on and in it, even though they weren't active *now*, it showed up as a ghostly negative image of itself. It was rocking slightly, as whatever-it-was pried at the back door. The lilac bushes also gave off a faint glow, since everything living produced a trickle of magic. The aluminum-sided garage beside the van was pretty much a solid black shape — but the alley itself glowed very, very faintly. It was old brickwork, and brick was clay, and porous, and all those pores were full of garbage dust and the microbes feeding on it.

Then the van stopped rocking. And although she listened as hard as she could, she heard nothing at all. If anything, that made her palms sweat more.

Then . . . it came from around the side of the van, and she froze.

It was more or less humanoid, but it was moving on all fours: smoothly, nimbly, with a sense of purpose. It was either naked or almost naked, not skeletal, but it gave that impression; there were long claws on its hands and feet. It kept raising its head and sniffing, and now she was *really* glad she'd killed her scent.

Then she got a look at its face. It looked like something the artist H.R. Giger might have designed. Eyeless, fanged, feral. She'd gone from sweating to chilled in the single moment when she saw that face. She didn't know what the creature was . . . but she had no doubt that it was murderous.

It made another prowl around the van, then swung its head back and forth as if it was trying to pick up something. Scent . . . *But what if it hunts by heat, too?*

She pressed herself back into the alcove and realized with relief that the brick was just about the same temperature as her skin. So she froze again, stilling her breath, hoping it couldn't hear her heartbeat. Because her heart was pounding with panic. And the thing was too close for her to whisper an alert into the microphone of her headset.

I can't run. And I can't fight. There was no question of her taking that thing on. Sure, she had her athame, her ritual knife that was also a black Fairbairn Sykes combat knife. But to use it, she'd have to get in close. And *that* thing was nothing she wanted to get close to. She wasn't wearing her 9 mil; *she* wasn't an FBI agent, after all, and the CPD would take a dim view of a teenager packing heat. *If there was something I could grab to use as a staff* . . . but there wasn't, at least not anywhere that she could see. All she could do was freeze, try not to move a muscle, and pray the thing would wander off far enough that she could make a run for it.

This had to be the thing that had taken down three Chicago cops and two ECHO metahumans. *Unless there's more than one of them.*

Just . . . don't . . . move.

Not moving was probably the hardest thing she had ever done in her life. Every bit of martial arts discipline she'd learned was concentrated on *not moving*, not even to shake with fear. On a hunch, she dismissed her mage-sight for a moment — and the thing disappeared, although it should have been clearly visible, right in the middle of the alley, with dim lights from the garages giving at least some illumination. She brought her mage-sight back up again, and there it was.

Well, that explains how it managed to get cops and metas.

It had moved a few feet down the alley, away from her, but toward the direction the others had gone in. Cutting her off from them. But . . . at least it was moving away.

Just . . . don't . . . move.

Every nerve was screaming in panic as it slunk down the alley. Twenty feet. Fifty. A hundred. Then, suddenly, it alerted to something she could neither hear nor see. Its head came up. And it skittered into the shadows between two garages.

She broke and ran.

She wanted to scream into her mike, but she whispered as she ran, making for the brick apartment building on the left-hand side of the alley. *Got to get up, up on the roofs. If it follows me up there, it won't be able to hide.* "Mayday, mayday, mayday!" she whispered urgently. "Unknown bogie. Visible only in mage-sight. Double-plus ungood. Was trying to get into the van." She went over the wall into the backyard of the apartment building, which was three stories tall with open balconies at each story. Perfect for getting to the roof. With a grunt, she swarmed up the brickwork; mage-sight worked just fine on this building, way better than real sight would have.

"Where are you?" asked her mother in that cold, calm voice that told Vickie she had just gone into maternal overdrive.

"Rooftops," she reported, as she made the leap for the edge of the roof and pulled herself up. "South side, West Dickens. Making for the park." If she was going to have any chance of using earth-magic, she had to get where there actually *was* earth.

"Roger." That was Mom. *"Get to the den."* That was Hosteen.

She didn't waste any breath with a reply. They knew she would, if she could. Now she had to concentrate on running. With her nerves on fire and the blood freezing in her veins, she ran, and jumped, and ran, and jumped, and at some point she sensed, rather than saw, that the thing was behind her.

It was an alien hunger behind her, and a sadistic enjoyment of the chase. Somehow it knew that she could sense and see it; it relished that. Relished the fact that *this* bit of prey *knew* it was coming for her, rather than tamely wandering within striking distance. The next house was the last on the block; she'd have to go down to the ground to cross the street. But so would it.

She made a leap for the tree she knew was there. Her hands

caught the top; it was a young pine, and the momentum of her jump made it bend down and carry her almost to the ground. She let go and dropped and ran, leaping over the wall into the backyard of the first house on the next block. Through the yard, over the wall, again, and again, until she sensed that it lost sight of her for a moment. And in that moment, she shoved herself into a nook under the steps of the apartment house and froze again, in shadows so dark they were like ink. *Freeze. Don't move. Try not to breathe.*

The nook contained eight electric meters, all of which hummed and ticked, effectively masking her heartbeat. She kept her eyes fixed on the top of the fence.

There was no warning, and no sound. One moment the fence was empty. The next, the thing was perched on top. Then it was dashing across the yard and over the fence on the far side. She waited for the count of thirty then ran between the buildings, over the bit of fence at the end, and came out on West Dickens. Then she ran flat out. Ahead of her she could see the tall ten-story apartment buildings that gave their inhabitants such a great, and expensive, view of Lincoln Park. Her breath burned in her lungs, and still she ran, across North Stockton and onto the grass of the park itself. She drew new energy from the earth, but didn't stop. She could sense the thing had found her trail again and, although it was back among the buildings, it would not be long before it would be in the park, too. Fear had every nerve on fire now. But glowing in mage-sight ahead of her was the stately brick entrance to the Lincoln Park Zoo, and now she could use her earth-magic to good effect. She headed for the lowest part of the wall — ridiculously high even for an expert parkourist, but not for her. She didn't slacken her pace one bit as she raced toward the barrier — she ran through the equations in a blink and thrust ahead with her hands and an earthen ramp appeared under her racing feet, taking her to within jumping distance of the top of the wall and crumbling away once her feet left it. She paused only a moment on the top of the wall before jumping down in a tumbling roll, leaping to her feet again, and pelting down the concrete walkways. The entire place was alive with the cries of animals objecting to this unexpected intrusion. This was good, it would cover the sound of her running as she headed straight for a particular chain-link-fence-enclosed space. The fence, with its inwardly curving top, was meant to keep its captives in, not a parkourist out. She went up and over it with no arcane assistance and landed on all fours in the middle of the Red Wolf den.

"We be of one blood, ye and I," she whispered, triggering the spell, and the growling from the sheltered den-spot stopped. Before the wolves could slink out to meet her, she was down in and among them, deep in the shadows, crouching beside the Alpha with one hand on his shoulder. Maybe, *maybe*, the thing on her track would be thrown off. But —

No. There it was, loping toward the fence as if it knew exactly where she was. The Alpha vibrated beneath her hand with tension, but did not growl. Two of the others whined with terror. She held her magic ready, heart pounding so hard it hurt her chest.

It jumped to the top of the fence and remained poised there for a moment. Then it leapt.

In the instant when it touched the ground, she turned the earth beneath it as soft as talcum powder. It unexpectedly found itself buried to its chest; caught off guard, it snorted and was about to spring free when she hardened the earth again to the state of cured cement.

Now it made the first real noise she had heard out of it, a snarl like the tearing of sheet metal. She'd hoped to trap all four legs; only the hind legs were fully caught, the left front was half buried and the right front was free, and it was clear from its frenzied struggles it had the strength to break out. "I'm in the den. It's caught, but working free!" she shouted into the mike, and dashed out of the den, looking around frantically for anything she could use as a weapon that could give her some distance on the thing. As if by some miracle she spotted an old-fashioned, heavy-duty, steel dirt rake that someone had left leaning up against the den rocks, out of sight of the tourists. She ran for it, feeling all the better for having it in her hands. She spun at the sound of growls and snapping to see the wolf pack had surrounded the thing, working as a team, one dashing in to snap at the thing's flanks when it was busy with the distractions of another. She dashed in to stand next to the Alpha, bashing at the thing's face and head and free claw with the wicked tines of the rake. It didn't seem to take much damage, but from the noises it was making, it didn't *like* getting hit, either.

But she could see the hind legs slowly breaking free of the grip of the ground. She paused long enough to try to solidify the earth again, but it wasn't cement, it was just plain dirt, and there was only so much she could do. It *was* going to get free, and when it did —

In a frenzy, she beat at the thing, cursing it in Hungarian, trying not to sob with terror, and backpedaled frantically when it got its other forepaw loose and tried to snatch the rake out of her hand.

She tripped and landed on her ass, staring in horror as the thing began to claw its way free.

Just then a howl split the night and a huge black shape, three times the size of the wolves beside her, leapt over the fence, landing squarely on the back of the creature and driving it face-down into the dirt. A pair of massive jaws closed on the creature's neck with a sound of shattering vertebrae, and Alexander Nagy, raging in werewolf form, shook the monster back and forth until it was as limp as a rag and as dead as last year's leaves.

Nobody really wanted to have to explain to ECHO and CPD why a girl who looked to be somewhere between the ages of thirteen and sixteen happened to be at a crime scene wearing an FBI consultant badge, so while Vickie's dad changed back to human — and into clothing — Hosteen made a call of another sort. Local agent Jo Sanchez, who'd worked with them before, came and got Vickie before anybody else arrived. *Plus ten, local knowledge*, thought Vickie as he stopped, without her even having to ask, at an open diner. He got repaid for his intuition, and his patience, when she came out around twenty minutes later with a big bag and a smaller one, and passed the smaller one to him without a word. "Patty melt, no fries, extra pickles, eat it now before it turns into a chilled grease sandwich."

"You remembered!" Jo said, sounding surprised and pleased. Vickie just grabbed a sandwich of her own out of the top of the bag and filled him in on what had happened between bites. Jo wasn't a magician, but he was a believer; he plied her with questions once he'd finished and got back on the road to the hotel. Finally, he shook his head as he pulled into the hotel parking garage. "That doesn't match up exactly with anything I ever heard of. Though maybe something Aztec?"

"I'm out of clues and operating on three cylinders," she confessed, grabbing the bag of food from the floorboards and opening the door. "Your best bet is to join the circus and see what the 'rents and Hosteen come up with. Thanks for the lift, Jo!"

Safely in the three-bedroom suite again, she laid out the

wrapped cold-cut sandwiches on a tray, got both pots of coffee going, and watched the sun rise, just letting her mind go blank. *I think this was the first time I've ever played tag with something I didn't recognize*, came the unbidden thought. *I hope it's the last . . .*

About 7 a.m. she heard the keycard in the door and Hosteen entered, followed by Moira and Alex. As soon as the door closed, they started talking, sounding as if they were resuming a conversation they'd been having in the van — in no way would a trained agent ever chatter about a case in an unsecured hotel corridor.

"You were *sure* it wasn't a Skinwalker?" Alex said.

Hosteen shook his head. "Positive. I've never heard of a Skinwalker able to turn invisible, I have never heard of a blind Skinwalker, and there was no trace of Witchery Way magic about it."

"Confirmed," Moira agreed, and noticed the buffet. "Oh sweetie, thank you! I wasn't looking forward to having to wait for room service."

"Thank Jo, he stopped at an all-night diner for me —" she began, then got the rest of what she was going to say squeezed out of her by her father's bear hug.

"First: good op. You didn't panic: you played it by the book. You *also* didn't go running to find out what was snooping around the van when you heard the thing; you held position and observed." Alex let her go. "Second: quick, what would you have done if you'd been *in* the van?"

"Doors were locked, glass is bulletproof. Assumed I could hold out till you got there, called for help, and grabbed Hosteen's shotgun and the bandolier and strapped myself into the seat in case it turned the van over. If it pried a door open, I'd have been pumping shells into it until I ran out of ammo." Hosteen Stormdance's all-purpose weapon was a shotgun that had been sung over by more than one of the Dineh Medicine People, with shells loaded with blessed salt, silver shot, iron shot, deer slugs, *silver* deer slugs, and something that was a secret known only to him. Since it would have been too conspicuous to carry openly in a Chicago street, he'd carried a handgun with equally creative loads and left the shotgun in the van.

"Good answer." Alex let go of her, and passed her to her mother, who kissed the top of her head and hugged her shoulders while Alex made a selection from the sandwiches.

"Well, if it's not a Skinwalker, what —"

Moira interrupted him. "What it is, is dead. Finding out what it *was* can wait. The first thing we need to determine is if there is more than one, and the second thing we need to do is track it back to its point of origin if we can."

"What's the *official* story?" Vickie asked.

Hosteen smirked around his roast beef. "Metahuman villain, what else? That's the answer for everything that no one wants explained." He turned to Alex. "Moira is going to tackle finding out if this was a solo beast. As soon as you're ready, I could use your nose with the tracking."

Vickie left them sorting out details and closed the door to her bedroom. She might still be needed, but for right now . . .

. . . for right now she was glad she wasn't on the payroll. That bed looked fabulous.

DAYTON WARD **DAY**
inspired by "Red Sector A" **TO DAY**

DAY 1

His hands raised above his head, Gabriel Ryder stared into the muzzle of the Pug's massive pulse rifle.

Glowering at him with large, bottomless black eyes set beneath heavy, pronounced brows, the alien shouted something unintelligible before shifting his weapon to aim at Gabriel's mother. Mirabella Ryder gasped, and Gabriel's breath caught in his throat as he imagined the invader's rifle discharging. Only moments ago he had witnessed the weapon's effects on human flesh, and the smell of death still lingered in the air. The Pug motioned with his rifle and Gabriel stepped in the indicated direction, keeping his hands above his head while his mother mimicked his movements.

"Don't make any sudden moves," he said. "We're unarmed, so we're not a threat." He hoped the words sounded more convincing to her than to his own ears.

Behind the alien was another Pug, his weapon held at chest level as he searched for targets. Aside from a long dark gray scar running down his face from the top of his hairless head to his jaw and bisecting a patch of puffy tissue that had once been his left eye, the second Pug looked no different from his hulking, gray-skinned companion. Bodysuits and equipment harnesses carried all manner of unfamiliar objects, stretching over their imposing physiques. Their mouths were wide and filled with irregular, jagged teeth. A pair of holes set into the middle of their broad, flat faces acted as their nose, and their ears were merely larger openings on the sides of their heads.

Shots — regular rifles and the Pugs' own weapons — rang out from somewhere behind his parents' house, and Gabriel flinched at the sounds of shouting from the backyard. Both One Eye and his companion turned toward the commotion just as two figures appeared from around the house's far side. David Ryder and his youngest son, Matthew, lurched into view, each wielding what Gabriel recognized as shotguns from the gun cabinet in his father's den.

"David!" shouted Mirabella before Gabriel grabbed her and pulled her to the grass. The two Pug soldiers were already aiming their pulse rifles at the new threats, but David Ryder was faster. His first shotgun blast took the first Pug in the shoulder and the alien staggered backward, but did not fall. Gabriel saw his brother raising his own shotgun and taking aim, but One Eye beat him to it.

The pulse rifle's energy bolt ripped through Matthew Ryder's chest. The man was dead before he collapsed to the ground.

"No!"

The anguish in his mother's voice and the shock racking her body struck Gabriel to his very core, and it took all his strength to keep her from charging toward the fallen body of her murdered son. Gripping her arms and holding her next to him, he watched as David Ryder turned his shotgun on One Eye just as the Pug fired again, and Gabriel saw his father's left leg ripped away below the knee. The older man groaned in pain, stumbling and tumbling to the grass. His face a mask of agony as he dropped his shotgun and reached for the stump of his ruined leg, David Ryder was helpless to do anything except watch One Eye advance on him.

"Dad!"

Pushing himself to his feet, Gabriel stopped when the other Pug, bleeding thick yellow fluid from dozens of small holes in his chest and left arm, turned on him and took aim with his pulse rifle. Gabriel held up his hands, furious at his inability to stop what he knew was coming.

Mom. You have to look after Mom.

His body trembling from rage and sorrow, Gabriel Ryder could only watch as One Eye aimed the weapon at his father's face.

DAY 324

The sirens began wailing, but Gabriel was already awake. Sitting up in his bunk, he used a rock to etch another notch on the metal slat above his head. It was the fourth such mark in this grouping. Tomorrow, he would be able to cross through the four scratches, and that would complete the marks he could make on this bed slat. He would have to start on the next one.

What would today bring?

The barracks compartment's single heavy metal door slid aside, allowing harsh light from the nearby guard tower to pierce the crowded room's near-total darkness. Stroking his unkempt beard, Gabriel counted off the five seconds he knew would pass before a hulking figure appeared in the open doorway, issuing the same command uttered each morning without fail.

"Assemble outside. You have sixty seconds to comply."

Like all Pugs, the guard was tall and muscled. A black form-fitting garment covered his hairless, ash-gray skin from his thick neck to the oversized boots encasing his feet. His large, oval shaped black eyes studied the room's crowded interior, missing no detail. Over his uniform was a gray bandolier, draped over his left shoulder and running across his chest to the wide belt around his waist. Though some of the Pugs wore helmets inside the compound, most guards charged with direct prisoner oversight tended to eschew the headgear. Gabriel had spent many a quiet morning or evening lying in his bunk and imagining what a larger rock could do to a Pug's unprotected skull.

The guard was gone even as prisoners reacted to his order. There was no need for him to remain and supervise, as every prisoner knew the penalty for disobedience. Gabriel moved to an adjacent bunk as its occupant pushed herself to a sitting position.

"Mom?" he asked. "You okay?"

"I'll live," replied Mirabelle Ryder, punctuating her answer with a wet cough.

As had long ago become the norm, her responses were short and lacking in anything resembling warmth. Once an outgoing, vibrant woman, she had withdrawn into herself following their capture, reeling from the emotional torture of watching her husband and younger son murdered before her eyes. Gabriel carried his own grief for his father and Matthew, but he had learned long ago to compartmentalize such feelings. It was the only way to survive, if one could call this simple, minimal day-to-day existence surviving.

Beats the alternative.

He had to believe that a chance at freedom would present itself sooner or later. A lapse in oversight was inevitable, either here in the camp or the quarry where he and his mother and hundreds of others toiled at extracting rock for use by the Pugs. On the other hand, it would be foolish to discount the prospect of dying from injury or illness, or perhaps radiation poisoning somehow would get him. While Florida itself had escaped the worst of the orbital bombardments, there was still fallout to consider; something he did every time rain fell from the omnipresent clouds. On the other hand, he had lived this long without any apparent debilitating effects, whereas there was the very real possibility that one of the guards would just kill him and it would no longer matter.

The sons of bitches were just going to have to earn that.

His mother coughed again as they proceeded to the door. Gabriel had heard her congested breathing during the night, and decided that what he thought might be a simple cold or perhaps the flu was instead sounding like a possible respiratory infection or worse. If that was the case and if she did not receive treatment, he knew her survival could be measured in days. As far as the Pugs were concerned, sick or injured prisoners were an inconvenience to be discarded.

"Come on," he said, casting aside the unwelcome thought and extending his arm so she could hold onto it as they exited the barracks. "Let's get outside."

It had rained during the night, and the ground was wet. The dirt had turned to mud, making walking treacherous for those with poor footwear. Gabriel could see his breath in the crisp morning air, and the chill was already seeping through his clothing and into his bones. Florida in October should be much warmer, but even the weather seemed to have surrendered to the Pugs.

Gabriel could not remember the last time the sun had done

more than peek through the occasional break in the otherwise relentlessly overcast sky. One day during the first weeks of his captivity, clouds rolled in and it rained, but then the clouds stayed. Before the media broadcasts stopped, he had heard weather and climate experts warning that the orbital bombings that had preceded the Pug ground invasion were causing irreparable harm to the planet. Some had even wondered aloud if those who soon would experience Earth's first artificially induced nuclear winter were less fortunate than those who had perished in the attacks that had set it into motion.

Maybe it's a toss-up, but I'll take my chances.

He and the other occupants of his barracks, all dressed in the same dull brown clothes issued to all prisoners, assembled outside the building, shivering in the cold, damp air as they organized themselves into four more or less even rows before the lone Pug guard overseeing them. Once they had gathered, the prisoners would march to the food lines and receive their paltry breakfast before being led to the quarry for the day's work detail. It was the same routine every day, without fail and regardless of weather or other factors. In this, as in so many other things, the Pugs were unwavering in their consistency and unrelenting in their monotony.

Towers rose above the squat barracks, spaced at regular intervals around the camp's perimeter as well as scattered in and around the other buildings. Each was fitted with motion sensors and pulse cannons mounted on rails that offered a 360-degree field of fire as well as the ability to angle upward or downward. Gabriel had studied the towers enough to know that their placement ensured the towers covered nearly every centimeter of the compound's open ground. A few blind spots existed between various buildings, but it was precious little protection when factoring in the guards. Nothing less than a full-scale revolt by the prison population had any chance of succeeding. Even then, there was nowhere to run, thanks to the electrified fences and tall metal walls surrounding the camp.

Now in front of the other barracks, twelve in all, similar prisoner assemblies were taking place. While some few prisoners held up their heads and carried themselves with at least a measure of confidence if not defiance, most of the men and women seemed to move about in a listless, defeated fashion, as though they had given up hope of ever leaving this place alive. Not for the first time, Gabriel cast his gaze in the direction of the camp's southern enclosure. There, children lived in separate quarters. As far as he knew, they were treated well, assigned to working parties but spared from most of the harsh conditions and even abuses visited upon adult prisoners. No one knew for sure what went on over there, so the lack of information served to fuel all manner of rumors and fears. As he often did, Gabriel breathed a sigh of relief that he had no children of his own.

Small mercies, I suppose.

Mirabella stood next to him in line, and Gabriel felt his mother leaning into him for support. With an anxious glance toward the nearest Pug, he gave her a gentle nudge, helping her to stand up straight. Only when the guard walked away, continuing to glare at other prisoners while searching for some perceived wrongdoing, did Gabriel allow himself to relax. Not for the first time, he eyed the massive sidearm in a holster along the alien's right hip. He had seen what happened when a prisoner attempted to snatch a guard's weapon, and he harbored no desire to serve as another example of the foolhardiness of such action.

His mother said in a low voice, "You'd think they'd be bored of this by now."

Standing on her opposite side, Gabriel's friend Dylan O'Connor replied, "What else have they got to do?" O'Connor was the first person Gabriel had met upon arriving at the camp, and the two men shared a common bond of prior military service and losing family members during the initial invasion. O'Connor lived in Tampa after leaving the Air Force and had fled with his wife when Pug ground forces swept the city. Though the other man never said anything outright, Gabriel had reasoned that his wife, Angela, had been killed at some point prior to his own capture.

O'Connor stomped his feet on the cold, wet ground. "I just wish they'd hurry up. It's the standing around that sucks. At least working keeps you warm."

The morning ritual was nothing new for Gabriel, who had endured similar banality throughout a ten-year career in the Marine Corps. Here, though, it seemed to be little more than another way for the guards to harass their charges, but even they seemed to go about the exercise in half-hearted fashion. It seemed that months of unvarying routine had dulled the Pugs as much as it had their prisoners. No actual head count was necessary, as each prisoner was injected with a subcutaneous monitoring chip at the base of their skull. In addition to acting as a translation device which allowed humans to understand the otherwise indecipherable gibberish that passed for Pug spoken language, the trackers transmitted their current location to a monitoring system located somewhere in the camp's headquarters. For this above any other reason, any attempt at escape was futile from the outset, at least not without a way to circumvent one's own chip. A handful of brave souls had tried, but the result was the same: the trackers had released a tampering alert and guards executed the offenders, leaving their bodies for days in the middle of the compound as a warning to anyone else who might consider similar mischief.

It had been almost a year since the Pugs' arrival, their massive ships taking up equidistant positions in high orbit around the planet. As far as he knew, no one even knew what they called themselves. To most humans they were just the "Pugs," so named because of their flat faces, and the moniker stuck. The aliens had no apparent interest in communicating their intentions, aside from the obvious, conveyed as that was in the form of orbital bombardments. Major cities had been the initial targets, most of them all but obliterated before people in those locations had any chance at evacuating. Entire populations — hundreds of millions of people, according to rough estimates — were lost on that first day. Those who survived found little quarter as they moved toward more remote areas, since by then Pug foot soldiers were on the ground.

There was no formal declaration of surrender, due in no small part to most of the world's governments being annihilated during the first wave of attacks, and the Pugs had taken less than a month to assume near-total control of the planet. This much was evident from those television, radio, and internet broadcasts that managed to elude the initial sweeps by Pug soldiers through those population centers that had escaped destruction. Reports abounded of survivors being collected and dropped into camps like this one, along with more disturbing accounts of mass executions when groups of Pugs needed to control the number of humans in their custody. Gabriel had reasoned that only blind luck had seen to it that he and his mother had escaped that fate and ended up here. In fact, following their capture he had no way of knowing how many people had been killed in the months since the initial attacks. Was it possible that the only human beings to survive now lived within these walls?

Lucky us.

"Damn," said another voice, and Gabriel looked past his mother to see O'Connor staring at something across the compound. "Looks like they're getting an early start, today."

Following the other man's gaze, Gabriel felt his heart rate quicken as he saw a pair of men being escorted from one of the other barracks under the watchful eye of two Pugs. Bulky metal clamps bound both prisoners' hands, the restraints heavy enough that they hobbled the men. Each of the guards carried pulse rifles aimed at the prisoners' backs, and the four walked at a brisk pace toward a metal wall standing alone near the compound's north end.

"These two prisoners were caught with materials stolen during their work detail. They were attempting to manufacture weapons," said the guard watching over the group from Gabriel's barracks. "There is but one penalty for such an infraction." The Pug's words, processed by his tracking chip's translator, made the guard's voice sound to Gabriel like fingernails on a chalkboard. It had taken him months to grow accustomed to the irritating tones whenever one of the aliens spoke.

He did not recognize either of the two men; they were no different from the hundreds of others housed here, dressed in clothing identical to the rest of the camp's population. One was older, the other far younger. Their clothing was worn and frayed and their hair and beards were as long and disheveled as his own, suggesting their internment here had been of similar duration. Who they were, what they had done before the Pugs or how they had come to be here did not matter. Now they were like him: indistinguishable from the rest of the population and ultimately disposable, as the guards were about to demonstrate.

"Oh no," Mirabella said, and Gabriel felt her grip loosen and slide down his arm until her hand rested in his. "How old is that one? He looks like . . . like . . ."

Like Matthew.

The pair of Pug guards led the two men to the wall, which bore the marks of weapons fire from previous "demonstrations."

Gabriel had watched this scene play out dozens of times since he and his mother had arrived here. Of course, he had witnessed similar killings even before the camps. The men looked at one another, then around the camp at the hundreds of prisoners assembled around them as though hoping for some reprieve or rescue. None would come, Gabriel knew. There would be no speeches, no calls for last words, no drums or other pomp and circumstance, as executions were performed with cold efficiency. As with everything else the Pugs did, it was all part of the routine.

Then the routine went to hell as the guard tower behind Gabriel exploded.

Gabriel felt the blast before he heard it, the shockwave washing across his head and shoulders. Still holding his mother's hand, he jerked her with him as he dropped to the wet, cold mud.

"What the hell?" cried O'Connor, who like everyone else dove or scrambled for cover. The Pug guards — most of them, anyway — were reacting to the blast even before alert sirens across the compound began droning. In front of him, Gabriel saw the guard from their group drawing the pulse pistol from his holster and starting to move toward the destroyed tower. He stopped when another explosion rocked the camp and another elevated platform along the perimeter fence disappeared in an expanding circle of fire and shrapnel.

Shouts of alarm and surprise were everywhere as two more blasts took out other guard towers, including one near the camp's main entrance. While numerous soldiers were running in all directions, some now were directing prisoners back to their barracks. Gabriel saw three men charge one Pug from behind, taking out the alien guard and driving him to the ground. Two of the men were kicking and punching the Pug while the third was trying to pull the alien's weapon from his grip. Other prisoners were starting to see the opening this new chaos had provided and were turning their attention to other guards, but now the Pugs were beginning to react. The first shots from pulse rifles filled the air, punctuated by cries of terror as prisoners began scattering in all directions.

"Come on," hissed Gabriel, pushing himself to his feet and pulling his mother with him. "Get back inside."

"What's happening?" asked Mirabella, just before yet another explosion echoed across the camp. This one was more distant, near the headquarters building, but it was followed up seconds later by the familiar hiss and whistle of something streaking through the air.

RPG.

Gabriel was just able to register the approach of the rocket-propelled grenade in the instant before the guard platform exploded. He dropped to one knee, covering his head with his arms as the concussion from the blast washed over him.

"It's an attack," said O'Connor. "Has to be."

Gabriel nodded. He now recognized that the explosions were timed and targets selected in a way that would throw the camp and its population into disarray as soldiers and prisoners reacted to what at first appeared to be random assaults. The Pugs were rushing to respond to each successive attack, only to be caught again with the next strike.

"Holy shit. Look!" O'Connor pointed to where Pugs were converging at the main gate. Fire blazed atop the elevated platform where its guard tower had been moments earlier, and Pugs in the remaining tower were firing their weapons at unseen targets outside the compound. The tower's pulse cannon was moving around to face that direction, but then Gabriel saw a smoke contrail before another RPG struck the side of the tower and the entire structure went up. Pugs were running in all directions, while others were dealing with prisoners who had not yet returned to their barracks or who had taken the bold step of attacking their guards. Looking around the compound, Gabriel saw how that had proved fatal for several people, but he also noticed the bodies of a few Pugs.

"Somebody's staging a jailbreak," said O'Connor. "Hot damn. Come on, Gabe."

Pushing himself to his feet, Gabriel shoved Mirabella toward the doorway of the closest barracks. "Mom, get inside and stay down." He ducked as weapons fire erupted on the building's other side. Given the proximity to the center of the compound, the Pugs had to be engaging attackers who had gotten over or through the perimeter walls, or else they were shooting at other prisoners. "We can't stay here."

The tower twenty yards from where they stood burst apart, and Gabriel and O'Connor each grabbed one of Mirabella's arms and continued hustling her toward the barracks. As they approached the door, Gabriel spied the body of a fallen Pug near the building's corner, and next to the guard was his pulse rifle.

Now we're talking.

Once Mirabella was at the barracks door, Gabriel retrieved the guard's weapon. It was heavy, at least twenty or twenty-five pounds, comparable in size to the M60 machine guns he had handled. He had never held a pulse rifle but had seen it in use by the Pugs enough times that he figured he could at least fire the damned thing.

"We're in the shit now, but good," O'Connor said, eyeing the pulse rifle as he snatched a pistol from the guard's belt holster.

He was right, Gabriel knew. Using anything as a weapon, let alone handling a rifle or pistol, was a capital offense for a prisoner. Then again, so was pretty much everything else, including attacking a guard or any other Pug. Assuming any prisoners survived the next few minutes, chances were good that those known or suspected to have taken part in the hostilities would be put to death.

Looks like we're going to test that theory.

"Where are you going?" asked Mirabella from where she stood near the door, her expression one of fear and worry.

O'Connor replied, "To find a way out of here."

"Damned straight." Gabriel turned to his mother. "Stay here. We'll be back once we figure out what's going on." He had to try linking up with their would-be liberators. Would they be at or near the front gate, or trying to get through the wall at some vulnerable point? Gabriel thought both were likely, along with other attempts at breaching the camp's fortifications if for no other reason than to keep the Pugs occupied and confused.

A cough escaped Mirabella's lips before she replied, "If you find a way out, you won't have time to come back for me. I'm going with you."

"Mom." Before he could say anything else, Mirabella held up a hand, cutting him off. "I'm not staying here. Either we get out, or we don't, but I'm done living day to day and waiting to die. I won't let them . . ." The words faded, but the look in her eyes was enough to communicate what she did not say.

What else could he do? The Pugs had already taken his father and brother. His mother was all the family he had left, and she was right. If today was the day they were to die, then better to die fighting, on their terms.

"Okay," he said. "Stick close." They needed to get away from the open ground of the compound's center and use the buildings for cover. Hugging the wall of the barracks, Gabriel led the way toward the building's far end. If there was a way out, it would be somewhere along the perimeter. That much seemed right just based on the exchange of weapons fire taking place at different points along the wall. Trying to keep the pulse rifle's muzzle level with the ground, he approached the nearest barracks' far corner and an intersection between four such buildings.

They were halfway there when a Pug soldier stepped into view.

Mirabella's gasp made the guard, who had not seen them at first, halt just as he walked through the intersection. Backpedaling, he turned in their direction.

Shit.

Gabriel held the pulse rifle against his hip and pressed the weapon's firing stud. Nothing happened.

Shit!

The Pug was raising his weapon when something howled past Gabriel and a bright red energy bolt struck the soldier's upper torso, driving him backward and off his feet. Fumbling with the pulse rifle, Gabriel saw O'Connor dart past him, the oversized alien pistol looking enormous in his hands as he trained it on the guard who, despite the ghastly wound in his chest, was trying to push himself from the ground. Still gripping his pistol, the soldier was lifting it when Gabriel found the rifle's safety and fired. His shot struck just below the Pug's neck, and this time the alien stayed down.

"Thanks," said O'Connor, moving to pick up the guard's pistol. Mirabella joined him and he handed the weapon to her. "Take it. If you have to, just point and shoot. It's got some kick." She accepted the weapon and Gabriel watched her handle it with confidence. Along with the rest of her family, his mother knew her way around firearms. Gabriel even thought he saw a flicker of new confidence in her eyes as she hefted the pistol, as though she were reclaiming some small part of her old self.

"I'll be fine," she said. "Let's go."

O'Connor was moving to take the guard's weapon when two more Pugs appeared at the far end of the alley, and Gabriel lifted the pulse rifle to his shoulder and fired. His shot struck the first Pug in the left shoulder, spinning the alien around and off his feet. The Pug lost his grip on his rifle as he fell to the ground, but Gabriel was already moving the rifle's muzzle to aim at the guard's companion. He sighted down the weapon's barrel, getting his first look at the second Pug and seeing the scar running down the left side of the alien's face.

One Eye.

"Dear god," Gabriel heard his mother say, from where she stood behind him.

So stunned was he by the unexpected sight that Gabriel froze in mid-motion even as the alien fired his pistol at O'Connor. With nowhere to go or hide, O'Connor had no chance to avoid the energy bolt. It struck him in the face, obliterating it along with his head and a good portion of his upper torso. What remained of his body toppled to the wet ground.

"Dylan!"

Move!

Gabriel's mind screamed the command, but his body would not obey. Arms remained locked in place, holding the pulse rifle with its muzzle pointed at One Eye. For his part, the Pug also seemed surprised by the odd encounter, but there was no way he would remember Gabriel or his mother, right? How many humans had he killed since arriving on Earth? Were they not all just faceless adversaries deserving of nothing more than incarceration or elimination?

Then One Eye smiled.

"You son of a bitch. You *do* remember."

Gabriel fired, and the pulse rifle unleashed a hellish red ball that drilled into One Eye's chest. The alien dropped to his knees, his eyes wide with shock as he looked down to behold the ghastly wound the weapon had inflicted. When he attempted to lift his pistol, Gabriel fired again and the second shot struck the Pug in the face, tearing away part of his jaw.

"Damn you!" shouted Mirabella Ryder, advancing toward the alien who had dropped his pistol and now was raising his arms in a weak, futile attempt to defend himself.

"Mom!" Gabriel shouted, but she ignored him. Stepping over the body of Dylan O'Connor, Mirabella lowered the pulse pistol until its muzzle was mere inches from One Eye's head. She said nothing, offering no words of regret or retribution as the Pug stared at her. Instead, she simply pulled the trigger.

One Eye's head exploded.

In mute horror, Gabriel watched the alien fall backward, yellow blood spraying in all directions from his mutilated body as it collapsed in a bloodied heap into the mud.

Moving to stand next to his mother, Gabriel eyed her. "You okay?"

Without looking away from the corpse of the fallen One Eye, Mirabella nodded. "I'll be okay."

Gabriel cast a forlorn glance at what remained of Dylan O'Connor, a decent man who had given his life without hesitation in order to save him and his mother.

Thank you, my friend.

"We need to keep moving," he said, gesturing ahead of them. He could still hear the reports of Pug weapons and human small arms fire. Numerous voices, many of them the Pugs' irksome chatter, were shouting somewhere beyond the barracks buildings. Sirens still blared, though they now were more distant.

"This way," he said, feeling his heart catch in his throat. "We're not that far from the fence."

Hefting the pulse rifle, Gabriel led them between the barracks, watching and listening for signs of movement. As they neared the corner of the last building, he flinched at the bark of a shotgun blast, the report followed by several human voices yelling something he could not understand. All of that was punctuated by the sounds of other Pug weapons. Reaching the building's far end, he risked poking his head around the corner, and saw it.

Freedom.

It was so close — less than twenty yards away — in the form of a gaping hole in the perimeter barrier. Twisted, scorched metal marked where an explosive charge had been used to penetrate the wall and electric fence. The bodies of Pugs and humans were scattered across the wet, muddy ground. From his vantage point, Gabriel saw at least two humans firing from positions outside the wall, doing their best to provide cover as more than a dozen people scrambled for the opening. He flinched as a harsh crimson energy bolt struck one escaping prisoner in the back, driving her to the ground.

"Gabriel," said Mirabella, and he felt her hand on his arm. "Listen. More of them are coming."

"They're pushing back. This is our only chance. If they find us now, they'll kill us. It's now or never."

Stepping around the building's corner, Gabriel saw the Pug who had shot the fleeing prisoner firing from a position of cover in the doorway of an adjacent barracks. He was raising his pulse rifle when the alien caught sight of him. The Pug was shifting his aim when Gabriel fired. The single bolt struck the Pug in the head and neck, driving him back into the building.

"Go!" he shouted, gesturing toward the gap in the wall, and Mirabella ran in that direction, moving as quickly as she could manage over the rain-slicked ground. The humans outside the fence fired into the compound, and Gabriel did not look back to see what they were shooting, but kept his head down and ran in a zigzag pattern toward the breach.

DAY 1

Gabriel was awake before the sun. Pushing himself to a sitting position, he rested his back against the wall of the abandoned department store their rescuers had chosen to spend the previous night. It was only a temporary shelter, but for now, it would suffice. Dozens of people lay around him, most of them still sleeping. For most if not all of them it was the first decent night's rest they had enjoyed in months.

What would today bring?

Looking to his left, Gabriel saw his mother sitting up and staring at him. For the first time in almost a year, she smiled. It was a small, weak smile, but it still was more life than Gabriel had seen since the day of their capture.

"Morning," she said. "You okay?"

He returned her smile. "I'll live." It took him a moment to realize he had not even heard her cough this morning. Instead, there was a light in Mirabella Ryder's eyes he had not seen for far too long. Gone was the air of defeat and resignation that had loomed over her for these many months. Her newfound resolve was palpable, and he drew strength from it.

"You realize we could be back in there before sundown," he said. "Or dead."

"And maybe we won't. What matters is that we've got a chance now. A real chance." She reached up and brushed the side of his face.

It was impossible for Gabriel to believe the Pugs would stand for such rank defiance. They would be coming, he knew, sweeping across the city and the neighboring countryside. He doubted he and his mother would survive to see the inside of another prison camp.

As though reading his thoughts, she said, "I'm not going back, Gabriel, one way or the other."

"Me neither," Gabriel replied, patting the pulse rifle that rested in his lap. Despite his own misgivings, there was no denying his mother's confidence.

"So, what do we do now?" he asked.

Again, Mirabella smiled. "Just survive."

DAVID MACK **OUR**
inspired by **POSSIBLE**
"Show Don't Tell" **PASTS**

I don't like watching people die, but sometimes it's part of the job.

The line shuffles through the elevator lobby, toward the security checkpoint. Around me are couples and pairs, people traveling in tandem for emotional support. I wish I could reach for my husband's hand and feel the comforting pressure of his grip. Instead, I step forward alone when beckoned by Officer Kassar, a dark young string bean of a policeman with a crew cut and a detection wand. He recognizes me but has to follow protocol. "Name and ID, please."

"Assistant U.S. Attorney Juan Robles." I hand him my credentials.

He scans them with his ocular implant and hands them back. "Very good, sir. I've been asked to direct you —"

"I know the way. Thank you."

Kassar ushers me past the checkpoint. On the other side, the spectators follow signs to the gallery. I wish I could join them, but I've been denied the comfort of such distance.

My shoes strike crisp echoes from the marble floor as I plod down a wood-paneled corridor with subdued lighting. I'm not sure what I'd expected this place to look like. Colder? More institutional, maybe? Then I remind myself this isn't some cinderblock edifice built for the Department of Justice, it's a corporate headquarters. Or, to hear my boss tell it, the capital of an invisible empire built on blood money and empty promises.

Must be nice to be so sure of one's opinions.

Half a minute's walk and I reach an open doorway. Posted beside it, a sign:

Psychotemporal Transmission Lab.

I see the room for what it is: an execution chamber.

Antiseptic fumes assault my nose as I enter. The lab is arranged like an operating theater. Bright lights blaze down from above the machine that dominates the space. It resembles an enlarged fMRI, a huge donut-shaped structure around a retractable sled for its victim — or "patient," to use the condemned's favored turn of phrase.

Strapped to the sled is Nguyen Anh Phuong. The sixty-eight-year-old Vietnamese woman looks frail and waifish in her paper gown, and beneath the lights' harsh glare her pallid skin is almost translucent. There is no fear in her eyes, only resignation.

My hands shake; sweat trickles down the nape of my neck.

I look up at the gallery. Through the angled window I see my boss, Deputy Attorney General Laura Kroeber, in the front row. Populating the seats behind her are members of the press and relatives of Ms. Nguyen's many victims. They all look down with hard, anxious stares.

Laura signals me to proceed. I turn back toward Nguyen and the machine. A technician whose name I don't know stands at a crescent-shaped control panel, awaiting my order to flip the switches that will end Nguyen's life.

I freeze. Not just because I doubt the justice of this moment, but because there is one more thing I've been compelled to do before it's carried out. Arrested by dread, I reflect on the case that led me here — and on all the questions it's left me unable to answer.

The office door opens. I stand as Ms. Nguyen walks in, followed by her attorney, an eager young criminal defense lawyer named Declan Chao. Ensconced behind her intimidating desk, Laura buries her nose in the case file. She points with her pen at the guest chairs. "Take a seat."

Nguyen sits, but Chao pauses to shake my hand. "Juan, I heard about what happened to Daley. I'm sorry for your loss."

I accept his condolences with a small nod. "Thanks." We have nothing more to say to each other, so Chao sits while I close the door.

As I return to my chair, Laura cuts to business in her husky smoker's rasp. "Thirty-eight counts of manslaughter, with a sentencing recommendation of thirty years."

Chao is offended. "Not a chance."

"Don't be stupid, Counselor. It's a fucking gift, and you know it."

"My client is sixty-seven. Thirty years might as well be life."

Laura sneers. "We've got enough to convict your client on over three dozen charges of premeditated murder, not to mention grand larceny, fraud, and conspiracy. You're worried about *life*? You ought to be worried about death."

Chao studies Laura. "Are you always this calm changing horses in midstream?"

Goddamn it. I knew he'd bring that up.

Laura bristles at Chao's verbal jab. "I asked Juan to take over on this case because his record speaks for itself. So let's stop wasting time, Counselor. What's your counteroffer?"

A shark's smile. "I don't have one. I just wanted to see how desperate you were to avoid a trial." He gets up and helps Nguyen to her feet, then aims a sly look at me. "See you in court."

After they leave, I say to Laura, "Thanks for the vote of confidence."

She dissects me with a scalpel-stare. "You ready for this?"

I shrug off her concern. "It's nothing I haven't done before."

"I just mean, are you okay to be back at work, so soon after —?"

"I'm fine," I lie.

She frowns but doesn't press me. "The good news is, Giudice did a bang-up job on jury selection before he had his stroke. You couldn't buy a better panel than this." She hands me the case folder. "Stick to the facts and nail that bitch's ass to the wall."

I'm not a superstitious man, but the night before a trial I observe a personal ritual. Sequestered in my home office after dinner, I reread the case file start to finish. I rehearse my opening remarks in front of the bathroom mirror. Then I pour myself three fingers of my best single-malt scotch and sneak out to the terrace to treat myself to a cigarette.

It used to piss Daley off when I smoked at home. He complained he could smell it in my hair and on my clothes, and he sent me away to de-stink myself or else sleep on the couch.

What I wouldn't give to hear his chiding now. To feel his sinewy arms around my torso. To revel in the tickling of his whiskered chin nuzzling the spot between my shoulder and neck. To laugh with him in the dark at some obscure in-joke only the two of us could ever understand.

For the past five weeks, I've slept on the living room couch by choice. It's easier than lying alone in the room we used to share. My first night alone in the house after he was killed, I had to sleep on his side of the bed just so I wouldn't see it empty beside me. It didn't help.

Every night I weep for what feels like hours before I sink into the embrace of nightmares, all of them reenactments of what I fear his final moments must have been: trapped in a fanatic's angry stutter of rifle fire, a marionette jerking in wild spasms before collapsing, stunned, into the street outside the metro station, surrounded by a dozen shocked strangers who all lie dying around him, islands of ruined flesh in a freshly spilled sea of blood.

Sleeping pills blunt my nightmares. I ponder downing the entire vial at my bedside, then recoil from my selfishness. Daley didn't get to choose his exit; why should I be so entitled?

I tilt my head back to gaze skyward. There's nothing to see but the peach-hued glow of light pollution reflecting off the city's omnipresent dome of smog. Then a cold drizzle descends.

Nostalgia plagues me. I recall the New Year's Eve party where Daley and I first kissed, a pair of fools standing outside in the pouring rain at the stroke of midnight —

Memories like broken glass pierce my veneer of calm. Tears

fill my eyes. Dwelling on what's lost rips the wound open anew. I need to stop.

I snuff my cigarette and down the rest of my scotch with one tip of the glass. Time to sleep. Tomorrow, I start telling a jury of twelve why they should condemn a woman to death.

There's just one problem: I'm not convinced she deserves it.

"Hear ye, hear ye!" The bailiff's voice pierces my hangover headache. "All rise! This court is now in session, the Honorable Jenise Rousseau presiding."

We all stand. The jury has first day stiff body language, and the packed rows of observers behind the spectator rail are a teeming mass of nervous energy.

On my right, Chao is a legal weapon ready for battle. The only person in the room who looks relaxed is the defendant, the one with the most to lose. Is she that confident? That good an actor? Is she delusional? Or does she just have a death wish?

Judge Rousseau climbs the steps behind her raised bench of dark oak, picks up her gavel in a wrinkled brown hand, and holds it in her lap as she settles into her high-backed chair. Her voice is deep yet slightly nasal. "Be seated." It takes a few seconds for the room to settle. Every audible word spoken here appears almost instantly on the automated court reporter display mounted on the front of the bench. "Call the case."

The court clerk hands the judge a digital tablet. "Criminal Action two forty-six eighteen, United States of America versus Nguyen Anh Phuong."

Rousseau adjusts her reading glasses and squints at the tablet before setting it down. Then she looks at me. "Mr. Robles, is the prosecution ready to proceed?"

Acid churns in my stomach. "We are, Your Honor."

She shifts her gaze to my opponent. "Mr. Chao? Is the defense ready to proceed?"

"More than ready, Your Honor."

His exuberance earns him a skeptical glare from the judge, who turns her weary attention back to me. "The court will now hear the prosecution's opening statement."

I rise from my chair. "Thank you, Your Honor." They jury watches me emerge from behind my table and approach their two-tiered box. "Ladies and gentlemen of the jury, good morning, and thank you for being here today. My name is Juan Robles. I'm an assistant U.S. attorney. My colleague Carlo Giudice had to withdraw due to a medical emergency, which is why I was asked to replace him as the lead prosecutor in this case.

"Over the next several days, you'll hear evidence against Ms. Nguyen Anh Phuong, who stands accused of thirty-eight counts of murder in the first degree, forty-seven counts of interstate wire fraud, forty-six counts of grand larceny, and four counts of conspiracy.

"You might wonder" — I pivot for a moment toward Nguyen, who remains saintly in her calm — "how could a woman so old, and so frail, have committed such heinous crimes? Simple. She preyed on the weak. The confused. The vulnerable. She told people with terminal illnesses that she could transmit their minds *through time*, enabling them to *cheat death*."

I arch one eyebrow and study the jury's faces as I let that detail sink in. Only a few of them react. One young woman mirrors my expression. After a few seconds, I continue. "Those people were so desperate that they trusted her. But her services didn't come cheap. She charged a high price for her brand of immortality. And after she relieved each of her victims of their cash and real estate, she put them inside a contraption she calls a 'psychotemporal transmitter.' But instead of sending them back in time, all it did was kill them by inducing a fatal neurological collapse. Unfortunately for the loved ones of those she killed, Ms. Nguyen doesn't offer refunds, or even apologies. She just goes looking for her *next* victim."

I shoot a withering look at Chao, who smiles. "The defense will try to convince you that Ms. Nguyen's time-travel box is real. That her customers got what they paid for. If you ask me, ladies and gentlemen, I'd say her thirty-eight *victims* got a lot more than that. Which is why I'll be asking you to give Ms. Nguyen what *she* deserves: the death penalty. Thank you."

The room is hushed as I return to my chair. Judge Rousseau looks at my adversary. "The court will now hear the defense's opening statement."

"Thank you, Your Honor." Chao stands, gives Nguyen a reassuring pat on her shoulder, then leaves his table to stand before of the jury. "Good morning, ladies and gentlemen. I hope you've come to this case with open minds, because the testimony you're about to hear and the evidence you'll be asked to examine are going to be *extraordinary*.

"First, let me point out the errors in the state's case. Ms. Nguyen didn't defraud anyone. She never lied to any of her patients. And what she promised them, she delivered. As for the charges of murder? Rubbish. Ms. Nguyen is a licensed provider of assisted-death services for the terminally ill, and in that capacity she provided her patients palliative care and a painless release from incurable suffering. The only reason for the state to call her methods murder is that they don't understand how the technology works. Which is understandable. It really does represent a major leap forward for science. But with your attention and patience — and the testimony of a few helpful expert witnesses — I'll make its workings so clear that even a child could grasp them.

"But what I most need you to understand is this: Ms. Nguyen did not defraud anyone, or murder anyone. And in the absence of those two crimes, the charges of grand larceny and conspiracy become not only absurd, but impossible. No crime was committed here, ladies and gentlemen. And once you see that as clearly as I do, it'll be your job to tell that to the state — by finding my client not guilty of all charges. Thank you."

Damn, he's good. I scrutinize the jury's reactions as Chao returns to his table. They're stonefaced. I've never seen twelve civilians so unreadable. I can't tell if this bodes well or ill.

No matter. Cases aren't won or lost by opening remarks. Those are just propaganda. In the end, what matters is evidence — and Carlo gave me enough to bury this woman.

For three days I build my case, point by point. I spend most of day one lobbing softball questions at the regal-looking Dr. Sara Hanzo, one of the country's most esteemed forensic pathologists.

It doesn't take much to get her going. She regales judge and jury with her findings from the thirty-eight post-mortem examinations she conducted on Nguyen's victims. The jurors wince at her descriptions of brains cooked into featureless mush by the defendant's lethal contraption. I struggle not to do the same. Only after I'm immersed in the trial do I realize how painful it is for me to plumb the details of murder and death. Each gruesome fact takes me out of the moment and makes me think of Daley. Then I struggle to regain my focus and continue my direct examination of the witness. By the end of it, I feel drained in both flesh and spirit.

To my profound surprise, Chao declines to cross-examine Hanzo.

On day two, I bring out my second expert, a pudgy, soft-spoken CPA named Adam Patel. Chao tries to quash Patel's testimony by claiming that none of the transactions he reviewed constitutes evidence of fraud. Rousseau overrules him. In answer to my open-ended queries, Mr. Patel elicits gasps from the jury as he details just how much money Nguyen siphoned from her victims in exchange for her fatal services.

Truth be told, Chao was right to object. People overpay for questionable services every day. They can't all be crimes. But the state needs the jury to see Nguyen as a thief and a killer.

Again, Chao shows no interest in cross-examining my expert. I'm not sure Nguyen is getting her money's worth from this guy. I've seen public defenders who put up more of a fight.

Day three, I go for the killing stroke.

My *coup de grâce* has a name: Anorah Whitcomb. Trim and articulate, she's a model witness. College educated, married, her record unblemished. Not even a parking ticket. She wears her light brown hair in a loose ponytail, lets her reading glasses slip halfway down her delicate nose, and dresses like the most fashionable librarian you've ever seen. The only hint of imperfection in her comely face is the lingering sadness behind her eyes.

She's a woman with a story to tell, and I want the jury to hear it.

After she's sworn in, I stand before the witness box, pause for a moment, and pretend to consult my notes. "Mrs. Whitcomb, was your mother Elaine Speath?"

She nods as she says, "Yes, she was."

"This court has heard testimony that your mother was a victim —"

"Objection!" snaps Chao. "Prejudicial terminology."

Rousseau glowers at me. "Sustained."

I clear my throat. "I'll rephrase. Your mother was a *client* of Ms. Nguyen, was she not?"

"Yes."

I reach toward my table. My associate Tynan Du Lac hands me a document. I pass it to the court clerk as I address the judge. "Your Honor, I would like to submit as People's Exhibit Seventy-Four the client-intake form Mrs. Speath provided to Ms. Nguyen."

Rousseau glances at Chao. "Any objection, Counselor?"

"None, Your Honor."

"Proceed."

The clerk logs it in as I continue. "Mrs. Whitcomb, your mother told Ms. Nguyen that she was dying of stage four pancreatic cancer. Did your mother tell *you* that she had cancer?"

Whitcomb shakes her head. "My mother *never* had cancer."

I face the judge. "Your Honor, I refer the court to Doctor Hanzo's post-mortem exam of Mrs. Speath. It found no evidence of cancer in any part of her body."

"Where are you going with this, Mr. Robles?"

I direct my next question to the witness. "Mrs. Whitcomb, did your mother suffer from *any* chronic illnesses that you knew of?"

"Yes. She fought depression most of her life. Two months before she died, she was diagnosed with dementia."

"How far along was her condition?"

"Far enough that the court gave me her power of attorney."

I throw a pointed look at Nguyen. "Did the defendant, or anyone acting on her behalf, ever contact you or one of your mother's medical providers for permission to put her in Ms. Nguyen's psychotemporal transmitter?"

Chao's on his feet. "Objection! Acts of fraud and misrepresentation by the deceased constitute an offense *against* my client, not wrongdoing *by* my client."

"Your Honor, I'm prepared to show relevancy."

The judge fixes me with a skunk-eyed look. "Quickly, Counselor." To the witness she adds, "You can answer the question."

Whitcomb nods to her, then faces me. "No one ever contacted me or my mom's doctor."

Tynan hands me a folder thick with pages. I relay it to the clerk. "Your Honor, I wish to submit these affidavits collectively as People's Exhibit Seventy-Five. Based on Mrs. Whitcomb's pretrial testimony, we interviewed the next of kin and primary caregivers of the defendant's dead clients. We found no record that any of the deceaseds' medical conditions had been verified by Ms. Nguyen or her associates prior to her provision of services. This chronic lack of due diligence constitutes an abrogation of the defendant's legal obligations as a licensed provider of end-of-life services." I finish with an accusatory look at Chao. "I believe this can also be construed as evidence of *mens rea*, in support of the people's charges of fraud."

Chao sinks into his chair as Rousseau declares, "I'll allow it. Continue."

"No more questions at this time."

The judge turns an expectant look at the defense. "Mr. Chao?"

He only half-rises from his chair. "No questions, Your Honor."

"The witness may step down." Whitcomb exits the witness box, and the bailiff escorts her out of the courtroom. The judge looks at me. "I see no more witnesses on your list, Counselor. Do you have anything else for today?"

"No, Your Honor. The people rest."

"All right. We resume tomorrow morning at 10." She lifts her gavel. "We're adjourned." The wooden hammer falls with a sharp report. The jury files out of its box and the spectators shuffle into the corridor. I pack my files into my briefcase and intercept Chao and his client at the railing gate. "Did you see the jury's faces, Chao? I *sank* you out there today." I direct a hard look at Nguyen. "She's as good as fried."

Chao's eyes narrow as he smiles, lending him a predatory mien. "The jury's only heard *half* the story, Juan." He shepherds Nguyen past me. "Starting tomorrow, they belong to *me*."

I pace my terrace like a beast new to captivity. In one hand I nurse a deep pour of scotch. With the other, I flip through virtual pages from the case file, courtesy of my eyeglasses' holochip. My mind circles like a raptor, trying to anticipate Chao's counterattack. On the one hand, I'm sure I dealt his case a lethal blow this afternoon, but in the back of my mind, doubt festers.

Or is it hope?

I scour the descriptions of Nguyen's machine. It's bizarre and complex and sounds like something out of a movie. And yet . . . Before law school I earned my degree in mathematics, and I was no slouch in physics, either. I'm not the genius Nguyen claims to be, but I know enough to realize there's a chance this machine of hers might really work. Of course, I can never admit that to the jury. Not without torpedoing my case and provoking a mistrial.

It's half past 2. My vision goes soft. My Glenmorangie bears part of the blame, but the real culprit is the dank fog that rolls into the yawning spans between the city's towers. I take my drink inside and clean my glasses. Able to see again, I call up the last page of discovery notes about the psychotemporal transmitter. I realize I'm searching it for proof of the defense's claims, grasping at its possibilities with the intensity of a drowning man flailing for purchase.

I wish it were true. But who'd want to go back to their childhood? Or even their teen years? I can't imagine reliving my own life. Decades of accomplishments erased, a blank slate filled with foreknowledge — but also foreboding. How much of the future would be changed just by the expectation of it? And even if I wanted nothing more than to live my life over again, how could I do it all the same as before, when one word or action could change everything?

Of course, what if changing everything is the whole point?

It's ridiculous; has to be. Fairy tales and technobabble. Just a postmodern spin on faith healing, cold reading, and snake oil. Another sham designed to capitalize on the grief of others, one more steaming heap of bullshit crafted to make the rich richer and the dumb dead.

Once more the doxepin calls to me from the coffee table, my nightly temptation.

I wash down one pill with the rest of my scotch and fall onto the couch, hoping I'm soused enough to lapse into darkness and languish there, free of dreams, until daybreak.

But I know I won't be that lucky. I never am.

The next morning I see Chao's final witness list. He's staking Nguyen's entire defense on two experts — a neurologist and a physicist — and one character witness.

I catch his eye as he and Nguyen pass by on the way to their table. "Three witnesses, Declan? You trying to throw the case?"

He smiles but isn't amused. "I could win with one, but I like to be thorough."

Judge Rousseau takes her chair as the bailiff calls the court into session. The spectators' murmuring fades to silence. "Mr. Chao, call your first witness."

"Your Honor, the defense calls Dr. Tariq Al-Hafaz, MD."

A trim man of middling years, Al-Hafaz enters the courtroom with long strides. The hue of his close-cropped hair and beard match his immaculate charcoal-gray suit. He takes his place in the witness box. There's a brief delay as the clerk searches for a Quran, upon which the good doctor swears his affirmation of truthfulness.

I tune out for fifteen minutes or so while Chao establishes Al-Hafaz's bona fides as one of the world's preeminent neurologists. They spend another twenty minutes educating the jury on the bioelectrical mechanisms of human memory. It's heady stuff, if you like that kind of thing.

The margins of my legal pad are packed with doodles of Einstein-Rosen bridges — wormholes, to the layman — by the time they get to something relevant.

Chao picks up a stack of papers in a clear plastic binder. "Doctor, I have here a paper you coauthored with my client sixteen years ago. In it, you speculate that it might be possible not only to map the synaptic links in human memory, but to actually read them remotely, by means of electromagnetic stimulation within a controlled environment. Do you recall that hypothesis?"

"Very well, yes. Though I'd no longer call it a hypothesis."

"Why not?"

"Because Ms. Nguyen proved it works. And she took the technology to the next logical step: not only can her psychotemporal transmitter read human memories the way a computer reads information off a hard drive, it can transmit them in the form of a signal."

Feigning a lack of understanding, Chao asked, "To what end, Doctor?"

"Properly calibrated, such a signal could be projected directly into the thalamus and amygdala of a target subject, allowing their mind to receive the transmitted memories."

"Could one send only selected memories?"

"Yes. Afterward, the recipient would be able to recall in detail one or more experiences he or she never had."

I notice jury members leaning forward. I thought this would bore them to sleep, but they're all hooked. I can see it in their eyes. Chao sees it, too — and panders to it like a pro.

"What would be the upper limit on such a memory transfer?"

"In theory, none. You could read all the contents of someone's mind and then beam it into someone else's head. But in practice, that's almost impossible. It's like an organ transplant — the new memories tend to get rejected, and the bigger the transfer, the faster it fails. The only stable way to effect such a large transfer is for the receiver's mind to be compatible with that of the sender — which, in practice, means they need to be the same person."

"And how does that relate to my client's invention?"

"She uses it to transmit a person's mind — memories, personality, and all — back in time to his or her younger self. Because it augments a patient's younger self rather than supplanting it, my research suggests such a transfer has a 99.7 percent chance of success."

Chao looks at Rousseau. "Nothing further at this time, Your Honor."

He returns to his table. I stand and approach the witness box.

"Dr. Al-Hafaz, to the best of your knowledge, what happens to a human mind when it is fully read by Ms. Nguyen's machine?"

He swallows. "The application of the electromagnetic field that stimulates the —"

"In layman's terms, if you please."

His face takes on a stern cast. "Their brain is erased, reduced to a blank slate."

"A blank slate. Curious. Tell me, Doctor: to the best of your knowledge, have you or Ms. Nguyen ever used her machine to read the full contents of a patient's mind, and then transmitted the contents back into their mind, to guarantee the fidelity of your transfer process?"

"I have not engaged in such experiments, no."

"Has the defendant?"

Chao springs to his feet. "Objection. The witness is not qualified to attest to my client's actions or lack thereof in his absence."

"I'll rephrase. Doctor, did you ever see the defendant conduct such a control study?"

"No, I did not."

"To the best of your knowledge, did the defendant ever tell you that she or someone acting on her behalf had performed such an experiment?"

"No."

"Then how could either of you be certain this protocol of yours would work?"

He regards me with contempt. "As I said: I believe my hypothesis to be sound."

"Oh — you *believe*. Thank you, Doctor. Nothing further at this time."

I return to my table thinking I've scored a victory — then I scan the faces of the jury, and I'm not so sure. Scowls of doubt, masks of indifference. Did I push Al-Hafaz too hard?

Two more witnesses to go — and then I'll have my answer.

I once read Tolstoy's *War and Peace* in less time than it's taken Chao's second witness, Dr. Liev Reichert, to explain to the court the interconnected nature of space and time. The judge and jury are losing patience. I have to confess, I sympathize.

Then, at last, Chao gets to the point.

"So tell us, Doctor: how do all these principles work together in my client's machine?"

The clean-shaven, aquiline-featured Israeli adjusts his wire-frame glasses. "There are three principal systems in the psycho-temporal transmitter. The first, which Ms. Nguyen developed with Dr. Al-Hafaz, is a functional MRI with quantum-state imaging. Its purpose is to excite the patient's brain with targeted radiation, enabling it to map and decode the patient's conscious and subconscious mind, and translate it into an uncompressed analog signal.

"The second major system in the device is the temporal signature scanner. Ms. Nguyen and I created it to isolate the patient's unique chronological profile, or CP."

Anticipating the jury's confusion, Chao asks, "What is a chronological profile?"

"A unique identifier," Reichert says. "More precise than a fingerprint or even a DNA scan. Each of us creates our own CP with every action and each decision, from the day we are born to the moment we die. Because no two persons can ever truly occupy the exact same point in space-time, each person's life becomes a unique four-dimensional Cartesian map."

Chao nods, as if he understood a word of that. "Why is this feature important?"

"It is used to track a patient's CP backward to whatever place and time he or she has selected for their return point. Most patients take Ms. Nguyen's suggestion and select dates and locations that are easily pinpointed, such as childhood homes at birthdays or major holidays."

"I see. Can the machine send a person back to any point in their personal history?"

Reichert cocks his head at a rakish angle. "There are limits. The farther back a patient goes, the harder it is to lock onto their past self. Dr. Al-Hafaz recommends not projecting back to earlier than age ten, or to later than age twenty-two. Any younger, and the mind cannot handle the strain of hosting an adult consciousness. Any older, and the mind might not be elastic enough for the transmitted persona to take hold."

"Interesting. And what's the machine's third key system, Doctor?"

"A wormhole generator."

"In simple terms, how does that work?"

"It pinches together two sets of coordinates in space-time and opens a narrow window between them — we are talking an aperture of a few centimeters, for a duration of only a few seconds. Just long enough to lock onto the CP of the patient's younger self and send their present-day consciousness in a single burst transmission into their younger self's mind."

Confusion knits the jury's brows, as well as mine and Chao's. But damn him, he plays the moment perfectly, with an irreverent smirk that elicits a laugh from the jurors. Then he asks Reichert, "If the patients' memories got sent back in time, why didn't they remember doing it?"

"Quantum branching," Reichert says. He lifts a hand to forestall protest. "I will spare you the math, but it works like this: to prevent time-travel paradoxes, the universe has a defense mechanism, quantum branching. When something happens that would change history, the timeline splits, like a fork in a road. One path leads to the history you know; the other leads to a new, alternate timeline we will never see. How different it eventually becomes from ours depends on how many changes a patient causes once they arrive in the new timeline."

"So, all of Ms. Nguyen's patients who've gone into the machine are still alive?"

"In a sense, yes. Their minds, their memories, everything they really were — they all live on, each of them transplanted to a new alternate timeline. Each of them gets to live his or her life over, maybe reliving their favorite moments, perhaps avoiding mistakes, maybe seeing what might have been had they followed the road not taken. But I assure you, they are all alive."

"Thank you, Doctor." Chao returns to his table and says to me, "Your witness."

I stand. Reichert's had most of the day to puff hot air into Chao's bubble of bullshit. My job is to put a pin to it. I plant myself in front of the witness box. "Dr. Reichert, is there any concrete evidence for the existence of alternate timelines?"

"There are numerous mathematical models, yes."

"I didn't ask if there were models, Doctor. I asked if there was solid evidence. Have you ever seen an alternate timeline?"

"No."

"Do you know of anybody who's ever visited one?"

"If they did, it would be a one-way trip. So, no."

"To the best of your knowledge, has anyone ever received a

communication that could be proved to have originated in another timeline? Or from the future?"

He hesitates. "No."

"So, other than your and Ms. Nguyen's own self-serving math, there is absolutely no proof of your assertion that her clients are still alive in alternate timelines — is that correct?"

A weary frown. "That is correct."

"Will you also concede that, regardless of any hypothetical possibility that the memories of Ms. Nguyen's clients might exist in some *other* timeline, their bodies are demonstrably deceased in *this* one as a direct consequence of being subjected to her machine?"

A disgruntled sigh. "Yes."

"Nothing further at this time, Your Honor."

The defense's final witness exudes grief and gravitas. Stately and gray, Carmen Blancaflor is a portrait in elegant emotional suffering.

True to form, Chao makes the most of the old Filipina's heart-wrenching tale: the deaths of her daughter, son-in-law, and three grandchildren in a Christmas Eve house fire, followed less than a year later by her husband's untimely demise due to a sudden, disastrous stroke.

I can tell her anguish resonates with the jury. It cuts me to the bone, too. I don't hide my tears from the court. I'm not some stone, some worse-than-senseless thing; I'm just a human being passing from one oblivion to the next, as we all are.

Chao shows her an open file folder. "Did you pay this invoice from my client's company, as a deposit to secure yourself a priority spot on her schedule?"

"I did. That's my signature."

"This is a steep bill — more than twice what some of my client's other patients paid. Yet you refused to swear a fraud complaint against my client when the prosecution asked. Why?"

Tears shimmer in the old woman's eyes. "Because hope is worth it, Mr. Chao. To see my Michael . . . to hold our daughter . . . to hear my grandchildren playing in the yard . . . I'd pay any price for a chance to live in a world where I might be with them all again. Just the *chance* would be worth a fortune."

A sad, reassuring nod from Chao. "I agree." He turns away. "Nothing further."

My heart sinks as I rise. I don't want to do this, but I have no choice. I step in front of the witness. "Mrs. Blancaflor, if I told you that I own an island off the coast of South America, and that on this island there's a natural spring with supernatural properties, one that can send you back in time to any moment of your life that you desire, if only you let me *drown you* first in my magic pool . . . would you deed the rest of your estate to me? Because I could use the money."

Her scowl could cut glass. "I didn't invest in a fantasy."

"How are my claims any more fantastical than the defendant's? If you apply Occam's Razor, ma'am, which seems more likely? That you bought a ride on a psychic time machine? Or that you got bilked by a con artist whose specialty is preying on the grief of others?" Her jaw trembles and tears streak mascara down her creased face. I don't need her to answer. I've made my point — and killed what was left of my soul in the process. "Question withdrawn, Your Honor. Nothing further." I return to my table.

Chao stands. "Your Honor, the defense requests a one-hour recess."

"Granted." Rousseau bangs her gavel. "We're in recess."

Chao escorts Nguyen out of the courtroom. He looks shaken; he should be. The jury's reactions were clear: his last witness backfired, badly. If I were a betting man, I'd say the odds are two-to-one they'll convict — and even odds that they'll give her the death penalty.

Twenty minutes later, I'm two heads from the front of the line at the new Korean-Cuban food truck that's taken up residence outside the court. My perusal of the menu is interrupted when an urgent text message from Laura scrolls across my field of vision, courtesy of my glasses' holochip: *Get to Rousseau's chambers ASAP*.

Fearing the worst, my appetite gone, I race back to the court building.

I rush into Rousseau's chambers to find Laura standing to the right of the judge's desk. Chao and Nguyen are parked in chairs on the left. He wears a grim look. The judge signs one page after another as I lurch like a mad bull toward her desk. "What the hell's going on?"

Laura intercepts me. "Juan! We've accepted a plea."

"Now? We're half an hour from closing statements!"

Her hand presses against my chest. "Calm down. This is a win for us."

I breathe and exhale, expelling my toxic pride. I hate to lose. It's part of what makes me a good prosecutor. Composure regained, I remind myself that I didn't think Nguyen deserved a lethal injection, anyway. Then I note Chao's glum countenance and wonder what he gave up to get his client a deal. "Why the long face? Couldn't get the sentence down to time served?"

He glares at me. "I advised my client against this. She didn't listen."

Confused, I pivot back toward Laura. "Hang on. What're the terms of the deal?"

"We drop the other charges and she pleads to thirty-eight counts of murder one."

The more I hear, the more baffled I become. "In exchange for what? Reduced sentence?"

No one looks at Nguyen. Chao aims a baleful stare at Laura, who looks embarrassed. "Nguyen offered to accept the death penalty without contest or appeal, on the condition that her psychotemporal transmitter be used as the means of execution."

I'm aghast. "You've got to be kidding me." I face Nguyen. "Why would you suggest a deal like this? What are you thinking?"

Her voice is low and brittle. "I am making the best of a bad situation."

Desperate to find an island of sanity, I look to the judge. "Your Honor, please tell me the court's rejecting this agreement."

"Quite the contrary, Mr. Robles. In my opinion, the proposed punishment fits the crime." She slashes her signature across another blank line. "It'll take awhile to hammer out the details with the DOC, and the AG has to sign off on it, but I'd say this looks good to go."

Alarm and suspicion drown out my thoughts. My gut twists like it did when I was a kid, facing off against con men running three-card monte games in my old neighborhood. It's the sense that someone's trying to put something past me. That I've become the mark in a scam.

But it doesn't matter what I think. They've already made up their minds.

"You're all insane." I nod at Nguyen. "You for suggesting

this." A glower at Chao. "You for not talking her out of it." I turn my last accusatory look at Laura. "And you for accepting it." I head for the door. "Best of luck with your travesty of justice."

I count myself lucky to walk out of this shitshow unstained. Or so I think.

Three weeks later, Nguyen afflicts me with her last cruel surprise.

And once again, the punishment fits the crime.

Her machine fills the lab with a palpable charge, a tangible undercurrent of danger. Mysterious components encased in shells of pristine white hum to life. Alone on the room's periphery, I hesitate to set fate's gears in motion.

The condemned beckons me with a subtle turn of her head.

As I near the toroidal core of the machine, a galvanic tingle travels up my spine, and the hairs on my forearms stand at attention. Aside from the chthonic pulsing of the machine, the room is eerily quiet. My palms are clammy with sweat. I wipe them on my pants as I reach Nguyen's side.

Her arms, legs, and neck are secured to prevent her from fleeing death's embrace. She smiles at me. "Closer," she whispers. Fear makes me slow to respond. I signal the technician to start the machine. He initiates the process and makes a swift exit.

Such was Nguyen's final condition: that I be present to hear her dying declaration.

"Closer." Only moments remain before she meets justice. At the end of my halting bow, my ear hovers above her pale, chapped lips. Her words caress my face: "I forgive you."

"For what? I didn't put you in this thing."

"No, but you'd have let the state put a needle in my arm, or condemn me to spend the rest of my life in a cell. I couldn't let that happen."

I turn a fearful eye toward her creation. "Like that's any better?"

A faint smile. "We'll see." She notes my surprise. "What?"

"I half expected you to say you've done this before."

"If I had, I'd like to think I'd have known how not to get arrested." A deep, lungsore cough shakes her frail form. "No, this is a leap of faith, Mr. Robles."

"You really think this is better than prison?"

The sled glides toward the machine. Her final words pierce my raw, wounded heart: "Better to die in hope than live in fear." She vanishes into the glowing white maw.

A mighty droning quakes the room. I retreat until my back hits the wall. Stricken and haunted, I watch in silence until the process ends, and Nguyen's lifeless body slides back out into the abrupt silence.

The spectators depart, and the medical examiner claims the body.

I ponder Nguyen's parting wisdom for what feels like minutes, but soon it's the middle of the night, and I'm alone in the lab, possibly the only living soul on this floor of the building.

A team is slated to scrap the machine in the morning. I wonder: will they be junking humanity's greatest invention or an overdesigned electric chair?

I access the trial transcript on my holochip and skip to the physicist's pretrial testimony. It's a user manual for how to configure the machine: what controls identify the patient's unique temporal signature, which keys activate and target the wormhole, what button starts the final process. It takes me less than twenty minutes to set the wheels of destiny rolling once more.

The retractable sled is cold beneath my back. I reach over to the control panel and start the countdown. I have sixty seconds to change my mind. Sixty seconds to choose fear and grief over courage and hope . . . It's not as difficult a choice as I'd thought it would be.

Emptiness surrounds me, reminds me of the unfillable hole in my life, the unbridgeable gap between all that I once had and the precious little to which I still cling.

Perhaps trying to do things over is a fool's errand. Can a perfect love, one that struck like lightning, really happen twice? There must be a million ways this quixotic mission can go wrong. Hell, maybe there's nothing at the end of this ride but oblivion. But even that must be better than the stew of rage and sorrow I've lived with since a lunatic robbed me of the man I loved.

My body shakes from adrenaline as the sled enters the machine.

Blinding light erases my hopes and fears, then darkness falls like a curtain . . .

. . . until I awaken, to a kiss in the rain.

LAST STEVEN SAVILE
LIGHT *inspired by "The Spirit of Radio"*

The speaker on Grace's black plastic radio crackled into life, bringing with it hope.

That was the worst of it, hope.

The last thing to die, they said, but that was a lie. Hope died on a daily basis. It didn't take a lot to kill it, either. Yesterday Grace took it with her. I'd been holding her hand when she died, but she didn't have a clue. Her eyes had that milky-white film of the blind as she looked up at the sky she couldn't see in search of stars to guide her home. It was harrowing. That's the only word that even comes close to describing the experience. One of the guys said sound was the last sense to go, so we kept on talking to her right until the end, telling her it was all right to leave us, that we'd be all right. Sy reckoned that was the kind of thing she needed to hear to move on. So that was what we focused on.

Ben said soothing things none of us believed anymore. There isn't a god, big G or small g. There isn't an Other Side. There is only this life, and it is what it is. He kept stroking her cheek with the side of his finger even as her mouth opened and those last few breaths dragged out through her twisted lips.

I couldn't do it. I just stared at her, tears streaming down my face, horrified by her last words, "No. No. No. I don't want to go." One moment she was there, the next she was gone.

And then there were four of us.

Ben, Sy, Max, and me.

Grace had been the best of us — we'd all loved her in our own way, not least because she kept us balanced. She was the rose between us thorns. Without her to act as a buffer to our sharp edges we knew we were all liable to kill each other before we ever found the Source. And that was all we thought about these long lonely days. The Source. She'd only ventured out because she thought she'd seen something, a glint on the water miles away. There had been whispers in the early days, a bunch of survivors living on the water, not staying in one place longer than a night or two before moving on. Not so many nights ago, a life like that would have been unthinkable. What law-abiding soul lived on a boat, always on the move, living off the grid? Of course, none of us had ever seen the boatman and his crew, so maybe they were just an urban legend for this new landscape? Those few minutes out there had been enough. She'd come into contact with one of them, the Lights, and been so badly burned it was a miracle she'd escaped with her life — even if it was only hers for a few more hours.

She wasn't the first to leave, either. There had been more than fifty of us at one point, survivors. But one by one they went stir crazy and needed to be out doing something instead of trying to wait out the end of the world.

That was why the little burst of static each morning was so important.

It began with a few seconds of music to set the morning mood, alternating flute and oboe, then those all-important words:

"Good morning, world, it's DM and Freddy coming at you this fine sunrise with music to soothe your mortal souls and, if you're lucky, save them." And for just a moment the DJ's voice was lost in another crackle of static. For one heart-stopping second I thought he was gone for good this time, but then his words cut across the white noise. "We know you're out there, somewhere, looking for us. We've got a message for you: we can't win this fight without you. We're going nowhere. We'll be with you every step of the way. And remember, it wasn't always like this. There will be a time after this, too, when all of this will be forgotten. But you must resist. Fight on. You are warriors, each and every one of you. You are our last best hope. And on that cheery note, let's make a joyful noise. Here's 'Better Days' to take you into the dawn . . ."

The music carried across the airways, reaching out toward the four corners of the world even if it could never hope to travel that far.

I listened from what we'd taken to calling the Bunker. That was Sy's grim sense of humor at play. That's the problem with the radio — it's one-way communication. DM and Freddy could talk to us every morning, filling us with hope that this too would pass, but we could never talk back, even when they urged survivors to call in and share their stories. Nothing. Not that I particularly wanted to know more about the hell we were living through. The brief glimpses I caught were more than enough. I was cursed with an imagination. Believe me, the last thing you want is to spend a few hours inside my head. I can't help it. I start to conjure up all sorts of monstrosities from the Frankensteinian collage that slowly forms one horrific piece at a time. Sometimes not seeing is better, believe me. Ignorance? Bliss more like.

Not that we ever come face-to-face with whatever is out there. The only one here who's ever been that unlucky was Grace. That contact cost her her life. So, yeah, there's that. We hide and we hope to make it through the night so we can hear those friendly voices one more time come sunrise. And for just a few moments, we stupidly dare to hope that today will be the day we are finally free of the threat.

Between ourselves we've taken to calling them the Wretched, mainly because of how they leave us feeling, but before she died Grace had called them Obliques. I hadn't understood what she meant, but, ever patient, she explained it to me. "Because of how they move. They don't run, they scuttle, phasing in and out of view as they do, as if they're shifting into and out of dimensions that run tangential to our own." She was always the smart one. Something comes running at you, blinking in and out of existence, I wouldn't immediately think they were fading between dimensions, I'd think, *Crap, now I'm in trouble*. Dimension-traversing critters with a taste for our blood? How do you win a fight like that?

Me, I tend to call them Lights because the few times I've actually come close to seeing them — properly seeing one of them — the only thing I've ever been able to make out was the afterglow that radiates from them, staining the entire landscape a hopeless shade of blue as it spills out from their cold cores.

I don't want to know if there's anything inside that light. I'm serious about that. I'll quite happily go to my grave not knowing what's inside it.

The Lights only move at night — that much I knew, or at least thought I did. Maybe that was the only time we could actually see them move? As soon as the sun goes down you can hear them constantly shuffling around out there, picking through the debris of civilization, their weird blue light bleeding out to fill the nightscape. It is the weird quality of that light that's so disturbing. It seeps into your dreams, I swear. Plenty of people reckon it's the end of the world, I'm not so sure. I don't think things will just end like this, but am I willing to bet my life on it? Nope. Well, not by choice. By choice, I think I'd find a rock to crawl under and hope it all just passes me by.

I don't know much about them. In the months since they came we've barely seen them from a distance, their eerie light spilling through the windows of the Bunker. We keep back from the light in case it is contagious. I don't know how they track, if they even track. It could be by smell or by sight or sound. Sonar? All I know is that they don't leave any survivors behind. If they catch up with you, that's the end of it as far as living goes. Darkness barely hinders them if the speed with which their ghost light shifts across the world out there is anything to go by, but at least it gives us a chance. We can see them. Right now, I'll take any hope I can get, no matter how small. I don't know how they kill. Grace's body was the only one of their victims I'd seen. They'd burned her badly. So maybe their light burned? Maybe that was it.

It's a mess out there. Rubble and ruined stones, the detritus of life all broken down and scattered. The Lights could conjure all manner of shadows and shadow-shapes from the jagged land-scape, making threats. Some phantom, some real. There's an old tea chest halfway between the Bunker's door and the crumbling section of wall that's been daubed with all sorts of inventive graf-fiti, prophets of our time promising the end of the world and star men offering ways out into others. I didn't want to think about what we had to do, but Sy forced the issue.

"Sooner or later we're going to have to venture out," he said. "We can't stay here forever. It won't work. They'll find a way in. Then we're sitting ducks. I don't know about you, but I don't intend to die here."

He was right, of course: the walls of the Bunker wouldn't hold forever, there were too many vulnerabilities that could be exploited, but it was hardly a plan. Right now we were safe here. Right now they couldn't get in. Right now we had supplies. Tomorrow was another day. Maybe we'd make contact with another group of survivors by then? That would change everything.

"No one's going to come and save us," Ben said.

We'd all been thinking it for days, of course, but saying it made it so much more real.

"So it's up to us to save ourselves," Max offered, "and if we can save a few others on the way, then we're heroes."

"Not me," I said. "I'm nobody's hero. Not even my own."

Which was true. Before all of this, I was a teacher, and not a particularly good one. There are those who can, and those who teach, and then there are those who really shouldn't be teaching, either. I fall squarely into that bracket. Not that we worry about something as old-fashioned as schools now. I'm not sure who is out there to pass on all of that useless learning to. And the idea of getting people to sit still long enough to listen to — never mind absorb — that kind of stuff? Laughable. To sit still now is to invite the Lights to find you.

Max was up on his feet, zipping up his parka and pulling on his gloves. No one else moved. We were all thinking the same thing, we wanted to get home, but the problem was we all knew there was no home to get back to. The world had changed on us. We'd all lost everything that had passed for normal. Now, with nothing left to lose there was an element of just waiting for everything to come to a natural conclusion. Max said as much. "I'm not waiting around here to die. There are people out there, we know that, at least two, DM and Freddy. I'm suggesting we go find them. If we die out there, we die doing something, and that's better than just sitting around here waiting for the inevitable." I knew it was just bravado, but one of us needed to show some balls. "Who's with me?"

"I am," Ben said. That only left Sy, and he'd been the one who forced the issue. I was outvoted, three to one. Not that we were a democracy. They'd have happily left me behind to fend for myself if I'd dug my feet in. But the simple truth was we stood a better chance of survival together, so that meant I was doing exactly what I didn't want to: I was opening the door and going outside.

"Suit up, Petey," Max told me. "I'll go and check out the lay of the land."

I wanted to tell him the greatest lie it could ever tell us was that there was even a chance we'd get out of this alive, but I kept that little gem to myself.

We had our own version of Evac Suits we'd scrounged up from the bowels of the Bunker and its endless supply of forgotten things. Once upon a time our suits had been designer outdoor gear with fancy labels on them that meant they commanded an unreasonable price. Now that we were reduced to the bare essentials, they kept us warm and were therefore some of the first things we'd salvaged in preparation for this day.

You're probably confused, thinking of the Bunker as some sprawling underground lair. A secret governmental silo or something, a warren of tunnels hidden away in the wilds of the Sierra Nevada. It was never that. Back before the Lights came, it was a vast shopping mall that spread out over almost a square mile.

It was a veritable Mecca to Material Things. There was a Super Church beside it that was just as big, with a parking lot that spread out as far as the eye could see and flagpoles that promised various kinds of redemption. Grace used to call it Six Flags over Jesus, like it was some kind of theme park. Just about all of it's useless now, regardless of the price tags or the prayers of the holy rollers. Strip the world down to basics and people quickly forget about fashion and the paraphernalia of wealth. Faith becomes simpler, too. You became obsessed with one thing: survival. Running around screaming *Praise the Lord* doesn't help, and even the staunchest believer can't argue with the fact that their Lord helps those who help themselves. In our case, that meant helping ourselves to ordinance from the back of the giant superstore, and hostile terrain gear from the survivalist section.

It always made me laugh that toilet paper was the first thing to go when people panicked about the end of the world, but when the Lights came no one gave a shit about toilet paper. They were all about guns and ammo. Funny that.

Max was the first to set foot outside since Grace had ventured out.

None of us knew what to expect.

We waited fifteen minutes for him to give us the signal to join him.

I was last through the door.

I didn't lock it behind me. There was no point. We all knew we wouldn't be coming back here.

It was bitterly cold out there. The wind stung my eyes and brought snot dribbling from my nose. That wasn't the worst of it: it was the way the air seemed to reach down inside my throat and rummage around in there. Even the follicles of my beard itched as my breath corkscrewed up in front of my face. Heads down, we walked on over treacherous ground. Something as simple as turning your ankle meant a single misstep could prove to be fatal. We all knew that. I don't know about the others, but there was a part of me that might have welcomed that. The Lights are just like any other apex predator, they pick off the weak and wounded from the herd. So what if we couldn't focus on them or reason with them? It didn't matter if we didn't know where they came from or what they wanted.

Maybe dead wasn't such a bad place to be, all things considered?

I had to stop thinking like that.

The dark skies meant we could see them coming. They gave us a chance.

We didn't speak. We didn't have the reserves to waste on words.

Ben and Sy pushed on ahead, scouting out the next stretch of the road.

The moon, low in the sky, was like a big wheel finishing off the illusion of the theme park. We had nothing to tell us which way to walk, so we aimed for the moon. The stars guided us, but none of us were wise. We weren't exactly royalty, either. If we had been we'd have stayed inside and had some other fools do the dying for us.

One hour turned into two.

We couldn't relax, not even for a moment. We constantly scanned the horizon looking for that telltale ghost light.

What we found instead was a shoe — or, more accurately, a shoe and the lower part of the owner's leg where it had been gnawed off just shy of the knee. It took me a moment, but I recognized the shoe; it belonged to Pye. He'd left us early, back when there'd still been about forty of us in the Bunker, completely losing it in the cramped spaces of the shopping mall. He'd wanted to take his chances alone. He might even have been the first one to talk about trying to find the boatmen. I don't remember. None of us stopped him. "Do we bury it?" Ben asked, looking down at the dead man's shoe. I wanted to laugh at the absurdity of it. That was the madness bubbling away just below the surface.

"What's the point?" I said, instead.

No one argued with me.

We found the rest of Pye's mortal remains almost four hundred feet away. Mushrooms grew out of his stomach. I had to look away. We trudged on following the map of the stars. Funny how once upon a time I might have dared to dream, pretending all the bright possibilities of the world were laid out up there in those thousands of points of light. Now instead of reading our future the stars mocked us, because, well, hell, that was where the enemy had come from, wasn't it? Out there, somewhere. Brought here by curiosity or hunger, or one of those stupid First Contact capsules we blasted out into space in the '80s.

We didn't encounter anyone or anything for the next hour, or the one after that. I would say there wasn't much to see, but I'd be lying. We were walking through a different world. The scars of the Lights were everywhere if you knew what you were looking for. Cables from the power lines twisted across the road like the dead skin of snakes where they'd been torn down. An old television set lay on its side, the cathode ray tube shattered. There were binoculars on the ground beside it, their lenses red with blood. Sheets of newspaper from so many yesterdays ago blew by like tumbleweed. By the side of the road someone had made a cairn of stones, balancing them precariously one atop another in the shape of a man. It was meant as a message. It had to be. Someone was trying to let us know they were out there.

For a little while it was possible to believe that we weren't alone.

That lie died when we saw the towering chimneys of the factory town up ahead. As we got closer it became increasingly obvious there was no smoke. The only light came from a pile of wood that had been stacked into a small bonfire. But it was smoldering, and that meant someone had been here not so long ago, even if there was no sign of them now. I don't know what they were thinking, though, lighting a fire. I quickly started trying to scuff it out, stamping on the charred brands and crushing the embers underfoot. There was no sign of whoever had lit it, but I couldn't help but wonder whether they were trying to drive the Lights away or draw them to the fire because they wanted to put an end to their wretched existence?

Sy hunkered down and fiddled with the radio, trying to pick up a signal. We were in a dead zone. The only sound coming out of the tinny speaker was white noise.

No, that wasn't true. Behind the static was the ghost of music trying to push through to be heard.

I noticed a relay tower on the top of a hill about three miles outside of town, a black finger pointing up at the moon. It had to be out, or the signal would have been stronger. I took that to mean we were still a long way from the source of the music and DM and Freddy, but, more importantly, that relay tower was a breadcrumb that would lead us to our journey's end. I had started to think of it as the Promised Land. I knew what we needed to do, and how we needed to do it, using the old radio to guide us there.

I explained my plan to the others. They looked at me like I was mad. "Can you do it?" I asked Sy. He was the more technically minded of us. Basically, what I wanted him to do was jerry rig some sort of signal strength meter we could use to track the signal from relay tower to relay tower, triangulating directional antennae with a strength meter in an "X marks the spot" kind of thing, working it all the way back to the Source, the studio where every morning DM and Freddy sent out their messages of hope.

"Probably, but it'll be so much more difficult if they're using some sort of mobile unit, keeping on the move so the Lights can't find them. I wish you'd thought of this before we set off. I could have found everything we needed in the Bunker. We're going to have to scavenge for stuff and hope we get lucky."

"We're due a bit of luck," I said, not bothering to mask the irony in my voice. No one argued with me. "Can you do it?"

"I can try."

"That's all I can ask. We've got about five hours till sunrise." I scanned the horizon, looking for the eerie blue precursor of the Lights' presence. We were alone out there. That was almost worse. "Let's make the most of it."

He gave us a list of what he needed and we divided into pairs, ransacking the abandoned houses that lined up so uniformly in the endless subdivisions that made up the suburban sprawl laid out before us. Back in the days before we all became tuned in and switched on, it would have been easy, we'd have turned to the directory and looked up the name of the radio station — that would have given us a place to start. But now everything was online, meaning everything was lost. Even the simple stuff such as the address of a radio station. So we had to resort to being clever, trying to cobble together some sort of battery-powered signal triangulator from bits of scrap. We moved quickly from house to house, rifling drawers, turning out closets and workshops in those weekend-DIYers' homes, assembling the raw components of what we hoped would be our salvation. It was the eeriest couple of hours of my life, which, given everything I've been through, is saying something. We were moving through streets, closer to the heart of the town. It should have been so alive, even given the hour, but it was deserted. In some places there was still food on the table, half-eaten, cutlery discarded beside the mold-covered plates. The townsfolk had left in a hurry.

I found the last thing on Sy's list on the back seat of a bricked-up red Ford. It was a beast of a car. I tried the door, but it didn't open, so I improvised, shattering the side window with a rock. Even as I reached into the back seat an ethereal blue light ghosted across the inside of the vehicle and I panicked. I snatched my hand back instinctively, and turned, expecting to be blinded by the overpowering blue Lights as the enemy scorched the driveway with its cold fire.

I was alone.

But the house behind me was lit up feverishly bright. One of the Lights — at *least* one — moved through the yard behind it.

I tried to catch Max's eye, signal him to ship out fast.

He didn't need telling. He was already moving away down the road, deeper into the wounded city. I yelled after him. He looked back over his shoulder, shook his head, then stumbled on, pushing himself to go faster. I didn't need to look around to know what he'd seen behind me. I could feel the chill of its light on my skin.

I didn't think twice, I didn't hesitate. I leaned in through the window and grabbed the coil from the mattress springs because without it Sy couldn't make his antenna gizmo, and without it we were lost.

And then I ran.

I could hear dogs out there in the night, their barks strangled as one by one the Lights silenced them. That moment of silence immediately after the frantic barking ceased was nothing short of chilling. It really did feel like the end of the world in the most primal sense. I had given up trying to work out what they were, how they'd got here, all that I could do was focus on surviving.

Every new dawn was a day won, and every day won was one more little victory against their evil. It was that simple.

I turned at the next corner, and then turned again, each time moving away from the Light. Cars lined up along the side of the road, abandoned to rust.

Max waited for me at the next corner.

He was breathing hard and red in the face, the veins of stress pulsing out like war paint across his cheeks and temple.

He gestured for me to follow him.

We'd arranged a rendezvous point with the others on the northern side of town. I didn't know what we were going to do when we got there.

I should have known that for one of us, at least, the answer was: die.

It was a trap.

The Lights learn fast, and we're nothing if not predictable as a species. We ran from one into the burning cold core of three others who emerged from different sidestreets and closed on us like a fist.

I thought I was going to go blind.

It was like looking into the heart of a blue sun. I couldn't bear to look at it for more than a heartbeat — less, the silence in between those beats — before I had to look away. Even then the halo effect from the sheer intensity of the cold meant I couldn't focus on anything. The cold fire stung tears from my eyes. Even as I blinked them back I heard Sy's scream and saw him reel away from the Light, half of his face gone just like that. Killing him would have been a mercy. I couldn't do anything. I froze. Ben and Max reacted almost simultaneously, yelling to try and draw the Lights' attention away from Sy so I could help him. It was brave and stupid, which summed that pair up perfectly.

The next thing I knew they were running, the boys leading the Lights in a merry dance down the street and away, firing off wild shots into the heart of the blue glow uselessly, and I was alone, on my knees, cradling my friend's head in my hands as he died.

It was quick, which was something, but it certainly wasn't painless.

I'd had two people die on me in twenty-four hours. There were only two other people in the world I cared about, and they were barely keeping ahead of the Lights, their bullets useless against the enemy. I couldn't be sure I'd ever see either of them again.

The wind chill was harsh, but nothing compared with the cold of the Lights. I turned my back to it and rummaged around in Sy's deep pockets for the transistor radio.

I took the radio from him. It was the only thing he had worth salvaging. The connection it gave us to DM and Freddy made it the most precious thing in the world. Of course, now we had a real problem as none of us knew how to finish building the triangulation gizmo that was supposed to guide us to the Source and bring us home.

I laughed at that, my voice manic in my own ears. A real problem? We'd had a pretty flaming real one for months now. All you had to do was take a look around you: the whole bloody world was going to hell.

I closed his eyes.

I don't know why we do that. It's not like it helped Sy, he was dead anyway, and it wasn't like it was going to stop the birds pecking away at his soft bits. There were no coins to pay the ferryman. No ancient rites to be upheld. I left him there at the side of the road, moving away through what little remained of the night. After ten minutes of running not knowing where I was going, I stopped to fiddle with the radio and see if I could pick up any sort of signal. I really needed to hear something.

I fiddled with the dial, holding the little plastic radio up above my head, turning and turning about until finally I picked up a burst of static and then the heartbreaking sponsor message promising that DM and Freddy would be back after this short break, only for it to lapse into scratchy silence after that. I couldn't risk draining the batteries and being left with no connection to what I still thought of as the real world, so I pocketed the radio again and pushed on, my eyes on the red fire hydrant at the end of the street. *Keep everything small, manageable*, I told myself. *Don't think about the fact the Source could be five hundred miles away. Just focus on the distance between here and the fire hydrant, then from the fire hydrant to the next obvious landmark, each little journey a victory of its own.*

There was no sign of the others. Presented with too many choices of where to go next, I had to trust my instincts. My gut said aim for the deeper darkness, away from the streetlights, never mind the harsher blue of the Lights behind the rows of buildings to my left. I needed the darkness to be my armor, even if that made me a knight without a sword.

I heard the roar of an engine, and a moment later saw headlights as a car came around a distant corner, fast. Its back end slewed wildly as it skidded all the way across the four lanes. The driver wrestled to bring it under control. A couple of seconds later, I saw Max behind the wheel, Ben beside him clinging on to the handrail for grim life as they came racing toward me.

And then I saw the Light.

It was no more than two hundred yards behind them and moving fast. Faster than their stolen car.

"Don't just stand there, pretty boy," Max said, hitting the brakes. I grabbed the handle and threw the back door open and clambered inside. There was no time for niceties, and I wasn't even halfway in before he put his foot to the floor and peeled away from the curb, putting precious distance between us. However much it was, I knew it'd never be enough. For now, though, it was effective.

"Sy?" Ben asked, looking at me through the rearview mirror.

I shook my head.

"Shit."

"That about sums it up." I held up the pieces of the antenna we'd scavenged, then shrugged.

Ben read my mind and said, "Double shit. What are we going to do now?"

"We'll do it the old fashioned way," Max said, not looking back. "We drive to the capital, and we use our eyes. This isn't some college radio thing. They're broadcasting from somewhere, there'll be a radio mast, we'll find it." He sounded confident, and he was at the wheel, so we had no choice but to trust him as he drove straight on into the morning.

"And if it's mobile? If they're in some sort of outside broad-cast van?"

"They're not. They wouldn't have the juice to keep broad-casting."

He had a point.

I curled up on the back seat and closed my eyes. Exhaustion claimed me before we'd left the town limits. For a while I felt safe, as if the world outside our steel cage couldn't touch us.

You can go a fair way on a full tank of gas, far enough to leave the factory town in the distance and have the bright shiny sky-scrapers of the big city look close enough to touch. But not far enough. We had to walk the last nine miles on foot. It gave us a chance to scan the horizon, looking for masts or anything else that might give DM and Freddy's location away. They had to be here. We were banking on it. Anything else would be soul destroying.

It was funny, not *ha ha*, peculiar, how we'd gone from a world of high technology all the way back to one of superstition akin to a new Dark Ages in a matter of months. Everything that made us *us* was useless. How many times over the last twenty or thirty years had someone said something like "Imagine what would happen if the power went out . . . we wouldn't be able to fend for ourselves because all of those old skills have died out." True, true, and true. The evidence was all around us. It was a grim skyline.

It started to rain.

And in time, worsen.

A shaft of lightning opened up the black sky, followed by a low rumble of thunder. Max joked that it was another one of *them* being born. That was a cheerful thought.

We didn't talk much after that.

We were all thinking the same thing: this was the biggest city in the land, if there were going to be survivors anywhere it should be here, shouldn't it? There should be some signs of life, of hope? But even from here we could tell it was bad. There was a wasteland where there should have been the Promised Land. All of the trappings of civilization were on display save for one very important one — people.

Setting foot inside the dead city was the last thing any one of us wanted to do. We put it off for a few more minutes, kneeling on the ground — as though in prayer — around the radio, and listened. I couldn't keep the smile off my face as I heard DM's voice through the tiny speaker, stronger than ever.

We were close.

I could feel it.

But there was something about what he was saying, the way he was filing the dead air. The rhythms of it. I'd heard it before, maybe not exactly the same, but in the snatches of broadcast we'd picked up on the way here it would have been impossible to know for sure. I might even have convinced myself I was imagining it but for the fact that I recognized something he said: "They might light up the sky, but we're the ones who have to shine a real light in the dark. We can't sit around meekly; then we're just dead men waiting to die," and Freddy chimed in. "So shine on." And that was the bit I remembered. Shine on. Not a lot. A couple of words like a catchphrase. Didn't DJs use catchphrases and stuff all the time?

"Where now?"

Big question. The Source was somewhere here — along with, we hoped, the base of whatever resistance humanity had to offer up against the Lights. That was all that had kept us going since we'd left the Bunker. There had to be an end to this. The three of us didn't stand a chance alone, no matter how powerful a band of brothers we'd become. "Look for a mast," I said. "There has to be some sort of antenna."

"Pity it's not like the old RKO logo where you can see the radio signals pulsing out through the air," Ben offered with a wry smile.

"That would certainly make things easier," I agreed.

Up ahead I saw movement but no light. It was the first time I'd seen any signs of life since we left the Bunker. It was a dog. A Dalmatian, malnourished to the point where it was nothing more than skin and bone, the spots seemingly sliding off its carcass as it hobbled across the road. Could he be our RKO signal? I mean, he was surviving, even if it was obviously a struggle. The dog knew where to find food, and maybe, just maybe, that meant he knew where to find people?

I resisted the temptation to say "Follow that dog!" but set off at an easy lope, keeping him in sight without scaring him off. It took the others a moment to realize what was going on, but they followed a few steps behind, keeping their pace easy and non-threatening. It didn't help. The dog took off, and we had to push ourselves hard with no hope of keeping up as it put on a burst of speed. We had to keep him in sight, and instead hope that his headlong flight would lead us toward some sort of deliverance. My head was filled with crazy thoughts, exhaustion and fear overwhelming me, but I kept thinking, *Dog is god backwards, dog is god backwards, dog is god backwards*, and while I didn't believe, I'd been praying for salvation forever. Wasn't this the kind of miracle that would prove I was wrong and that there was at least a small-g god out there looking out for us?

All the buildings around us looked the same, a bland mix of concrete, glass, and steel. There was no personality to any of them. Nothing that said they were going to stand there as a lasting reminder of the human race. It was a far cry from any kind of monument to civilization our generation would have wanted to leave behind, I'm sure. Not like those builders of the sixteenth and seventeenth centuries who created so many amazing and baroque works of art to the glory of mankind. Everything here was so much more functional and, in the end, soulless. After five minutes of running, we slowed down, lungs burning, hope burning out. I scanned the rooftops but realized it was an impossible task. The buildings were just too high for use to see any masts on top, and almost all of them sported some sort of aerial anyway.

I wanted to curl up and just give up. We'd come all this way for what?

Blind alleys and dead ends, that's what.

"I need to listen," I said. I didn't explain why. I didn't need to tell them that I needed to hear DM and Freddy again, to renew my faith, or that I needed to hear a song, any song, to save me.

They got it.

We sat at the side of the road and listened to the sound of salesmen peddling their wares, promises of discounts at the jewelry store, cash back for the computers and tablets, guarantees of lightning-fast broadband from the telecom giants, and secondhand cars that were going fast, so fast the idiot was practically giving them away, a few minutes of commercials encapsulating everything that had been wrong with our world before the Lights descended.

Then it struck me: why were we still listening to these words from our sponsors? They couldn't be paying for the privilege, could they? Why would they? I mean no one was using any of the machines now, with no power to juice them. So why were DM and Freddy filling the air with their meaningless words unless they weren't? I was beginning to make sense of things, and realize just how naïve I'd been.

I didn't get confirmation that I was right until we found the radio station — after almost ten hours wandering the streets, looking at the signs above the doors and windows (most of which were shattered, the result of those first few nights when looters hadn't realized just how pointless scavenging all of those material things would be) for the tell-tale letters of the station's call sign, CFNY-FM. Walking the streets of the city was as low-tech as it got, but we were methodical, turning the city into a grid, walking each piece of the grid one street at a time, and it worked.

It didn't look like much in the end.

It certainly didn't look like the Promised Land.

I pushed open the door and went inside.

The fact that there was no one manning the reception foreshadowed what we'd find upstairs. The expensive high-tech barrier was no obstacle without guards behind it to stop us clambering over.

"I don't like it," said Ben, the last one over.

We checked the building's directory for the floor, then walked to the bank of elevators. Unsurprisingly, none of them were working. "How are they broadcasting if there's no power?" Max asked.

I had the answer. I'd figured it out awhile ago. "Back-up generator."

"Makes sense. And they'd only use that to juice the studio, not waste it lighting up the reception. Smart. And it doesn't draw attention to them. Anyone walking past outside will just assume this is another abandoned building." I nodded, knowing that he was only seeing half of the picture. The rest would come clear soon enough.

We climbed the stairs, making our way up the fourth floor, looking for studio 56, where DM and Freddy were talking to the world.

We found it soon enough.

The On-Air light was on. That didn't stop me. I opened the door.

The air tasted strange as I stepped inside.

I knew the smell. It was unmistakable. Rot. Decay.

The room itself was nothing special. It was small, with banks of equipment lined up on one side, a desk with a spider-like stand of microphones set up, spit guards in front of them, and posters on the wall from some of the acts DM and Freddy obviously loved, the album covers and gold discs a window on our vanished time. We could hear the music as one track shifted into another. There were two high-backed leather chairs at the desk, and dead men in them, their skin mummified by the lack of air in the place.

On the wall, I saw someone had written:

The Liberators are nowhere.

It was a damning line, one that absolutely wiped out any last lingering hope they had had that there was anyone out there, that they had any hope of salvation, that there was anything more than this . . . it wasn't hard to imagine the last man, broken to the point of absolute despair, standing in front of that wall and writing those words, giving up.

But the message was wrong.

I wanted to change it.

There were marker pens on the desk between the dead men. I took one and walked over to the wall.

Using the same letters in exactly the same order, I told the truth:

The Liberators are now here.

Because we were, weren't we?

We were exactly what DM and Freddy had been calling out for, day after day, even if we hadn't realized it. We'd pictured them as our redeemers, but that's not the way it was at all. They weren't our saviors. We were theirs.

Or we should have been, but it had taken us too long to find our way here.

Their voices were reduced to loops of digital information in our once again analog world, but dead or not, they'd managed to keep us going. They'd given us hope. Day in, day out, they'd given us a reason to think there was a way out of this hell we found ourselves in. That it wasn't always going to be this way. Even when they'd know there wasn't a way out for them, they'd taken steps to keep the show on the air, running loops of saved broadcasts, and having the computer make random choices in terms of track lists so it felt real to anyone listening. That was why they never told us what was going on out there in the real world, because they had no idea. They couldn't tell the future. They weren't prophets. They were ghosts. Spirits. Their voices were all that was left of them, haunting the world's last working machine.

It should have been soul crushing to see their corpses, but it wasn't. It gave me the answer I'd been looking for.

There were three of us. Max, Ben, and me, and there was an entire city out there, with bountiful supplies, clean water, and dried and tinned food that would last for years. That had to be time enough, didn't it? Time to know for sure if we were the last ones to survive. I looked at my friends. It didn't bear thinking about. Could we really be the last of our kind? No. I refused to believe that. In place of a plan, a proper plan, I needed hope. We had a good position here. We could batten down the hatches. Hunker down, make a new Bunker. We had the radio, we had the generator. That meant we had a way to reach out into the silence and let the others know we were here. They had to come. Had to.

I knew what we had to do. I knew why we'd come here.

"What now?" Max asked.

"We do what we came here to do," I said.

Max shook his head, not understanding. In his world we'd still come here to be saved.

I corrected him. "We only ever came here to do one thing," I said, taking over the controls. I didn't look at the dead men in their chairs. We'd have to deal with their bodies soon, but for now it felt like their spirits were still in the room with us. I liked that. "We were just looking at it from the wrong side. This place is vital. You know that. We would never have made it without the messages beaming out of here. So what if the guys are dead? It doesn't matter. It's the friendly voice that's important. It's the promise that you're not alone out there. That's why we came here. To keep the spark of hope alive."

I pressed the green Talk button in the center of the console and leaned toward the mike. "My name is Pete. I'm going be with you as long as you need me," I said, not knowing if anyone could hear me, but wanting to believe that there had to be more people out there like us. "That's my promise to each and every one of you out there listening. I refuse to believe no one is listening. That possibility is too bleak to even comprehend. You are out there listening to me. I know you are. It's —" I checked my watch, an old reliable wind-up. There was a small golden angel on the face. "Twelve minutes past nine. Why am I telling you that? So you know I'm here. Right now. And I'm not going anywhere. I'll keep talking to you and playing music so you can find your way home for as long as there's breath in my body and juice in our emergency generator to keep the turntables spinning. In return, I only ask for one thing: that you keep on fighting. Don't give in. No matter how dark it gets out there, find a way to fight. We can't win if you don't fight. And I know it feels like we can't win, trust me, I know, but, like Freddy used to say, shine on. We're here with you every step of the way. As long as you've got batteries for your radios, you'll never be alone. I can't tell you where we are, in case they are listening, but you're smart, you must be, because you're still alive, so use your head. Find us. Together we can fight. Together we can survive."

We could do it in eight-hour shifts, someone always awake to man the microphone and offer hope to anyone who could hear us. The two others could venture out into the city, bring back what we needed to keep going. It wasn't much of a plan, but it was a start. We had to believe there were others out there like us. It didn't matter if we didn't know what to say, really, even if it was just "blah, blah blah, blah blah, blah . . ." All that mattered was that one of us was always there, talking, playing music, keeping the spark alive. Every fire needed a spark if it was going to ignite.

All we needed was one person to come. That was all. Just one. Then another would turn up at our door, and eventually there would be others, drawn in from far and wide to the Source just as we had been. From that we could form a resistance and start to fight back against the Lights. That was the message I intended to send out over the invisible airwaves every day and all through every long night: Humanity could survive.

2113 *inspired by "2112"*

I

High above Earth, a portal tore open from a parallel universe. The moonstone gate spread wider, shimmering with both possibilities and threat — the largest gateway the Elder Race had ever created.

Coming home.

Similar doorways opened above the domed lunar base, the sprawling Mars outpost, the mining stations on the moons of Jupiter, the outposts in the rings of Saturn, even the artificial habitats drifting above the hostile clouds of Venus.

An armada of dreamships crossed over, passing through the gates: titanic vessels made of ethereal arcs and lines that fit no standard design. An overwhelming force, one ship after another — the Oracles knew they would not get a second chance.

On the bridge of the lead dreamship, the pearlescent viewing wall cleared to show a magnified view of the crowded cities of

Earth below. Seated in white robes on his command dais, Oracle Fulcrum studied the rigid metropolis with disappointment. "We heard the call, but I only hope that the spark hasn't already been snuffed out."

Beside him, Oracle Anchor said, "We thought this branch of humanity had withered and died. I had surrendered all hope for Earth."

Fulcrum stroked his silky beard. "We must never surrender hope, for then we surrender everything." He gazed at the landscape as the dreamships cruised over North America. The identical blockish buildings and the precise geometrical layout sparked a deep, sharp sadness in him. This Earth, one of the original birthplaces of mankind, was now just a dry, brittle remnant of the human spirit. "Our ancestors abandoned them, but maybe there is something worth saving down there."

Looming tall in every city on the continent, like threats erected in perfectly cut stone, were the implacable Temples of Syrinx, each mammoth structure crowned by a glowing Red Star — the only splash of color in a gray and ordered world.

The metropolis was a hive of identical gray buildings constructed according to an uncompromising master plan. Fulcrum saw no sign of the grace or imagination of the human heart. That alone angered him. Human beings were not drones to live in a beehive.

As the dreamships descended through the atmosphere and awakened the stifled cities, the optical lenses flexed to expand the image. The view rocketed downward through the clouds so the Oracles could see swarms of people in the streets, all of them wearing specific uniforms to denote their classes, their professions. In wonder and fear, they looked up as gigantic dreamships filled the skies, dwarfing even the enormous temples.

"Somewhere among those great masses there was a spark," Fulcrum said. "We have to find it and nurture it."

"Or create other sparks," said Oracle Axis, who was always the most optimistic of the group. She did not seem so disappointed to see the stagnation. "Those people can be rescued — and it's long-past time."

History had become myth, simplified and clarified by many retellings. Centuries ago when a dark starvation settled over the Earth, when rigid rules and intolerance began to strangle freedom of expression, all the dreamers — musicians, artists, writers, poets, architects, engineers, theoreticians . . . anyone who represented the great sweep of civilization — had become targets. They were rounded up, locked away, and punished for their questions and their creativity. Harsh leaders tried to stamp out any spark of imagination, convinced that rule-followers were easier to control.

There could have been a long and bloody purge — but the dreamers fought back in a different way. By creating the moonstone gates, they could slip away to a parallel but different universe, and they all simply . . . *left*. The imaginers, the creatives, and the rule-breakers had flooded away by the millions, taking with them their vibrant songs, poems, and ideas — the very heart and soul of the human race. They left the rest behind, like a snake shedding a useless old skin.

Those days had been lost in the mists of legend and the exaggeration of centuries. In their new home, the refugees built a stunning and glorious civilization, everything a person could aspire to, guided and encouraged by the Oracles. Some debated among themselves whether the castoff remnants of humanity would ever emerge from their self-inflicted dark ages, but after the silent passage of so many years even the debates had faded into esoterica . . .

Now, though, millions of people stared up at the dreamships with wide eyes. They were like sheep. They had forgotten how to understand the extraordinary.

Oracle Anchor whispered, "A seed can lie dormant for years before it germinates. We know the seed is still down there, if we can find it."

Fulcrum received a transmission from the rest of his armada throughout the solar system. All dreamships were in position. He rose to his feet from the dais, and when he activated the communication crystal, his voice boomed across all the frequencies controlled by the Temples of Syrinx.

Fulcrum wore a grim expression. "Attention all planets of the Solar Federation — we have assumed control."

II

As the other Priests of Syrinx responded with panic, Father Brown just shook his head. "We never should have excavated Red Sector A." The weight of dismay felt as heavy as the cyclopean temple walls around him. "The workers found something there. We knew it was a dangerous area."

A frantic Brother Theo stared at the wall imagers that showed gigantic dreamships closing in. "Red Sector A? That was just a routine expansion for a new Temple District. How does it concern us now? We have to fight these invaders!"

Brother Adam could not believe what he was seeing on the screens. "What is this enemy? Who are they?"

For some time, Father Brown had dreaded that his earlier actions would trigger a dangerous retaliation. He had asked the computers to run probability calculations, and he had expressed his concerns in private with the Great Face. Ever since that naïve young man had appeared before them with the ancient guitar he had found in the rubble . . .

"It's the Elder Race," he said. "They've come home at last."

Brother Simon let out a hysterical laugh. "That's just a myth whispered by weak-minded fools!"

"Do those ships look like myths?"

Father Brown had known that forbidden remnants of the past were buried beneath Red Sector A, but the Temple computers had chosen that area for the next expansion. One of the excavation workers had indeed found a very dangerous artifact, showing it off to the Priests, proud of the music he had taught himself to play. Father Brown had put a stop to that as soon as he saw the risk, but such things were like noxious weeds and not easily eradicated.

Now, the Elder Race had returned.

The synergy screens in the main hall projected panicked reports from the Priests on the lunar colony and on Mars. Within hours, due to the signal lag, he would likely receive similar alarmed calls from the rings of Saturn, the moons of Jupiter. The Solar Federation was overwhelmed.

Father Brown's priority, though, was to save Earth — and save himself.

First order of business, he evacuated the sycophants from the Temple and closed the thick vault doors, turning the main Temple into a fortress. Or a prison.

He activated Earth's planetary defenses, which were too small and too late. He launched squadron after squadron of defensive Nforcer gunships, which launched from their fenced hangars like a flurry of angry wasps. They soared skyward with conventional weapons blazing against the incomprehensible dreamships, but the Nforcers were trained to quash civil unrest, hold the Red Star high, and keep the populace content. They were not meant to fight a full-scale military action.

Outside, the milling mob beseeched the Priests for protection and guidance. Inside the Temple, though, the rest of the Priests looked to Father Brown to save them — but *he* always looked to the computers, the Halls of Wisdom and Calculation that guided every aspect of daily life.

"With me!" he said. "We need to consult the Great Face."

Hurrying through a labyrinth of thick-walled catacombs, Father Brown descended into the heart of the enormous structure until they reached the sacred computer core. Inside the holy vault, the walls gleamed with hypnotic and arcane patterns, circuits etched with hieroglyphic engrams.

A crackling ball of energy in the chamber coalesced in the air to form a benevolent human face, an old man with a paternal, yet also terrible, expression. It hung suspended there, staring at the visitors.

Brothers Theo, Simon, and Adam fell to their knees, beseeching the cybernetic god, but Father Brown stood straight and faced the computer deity. "We are under attack. Tell us what to do."

After he'd been ordained as High Priest, Father Brown was granted access to the most secret records of ancient humanity, a hidden vault of treasures and mysteries beneath the computer core. There, he had seen the relics left behind by the Elder Race, as well as even more ancient libraries. He knew this projected image of the Great Face was taken from an ancient film called *The Wizard of Oz*.

The paternal image brightened. "My sensors detected these enemy ships, but I cannot analyze their capabilities. Their technology is far superior to our own."

"Our citizens will look to the Priests to save them," said Father Brown. "We must tell them something. We must *do* something."

The Great Face said, "The people look to us for every decision, every action. This does not fit the plan."

Brother Theo cried, "How do we defeat them? We must drive away the invaders."

"I have run projections, followed many paths of probabilities. All conclusions are the same." The kindly holographic face frowned. "There is no probability of our victory."

Father Brown felt as if a brick had fallen on his heart. He thought again about the discoveries in Red Sector A, a haunted place that had been left abandoned since the Elder Race departed. Too many memories were there, too many relics . . . too much danger.

He did not dare cast blame on the computers, though, as he faced the benevolent image. Again, he remembered the young man expecting to be rewarded for his forbidden music. That incident, Father Brown knew, was merely the tip of the iceberg. He wondered what else the young man had found down there . . .

III

From a journal found in Red Sector A:

I'm writing this because I need to document what I found and what happened afterward, and I don't know how else to do it. This isn't a report I can file with my supervisor, not something I can share with my fellow excavators. I don't understand it myself.

It delights me. It fascinates me. It terrifies me.

A job like any other job, on a day like any other day. I woke to the approved morning fanfare. My small apartment contained everything I could want — and how could I possibly want much of anything? Everyone had the same apartment based on the same design; my living arrangements as a single man wouldn't change until a marriage approval came from the Temples, and then my wife and I — whoever she might be — would move into a new apartment, identical to what all married couples had, until we started a family, and then we would move into the approved couple-with-family apartment design.

At my bedside was that month's approved novel. Everyone was reading it, and I dutifully went through a chapter a night. The story resembled the previous month's novel, but the character names were different; therefore, it was an entirely new story.

I put on my standard uniform as a mid-level excavator; I was pleased to display the Red Star on my right breast. My crew cleared away old debris to make room for immense new temples and countless living structures. It was a job to take pride in . . . just like everyone's job.

Heading toward work, I followed the flow of people along arrow-straight boulevards. A peppy morning march played on speakers mounted on the buildings so that everyone walked with the same rhythm, the same smiles. Cruising the skies overhead but low to the buildings, armored Nforcer patrol cars made us all feel safe.

Arriving for work, I joined my crew, which had been assigned to a new expansion project in Red Sector A. We would open up an old section of ruins to be paved over as the foundation for another gigantic temple. I liked seeing progress. What a nice contented world.

As we rolled out to the work site, I sat in peaceful silence next to my co-workers. I knew them well enough, but we were not encouraged to form friendships. We did our jobs like busy little honeybees.

The tallest ruins in the sector had already been leveled by large destructor equipment, broken shards and girders hauled away to be recycled into new construction material. My crew of excavators was trained to explore beneath the surface; we mapped the voids, followed the intact passageways, and found unstable chambers left behind by the Elder Race, who had departed centuries before and left the rest of our race to clean up their messes.

Excavators wore helmets and tough clothing; we carried lights, tools, and logbooks to keep a careful record of our explorations. Each excavator was assigned a territory and range, given a generalized map. After checking in with our prime supervisor, we split up and headed into the ruins. No one questioned the assignment. The Priests would not have sent us here if it was unsafe.

As I descended into the initial shaft, I hummed to myself the tune of that week's featured song. I was clear-eyed and devoted to my task. I had done this work many times, but never in a place so full of dust and buried memories.

For the first three hours I made my way through typical shafts, following basement vaults, documenting underground structures, and measuring the stability of the walls. My helmet light pierced the air, creating a cone of suspended dust motes. The thick concrete walls were sturdy, the ceilings stable, and I laid down a detailed map of my solitary explorations.

No one had been down here in centuries. When I saw a handprint on the wall I wondered if it had been made by a wild-eyed barbarian of the Elder Race. I placed my hand on top of it, curious, and found that the outline matched mine; when I took my palm away, the edges were smudged, and I could no longer tell what was my print and what belonged to that long-forgotten person.

I opened doorways that shrieked on rusty and corroded hinges; I descended unstable metal stairs to even deeper levels where I could feel the oppressive weight of years above me. I finally reached a dead end where the ceiling and walls had collapsed in a pile of debris. I marked the location on my log, and I was about to turn back when I heard a trickling noise — running water. When I moved some of the fallen slabs of artificial rock, the sound grew louder, coming from the darkness behind the cave-in, and when I inhaled, the air was a rush of pure moisture, like a fresh breeze after a spring rainstorm.

With my curiosity piqued, I had to see for myself. I cleared more rubble, shone my helmet light inside, and discovered a large chamber, like a cave full of shadows and treasures. A ribbon of water streamed through a ragged hole in the ceiling, a waterfall that filled the mysterious place with a flowing peace. Either I had gone so deep beneath the surface that this was a natural underground stream, or more likely a water conduit had broken above, spilling through the tunnels until the water found its way here, where it drained through the floor of the chamber.

Intrigued, I wormed my way through the rubble until I emerged into the chamber. It was like a museum. I found incomprehensible machinery, unusual objects that looked like framed mirrors, lenses connected with wires and long-dormant generators . . . sculptures, tapestries, and fabrics nearly disintegrated with age.

Paintings leaned against the walls, portraits of long-vanished people in ancient costumes, brooding expressions, and a regal bearing. One painting looked like an old king — but it was entirely different from the benevolent grandfatherly Great Face of the computers that watched over the Solar Federation. I stared at the portraits, and they seemed to stare back at me.

My first instinct was to rush back to report to the prime supervisor, but some indefinable caution struck me. What if the Priests destroyed all such objects? I wanted to cling to these things, to explore and experience them. I could always report them later.

I came upon a clutter of books, volumes filled with stories, essays, poetry — titles I had never seen on the approved list. And I found one bound volume that was empty, blank pages and no title. Why would anyone publish a book with no words? It seemed to be waiting for someone else to write a story.

That is what I am doing now.

IV

The dreamships from the Elder Race engulfed the cities of Earth in a show of color and force. At the helm, Oracle Fulcrum studied the gray-clad stick figures that stood confused, afraid, and waiting for guidance. The citizens looked meek, without ambition. That drive had been bred out of them long ago, and their creativity had atrophied. As Fulcrum viewed the ominous temples and the blazing Red Star, he vowed to reawaken these shadowy scarecrows and restore the human spirit.

Following commands issued from the Priests, squadrons of overconfident Nforcer airships roared out to face the strange vessels. The security troops were incapable of imagining the weapons and exotic defenses that had been developed by the Elder Race throughout centuries of creative freedom and exuberant experimentation.

Before traveling through the moonstone gates, the Oracles had agreed there would be no senseless killing. However misguided and grim these people were, they were still humanity's long-lost stepchildren. The signal they had received from the awakened dream amplifier showed that at least someone here still had a spark of creativity.

As the Nforcer gunships opened fire with weapons that merely skated across the slick pearlescent surfaces of the dreamships,

Fulcrum directed his crew. "Deploy shrouds. Remove those ships from the conflict before they cause any more harm."

The dreamships launched glowing soap bubbles that struck and surrounded the Nforcer craft, bottling them up. The shroud-fields rendered the security troops impotent, but did not physically harm the soldiers inside. Engulfed by the soap-bubble shrouds, the Nforcer gunships dropped to the ground, where they lay like pearls.

Oracle Axis suggested an important symbolic gesture, and the dreamships flew toward the main Temple of Syrinx, where they unleashed one of their rare destructive weapons and blasted down the glowing Red Star. Fulcrum took immense satisfaction from the act.

Even as more bristling Nforcer gunships closed in, Fulcrum knew the rest of his armada could easily take care of the resistance. In the meantime, he had a more important goal. "We need to find the one who sent us the signal. He may need help."

Leaving the rest of the dreamships to close around the Great Temple, Fulcrum guided his own vessel to track down the triggered dream resonator, a relic left behind the great exodus, perhaps in hopes that worthy dreamers might someday awaken.

After his dreamship landed in the barren flats where destructor machinery had leveled the old ruins, Fulcrum, Anchor, and Axis emerged with a crew of acolytes. Fulcrum pointed at an access passage leading underground. "A vault is down there. We need to find it."

Working together, they picked their way into the cleared catacombs, exploring deeper until they came upon a pile of rubble that blocked a much larger chamber. Oracle Fulcrum helped the acolytes clear the obstruction, and they climbed through into a vault that was filled with ghosts of disappointment and the smell of death. To illuminate the room, they dispatched a swarm of lightspheres that darted around the relics, which included an antique but still functional dream resonator.

A dead body lay sprawled on the floor. He had been there for some time.

"Too late," said Oracle Anchor.

Fulcrum felt the heat of anger in his blood. He knelt beside the body. "Despair can be as powerful as a dream. If you are the only one in an entire world who hears the dream, that makes the despair even more powerful."

A book — a journal — lay beside the body, as if the young man had placed it reverently there before the end. As his anger toward the Priests of Syrinx grew, Fulcrum picked up the diary.

V

From a journal found in Red Sector A:

I don't know exactly why, but I made no notation of the vault in my official report for that day. As far as the prime supervisor knew, the catacombs dead-ended in the rockfall and there was nothing beyond. Such a report would call no attention to the place and give me time to investigate further.

A chime in my helmet informed me that my shift was about to end and that the rest of the excavation crew was to report back to the rendezvous point. I was disappointed because there seemed so much to learn from the items in the grotto.

The next day I reported for work with a greater anticipation than I had ever experienced. While the rest of the excavators worked through other tunnels beneath the ruins, I came back to my secret chamber. Something changed inside me as I saw all the ancient miracles. I didn't understand what was happening to me.

In a corner, I discovered a strange device covered with dust. It had a long neck and a large resonating box that was strung with wires. When I picked it up, unable to imagine what it was for, the strings startled me with a tone that was instantly pleasing. I touched the other strings, then plucked them, realizing that each string made a different note. Was that what this artifact had been designed for? For communication? When I plucked the strings in sequence, I suddenly realized — music! This device created music.

It was called a *guitar*, I learned later, and I began to experiment. If I plucked the strings simultaneously, I could make combined tones; or I could strum them all with a different rhythm. If I moved my grip and shortened the strings, that also changed the sound. It was amazing how many pleasing tones could come from only six strings.

Excited about my discovery and wanting to tell someone, but not knowing who might appreciate it, I chose to write down my activities in the empty book. The journal seemed to have been left there for just this purpose . . .

On my way to the work site the next day, the transport vehicle played a familiar background melody that was always there but rarely listened to. I thought of the stringed musical instrument and wondered if I could play those notes myself.

Once I returned to the marvelous vault with the waterfall, I picked up the instrument and brushed it off, removing the dust, thinking that a little bit of care might make the sounds brighter or fresher.

As I plucked out melodies on the guitar, each tune was a new discovery. At first I fumbled clumsily, but soon I learned how to play, and the music gave me great joy. I *created*, which was such a satisfactory experience that I wanted to share with my crew-mates and my prime supervisor. This was something so precious, so unexpected, it could change the world! Had the Elder Race stolen real music from us when they left Earth? Had the Priests forgotten how to make new music?

This was far too important to show my comrades in the work-place. No, this was something vital. As a good citizen, I had to present my marvelous discovery to Father Brown himself in the Great Temple. I would show all the Priests of Syrinx and give them the joy that this guitar gave me. Yes, I was galvanized now. I knew what to do.

I practiced until my fingers were sore. I developed complex and joyful tunes, and then with a spring in my step, I left my secret cave carrying the guitar. I had a mission.

VI

Surrounded by the shimmering circuit-board walls inside the computer vault, Brothers Theo, Simon, and Adam begged the Great Face that hovered in the air. "Please tell us how we can drive away these invaders."

"We have nothing that can fight against them!"

On the synergy screens, they had watched the full squad-rons of gunships so easily neutralized, and the giant invading vessels simply landed wherever they liked. The Priests did not have a gigantic military force, since the days of large-scale battle had faded long ago with the perfect consolidation of the Solar Federation. The Nforcers were in no way equipped to defend against a massive external armada, their weapons designed instead to monitor the citizenry and snuff out any signs of unrest.

The paternal image of the Great Face blinked as if giving the matter some thought. "I have recalculated, added further data. The situation is even worse than previous projections. Given the technologies the invaders have already demonstrated, no favorable outcome is possible for the Temples of Syrinx."

Father Brown had expected nothing else. The Priests and their computers had made a fatal oversight in assuming that the Elder Race would never return. "This could end in surrender, or in violence," he said. "But it will end."

Unlike his fellow Priests, Father Brown had seen the true threat posed by the young man with his shining eyes when he came to play his beautiful, dangerous music, expecting to be *rewarded* . . .

Nothing in the young man's prior service record showed him to be unduly imaginative, nor offered any indication that he was dissatisfied with his contented world. He had given the Priests no cause for concern — until he appeared before them, bold, energized, and showing off what he called an "ancient miracle" that he had discovered in the ruins beneath Red Sector A. "I know it's most unusual . . ." He held up a musical instrument from ages past and began to play the strings with intense concentration. He plucked out tones, found a melody, and grinned as he played it again.

The other Priests listened, at first more confused than horrified, and, when he was finished, the young man grinned stupidly. After the silence fell, without music, without comment, the young man struck up another song, as if that might help his case rather than increase his own danger.

The poor naïve fool!

"What is the purpose of this?" asked Brother Theo, finally. "We already have music. Why do you need more?"

"But this is *my* music."

Father Brown rose, pulling his powerful presence around him.

"What use would the average citizen have for such things? Should they all start to make their own music?"

"But . . . listen," the young man pleaded, then started to play again.

"Stop! Those relics were buried deep in the tunnels — where they belong. *Buried!* The Elder Race abandoned us, and they took their sickness with them. After centuries of united effort, we created the stable Solar Federation. We made the Red Star a symbol of consistent happiness. We do not need these frivolous distractions. We have our work to do — and so do you."

The other Priests took their cue from Father Brown, glowering at the young man, but the fool didn't know when to give up. Although his face fell and his eyes stung with tears, he refused to turn away. "But there's something here, Father. Let me play another. I know it will reach you." He began to strum again, but Father Brown strode forward, furious, terrible, and knowing he had to crack down on this crisis. He hoped and prayed to the computer god that he had acted in time, before this insanity infected others.

He ripped the guitar from the young man's trembling hands. "Don't annoy us further. Your purpose is to serve the Solar Federation. Your masters are the Priests of Syrinx. This . . . noise is a waste of your time. And ours."

Knowing that it would devastate the young man — but better one citizen than all of civilization — Father Brown smashed the guitar across his knee, snapping the stem, jangling the wires. He tore it apart, dropped the resonating box on the stone floor, and stomped the rest into splinters.

The young man stared in horror, as if the Priest had broken him in half and likewise ground him under his heel. Father Brown summoned uniformed Nforcers to escort the man away. Their heavy boots thundered across the floor of the Great Hall, whisking the man out but leaving the destroyed shards of the guitar.

The other Priests were confused by Father Brown's extreme reaction, but he kept his face a stony mask, secretly terrified that this young man's discovery would still cause a great deal of trouble . . .

And his worst fears had come to pass.

A report came in from one of the besieged Venus habitats, and the walls of the computer vault resolved into images. Sparks flew behind a panicked High Priest in the control chamber of the sealed orbiting habitat. "We are overwhelmed! Enemy ships brushed aside all our weapons, and they are swarming our habitat with small ships. They've attached to our hull!" The distraught Priest drew a deep breath and found the steel of resolve. "We cannot let our citizens be corrupted. This is our final play."

The High Priest of the Venus habitat set his station reactors on a slow buildup and overload — and within ten minutes the entire habitat exploded, terminating the transmission. Inside the computer vault, the screen reverted to the Red Star logo, while the Great Face hovered in the air, expressionless.

Commandeering the communication systems inside the vault, Father Brown sent out a broadcast to any remaining defenders of Earth. He understood that this Temple would be their last stand. In order to let his cadre of Priests survive just a little longer, he recalled all operational Nforcer armored ships, all ground fighters, all uniformed soldiers and ordered them to form a cordon around the Great Temple.

"Yes, that will be enough!" said Brother Theo. "It has to be enough. We can hold them off."

"We'll be safe in here," Brother Adam echoed, as if to reassure himself. "We'll withstand the invaders. No one can break into this fortress and harm us."

In the center of the vault, the benevolent visage of the old man closed his eyes, then winked out as all the great computers shut down.

VII

From a journal found in Red Sector A:

After the Priests of Syrinx crushed my dreams, I was shaking so badly I could barely walk. My heart felt cold and empty. I should have returned home, but my assigned apartment was not home to me. The reminder of my colorless existence would only emphasize how bleak this world was, and how silent it was without the joy of the music I had discovered.

Now that Father Brown had destroyed my precious guitar, I didn't even have music of my own. Why couldn't the Priests hear what I heard? How could they not feel the wonderful energy evoked by those bright silvery notes? How could Father Brown dismiss that ancient miracle as a mere toy?

And how could *music* have destroyed the Elder Race? It didn't make sense to me, but questions were not encouraged in our contented world.

The city streets were empty, unwelcoming. I rode the automated transport lines and then walked for hours through the dark until I made my way out to Red Sector A. I had the haunted treasure-filled place all to myself.

When I reached my beautiful serene cave, the trickling sound of the waterfall tried to comfort me, as did the memory of my music. I stared at the ancient portraits of anonymous people, but they were strangers offering no sympathy and no support.

My heart had been broken. I was lost, exhausted. My mind seemed to shut down, as if Father Brown had smashed a bridge of hope just as he had smashed my guitar.

Unable to face even my own company, I lay down on the hard stone floor next to the waterfall and retreated into sleep. As I drifted off, the strange connected mirrors and lenses from the ancient devices nearby began to hum and glow. But rather than waking me, the thrumming light enfolded me and dragged me deeper into sleep . . .

That night I experienced a dream unlike any other. At first I heard guitar strings playing music *my* music — then the murky dream images turned into a vivid landscape, a wondrous vision of paradise with colorful towers, majestic architecture. I had never seen or even imagined a place like this, so how could I be envisioning it?

I found myself transported — there was no other word for it — to a spiral staircase that seemed to overlook infinite possibilities. Atop that staircase a wise bearded man in a gleaming white robe stood before me. He spread his hands wide to encompass all that he and his people had accomplished. "The dream has awakened at last," said the Oracle. "And the dream is you."

"Yes . . ." I replied. "I am dreaming."

"More than dreaming. This is real, but a different reality." The Oracle swept his hands aside and showed me the panorama of a vibrant world that made my very existence ache with color, music, scents, blossoms, and fireworks of the imagination.

"We departed from the original Earth long ago, and we have thrived," the Oracle explained. "Look at all we have done . . . and the human spirit is just beginning. You are part of it. This is what your life might be. This is what your world *could be*, if only you all would open your eyes and your hearts again."

My heart swelled with the impossible possibilities, surging so bright in my mind that I was thrust back into wakefulness — and I sat up blinking in the cave.

I know the Oracle was trying to give me hope, but when I emerged from my fitful sleep, the dream and the Oracle had done me no service. Before, I had not known such a place could ever exist . . . but now I had touched it, tasted it, experienced it.

And it was gone.

My world was gray and monotonous. The music was all the same. The Priests of Syrinx mistook a numb and soulless world for a contented world.

And I knew I could never have what I had seen in that dream . . . I huddled in my secret chamber for days. I had brought some food and my excavator's toolkit with me, but nothing else. I drank from the waterfall, but it had a metallic bitter taste. I wasn't hungry. Nourishment didn't interest me, when I knew I was starving for other things. I grew weaker day by day, and my broken heart was even heavier in my chest.

After Father Brown had cast me out of the Great Temple, I had not returned home, had not reported to work. I would face severe punishment if I decided to go back and pretend that nothing had happened . . . but how could I return there? Under the Red Star, there was no life, no existence that I wanted to have. The wonderful cruel dream had shown me everything I was missing, and those hours of sleep were the only time I had ever felt truly alive.

In the depths of my despair, the only spark I clung to was that I could somehow return to that world in my dreams. Permanently. I know I can never get there in this life; perhaps the path to that wondrous place lies through another doorway entirely. A sleep from which I cannot awaken.

I have a sharp cutter in my toolkit, and I'm sure it will be swift.

This will be the last entry in my journal.

VIII

As Oracle Fulcrum finished reading the poor man's last words, the simmering uneasiness and disappointment inside him became a bright fury. With reddened eyes, he turned to the others. "So much lost here. So much potential. Just think of what these people could have created if they hadn't been smothered by the Priests of Syrinx."

Anchor was openly weeping, and Axis comforted him. "We don't even know his name," she said, taking the journal and rereading some of the pages.

"He is all of us, and every person here — or who they might have been." Fulcrum felt heartsick that this victim would never again hear music, nor experience the wonders that the Elder Race were bringing back to this Earth, or the *new* things this prodigal arm of humanity could create once they were liberated.

Fulcrum's anger became a white hot determination. He gestured for the others to join him. "We will build a memorial for this young man, and he will become a symbol for the new world. But first . . ." He narrowed his eyes and saw the steel in their eyes as well. "Before the forest can thrive, we have to clear out the deadwood."

As their dreamships converged above the Great Temple, Fulcrum received reports from the other dreamships across the Solar Federation. He was saddened to learn that one of the orbiting Venus habitats had chosen to self-destruct rather than surrender. The other two habitats were now under the control of the Elder Race; the frightened inhabitants were disoriented, not sure what these new masters would bring.

A dreamship signal from stations in the rings of Saturn pronounced victory, as well as outposts on the moons of Jupiter. Fulcrum was surprised to hear from the sprawling colonies on Mars, where previously unexpected resistance groups seized the opportunity to overthrow the Priests themselves in spontaneous internal uprisings.

But Oracle Fulcrum needed to see the Great Temple fall. He would be among the conquerors as they surged into the hall. After reading the young man's journal, he would confront Father Brown in person.

As armored Nforcers converged around the Temple in a last defense, Fulcrum and his comrades moved through the streets. He looked at the citizens, sure that some of them at least must have hungry minds.

Axis and Anchor directed the acolyte soldiers to tear down the Red Star banners and replace them with bright makeshift pennants — the design didn't matter, so long as it was an outpouring of colors and imagination. Celebratory fireworks exploded and sparkled like chrysanthemums in the sky.

Every citizen of the Solar Federation had followed instructions for so long, facing no choices or concerns, that they didn't know what to do with freedom. How many of them had dormant dreams like that young guitar player? How many of them secretly wrote poems, or drew sketches, but were afraid to show them to anyone? Now, they no longer needed to be afraid. They could achieve anything they liked, create anything they might imagine. They just needed to be shown how. They needed to be granted *permission* to unlock their imaginations.

As the returning members of the Elder Race marched through the city, they were all smiles and exuberance. Next to him, as they closed on the Great Temple, Oracle Axis hesitated. She lowered her voice as she stared at the uniformly clad men and women, their averted gazes. "It's a barren creative desert instead of a lush rainforest of ideas. I never imagined it would be so . . . desolate."

"Even a desert bursts into bloom after the rain," Fulcrum pointed out. "And we bring the rain."

"But they're so . . . meek," said Anchor, keeping his voice low.

Fulcrum did not agree. "Dreamers have a hidden strength that is often mistaken for meekness by those who have power."

The landed dreamships opened and played music. Representatives and counselors emerged, talking to the citizens, reassuring them. It was just a start.

When the armies finally arrived at the Great Temple, a wall of armored Nforcers blocked them, but Fulcrum did not have the patience to use a gentle hand. "We won't caress the boot heel that crushed the life out of these people. This has been much too long in coming."

From forward weapons ports, the dreamships emanated a rippling rainbow wedge that pushed through the cordon of armored vehicles and defensive barricades. The clustered Nforcers fired their weapons ineffectually against the shimmering shield, but the colorful wedge split them apart like a divided sea, clearing the way for the Elder Race to enter the mammoth Temple.

"Bring it down," Fulcrum said.

Over the centuries, the Elder Race had invented matter-manipulation devices that allowed sculptors to work on the scale of mountains, to build and assemble anything they could design. The same constructor tools could be used to rearrange the massive block walls, and like a sculptor working with soft clay, the matter manipulators carved away the stone and split open the Temple of Syrinx.

Oracle Fulcrum led his people as they surged inside. "This is the day that dreams begin."

IX

After the benevolent computers shut down and the paternal Great Face faded, abandoning the terrified Priests in the core chamber, Brothers Theo, Simon, and Adam were nearly catatonic. For centuries the Priests of Syrinx had ruled the people — but even the Priests relied on the great computers, and now they were thoroughly alone. They could not react to the emergency, could not solve the problem for themselves.

Father Brown could rely on no one but himself, but he could use these men for now. Taking charge, he ushered the other priests out of the core chamber. The three stumbled as they moved, their knees quaking. The Temple was a cacophony of chaos, which grated on Father Brown. Countless robed Priests ran around in panic inside the sealed structure, which was being bombarded from outside.

Tall synergy screens on the walls showed the turmoil in the streets, and the skies overhead were full of dreamships. The invaders were sweeping everything away without understanding, without the slightest grasp of who these poor people were. They needed someone to guide them, to think for them, to create a perfect world where all could be content . . .

Sickened, Father Brown shook his head. Despite their grandiose dreams of liberation, the Elder Race did not comprehend what Earth had become. The citizens had no ability to take care of themselves — independence had been bred out of them over the centuries. To grant them complete freedom was like giving a child sharp knives to play with!

The Elder Race thought they could simply open the floodgates of freedom, and the people would know what to do? Simply *telling* a person he was free did not *make* him free. And did the citizens even want that? Father Brown understood these people far better than the arrogant Oracles did.

With the armada of dreamships and their incomprehensible weaponry, he had no question that the invaders would succeed . . . but he doubted they knew what they had done. A utopia did not create itself, and there were conflicting definitions of what constituted a perfect world.

The Red Star had fallen. The Solar Federation was doomed.

Father Brown made his decision. After the centuries of effort it had taken to create this contented world, he had another obligation. He placed his hands on the trembling shoulders of Brother Theo and Brother Adam. Dozens of Priests had gathered in the Great Hall, staring at the open empty air and praying for the computer god to reappear and give them instructions. Like the citizens they ruled, they could not think for themselves, either.

Father Brown spoke in a firm, commanding voice to Theo, Simon, and Adam. "Be strong — that is what you must do. Go and meet the Elder Race. It is your only chance. Make peace — they will accept you."

"But, you have to lead us!" cried Simon. "Please, Father Brown."

He shook his head. "I have another mission. It may not succeed, but I have to try. This world did not turn out the way I envisioned, but maybe there is a second chance."

Brother Adam's face formed a grim mask as he struggled to defeat the fear inside him. "If anyone can do it, Father, you can."

Then he, Simon, and Adam marched forward, leading the lesser Priests to the grand archway as the walls of the Temple crumbled and fell. They went to meet the Elder Race.

After they had left, Father Brown retreated into the computer vault — his only chance. The heavy vault door slammed shut, protecting him, giving him time . . . but he knew the Temple defenses would not last long against the invaders. He had to hurry.

Behind the engram-enhanced silicon walls, he ran his fingers along the circuit paths, tracing an emergency pattern no one else knew. He had planned for this ever since he began to fear what Earth might face. Now that the computers had shut down, he used the last flickers of energy to activate a code.

With a sound like a defeated sigh, a hidden access door slid open to reveal the secret vault that contained remnants of ancient technology considered far too dangerous for the average to see.

Earlier High Priests had locked all that equipment there, relics discovered by excavators as they rebuilt ruined sections of the city. In the past, citizens were fearful enough to surrender any such objects, but it was only a matter of time until someone decided to toy with them . . .

The forbidden technology of the dimensional gates had not been tested in countless years, and even Father Brown didn't understand it — thought amplifiers, resonance lenses, sensory prisms. He did know though, about the moonstone mirrors.

When the Elder Race left the world so long ago, all the dreamers had built countless dimensional gateways for their exodus. They had traveled to an alternate Earth, a place where they had apparently thrived for centuries.

Some of those moonstone portals remained, though, and now Father Brown stood before one deep in the secret vault, saw the faint pearlescent glow of its latent energy. The Priests of Syrinx had suppressed any further investigations, but according to the theories left behind, there were countless similar worlds. Infinite possibilities. Anywhere but here . . .

As the portal shimmered, Father Brown stared at it. He had to escape, had to take his knowledge with him, but he didn't dare go to the parallel world where the Elder Race had built its great civilization. He needed a fresh start. Instead, he adjusted the portal, found a random mirror image of different possibilities.

Father Brown had always been a man of firm convictions, untroubled by doubts, unwavering in his straightforward path. All answers were clear when one didn't bother with questions. Now, though, he paused to stare at the gateway that would take him away from this collapsing civilization. There would be no turning back.

It was his only chance.

Above him, behind the sealed door of the vault, he could hear pounding noises, then shouts as the invaders breached the chamber. They were coming. Father Brown could no longer wait.

Without looking back at the fallen Red Star, he stepped through the moonstone portal.

X

When he emerged on the other side, in another world, his great city was gone, and he saw no sign of the Great Temples or the geometrical dwelling units that sprawled as far as the eye could see. Instead, he stood on a rolling green hill looking down toward a village in a valley below — but he also saw fire and smoke. Many of the small quaint dwellings were burning. From where he stood, he heard distant shouts and screams, saw marauders charging through the streets while villagers evacuated in panic and ran into the hills.

Father Brown took shelter under a tree so no one would see him, and he watched, gathering information. He was surprised when a man, a woman, and two raggedy children crashed through the trees behind him. The refugee family stared in terror at his strange appearance, but even Father Brown in his Priest's robes was not nearly as terrifying as the marauders attacking the village. The mother gasped and snatched up her children, gathering them protectively while the man stood before them, ready to fight. "Who are you, sir?"

Father Brown raised his hands. "I'm just a visitor. I mean you no harm."

The man looked at him suspiciously, then jerked his gaze sideways, interrupted by the sharp icepick sounds of gunfire, the shouts and explosions from the village. He looked sickened and terrified. "You're not one of the bandits, then?"

"No . . . I don't think so," said Father Brown.

"They prey upon our village every year," said the woman. Tear tracks cleared lines down her soot-stained cheeks. "Many of us escape, and we spend months rebuilding. When we beg the nearby towns for help, they only see our weakness and then they steal our stored crops. It never ends."

The man's brief laugh had no humor. "Last year, the bandits raided during fever season — and they also stole our sickness, so their numbers are smaller this year." He spat on the ground. "Not that it does us any good."

Father Brown was appalled to see the barbarism, the chaos. "It sounds terrible. Complete anarchy! Don't you have a leader to bring everyone together? To show you how to make the world an efficient place?"

The ragged, forlorn family looked at him, uncomprehending. The mother shook her head.

"It sounds like you could use some stability," said Father Brown. "What is the name of this land?"

The man frowned, wondering if the question was a trick, but one of the children piped up, "Albion. It's Albion."

Father Brown nodded. And the wheels began to turn like clockwork in his mind.

ABOUT THE CONTRIBUTORS

KEVIN J. ANDERSON has published 130 books, 54 of which have been bestsellers. He is best known for his *Star Wars*, *X-Files*, and Dune novels; his Saga of Seven Suns series; and his humorous horror series featuring Dan Shamble, Zombie PI. Rush fans know him best for the steampunk fantasy novel *Clockwork Angels*, developed and written with Neil Peart, based on the Rush concept album. He and Peart adapted the novel to a full graphic novel published by BOOM! Studios with artwork by Nick Robles, and in 2015 they published an ambitious companion novel, *Clockwork Lives*, which expands on the characters and the world of *Clockwork Angels*.

Kevin has edited numerous anthologies, including the Five by Five and Blood Lite series. He and his wife, Rebecca Moesta, are the publishers of WordFire Press, with over 200 titles in print and eBook format. He also wrote and produced two prog-rock CDs based on his Terra Incognita fantasy trilogy, which were performed by Roswell Six, featuring legendary rock performers from Dream Theater, Kansas, Saga, Asia, Shadow Gallery, and Sass Jordan.

RON COLLINS is an award-winning author whose most recent publication, *Saga of the God-Touched Mage*, spent a couple months at the top of Amazon's Dark Fantasy bestseller list. Ron has been a Rush fan since he was a kid playing air guitar in his basement. He has contributed nearly one hundred stories to premier science fiction and fantasy publications, including *Analog*, *Asimov's Science Fiction*, and Mercedes Lackey's Valdemar and *Elemental Magic* collections. He is a Writers of the Future prizewinner, and in 2000, CompuServe readers named his story "The Taranth Stone" their best novelette of the year. You can find his collected science fiction in *Picasso's Cat & Other Stories*, and his collected fantasy in *Five Magics*. His website is Typosphere.com. His Twitter handle is @roncollins13.

LARRY DIXON's thirty-two-year career in science fiction and fantasy includes novels, short stories, and nearly three hundred convention guest appearances worldwide, and he is one of the premiere black-and-white book illustrators in America. Larry's been a firefighter, race car driver, falconer, raptor rehabber, editor, stormspotter, concept artist, mentor, and charity worker. Larry's well-known knack with birds of prey led to his work on the *Lord of the Rings* and *Hobbit* films as Weta Digital's Great Eagles expert. Most recently, he's done creature design for Disney. Larry Dixon is a race marshall for several high-tech international racing series, including the FIA WEC, Tudor, Lamborghini Trofeo, ALMS, and Formula 1.

DAVID FARLAND is a *New York Times*–bestselling author who has won numerous awards, including several Best Novel of the Year awards in fields as diverse as historical fiction, science fiction, and young adult fiction. He is the lead judge for one of the world's largest writing contests and has helped discover and mentor such #1 *New York Times* bestselling authors as Brandon Sanderson (Mistborn), James Dashner (The Maze Runner), and Stephenie Meyer (Twilight). Dave has also worked as a screenwriter and movie producer. He is currently writing the final installment of his popular Runelords fantasy series, and has recently been hired to produce the first of the Runelords movies through L.A.B. Studios.

RICHARD "RICK" FOSTER retired in February 2013 after serving as chief actuary for the Centers for Medicare & Medicaid Services since 1995. Foster has testified before Congress on numerous occasions and has made more than two hundred other presentations on Medicare, Medicaid, national health insurance, and Social Security issues. Rick has received a number of awards, including the UMBC Outstanding Alumnus of the Year in 1997, the Presidential Meritorious Executive Award in 1998 from President Clinton, the Presidential Distinguished Executive Award in 2001 from President Bush, and the College of Wooster Distinguished Alumni Award in 2006. In 2007 through 2012, the readers of *Modern Healthcare* voted Mr. Foster one of the 100 most influential persons in health care in the U.S.

He has enjoyed forty-four years of marriage with his wife, Nancy, and they have traveled to England, France, Italy, Switzerland, Germany, and Austria. Rick has been a lifelong car enthusiast, and he raced with the Sports Car Club of America for ten years, winning the Mid-Atlantic Road Racing Series Championship in 1986 and 1987 in the Spec Racer class.

BRIAN HODGE is one of those people who always has to be making something. So far, he's made ten novels and is working on three more, as well as 120 shorter works and five full-length collections. His first collection, *The Convulsion Factory*, was ranked by critic Stanley Wiater among the 113 best books of modern horror.

He lives in Colorado, where he also likes to make music and photographs, loves everything about organic gardening except the thieving squirrels, and trains in Krav Maga and kickboxing, which are useless against the squirrels.

Recent works include *In the Negative Spaces* and *The Weight of the Dead*, both standalone novellas; *Worlds of Hurt*, an omnibus edition of the first four works in his Misbegotten mythos; an updated edition of *Dark Advent*, his early post-apocalyptic epic; and his next collection, *The Immaculate Void*.

BrianHodge.net.

MERCEDES LACKEY was born in Chicago, Illinois, on June 24, 1950. The very next day, the Korean War was declared. It is hoped that there is no connection between the two events. She was raised mostly in the northwestern corner of Indiana, attending grade school and high school in Highland. She graduated from Purdue University in 1972 with a Bachelor of Science in Biology. This, she soon learned, along with a paper hat and a nametag, will qualify you to ask "Would you like fries with that?" at a variety of fast-food locations.

In 1985, her first book was published. In 1990, she met artist Larry Dixon at a small Science Fiction convention in Meridian, Mississippi, at a television interview organized by the convention. They began working together from that time on, and were married in Las Vegas at the Excalibur chapel by Merlin the Magician (a.k.a. the Reverend Duckworth) in 1992.

They moved to their current home, the "second weirdest house in Oklahoma," also in 1992. She has many pet parrots and the house is never quiet. She is approaching one hundred books in print, and some of her foreign editions can be found in Russian, German, Czech, Polish, French, Italian, Turkish, and Japanese. She is the author, alone or in collaboration, of the Heralds of Valdemar, Elemental Masters, Secret World Chronicles, 500 Kingdoms, Diana Tregarde, Heirs of Alexandria, Obsidian Mountain, Dragon Jousters, Bedlam Bards, Shadow Grail, Dragon Prophecy, Elvenbane, Bardic Voices, SERRAted Edge, Doubled Edge (prequel to SERRAted Edge), and other series and standalone books.

Mercedes Lackey is a race marshall for several high-tech international racing series, including the FIA WEC, Tudor, Lamborghini Trofeo, ALMS, and Formula 1.

TIM LASIUTA is a Canadian writer whose first introduction to Rush came through a garbled eight-track of *2112* in a Chevy Nova. "We are the Priests . . . click . . . of the temples of Syrinx." The rest is history, or the future.

His work can be found in the *Innisfail Province*, *Comic Buyers' Guide*, *Mad Magazine*, Graphic Classics ("The Hold Up," "Nosferatu"), and in Moonstone Books' Zorro, Lone Ranger, Green Hornet, and Captain Midnight anthologies. He has penned *Brushstrokes with Greatness: The Art of Joe Sinnott*, *Misadventures of a Roving Cartoonist*, and *Collecting Western Memorabilia* with an upcoming volume for Hermes in the offing.

In addition to working as a writer, he hosted *Comic Zone*, an internet radio show, and is on the board of the Museum of Comic and Cartoon Art in New York.

He has been married to Karen for twenty-eight years and they have four children.

TimLasiuta.weebly.com.

FRITZ LEIBER is a classic SF and fantasy author best known for his Lovecraftian horror and his swords-and-sorcery epics, particularly the Fafhrd and the Gray Mouser cycle. Some of his best known books are *The Swords of Lankhmar*, the science fiction disaster novel *The Wanderer*, the satirical *A Spectre Is Haunting Texas*, his late short fiction, and the fine horror novel *Our Lady of Darkness*. Leiber's story "Gonna Roll the Bones" was part of the seminal science fiction anthology *Dangerous Visions*, edited by Harlan Ellison.

Grace Under Pressure was the album that converted MARK LESLIE into a Rush fan. From there, he moved to *Signals*, then sequentially from the band's first album up through every one ever since. He remembers how excited he was to discover the short story "Drumbeats" that Neil Peart and Kevin J. Anderson co-wrote in the 1990s, and which he republished in *Tesseracts Sixteen: Parnassus Unbound*, a collection of speculative stories inspired by art, literature, music, and culture. Mark writes *Twilight Zone*–style fiction, horror, and thrillers, and his first published horror story, "Phantom Mitch," earned him Honorable Mention in *The Year's Best Fantasy & Horror*. Mark's fiction books include *One Hand Screaming*, *Evasion*, and *I, Death*. Mark also writes non-fiction explorations of the paranormal, the latest of which is *Tomes of Terror: Haunted Bookstores & Libraries*. "Some Are Born to Save the World" is Mark's second published short story inspired by "Losing It." Mark's dark-humor story about a ghost who can no longer properly haunt ("Hereinafter Referred to as the Ghost") was published in *Tesseracts Seventeen* in 2013.

DAVID MACK is the *New York Times*–bestselling author of thirty novels, including the Star Trek Destiny and Cold Equations trilogies. He developed the Star Trek Vanguard series with editor Marco Palmieri. His first original novel was the critically acclaimed supernatural thriller *The Calling*.

Beyond novels, Mack's writing credits feature more than a dozen pieces of short fiction and span several media, including television (episodes of *Star Trek: Deep Space Nine*), film, and comic books. He also co-authored Bryan Anderson's Iraq War memoir, *No Turning Back: One Man's Inspiring True Story of Courage, Determination, and Hope.'*

Mack's latest published novels include *Star Trek: Seekers #3: Long Shot* and *24: Rogue*, and his novelette "Hell Rode with Her" is featured in the anthology *Apollo's Daughters*.

His upcoming works include the short story "The Ghost Rider" in horror and dark-fantasy anthology *Out of Tune, Vol. 2*; a new series of original novels set to kick off with *The Midnight Front*, a World War II–era fantasy adventure; and a new *Star Trek* novel that will be part of Pocket Books' salute to the fiftieth anniversary of *Star Trek: The Original Series*.

DavidMack.pro.

JOHN MCFETRIDGE has enjoyed wide critical acclaim for his Toronto series novels. *Everybody Knows This Is Nowhere* was named a book of the year by *Quill & Quire* and *Tumblin' Dice* was an Amazon.ca Editors' Pick. His new series features Constable Eddie Dougherty and is set against actual historical events in Montreal during the turbulent 1970s. The first Eddie Dougherty novel, *Black Rock*, was published in 2014 and the second, *A Little More Free*, was published in fall 2015.

John began his career in 1996 with the CBC feature-length radio drama *Champions*, which tells the story of Jackie Robinson breaking baseball's color line with the Montreal Royals. John was a story editor for the CTV/CBS television show *The Bridge*. A graduate of Concordia University and the Canadian Film Centre, John lives in Toronto with his wife and two sons.

STEVEN SAVILE has written for *Doctor Who*, *Torchwood*, *Primeval*, *Stargate*, *Warhammer*, *Slaine*, *Fireborn*, *Pathfinder*, *Arkham Horror*, *Rogue Angel*, and other popular game and comic worlds. He won the International Media Association of Tie-In Writers Award for his novel *Shadow of the Jaguar*, and the inaugural Lifeboat to the Stars Award for *Tau Ceti* (coauthored with Kevin J. Anderson). Writing as Matt Langley, his young adult novel *Black Flag* is a finalist for the People's Book Prize 2015. His latest books include *Sherlock Holmes and the Murder at Sorrow's Crown*, published by Titan, *Sunfail*, an apocalyptic thriller published in the U.S. by Akashic Books, and *Parallel Lines*, a brand new crime novel coming from Titan in 2016.

BRAD R. TORGERSEN is a full-time healthcare tech geek during the day, a United States Army Reserve Chief Warrant Officer on the weekend, and an award-winning science fiction writer at night. He was a triple nominee for the Hugo, the Nebula, and the Campbell awards in 2012, and is a winner of the Writers of the Future Award, the AML Award, and is a three-time winner of the *Analog* magazine AnLab Readers' Award. Married for twenty-two years, Brad resides in the Intermountain West.

GREG VAN EEKHOUT writes books and stories for ages spanning from middle-grade readers to adults. His works of science fiction and fantasy include the novels *Norse Code*, *Kid vs. Squid*, and *The Boy at the End of the World*. His Daniel Blackland trilogy (*California Bones*, *Pacific Fire*, and *Dragon Coast*) is about wizards who gain their powers by eating the bones of dragons and griffins from the La Brea Tar Pits. His work has been nominated for the Nebula, Andre Norton, and Locus awards. He has not missed a Rush tour since *Power Windows*. WritingAndSnacks.com. Twitter: @gregvaneekhout.

DAYTON WARD is the *New York Times*–bestselling author or coauthor of nearly thirty novels and novellas, often working with his best friend, Kevin Dilmore. His short fiction has appeared in more than twenty anthologies, and he's written for magazines such as *Kansas City Voices*, *Star Trek*, and *Star Trek Communicator*, as well as the websites Tor.com, StarTrek.com, and Syfy.com. Until recently, Dayton was a software developer, having discovered the private sector and the perpetual fear of outsourcing after spending eleven years in the U.S. Marine Corps. When asked, he'll tell you he joined the military soon after high school because he'd grown tired of people telling him what to do all the time. Whoops. Though Dayton lives in Kansas City with his wife and daughters, he's a Florida native and maintains a torrid long-distance romance with his beloved Tampa Bay Buccaneers. Visit him on the web at DaytonWard.com.

MICHAEL Z. WILLIAMSON is a longtime Rush fan, and guitarist and occasional bassist, who realized he was marginal at instruments and much better with words. He is an American who was inadvertently born a native of the U.K., which he corrected in front of a U.S. District judge right before enlisting in the USAF. Also a veteran of the U.S. Army, he mostly writes about planet-killing explosions and futuristic technoninjas, but occasionally dabbles in fantasy, satire, and contemporary action adventure. He has written fifteen books, parts of some others, and dozens of short stories and articles. His works have been nominated for several awards and translated into a few languages other than English. As a consultant, he's worked with productions for Discovery, National Geographic, Science Channel, and the Outdoor Channel, as well as private clients and occasional government agencies. When not writing, he's a bladesmith, gunsmith, and armorer for relaxation.

DAVID NIALL WILSON has been writing and publishing horror, dark fantasy, and science fiction since the mid-eighties. An ordained minister, once president of the Horror Writers Association, and multiple recipient of the Bram Stoker Award, his novels include *Maelstrom*, *The Mote in Andrea's Eye*, *Deep Blue*, the Grails Covenant Trilogy, *Star Trek Voyager: Chrysalis*, "Except You Go Through Shadow," *This Is My Blood*, *Ancient Eyes*, *On the Third Day*, *The Orffyreus Wheel*, *Vintage Soul*, *My Soul to Keep & Others*, *Kali's Tale*, *Heart of a Dragon*, *The Second Veil*, *The Parting*, *Nevermore: A Novel of Love, Loss & Edgar Allan Poe*, *Killer Green & Crockatiel*, the newest novel in the new series OCLT. David has also coauthored the *Stargate Atlantis* novel *Brimstone*, with Patricia Lee Macomber, and *Hallowed Ground*, with Steven Savile. He has over 150 short stories published in anthologies, magazines, and five collections. His work has appeared in and is due out in various anthologies and magazines. David lives and loves with Patricia Lee Macomber in Hertford, NC, with their daughter Katie, and occasionally their genius college daughter Stephanie; three sons serving in the USN, Will, Zach, and Zane; their ridiculous Pekingese Gizmo; their spaz of a Cocker Spaniel, Callie; their not-so-vicious cat, Sid; a never-to-become-a-coat chinchilla named Pook Daddy; and various other creatures. David is CEO and founder of Crossroad Press, a cutting-edge digital publishing company specializing in electronic novels, collections, and non-fiction, as well as unabridged audiobooks. Visit Crossroad Press at store.crossroadpress.com.

Published by ECW Press
665 Gerrard Street East
Toronto, Ontario, Canada M4M 1Y2
416-694-3348 / info@ecwpress.com

The publication of *2113* has been generously
supported by the Government of Canada
through the Canada Book Fund.

PRINTED AND BOUND IN CANADA

LIBRARY AND ARCHIVES CANADA
CATALOGUING IN PUBLICATION

2113 : stories inspired by the music of Rush / edited
by Kevin J. Anderson and John McFetridge.

Issued in print and electronic formats.
ISBN 978-1-77041-292-7
also issued as: 978-1-77090-860-4 (PDF);
978-1-77090-861-1 (EPUB)

I. Anderson, Kevin J., 1962–, editor, author II.
McFetridge, John, 1959–, editor, author III. Title:
Twenty-one thirteen. IV. Title: Two thousand one
hundred and thirteen. V. Title: Two thousand one
hundred thirteen.

PN6120.2.T86 2016   823'.0108092
C2015-907297-2   C2015-907298-0

Cover design: Michel Vrana
Cover images: stars © pixelparticle / iStockPhoto,
young naked man in lake © egorr / iStockPhoto

Canada

PRINTING: FRIESENS   5   4   3   2   1

At ECW Press, we want you to enjoy this
book in whatever format you like, whenever
you like. Leave your print book at home and
take the eBook to go! Purchase the print edition
and receive the eBook free. Just send an email
to ebook@ecwpress.com and include:

- the book title
- the name of the store where you purchased it
- your receipt number
- your preference of file type: PDF or ePub?

A real person will respond to your email with
your eBook attached. And thanks for supporting
an independently owned Canadian publisher
with your purchase!